Late Bloomer

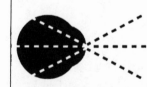

This Large Print Book carries the
Seal of Approval of N.A.V.H.

Late Bloomer

Melissa Pritchard

Thorndike Press • Waterville, Maine

Portions of *Late Bloomer* appeared first in *Washington Square* (no. 12, Summer 2003), New York University, and in *Blackbird* (vol. 2, no. 1, Spring 2003), Virginia Commonwealth University, Richmond.

The author gratefully acknowledges permission to quote from *Reading the Romance: Women, Patriarchy, and Popular Literature* by Janice A. Radway. Copyright © 1984, 1991 by the University of North Carolina Press. Used by permission of the publisher.

Published in 2004 by arrangement with Doubleday Broadway Publishing Group, a division of Random House, Inc.

Thorndike Press® Large Print Basic.

The tree indicium is a trademark of Thorndike Press.

The text of this Large Print edition is unabridged. Other aspects of the book may vary from the original edition.

Set in 16 pt. Plantin by Elena Picard.

Printed in the United States on permanent paper.

Library of Congress Cataloging-in-Publication Data

Pritchard, Melissa.
    Late bloomer : a novel / Melissa Pritchard.
      p. cm.
    ISBN 0-7862-6755-0 (lg. print : hc : alk. paper)
    1. Love stories — Authorship — Fiction. 2. Comanche Indians — Fiction. 3. Women novelists — Fiction.
4. Arizona — Fiction. 5. Large type books. I. Title.
PS3566.R578L38 2004
    813′.54—dc22   2004052274

For
My Father
Clarence John "Jack" Brown
D. D. D. L.
April 17, 1918–June 13, 2002

and

Joseph Wolves Kill
Kultseena Peeka

Nu Ahapa Puya Meon
Walk in God's Love

As the Founder/CEO of NAVH, the only national health agency solely devoted to those who, although not totally blind, have an eye disease which could lead to serious visual impairment, I am pleased to recognize Thorndike Press★ as one of the leading publishers in the large print field.

Founded in 1954 in San Francisco to prepare large print textbooks for partially seeing children, NAVH became the pioneer and standard setting agency in the preparation of large type.

Today, those publishers who meet our standards carry the prestigious "Seal of Approval" indicating high quality large print. We are delighted that Thorndike Press is one of the publishers whose titles meet these standards. We are also pleased to recognize the significant contribution Thorndike Press is making in this important and growing field.

Lorraine H. Marchi, L.H.D.
Founder/CEO
NAVH

★ Thorndike Press encompasses the following imprints: Thorndike, Wheeler, Walker and Large Print Press.

Acknowledgments

Grateful thanks to the Women's Studies Department at Arizona State University; to my darling, oh, for-Pete's-sake-and-heavens-to-Betsy mother, Helen Reilly Brown; and to the two most everlasting blooms in a mother's garden, Noelle Pritchard and Caitlin Pritchard. Thanks to Oralia and Victor De La Cruz at the V/O Stables; to Eddie Webb for inviting me to my first Sun Dance on the Yacqui reservation and first sweat lodge on the Gila reservation; to Laura Tohe, *Shideezhí, nízhóníyee'* (My younger sister, you are beautiful); to Jillian Robinson, who stood beside me at a transcendent time; to Keith Tolagai, for inviting me to the first Sacred Mountain Sun Dance in 1989; and to his courageous, gracious mother, Sarah Begay; to Jake Metz at Borders bookstore for the translation of his Celtic tattoos; to Will Johnson at Staples and William Summers at Remac Computers, Inc., for swift technological rescue; and to Garrison Tahmahkera.

Respectful thanks to Servando Trujillo and to the Sun Dancers, their families and supporters at the Sacred Mountain Sun Dance in Pinon, Arizona, most especially the Begay and Looking Horse families. *Mitakuye Oyasin.* Loving thanks to Anne Merrow; to my agent, Joy Harris, for her gardener's determined and ever-optimistic heart; and to my singularly splendid, inimitably wise editor, Deb Futter.

The romance's conclusion promises her that if she learns to read male behavior successfully, she will find that her needs for fatherly protection, motherly care and passionate adult love will be satisfied perfectly. The explanatory structure of this argument is represented in Table 4.2.

— Janice A. Radway,
Reading the Romance:
Women, Patriarchy, and
Popular Literature

TABLE 4.2 / THE NARRATIVE LOGIC OF THE ROMANCE

1 The heroine's social identity is thrown into question.

2 The heroine reacts antagonistically to an aristocratic male.

3 The aristocratic male responds ambiguously to heroine.

4 The heroine interprets the hero's behavior as evidence of a purely sexual interest in her.

5 The heroine responds to the hero's behavior with anger or coldness.

6 The hero retaliates by punishing the heroine.

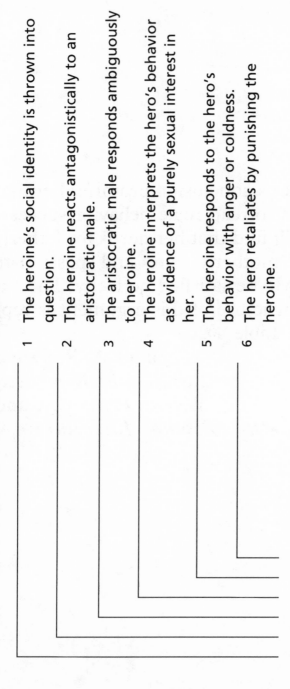

This explanatory link is revealed only later.

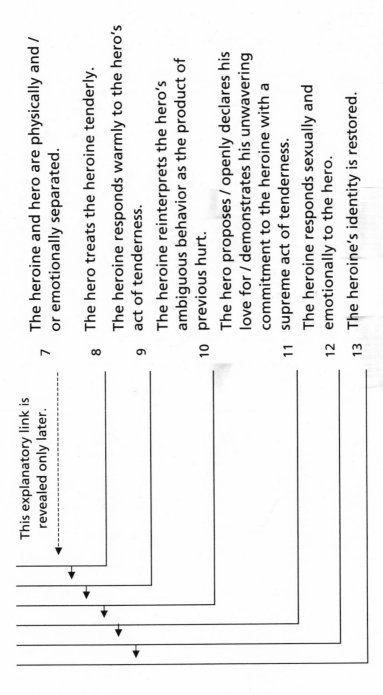

7 The heroine and hero are physically and / or emotionally separated.

8 The hero treats the heroine tenderly.

9 The heroine responds warmly to the hero's act of tenderness.

10 The heroine reinterprets the hero's ambiguous behavior as the product of previous hurt.

11 The hero proposes / openly declares his love for / demonstrates his unwavering commitment to the heroine with a supreme act of tenderness.

12 The heroine responds sexually and emotionally to the hero.

13 The heroine's identity is restored.

Saturdays, not every but most, Prudence True Parker visits her local library. Like a backwoods dowser, she moves lithe among the stacks, aisles and shelves, alert and poised as if she were in a hushed, damp primeval wood, her hand casually brushing book spines, the whorls of her fingertips buzzing, until one gives off an odor, a heat, until a voice bleeds, a revenant's whisper, a cuckold's lament, a poet's elegy, a theologian's bleat, a cook's plea for purity of ingredient. She stops then, seizes that book, takes it home, its pages containing some stoical, patient secret intended only for her. Occasionally the library is barren of message, its books mute catacombs, its words ash. At those rare times, she goes home empty-handed. Sometimes, though not often, she staggers out, knees buckling under the sheer bounty of clothbound wisdoms spilling from her arms. The titles of these books are various, their contents offer up innovations, peculiar methods of stalking the elusive self, shepherding her along fresh, wild paths, tributaries inward.

Prudence has yet to prepare a syllabus, a study guide for her fifteen-week community college course, Advanced Personal Journey. She knows she can fudge the first six weeks, reuse exercises from old syllabi — *mirrored passageways leading to the mysterious and majestic Labyrinth of Self.* After that, she will have to create something new, something to follow on the heels of:

1. Ripley's Believe It or Not: Uncover Your Own Uniqueness
2. Body Mapping: Freud Confronts His Dreams
3. House Blueprint: Cellar Is a Hero's Word
4. From Seed to Bloom: Horticultural Encounter
5. Masks: Whose Side Are You On?
6. Oddballs Lead No Humdrum Lives: A Personal Collection

So on a blistering Saturday afternoon in late July, Prudence parks her car in the library's newly macadamized parking lot and marches past the freshly installed

14

water sculpture, a city map of Tempe bordered by a raggedy queue of teddy bear cactus, a monstrous stonecutting suggesting nothing so much as angular chunks of spew in shades of fried, half-burnt Spam. Even the tepid glaze of fountain water trickling over its porcine pink face doesn't help; the sculpture nauseates Prudence. Averting her eyes, she stares stolidly toward the library's entrance, where a throng of women streams like slow, mottled smelt, garbed alike, with similar haircuts, wearing identical shoes. The mystery is solved when Prudence steps into the cool, darkened foyer of the library and happens upon a bold-lettered announcement:

MILDRED CRAWLEY,
ACCLAIMED AUTHOR OF THE
SAVAGE PASSION SERIES,
READS FROM HER
NEWEST BEST-SELLER,
SAVAGE SUNRISE.
4 P.M. FREE TO THE PUBLIC.

A romance novelist? The dowsing stick of her body falls dead at the very suggestion. Romance novels were lurid bromides, foul sop. Shouldn't one live one's romance, not read about preposterous imaginary ones? Who could help but typecast the sort of females converging by the dozens, streaming downstairs to the library's auditorium? Sparrows, every one. Drab, rumpled dowdesses. Look, there goes one now: wan, endomorphic, with bowl-cut brown hair, and a grayish complexion, sporting polyester slacks in sludge brown, a white bow-tie blouse and rustic Birkenstocks. She had taken note of such women in public areas, on buses or trains or airplanes, shamelessly gobbling up their romances, and it had long been Prudence's covert theory that the more romance novels a woman devoured, the more drab and colorless her own life was destined to become. Who was Mildred Crawley? Avatar of phony passions, sower of blight, draining women of life and color, their blood exchanged for the thin, addictive treacle of romance? Millionaire Crawley no doubt reaping high profit from such warped exchange! Prudence feels perversely tempted to follow the dull-plumaged multitude down the steps just to see the horror unfold, but with her class set to begin in a few weeks, she requires inspiration, not outrage. First, though, she needs to go into the bathroom and rinse out her right contact lens, clouded over with an opaque smear — a smear of distaste, no doubt. From her habitual trips to the library, Prudence knows of a wheelchair accessible bathroom tucked away behind the large-print editions, the blue handicapped logo on its door, a clean unisex bathroom, scarcely used.

Someone is in one of two oversized toilet stalls, a female with extremely large feet encased in suede maroon pumps with giant silver buckles. Pilgrim brogues. Cotton Mather shoes. The sound of this woman's urination is thunderous, prolonged and horsey. As the torrent of splash dwindles to a glassy tinkle, Prudence stands before the sink mirror blinking her right eye and hearing a voice, husky, peevish, irritable: *Hell's bells, no toilet paper, no paper in a library for Christ's sake, none at all.*

Prudence raps on the pale blue door. She has torn off a dry, neat length from the toilet roll in the adjacent stall and now waves it under. A massive hand, heavily beringed, snatches the wad of paper. Prudence sees dark hairs along the knuckles, vampire-length scarlet nails. "Thank you," the voice turns airy with gratitude. "You have no idea. I am obsessed with hygiene.

17

Without toilet tissue, my afternoon would have been irretrievably ruined. Speaking of ruin, these thigh-highs, the silicone tops are coming down, the left one is simply dropping like a rock to my ankles. Why in god's name did I say I would do this? What was I thinking?"

When the stall door unbolts, Prudence has both contact lenses out and can't see. The massive figure comes up, grips both her hands with bearlike force. "A thousand thank-yous. What is your name? Prudence? Prudence what? Parker? I'd like to properly thank you for coming to my rescue, but for the moment I must scoot as I am heinously late. May I locate your number in the phone directory, P for Parker?" Prudence, still blind, nods. "Fine then. Expect to hear from me. Tootles and tah-tah — I must be off!"

After Prudence has both eyes back in, it occurs to her whom she has probably just spoken with, passed hygienic toilet tissue to. The tall, broad woman with large feet, draped in massive swags of maroon cloth, heavily rouged and powdered, with a hairstyle reeking of wig, the woman with the chalky voice who would be looking up her name under P in the phone directory, had to have been Mildred Crawley, author of the Savage Passion series. Prudence's body begins dowsing like mad, thrumming like a tuning fork. Emerging from the bathroom, she bolts straight down the steps to peek into the lower-level auditorium. The large room is awash in monochromatic rows of females, a somber-feathered flock managing a thunderous ovation for Mildred Crawley as she approaches the podium, passing stacks of gaudy, glittering paperbacks awaiting her signature. The author of the Savage Passion series faces her wildly applauding audience. Pulled to full regal height, hands clasped modestly, head bowed graciously, she humbly surrenders to the noisy adoration of her fans. Standing near the back of the room, Prudence notes the rascal stocking, like a little black O-ring, a mourning band, dropped around the romance novelist's thick right ankle.

Part One

Part One

Tempe, Arizona

Clad in boxers patterned with glow-in-the-dark pumpkins and a Garfield "Easy Rider" tank top, clothing belonging to her daughter Fiona, Prudence stood, two mornings later, before her open refrigerator, unable to fend off the realization that something in her life was off-kilter. Incontestable evidence presented itself in the one egg, two heels of twelve-grain bread, bag of rubbery carrots, and sad knob of old butter. Outside the icebox and inside her head (that overcrowded, bony box) lurked the reluctant awareness that (a) she did not have money to buy groceries, (b) she would not be paid for three more weeks, and (c) while she had been busy helping others, no one had thought to help her. Entrenched within Prudence's moral foundation was a certain unchecked generosity, a self-destructive impulse toward charity. *Give, woman, give, to the headstrong, plunging world* . . . At fourteen, Prudence Parker had copied down this anonymous quote in her diary, a virtue thereafter subscribed to and left unexamined, a virtue leaving her, decades later, feeding others while starving herself. Martyrdom, an incremental, dishonest way to die.

Scrambling her solitary egg, toasting both grainy heels, Prudence mentally calculated the credit remaining on her card. Her penury, even to herself, was scarcely credible. She was a teacher at a community college, wasn't she? She lived in a reasonably attractive home with a brick fireplace and a newly fiberglassed swimming pool, didn't she? Aside from the cavernous icebox, the refrigerator busy chilling nothing, there were no outward, visible signs of monetary distress. Even Prudence had overlooked her own plight until there was no food, no money, and her daughter, Fiona, was due home, set to begin her senior year in high school. Since Prudence and Powell's divorce eight years before, Fiona had spent summers with her father in Taos, always flying home the day before school started. Eight summers of the same wrenching farewells and queer, ensuing silence, driving home from the airport without her child, the gradual adjustment to solitude, until, just as she'd developed a mostly pleasant routine, when silence no longer felt adversarial, the summer passed and Prudence had to re-adapt, make room for Fiona's return.

According to her late father's Pragmatic Book of Life, one should never admit budget failure. A person should cut out one's tongue rather than confess the deep embarrassment of fiscal idiocy. Thus it was with little discernible enthusiasm she plucked the day's mail from its black metal box, tossing plant, clothing and cookware catalogs and past-due bills into the trash, pausing only to tear open a large lilac envelope hand-addressed in violet ink, a masculine scrawl. Inside, a formal invitation to Mildred Crawley's home for afternoon tea. Tea, just for sharing toilet tissue? Prudence checked the address. Camelback Mountain. Her body began its low-pitched dowsing thrum, not in response to a library book, but simply from holding the blowsy, empurpled signature of a romance writer in her hand.

Mineral monstrosity! Luxe behemoth! A few scant hours after receiving her invitation, Prudence paused in her little two-toned, sunbaked Nash Rambler, hands on the steering wheel, neck craned up at the red rock castle gouged imposingly into one flank of Camelback Mountain, twin turrets jutting out, rugged, frank statements of penile aggression. She was only halfway up the winding ascent, a vertiginous climb steeper than the parking spiral at the Phoenix airport. After a series of hairpin turns, she arrived at the top, counting six garages built into the bottom layer of the castle. She parked in the pencil-thin shade of a dying saguaro, walked across a wooden drawbridge, a dry, rocky, waterless moat, and knocked on a massive timbered door fit for giants, a fee-fi-fo-fummish door. Ushered into the castle by a grim-faced old toad wearing a starched white nurse's uniform, Prudence trailed the toad's squeaking rubber shoes down a vast, parqueted hallway into a large circular, cavernous room with round recessed windows set high along one wall. In the center of this dank, echoey rotunda noised an impressive, deafening waterfall, backlit with gel lights, green, red, yellow and blue sweeps of garish color passing in monotonous rhythm across a botanical jungle suggestive of the Pleistocene era. With neither fanfare nor courtesy, Prudence was seated at a small garden table made of white, floridly patterned wrought iron. The nurse squeaked off, and moments later the boxy creature Prudence remembered meeting in the Tempe library's handicapped bathroom stood before her, extending a broad hand with its fleet of dark hairs and vampire-sharp glue-on nails. Outfitted in a maroon silk smoking jacket, black silk pajama bottoms and sleek black slippers, sparse, snowy hair cropped close to the skull, Mildred Crawley was incontestibly, inarguably, a man.

"Delightful of you to arrive on such peremptory notice, Ms. Parker." The familiar chalky enunciations. "What you see" — here Mildred (Prudence knew no other name) gave a lordly, operatic gesture with silk-robed arms — "is my recompense for helping lonely female souls, one page at a time, one book at a time, one series at a time, find asylum from mundane and otherwise socially wretched lives. Casa Crawley has twelve bedrooms, six and a half bathrooms, a fully outfitted dungeon, an Olympic-size pool along with a spa for twenty. I admit to hedonism, gluttony and a sybaritic excess of lovers who have kept pace with my literary output, a boy for every book, not intentional in the least. Until she died at noon on Secretary's Day, 1992, my mother, Glorianna Jean, lived here with me. And as melodramatically as the truth may fall upon your unassuming, innocent ears, Ms. Parker, I have not long to live myself, less than six months. Perhaps only three. The Mildred Crawley you see before you, née Digby Deeds, totters on the last of her pathetic, shopworn legs."

Colors swept like klieg lights across her host's face, turning it jaundiced, sickly green, hellish-lit or moody blue by turns. He scraped back a dainty iron chair and sat fussily down just as the nurse trundled in a tea cart, the kind Prudence associated with five-star hotels, fully linened and loaded with tea sandwiches, French pastries and a silver tea service. Ravenous, Prudence heaped her plate as Digby began his story, after helping himself to nothing but a cup of green tea and a paper-thin slice of kiwi which he left untouched. "Twenty-five years ago, on a drunken dare, I dashed out my first Mildred Crawley romance, *Beauty, Her Dark Beast*, a mere lark, with my partner, Edgar, who has been irredeemably and unforgivably dead, leaving all the drudgery to me, for more than ten years now. *Beauty* was a positive horse plop of clichés, a monstrous success, manna for the booboisie, that apt coinage of Mencken's. I found myself shackled to my nom de plume, Mildred Crawley, having accepted a wildly lucrative contract for the Savage Love series, to be followed by the Savage Dream and Savage Passion series, a ride straight to the top, where I have lived, in outrageous splendor, ever since. My newest agent, a dreadful little fellow who insists on wearing fruit-colored leisure suits, induced me to appear at your quaint little *bibliothèque* — sales, he insisted, were dipping, and I owed my readers, no less than *semper fi*, one of my rare appearances. Meeting you in a public toilet, Ms. Parker, was worth every misery of that arduous afternoon, even perhaps the divinely ordained reason for my appearance. To be perfectly blunt, I have been seeking an heir. Someone to complete the final forty plots of my Savage Passion series. And like a Hollywood starlet discovered waitressing at a drugstore counter or checking hats at the Ritz, I feel in my dying bones that I have discovered you, Prudence Parker. My starlet. My heir."

"How flattering," Prudence mumbled. How ludicrous, she thought.

"I further confess, when I emerged from that nasty stall and saw you, so manqué, with a certain irresistible *je ne sais quoi* look of genteel, Bronte-esque poverty about you, it was as if you had emerged, full-blown, from my dreams."

Prudence bent down to retrieve her linen napkin from the floor where it had slipped from her lap. I looked manqué, she thought, because I was blind. The man is mad.

After they had eaten, or rather after Prudence had hoovered up every single cucumber and shrimp paste sandwich, giving mumbled answers to Digby's few questions about herself between mouthfuls, he led her up a steep, winding marble staircase to his author's turret, a circular chamber with a panoramic view of Phoenix, cloaked in its usual sulfuric caul of bilious, industrialized air.

"Following Balzac's lead, though spared his genius, I wear a white silk robe, drink strong black coffee and write from midnight to dawn, five days a week. I finish each of my books in ninety days; an utterly methodical, cold-blooded process. Because of failing health, my output, in the past year, has declined significantly. What I have done instead, to amuse myself as well as pave the gold brick road for my heir or heiress — perhaps you, Ms. Parker — is to draw up plots, detailed plots, blueprints, for forty additional novels. This will require someone to simply fill in the blanks, someone, after I am cast out into the cosmos, to carry on the Crawley name. I know little of your personal life, Ms. Parker, but judging from the fact that you were alone in a library on a Saturday evening, and further judging from the look of your car" — they stood staring out a deeply recessed turret window at Prudence's faded aqua and beige Rambler — "this may be welcome news. Each of my books earns an advance of ten and royalties of upwards of twenty thousand dollars. And though what I view as destiny you may view as bizarre happenstance, a chance encounter in a toilet stall, the figures may still impress you. It is equally true you may, at this very moment, be scrambling for an excuse to escape." He peered at her. "Are you?"

What about the dungeon? Fully outfitted. What was that about? Prudence felt anxiety mixed with greed over such dangled sums of money, an overall giddiness, perplexity, a bungled sense of wonder. As she often did in crisis, she heard her mother's voice — *Nothing's free in this world, Prune, don't be a naive Nancy!*

"I don't quite know what to think. I —"

Just then the bashing, assaultive sound of heavy metal music leapt up the spiraled staircase. Wearily, Digby brushed a sallow hand over the top of his white cropped hair. "He'll be the death of me, I know it."

"Your son?"

"Hardly. Let's trudge down, shall we?"

"Therron is a fledgling Navajo poet," Digby's voice floated backward as Prudence trailed him down the staircase. "An exquisite piece of human furniture. He is with me for my fortune, and pretends, not very convincingly, otherwise." In a living room the size of a resort lobby, its oak floor saturated with animal skins and pelts, its polished rosewood walls studded with mounted heads of game animals, moose, deer, elk, and an entire family of molting javelina, they stood gazing out one of several velvet-swagged, leaded windows watching a copper-skinned young man, completely naked, with stylishly short bleached hair swan-dive into an Olympic-size pool. "Therron is the only one to have gone completely aquatic," sighed Digby. "He is the perfect one-night stand. One night after another."

"Couldn't he write your series for you?"

"He's a fledgling poet, my dear. Taking on the Mildred Crawley mantle would be tantamount to suicide. Stabbing himself to death with his own pen."

It was dusk by the time Prudence trawled back down the mountain, having ended her visit by thanking Digby but refusing his generous offer. How could she possibly churn out such dreck, color in the stiff plot points of romance, betray her own aesthetics? Digby simply urged Prudence to give herself time, to sleep, as it were, on his offer. Not wishing to insult the wishes of a dying man, Prudence found herself exiting Casa Crawley with a heap of Crawley romances, both hardback and paper, sliding about in the backseat (having been shouldered out by taciturn Therron, clad in nothing but the electric blue Speedo he'd hastily snapped on, Prudence assumed, for her sake). The only way she could consider carrying on Digby's Savage Passion series was if it were a secret pact between them — and if, like Digby, she could learn to flip out romances, fast as hotcakes, in the middle of the night. What was it he had said? Crawley's Foolproof Formula for Best-Selling Romance: four sex scenes per book, understanding that emotional intimacy is far more dangerous than physical contact, and on the final page of every Crawley romance, the woman always, always, wins.

Waikaloa, Hawaii

The minute her plane rose up over the five islands only diehards, dreamers and prairie dwellers still called paradise, Prudence True Parker regretted what she had let her mother, Deleanor, do to her hair. Hadn't the entire length of her adolescence been demoralized, derailed by hapless, wanton crushes on wide-shouldered boys with butter-colored hair, covert infatuations with platinum-haired girls, sleek and haughty as seals? Prudence True Parker had grown up buck-toothed, chipmunk-cheeked, flat-breasted and flame-headed at a time when redheads were thought to be hot-tempered viragos, fractious and full of sass. Prue, or Prune, as her mother liked to call her, had been a timid, photo-sensitive child. Sunlight had made her dizzy and weak. Sunshine, along with her own emotions, had caused her to overbreathe, see spots, hyperventilate. Decades later, her mother still prized a rare snapshot of Prudence at sixteen, holding a sun-drenched pose on the back lawn, languid, odalisque, and wearing a white piqué "bikini," the old-fashioned kind, a one-piece suit snipped boldly in half. In that chemically faded Polaroid, Prudence's poached, milky collop of stomach was indistinguishable from the two white squares of dry, dimpled fabric. And now, because of Deleanor's buying the wrong box of Lady Clairol off a closeout table outside Wong's Pharmacy, and because of her own inability to deny her widowed, grieving mother a thing, Prudence had turned, overnight, into the very creature she had so strenuously envied and lusted after in youth — a blonde.

"Say, would you get that stewardess to give me another fork? Mine snapped."

Prudence was belted in beside a squat cylinder of a woman in a man's polyester shirt, green and orange boomerangs whizzing across its cream background. The shirt reminded her of a Klee painting. Cylinder, whose iron gray hair snapped up from her scalp in wiry terrier tufts, crackled open her cellophaned crackers, chewed with square-jawed, methodical greed, latched onto the procured fork with burly, thankless zest.

"Been on vacation?"

"Visiting my mother."

"She lives there in Hawaii? Lucky duck."

"She's newly widowed." Prudence felt thonked by a tiny mallet of grief. Banana cake stuck in a moist clump to her palate. "They were married sixty-two years." And loved each other. She didn't add that, it seemed too private.

With hamlike arms and pudgy cone-shaped fingers, the Cylinder beat butter onto her dinner roll with a plastic knife that looked as if it wanted to snap, too. She fixed a stern, gimlet eye on Prudence.

"Your parents were fortunate. They had each other all that time. Do you know how many old folks" — she cocked her chin toward the airplane window — "are out there alone?" Following her gaze, Prudence half expected to see old people drizzling past, sad, brittle-boned, desolate.

The tiny mallet struck again. *I'm the one alone.* Selfish thought! She should be thinking about her mother. Prudence arched her tense neck, closed her eyes. Two weeks ago, on her flight from Phoenix to Kona, she'd been sandwiched between a retired nurse and a delegate to the Home-makers of America Convention. The homemaker's husband, who ran a small cattle operation outside Truth or Conse-quences, New Mexico, had refused to accompany his wife to paradise. If he'd never traveled past Albuquerque, he'd argued, why should that change now?

"I froze him a week's worth of dinners," the homemaker told Prudence. "Salisbury steak, chicken fried steak, glazed ham loaf, battered cod. Not one night apart in twenty-seven years. I'm worried he won't eat or remember to feed my gladiolas."

"Trust me, hon, he'll annihilate your gladiolas before he lets himself starve," the nurse interrupted the rancher's wife, busy using her homemaker's thumbnail to deftly slice open a blue packet of Mauna Loa macadamia nuts. Prudence marveled at the small competencies of people, their sturdy declarations of accomplishment, their pride, for instance, in having slept beside the same man for twenty-seven years, or in her mother's case, sixty-two.

"What do you feed your gladiolas?" Prudence pictured the rancher, hunkered down, tossing his wife's flowers small scraps of beef.

"Bonemeal."

Bonemeal. Powdered bone. Of course. What her dead father, an amateur horticulturalist, tender of old-fashioned roses, had finally become. Food for bulbs.

★ ★ ★

When the plane landed, blump, a shiny tumescent pod, onto the runway of the small airport in Kona, it was past sunset, nearly dark, but Prudence picked out her mother's familiar shape, waiting as if her forty-nine-year-old daughter was still in need of tender maternal harbor, which, Prudence supposed, she was. Descending the plane's short metal staircase, crossing the soft black tarmac, she bent her neck to accept the chilled lei of pink and yellow peikeili blossoms her mother always greeted her with. Back home, Prudence had a pottery jar full of Deleanor's dried, faded leis.

"Prune, your hair! It's gone the strangest shade on top!"

"It's gray, Mom." She kissed her mother's cheek. "I'm getting old."

"Pishposh!" Deleanor dismissed her child's nonproductive, negative thinking. "Mind over matter, peanut. If you don't mind, age won't matter."

Prudence slouched in the plush upholstered passenger's seat of her father's luxury Cadillac, a familiar position sequentially occupied, first as a wan, squirmy child, then as a mopey, thick-rumped teenager, a dreamy, bookish college student, domestic, pert wife, housewife flailing and discouraged, single working mother, and now as herself, aging, debt-ridden and thin-shelled as a blown egg, staring out the window as Deleanor steered Walt's lime green sedan through a tropical Wuthering Heights, interminable bleak miles of harsh-pored black volcanic rock hulking into a brumous, inky sky and beyond, the slight westerly relief of a rumpled, satiny ocean. As they floated up the driveway into the nearly empty garage of her parents' home, a home that reminded Prudence of a pristine white jewel box, she noted the Island Realty sign, hanging listless from its whitewashed post on the sloping lawn. Over the past six months, Deleanor, having decided to move to Arizona to be near her daughter and granddaughter, had gone through five realtors, blaming each, personally, for what could not be helped, a sluggish housing market. When her contract with the divorced orthopedic surgeon from Queens had fallen through two days earlier, that did it.

"Walt's trying to get me to stay put. Bloom where you're planted, Del — I can just hear him, talking in bumper stickers. H-E-double-toothpicks. I told him on my walk this morning, that's what I'll do if that's what he wants. Stay put." Deleanor said this as she led Prudence down the hall. The walls were soft white, the carpet pale gray. Prudence had forgotten how immaculate her mother was, how tidy.

The guest room was done in soporific blues and creamy vanilla, sentimental French decor down to the ribbon-tied sprays of lavender, Provençal lamps, Provençal duvet, lace café curtains, Monet and Manet framed prints on the mild blue walls. Hefting her suitcase into the lavender-scented closet, Prudence felt tranquilized by her mother's aesthetic, by the same sweet, soothing symmetry that over a year ago, when she had come here for Walt's funeral, had caused Prudence to scuffle her hand down the gaping, linted throat of her purse, hoping to pinch up a stray Valium or two. But now, having run out of money, men and bright ideas, with no rosy plan or ambitious perspective, all Prudence wanted was to ploff down into Deleanor's crisp French country ambience and never emerge.

"Prune! You're as piebald as old Grandma True!"

They stood in Deleanor's spotless white kitchen, sipping from plain white mugs of Sleepy Time tea, discussing the mottled, milky spillage on Prudence's hands and forearms. Earlier that evening, in the guest shower, Prudence had come upon a new patch on the back of her left calf, refrigerator white, shaped like a puzzle piece.

"Vertigo? Vitalo? Vit . . . vitiglio? Anyway, with Grandma True, the family called it piebald."

"It's vitiligo, Mom. Same disease Michael Jackson has."

"Now don't go comparing yourself to him. You're shedding pigment. Losing melanin. Here. Have a ginkgo biloba."

"What for?"

"To help you remember to keep out of sunlight. The sun aggravates what you've got. I don't forget a thing since I've been taking this stuff."

Deleanor began rattling an army of short-necked vitamin bottles out from the lazy Susan built into her corner cupboard, tapping out two equal humps of dun- colored bullets, molehills of health, one for her, one for Walt.

"Your father and I always did great for our age, but we didn't know which of these pills was doing the trick. If we stopped taking this one or that — hoo! — Mr. Reaper! So down the hatches, we'd pop them all."

Prudence swallowed one army-colored

ginkgo. Her father had been dead sixteen months, and it seemed as if Deleanor, gulping down first Walt's vitamins then her own, hadn't fully noticed. Things revolved around him now, even more than they had when he was alive, when Deleanor used to complain he was always underfoot, dragging dirt clods into the house on the bottoms of his canvas gardening shoes. In death he had become her resident deity, consulted daily, an oracle, the entire house a reliquary given over to his memory and rote presence. It worried Prudence a little, but what would she know about being married for nearly half a century? She didn't know ten years.

"Those Japanese have all the bright ideas. They use umbrellas for rain and sun. That's the ticket, Prudence. Buy a bumbershoot."

"Bumber—"

"— shoot. Brit word your father and I picked up on our last garden tour. The Sackville-West garden. The year after Giverny."

Prudence pictured plodding about campus balancing a slim-stemmed umbrella above her head. Why not one of those brightly striped umbrella hats with a built-in misting system? No, she'd never wield an umbrella, she'd look like Mary Poppins fending off sunstroke. She wouldn't even use a rolling briefcase the way most of her colleagues did, looking as if they were dragging flat, recalcitrant pets along; she preferred lugging books and papers the old-fashioned way, in her arms.

"OK if I sleep late?"

"Late as you like, lovey. I'm up with the birds at five, Dad's up at six, doing his crossword, there's no rush to do a thing. You're on island time here."

Prudence chose to overlook her mother's comment about her dead father's hour of rising. Instead, and for the next two weeks, she would wallow and flop in her mother's old devotions, rolling about like a dog in clover, letting Deleanor wash and iron her clothes, hang her blouses and dresses neatly on fat satin hangers, ply her with warm homemade oat bread, spicy ginger cookies, slices of island fresh papaya, guava, pineapple. For the first time in her adult life, Prudence did not resist Deleanor's domestic fussing.

Waking early that first morning, Prudence put on her mother's pink gingham guest robe and drifted out onto the screened veranda to join her father, where he sat boxed on the glass-topped table beside his sharpened pencil and neatly folded crossword from the morning's newspaper. Sipping Kona coffee, Prudence watched a scatter of bright yellow birds, small as minutes, dart in and out of the bougainvillea, perch on the granite birdbath, ruffle and snap their sharp, vitelline wings. Her mother was out exercising. Eighty-four-year-old Deleanor practiced yoga, bench-pressed, scudded up and down hills for an hour each morning, each hill one in a series of geriatric obstacles she was resolved to conquer. The amazing Deleanor True Parker. Powerhouse. Hannibal. Atatürk. Widow of Might. Yawning, Prudence leafed idly through the *Honolulu Advertiser.* She loved small-town papers, especially the police reports. WOMAN REPORTS SEEING MAN URINATE ON GOLF COURSES* *Miss Addie Perch, 68, called police upon seeing a man approach the ninth hole at the Kona Golf Course and begin to urinate. The man, she reported, emerged from a stand of eucalyptus trees, and when he was finished, stepped back into the trees. Miss Perch witnessed this from her backyard, just after her usual luncheon, at approximately 2 p.m.*

44

★ ★ ★

With its showy, scarlet-bloomed hibiscus, waxy tangle of philodendron, wild orchid and banana trees, its narrow graveled paths meandering beside koi ponds and insistent, plashing waterfalls, the clinic's grounds resembled a lush verdant botanical garden more than a medical complex. Inside, however, the chilly, blue-carpeted halls and sterile, fluorescent-lit examining rooms were no different than those in any stateside medical building. When Deleanor's routine checkup revealed sky-high blood pressure, her mother confessed to having had "little wingdings," occasional dizzy spells. They waited an hour to see a specialist, another hour to get a prescription, with Deleanor swatting the prescription slip sticking out of her purse, insisting she wouldn't take whatever it was they were going to try to kill her with this time. After getting her mother's blood pressure pills, Prudence suggested lunch in the clinic's cafeteria, a large room filled with Formica-topped tables and unoccupied benches. The coral pink walls, swagged with brown fishnets, bulged with clear glass balls that looked like gloomy, sadsack testicles. Going down the cafeteria line, shoving along pink plastic trays, they chose blackened hot dogs striped with mustard and relish, Doritos and Diet Dr Pepper. Sitting down, Deleanor fixed an eye on her lunch, a reckless truant, greedy for forbidden foods (*Anybody tell you what wieners are made of, Prooster? Hearts, tongues and snouts, hearts, tongues and snouts*). A self-declared health nut during the last years Walt was alive, her mother had mastered the sober, guilt-scored language of grams and sodium, mono- and diglycerides, hydrogenated and nonhydrogenated fats. (Sneak- ing a surreptitious forkful of something tasty, Prudence would invariably be caught out, subjected to Deleanor's recitation of statistics handed down by her favorite newsletter physician, Dr. Sinatra, Dr. Sinatra this, Dr. Sinatra that.) But death tested faiths democratically, and it had not escaped Prudence's notice that her mother rarely mentioned food as the pathway to longevity anymore. Leaving the cafeteria, Prudence stopped at one of the vending machines to purchase two foil-wrapped Eskimo Pies.

"Crammed with fat, wax and god knows what all," her mother said, tearing off the crinkly silver wrapper. "Why do they call these pies? They are squares. Eskimo squares."

"And one little square won't kill us," Prudence said, flicking a bit of chocolate off her mother's downy chin.

Prudence and Deleanor sat at an open-air table, the dark sea roiling behind them. A tall, muscular Hawaiian man sprinted past, dressed in nothing much and bellowing on a conch shell, part of a nightly show put on by the Japanese-owned resort hotel. By the light of a string of tiki torches, flaring along the outdoor patio like a fiery amber necklace, Prudence and her mother ordered mahimahi, fresh from the sea that day, with a coconut, ginger and macadamia nut sauce, drank expensive Chilean merlot (Walt's favorite), ending their meal with a shared plate of Mauna Loa Fudge Volcano cake. A bit of Walt tagged along in Deleanor's new small plastic prescription bottle, her blood pressure pills having been flushed down the toilet the minute she'd gotten home from the clinic that afternoon. The amber pill bottle lay on its side near the white-napkined basket of dinner rolls, as if resigned to an endless afterlife of vicarious longing.

At home, Deleanor appeared hale and fit, yet in public, her mother had begun to seem frail, peripheral, even spectral. Prudence had her own days of periphery now, falling-behind days, entire sluggish hours, when everyone else seemed glossy, comically swift, ambitiously paced. Their waiter, his tropical shirt neatly belted into pressed khaki shorts, afforded Deleanor the arrogant, glancing condescension reserved by the young for those who had failed life by growing old and unsavory, those with one foot in the grave. Prudence wanted to hiss at this muscle-pumped youth with his gelled, porcine hair after he coldly ignored Deleanor's joke, actually one of Walt's (*Young man, do you know what the snail said, riding on the turtle's back? . . . Wheee!*), you'd better hope someone a bit smarter, a bit kinder, is around when you are old one day. She recalled a time two years before when she, Walt and Deleanor had driven the two-laned slice through the island's black volcanic rock to a run-down seventies-era shopping center (its indoor food court like a pet shop aquarium with finger-smudged glass and murky atmosphere), the three of them standing in line, ordering vanilla cones dipped in chocolate (paraffin, Deleanor sniffed, eager for hers), bearing their treats out to a table overlooking an artificial lagoon. Deleanor's cone had broken at its tip; a rivulet of melted ice cream puddled in her lap, staining her alice blue, white-flowered muumuu, and Walt had taken the dripping cone and gallantly handed Deleanor his. Wrapping the defective cone in a thick diaper of napkins and limping back into the food court (using the cane Prudence had bought him as a gag one Christmas; she'd loved how the brass knob pulled apart to reveal a compass, admired the slender flask covertly fitted into the hollowed top length of the cane), her father waited in line, composed, resolute, holding Deleanor's soggy-bottomed cone, his parrot's crest of white hair adding to his already imposing height. A teenager with a pitted complexion, shaved head and double nose rings waited on the counter's other side, impassive, and hostile as her father requested, confident in the rightness of his case, a refund. Prudence remembered watching his large hands tremble as he'd carefully pocketed each coin, how she'd held the door as he used his cane to navigate back to Deleanor, waiting in her stained muumuu, a partial mustache of ice cream gleaming across her upper lip, a smile of open, heartbreaking trust upon her face.

They packed towels, sunscreen, water bottles, books (which they never read), snacks (which they always ate) and the ubiquitous bit of Walt (Deleanor making sure that, even if he just sat in his pill bottle on the dash, her dead husband was afforded a view). Each morning, Deleanor drove the unpaved, hilly road to a local private beach, where she and Prudence laid identical blue-and-white-striped towels on a silken hummock of sand, set down identical straw bags on the soft gray picnic table half hidden in the cold shade of a low-branched, spreading tree, and walked the shoreline, bare feet slipping and rising in the night-damp, cinnamon-soft sand, wearing identical tomato red boy-legged suits, because if Deleanor liked a thing, she often as not bought two, and because Prudence, who usually skinny-dipped in her pool back home, did not own a swimsuit. On one morning's stroll by the sea, they came upon a broad-backed ocean turtle, washed ashore and motionless. Squatting down, Deleanor rapped lightly on its mottled shell. A turtle, she said, could feel the slightest vibration through its horny, greenish brown carapace. In a torpid yet strangely telescopic motion, the turtle extended its neck, turning the scaled greenish stalk and fixing one eye on Deleanor with glassy, unnerving directness.

"The eye, Prudence. The expression. It's Walter."

"Should we carry him back into the water?" Surely her mother wouldn't decide to lug this new embodiment of Walter home with them. Prudence had been humoring Deleanor in all this carting around of Walt's ashes, arranging his place at the table, setting his daily crossword on the patio table each morning, placing the remote on his chair each night, and now, confusing him with a turtle. At night, Prudence heard her mother chatting away — to Walt — in their bedroom. She had listened with eroding forbearance to Deleanor's stories of losing an object, of hunting high and low, then coming upon it placed in such mischievous fashion it could only be Walt, Walt's spirit, playing with her, letting her know he was around. She had tried not to presume the eccentricities of human grief, but this time she hoped Deleanor would not insist on bringing Walt, as a terrapin, home with them.

"We can't pick him up, Prune. If he has a human scent, the others will reject him."

With Deleanor waving, blowing kisses to the turtle, they moved off down the beach.

51

Coming back an hour or so later, they found their friend vanished, though Deleanor spied flipper marks, curving scuffs in the sun-brightened sand, headed in a sure straight direction back into the sea.

When she swam, Prudence stroked sideways, absurdly close to shore, knees bumping the sand. Deleanor didn't swim at all, but strode right in as if to confront the long, flat horizon, letting the waves hike her thighs, leave salty tendrils on her skin. She looked glorious, lightly planted in the sea, with slim tanned legs, a billowing white shirt, one hand pressed to the crown of her flat-brimmed straw hat to keep it from flying off. A violet craze of veins broke across Deleanor's slender legs, her arms bore dun, yellowing bruises from minor bumps, her skin, after nearly a century, was ropy, swagged, hatched and scored with wrinkles. Her mother's refusal to allow the slow, fated ruin of simple flesh keep her from enjoyment, from full, sensuous pleasure, was, to Prudence, marvelous instruction, and thrilled, she took pictures. One photograph she would frame and keep on her desk at school — Deleanor, against a glittering aquamarine backdrop of sea, hands on hips, wearing her wide-brimmed hat with its fluttering swallow's tail of black grosgrain, her poet's blouse, grinning into the camera with the gleeful, profligate wiles of a survivor and a sensualist (*What a god-awful picture . . . why on earth did you take that? Lordy, Prune, don't show that to anybody, I've gotten so many more wrinkles since Walter died, I swear I look one hundred years old!*).

Behind the wheel of her late husband's Cadillac, Deleanor rivaled *The Twilight Zone*'s character of Mr. Death. Blithely waving at cloud formations or pointing toward a squat black slope of volcanic rock, pimples of white rock spelling out on its surface WAYNES* LOVESS* RHODAS*, her mother would rocket the car off the road, dust spewing up around its windows, or worse, womble into the opposite lane before righting her course with a sharp jerk of the arms. Cautionary articles had been written about the dangers of elderly drivers, how they resisted the surrender of their keys, fought the loss of their freedom, resented being jostled toward a more democratic destination, death, which required no license and very little skill. For the sake of public safety, adult children needed to step up, take charge, firmly take the keys. Well, Prudence would probably let her mother kill them both before she would have the nerve to do such a thing. This time it was night, with her mother's beringed hands clamped on the steering wheel at eleven fifty-eight and eleven fifty-nine as they arrived, unscathed and still blessedly alive, on a blustery hilltop and walked toward a modest one-story nondenominational church, both of them buffeted, danced along by a freshly risen island wind.

"Looks like the whole henhouse blew in," Deleanor muttered. Waiting in line, Prudence counted twenty women over seventy seated in the large nondescript room, many of them turning to smile or wave at her mother. The wind, howling now, slammed and tore against the windows of the building, shook the walls and lent a kind of shipwreck intimacy to the group of females sheltered inside. "I take my yoga here three times a week, that's how all these old biddies know me," Deleanor hissed. Paying the small admission fee, Prudence located an empty seat among rows of tan metal folding chairs as her mother, in her short-sleeved pink unitard and denim skort, stood listening to a handsome silver-haired Hawaiian woman describe her husband's second hip replacement.

The sole man in the room, pigeon-breasted and potbellied, wore a too-snug polo shirt and linty, ballooning black slacks. As Prudence watched, he shambled up to the front of the room with a stout woman in a bamboo-patterned green shift, stretched like Saran wrap against his plump left hip. The woman's hair, the shade and stringiness of overdone pot roast, dropped like tent flaps on either side of two cross vulpine eyes overlaid with gigantic black-framed glasses resembling empty TV sets. Quig, followed by his wife, Karma, began to speak, sharing the cosmic destined ways they'd been led to their work as a spiritual couple (*And may I tell you, ladies, life with Karma hasn't been a stroll in any normal park, winked Quig*). The Master Toning Workshop began with the elderly ladies all tittering as Quig instructed them to find a comfortable spot on the gray-carpeted floor, to lie down on their backs and close their eyes. Karma took over from there, ordering the women to breathe in unison from their navels. This is like a bank robbery, thought Prudence, staring at the blank ceiling. With all twenty or so senior ladies strewn about on their backs, feet splayed, eyes shut, bellies breathing, Quig, who boasted having once been a cattle auctioneer in Omaha, drew himself up before the prone forms (Prudence watched through her lashes), inflated his already orotund belly, and with pursed feminine lips let forth a measured, gaseous conch-shell blast of sound. BAAAAAH-ROOOOOM (bathroom without the t, Prudence thought). Karma then commanded the blind, supine flock to tone along with Quig. BAAAAH-ROOOOM. Prudence's mind hopped like a gnat. Her feet itched. Reluctantly, she added her voice to the bloated, asinine sound boiling off the floor. BAAAAH-ROOOOM.

After some minutes of this, a thrumming silence ensued during which they were instructed by Karma to sit up, open their eyes and share. One woman emphatically related how her spirit had left her body and gone to sport with dolphins in the sea. Another said she had experienced a profound love for all deceased beings. The silver-haired Hawaiian woman spoke tearfully of her husband's physical suffering. When Prudence's turn came, she quietly said she had glimpsed the color lavender and been urged by a mysterious inner voice to eat more carrots and cut back on dairy. Deleanor, who had stayed disobediently upright throughout the exercise, perching on a chair near the fire exit, spoke last.

"I feel dull as a ditch, the rest of you having had so many religious and health messages. I'm antsy, that's my whole problem. Can't sit still. My daughter over there, the one in white, she's a schoolteacher back in Phoenix, Arizona. Prune honey, that voice you heard was probably me telling you to eat your carrots and knock off the ice cream."

Everyone laughed except Karma, who interrupted the general gaiety, commanding everyone back on the floor, eyes closed, navels breathing. Prudence lost count of the monotonous string of BAAAAH-ROOOOM-ings and sharings before the workshop finally concluded with a Q&A encompassing subjects from space aliens to the lost city of Atlantis, from iridology to toning for relief of constipation, capped by a strong-arm pitch from Karma to buy their newest cassettes and toning pamphlets. She and Quig flanked the exit doors, tirelessly pushing cheap trifold brochures, *Toning for Weight Loss*, *Chanting for Prosperity*, into the departing women's hands. Scuttled along by near-gale-force winds, Prudence and Deleanor blew back to Walt's pale, mystic-looking green Cadillac. Steering by the red tail-lights of exiting cars, Deleanor wavered down the unlit hill as Prudence, over- oxygenated, began to giddily BAAAAH-ROOOOM at the top of her lungs. Deleanor drummed her palms on the wheel, hooting. "Don't breathe a word to your father. He'd never let me live it down. Bunkum, he'd say. Flake-o. Pure hogwash."

Represented by the slim black slipper of the remote, set atop a freshly ironed pair of baby blue boxers, Walter Parker waited up in the den in his plaid wing chair, watching a special about history's worst circus fires. "I don't know how you can bear to watch. Poor burning creatures. Pity's sake, look at those camels. Historical or not, I can't watch. Prune, can I take you up on that treatment you offered? That Reiki thing? I'm about to jump out of my skin."

Prudence dimmed the matching brass table lamps in her mother's living room, put on the CD she'd brought at Crystal Magick, a solo cello accompanied by cracks of simulated thunder and a blurring of hypnotic rain. Still in her pink unitard, Deleanor lay face-up, belly inflating, a beach ball, deflating with each exhale. All at once, Deleanor stuck her arms straight above her head and began bumping her hips around. "What am I, Pruey?"

"Mom, with Reiki —"

"A piece of chewing gum!"

"— you're supposed to lie still. Relax." Prudence wasn't sure she liked the CD's irritable thunder, the plaintive, whining cello.

Arms stiffened above her head, Deleanor began writhing, making popping, spitting noises. "Now guess."

Prudence kept silent.

"A strip of bacon frying!" Deleanor kerplunked her arms, palms down, to her sides. "All right. I'll be good. Truth is, Prune, I'd hoped at that dumb Toning thing to hear some kind of message from your father. That's why I went in the first place. I thought maybe he'd be able to reach me there. I talk to him all day long and never hear a word back."

Prudence remembered her father in his last years as a quiet, round-shouldered man with silky white hair and sharp blue eyes, pottering among his turgid-bloomed old-fashioned roses, or sitting in his wing chair in front of the television, or showing up like clockwork, three times a day, at Deleanor's kitchen table to eat whatever nutritive challenge she set before him. Fading, like an old snapshot, colors leaching, outlines dimming, her father had begun to talk less, move less, until he was gentle, silent and mostly still. Now Walt was eternally quiet, moodless, not even naked, just ashes in a Hershey's-colored box, and the few flakes of marrowed bone Deleanor carted about with her in a pill bottle. Not so different from those last years, really, when Deleanor used to grumble to Prudence how Walt never talked anymore, never listened either, never wanted to go anywhere or do anything, the only thing he cared about were those g.d. roses of his, which by now she had begun to nearly hate the sight and fragrance of, imagine that, feeling that way about roses, the flower of passion.

Prudence sat tailor fashion, hands cupped above the crown of her mother's head. Slow heat rose from her palms, a buzz of healing warmth. When the heat subsided, she moved her hands, cupping them next over her mother's ears, eyes, throat, chest, methodically moving down her body. Prudence had gone to a Reiki workshop the summer before, and after some brief beginner's enthusiasm, rarely practiced it. She had been taught to use it on herself every night, but invariably fell asleep, arms aching. With her face now inches from Deleanor's, she studied her mother, the closed eyes, the hair wisping up from the child-sized skull, the same "youthful" champagne tint she had dyed it for the past quarter century. Prudence, who could not recall ever having seen Deleanor this motionless, this stilled, suddenly imagined her mother dead, a corpse, watched her lighten, burn to ash, join Walt. Her parents, once human and married, arguing and traveling and sleeping together, horsing around, had turned into ten-pound boxes, paired identical bookends. Oblivious to her daughter's morbid thoughts, Deleanor began expelling little puffs of air, her mouth relaxed, slightly agape. Her mother was not dead. She was snoring.

Prudence quickly settled into her childhood routine, in bed by nine, read until ten or so. One night, exasperated with a murky Irish novel, Prudence remembered a second book, Bachelard's essays on the phenomenology of objects, left on the ledge of the tub in the guest bathroom (*And what thoughts we have, what daydreams, when we eat the germs of plants!*). Opening the bedroom door, hearing only oppressive silence from her mother's bedroom, she paused, remembering the last sudden visit, for her father's funeral, when all she'd heard from Deleanor's room night after night was piteous, constant weeping. And the visit before that, with her father still very much alive, when she'd gotten up to use the bathroom one night and overheard her mother's high-pitched giggling, a sudden, girlish shrieking from her parents' darkened bedroom, followed by her father's rare, teasing voice — *Here Mommy baby, here Mommy baby!* Her parents! Horsing around! Shocked and strangely envious, Prudence retreated to her room and closed the door, thinking of her mother's recurrent, infuriating complaint: *Such a shame you divorced Powell, an awfully nice man when you consider what's out there these days. Judging by the snapshot he still sends us every Christmas, that new wife is no great shakes, under what rock did he find her, even at your age you're a thousand times more attractive — he's still a dead ringer for Clint Eastwood, your father's all-time favorite movie star.* Deleanor magneted each holiday snapshot of Powell to her refrigerator door, mincing no words about the loss of her good-looking son-in-law, occasionally saying outright that Prudence had lacked good common sense, not putting up with ordinary male misbehavior, mere "peccadilloes." Her own marriage had lasted sixty-two years because she, Deleanor True, had put up with a host of Walt's failings, had learned to look the other way. Prudence's whole misguided, self-indulgent generation had failed to value the old-fashioned art of denial. To shut out the sounds of her parents cavorting that night, to stifle her own sobs, Prudence had taken a Japanese pillow stuffed with buckwheat hulls and clamped it over her face.

On this newest visit, after a sleepless night (not even Bachelard's book, retrieved from the tub ledge and diligently pencil-checked — *The tree is alive, reflective, straining toward God* — helped), Prudence surrendered to her mother's bold suggestion the next morning. Perched on a chrome-legged stool in Deleanor's tidy kitchen, a sky blue towel draped over her vitiligo-splotched shoulders, Prudence allowed her mother (wearing nothing more than the oversized Hawaiian shirt Walt had had on the day he died, and whistling one of his favorite songs, "Moon River") to dye her shoulder-length graying hair Tropical Blonde. *I just want you to find someone as good as he was, sweetie. As good as Walter. I just don't want you to be all alone.*

On the last day Prudence would see her parents alive together, on the day of her flight back to Phoenix — her mother's left bicuspid, like a badly timed practical joke, lodged itself in her tunafish sandwich. Calling the local dentist and leaving a frantic lisped message with his answering service, Deleanor suddenly decided, as long as Walter was busy watching the Tour de France, this was as good a time as any to conduct Prudence through yet another walking tour of her worldly possessions. So as to better fortify herself, Prudence snuck into the kitchen and hastily downed a glass of warm merlot. The tour began in the living room, with Deleanor confiding what year she'd acquired her antique French chair (1972), the secret table drawer where her "real jewelry" was hidden, her cloisonné vase (1983), where her pair of ceramic elephant bookends had come from (Saigon), her brocade place mats (Lima), copper kettles (Ankara), lithographs (Beirut), poncho/tablecloth (Guatemala).

Like a museum docent, Deleanor lisped forth the convoluted history of her hand-painted Italian roosters and Turkish copperware, named the thirty-five countries each of her hand-painted dessert plates came from, countries she and Walt had dutifully, guidebook in hand, explored. The unspoken inference in all of this was inheritance. As a beneficiary, Prudence was a poor choice. She was not acquisitive, and had spent much of her current summer pitching negative reminders of her past out windows and doors, into garbage cans and Salvation Army drop-off bins, gifts from ex-fiancés, old boyfriends, one ex-husband. She felt no bitterness doing this, only solid, unsentimental relief. Pared down to a gratifying monastic sparseness, along putzes Deleanor, eager to load her up with the small histories of hundreds of foreign knickknacks, curios, each with its documented tale of discovery and purchase. Guilt rode like a tossed brick in Prudence's stomach, and beneath the brick, resentment. Did her mother honestly expect her to enshrine, marvel over, polish and feather-dust all these things? Wedged beside Deleanor in the storage closet, listening to the origin of her mother's six sets of miniature andirons, the moment Deleanor bolted out to answer Dr. Teeter's phone call, Prudence, too, crept out of the fig-scented closet and scooted around the corner and into the kitchen to gulp down a second glass of merlot, after which she fled to the den and plunked tipsily into her mother's matching plaid wing chair, a few feet from Walter's. She was staring at a pointillist streak of hurtling bicyclists, one crashing now and again, pitched over the handlebars and flung into the hedgerows, when, without warning, Walter muted the TV. He needed, he said, to talk.

"If I kick the bucket first . . ." he began, outlining a grim, terse vignette Prudence scarcely heard through the sudden bloom of alcohol in her blood. "On the other hand, if your mother goes first . . ." "Believe me, Prue, if I go before her, the first thing your mother will do, after burying me, of course, is go out and buy herself a face-lift. If you want your inheritance, you'd better scare her off that cockamamy idea, or be prepared to watch your money disappear straight into her face. She's terrified of getting old, poor thing. I feel sorry for your mother. She's got more phobias than you can shake a stick at."

Here was one subject Prudence and her

father discussed occasionally with a certain common relish — Deleanor's eclectic fears of moths, poverty, swimming in ponds, age and infirmity. "Has she gotten worse?"

"Oh lord, yes. Lately I catch her talking to herself. Whole conversations. It's an eerie, eerie thing, Prudence." Walter limped to his desk, opened a drawer, removed a large manila folder which he then handed to her. Prudence clutched the oversized folder as her father summarized the whole of his green, neatly graphed financial fiefdom. She tried to heed his cheerful, byzantine assessments, his convoluted projections of fiscal profit and loss. A retired accountant, Walter was as animated by his subject as Prudence was confused. The entire scene had the dry sensibility and stamp of a Jane Austen novel. *An heiress, my dear,* the antique phrase sprang open, like a jeweled trap, in her head. The truth her parents neither knew nor suspected was that Prudence's funds were as exhausted and depleted as she was. Since her divorce, she had planned badly, overspent, raised Fiona largely on credit, accumulating the sort of debt Walt and Deleanor vocally deplored in others, counted among the basest of modern sins (*All these young people, not a thought in their heads, charging like there's no tomorrow*). Muzzily, Prudence clutched her father's folder, the shifting maps of his wealth, nodding as if she understood, as if she had no moral argument with the shabbiest conversion in the world, death into cash.

As they watched the winning cyclist, a ruddy-faced American who had earlier triumphed over testicular cancer, being hoisted onto the sweating shoulders of his fellow cyclists, Prudence took a slightly drunken nosedive into the day's ongoing grim theme.

"Um, awkward, Dad, but have you and Mom ever discussed, um, where, ah, how you'd like to be, uh, buried?"

"Cremated," Deleanor chirped from the doorway. Prudence turned. How long had she been there?

"But where —"

"Tweedly-dee, tweedly-dee, in the sea."

What sea? Where? Prudence hadn't the will to press on. Instead the three of them watched Dan Rather.

"How much work do you suppose that man's had done to his face?" Deleanor asked. "He's right up there with Phyllis Diller, Dick Clark and that awful woman with the pointy face. That loud woman."

"Joan," Prudence said. "Joan Rivers."

"Bingo, that's who your mother's talking about." Walt reached for a handful of the pretzels Deleanor had brought him. "No one knows when to retire anymore, back off, when to step out of the limelight."

"I've been reading to Walt about cryogenics, how you can freeze two heads, say a husband's and wife's, then later on attach two bodies, other people's bodies, so the husband and wife get to have a whole new life together. That could be you and me, Walter."

"Grafting eighty-year-old heads on twenty-year-old bodies — sounds pretty bad to me." Walter grunted. "People don't know when to die anymore. When to make room."

Prudence thought of those visual gag books for children, each page cut into threes so you could mix up animals in zany combinations, a giraffe with a hippopotamus's bottom, a polar bear with a rabbit's head. Genetic bioengineering. The future. Just recently a scientist splicing duck and quail genes had come up with a quail having a duck's bill and a duck with a quail's head. Just as Prudence was about to get depressed by science, it was time to turn off the TV, time for Walter to heft his daughter's suitcase into the trunk of his new Cadillac and drive them all down into Kona for her farewell dinner.

Outside the Kon Tiki restaurant, Walt snapped a photo of Deleanor and Prudence snugged against opposing sides of a life-size sea captain, rough-hewn from a block of wood. With her head coyly tilted against the captain's dry rotted shoulder, Deleanor, who had sworn not to smile until she got her tooth fixed, suddenly grinned, impish and fey, into the camera. Prudence borrowed the camera to snap one last picture of her parents, followed by a second for good measure. Six months later, the second photograph, enlarged and framed in silver, would stand beside Walter's printed memorial service, near a bouquet of his flushed late-season roses, apricot-hued, and of a honeyed fragrance Prudence would forever afterward avoid, associating such gorgeous redolence and scent with death, grief, loss.

After dinner, Walt drove Prudence to the little outdoor airport in Kona. Her father's leg was bothering him, he used his cane all the time now. Since her visit the summer before, he had developed the beginnings of emphysema. Now he sat on the edge of a wooden bench, catching rough breaths, while Deleanor went to the flower cart and brought back a lei of lilac orchids, pale, cool blooms she arranged carefully around Prudence's bare neck. At the gate, her parents hugged her, Walt stoical, Deleanor sniffing, both careful not to crush the fragile necklace. Prudence, walking backward a few steps toward the waiting plane, blew kisses, turned, climbed the metal steps, then stopped at the plane's doorway to turn and wave a last time.

For the old, the world declines into doctors' offices and hospital visits, things move too fast and grow too quiet, no one calls, has the extra hour to visit. The old are spoken to by doctors, nurses, salespeople, realtors, waiters, sometimes by a kindhearted person or a grown child, resentful of fast-approaching, eclipsing loss. My wish, thought Prudence, waving to her parents, is selfish, plain as a child's. I wish them immortal. I want them, my mother and father, never to die.

Her father would die, suddenly, of a stroke, in his garden, among a scattered late bloom of dusky-hued roses, a garden Deleanor would at first let go wild, then pay the neighbor's newest Filipino gardener to dig up and resod with neutral, short-cropped emerald turf.

Tempe, Arizona

Home from Hawaii, Prudence stood holding her Wal-Mart suitcase in one hand and in the other an orange plastic net shopping bag containing Walt's canvas gardening shoes, the shoes he'd been wearing the morning he died, along with *The Gardener's Dictionary of Horticultural Terms*, by Harold Bagust, the last book her father had kept by his bedside, dog-eared and earth-smudged. She stood on the same blindingly bright street she had lived on, with geographical inertia, for nearly ten years. The Tempe fire chief lived on the southeast corner, a hairless pale meat of a man who sported skimpy red spandex shorts whenever he trudged his mower with immaculate accuracy across his front lawn. To Prudence's left lived a retired Dutch hydrologist; to her right, an ermetic, frightened widow whose plastic flowers marched in stiff, sun-bleached adornment up the curved, cracking walkway to her tightly shuttered, locked home. Up and down both sides of Prudence's short block lived an involuntary society, a sodality of widows. With the exception of the fire chief and the hydrologist, husbands, men as a group, didn't seem to last long on La Diosa (the Goddess) Street.

Setting down her suitcase and shopping bag, with Deleanor's orchid lei drooped like a pale, sweaty noose around her neck, its sweet, humid petals already browning in the shock of desert heat, Prudence turned the front-door key in its lock, noting as she did that her bustling red geraniums, in their clay pot under the mailbox, had perished on schedule, their sere, crumpled leaves brown as bran flakes. With one knee she bumped her suitcase over the threshold and into the dim tiled entryway. Carrying the shopping bag, Prudence shut the door behind her and stood very still. Something was wrong. The house was dark, the drapes pulled, everything the way she had left it, but Prudence couldn't catch her breath. She felt smothered under some imaginary gigantically hot, gloomy armpit.

In the shuttered false twilight of her kitchen, Prudence fumbled the massive city phone book out of its drawer and paged through, fingertips sticking to the thin yellow pages, until she found the boldest ad under Air Conditioning. POLARS★ BEARS★ KLIMATES★ KONTROLS★. With sweat beading, rolling down between her breasts, Prudence dialed, was put on hold, taken off hold. *A Polar Bear serviceman would not be available until the following morning. Units all over the city were blown. Is there an infant or elderly person in the home?* a nasally female whine, a tone of bored vexation. Prudence was tempted to answer, Hold on, let me check — surprise! I just located two infants asleep under my piano bench and one old man left for dead in my broom closet. But no. She was an adult, whole-bodied, expected to last. Prudence took the only remaining appointment, an ungodly hour the following morning, hung up, pressed her voice mail button. *Hey there, angel girlfriend, Holt and me'll be at the airport tomorrow to get you, so bring your broomstick skirts and those bad-ass cowgirl boots of yours. Maybe we'll snag you a good Indian man — a contradiction in terms these days, gorgeous though they are. I did a little flirting yesterday with Amos Yellowhorse — that old sweet fart pure and simple adores every sidewalk I waltz my behind down, so we now have the best booth space in the entire exhibit hall, the only one with a standing fan.*

Samantha Hill, a seventh-generation Texan transplanted to Oklahoma, had a history of marrying and unmarrying, her fourth and loosest connubial knot having landed her *in Enid-of-all-pie-holes, Oklahoma, my fate no different from that of some jackass who's been shot blindfold out of a circus cannon.* Sam's message went on to reassure Prudence, for the second time, that she would be at the Oklahoma City Airport, on time, along with Holt Able, her newest honey. Willis Bulliebush, Sam's fourth husband, had been unemployed and catnapping inside his ramshackle pink house one afternoon last spring when it got sideswiped by the second in a series of mild tornadoes. Months later, the pink house was still unrepaired, and hopping with mice, with Willis still yawning and waiting around "for his brain to kick in." Fed up with his shiftlessness, Sam swapped Willis Bulliebush for Holt Able, whom she'd met in the airport lounge on the Fourth of July (*my day of independence, girlfriend!*). Before she'd left for Hawaii, Prudence had protested Sam's naming her codirector of Sam's partially realized dream, Native People's Circle. The vision, full-blown, had come upon Sam in a budget motel room in Anadarko, Oklahoma, in the midst of her second heart attack, as she lay on the damp, mildewed bathroom floor waiting for the ambulance she had managed to summon before collapsing. God poured instructions into her ear that fateful night, as dramatic as any story from the Old Testament. She was to build shelters for battered women and children on every Indian reservation in the entire state of Oklahoma and beyond. Now, due to Sam's unpaid, unstinting labor, Native People's Circle had achieved tax-exempt status and accepted its first charitable donation from an Episcopal church group in rural Pennsylvania, their cash gift arriving just in time (*God's time*, Sam crowed) to buy a company car and rent booth space at the Sixty-eighth Annual Indian Fair and Exposition in Anadarko. As codirector of an organization existing mainly as a God-inspired blueprint in Sam's head, Prudence's charitable activities would include sitting in the NPC booth, handing out domestic violence prevention brochures, spreading the word about NPC's mission, and selling autographed photos of the Bolivian movie actor Enrique Paz, the same celebrity Sam had snagged the year before for her very first NPC booth at the Red Earth Pow-Wow in Oklahoma City. This year, she had flirted with those members of the exposition's board of directors vulnerable to her charms, harangued impervious others until she eventually maneuvered Enrique, as NPC's spokesperson, into coveted Indian of the Year status. That victory under her hand-tooled western belt, Sam fixed her sights on an abandoned Methodist church camp five miles north of Anadarko. This, God showed her, would be NPC's first shelter site. A single afternoon's pleasant chat with the Methodist minister had yielded a one-year option on the ten-acre property — after that, the Reverend Learned Boyle told Sam, it would be sold off to a casino developer from the Philippines.

Prudence's friend Trish Yazzie managed to squeak a last clipped message onto the end of the voice mail. Could Prudence meet her at Victoria's Secret at five? *Remember that cute oboist I met on my flight from Cedar Rapids, well, he's* — the message beeped off.

So Prudence decided to leave her dim, sweltering house, buy a late birthday gift for Trish, meet her at Victoria's Secret, have dinner, come home, maybe wrap herself in a wet sheet the way Arizona's old-timers used to, sleep on a chaise lounge by the pool, and in the tepid dawn watch for the Polar Bear repairman as she unpacked, washed a few things, and repacked for her trip to Oklahoma, where, Sam had warned, folks were suffering the worst heat wave since 1902.

The Crystal Magick Metaphysical Shop, located in a low-rent strip mall, was squeezed between a tae kwon do studio and an X-rated shop called Smokin' Lingerie. There was also a sports bar, Horse and Hound, a wine-tasting shop, Cork 'n Cheese, and a medical uniform supply shop called Scrubs. Pushing open Crystal Magick's heavy glass door with its purple-tasseled brass temple bells, Prudence passed three cubicles marked *Private Readings* and paused at the message board, a choppy, desperate-seeming blizzard of overlapping flyers and business cards: *Wanda Fulkerson Channels Messages from Torina, Aura-Soma Level I Certification: A Rainbow Experience (discover within 100 jeweled aura-soma equilibrium bottles, brilliant tools for evolving consciousness), How To Channel Your Akashic Records, New!!! Metaphysical Singles Nights (group activities center around relationship compatibilities, focusing on soul mate attraction, aura soul*

*colors, palmistry, astrology and past-life con-
nections to match up with other attending singles), My Life's Purpose (too many of us, my
friends, are rudderless ships, adrift on life's sea
of possibilities), Journey Through the
Chakras: Remote Viewing Level II (RV is a
recently declassified government data collection system that allows the viewer to retrieve
accurate data remote in time and space),
Money Rituals That Work!!!, Channeled Messages from the Fairy Kingdom by Celeste,
Gong Attunement with Serge (gong, the only
instrument the mind has no defense against,
allow it to massage you on a molecular level:
experience your energies rising!).*

A bluish, lotus-smelling haze smogged
the shop. Behind the sales counter, a wan
clerk, scratching at her scalp with the
eraser end of a clear pencil filled with tiny
moving bits of colored glass, responded to
Prudence's inquiry by handing her a
plastic packet of Ancient Temple incense
cones. Sniffing the packet, Prudence
browsed through other packs of incense,
cones and sticks — Ebony Opium, Heavenly Bodies, Tropical Rain, Illuminating
the Soul, Rebirth and Regeneration, Sensual Dreams, Jungle Fever. What's today's
music, Prudence asked. The clerk jabbed
her rain-stick pencil in the direction of a

plastic jewel case propped on a tiny, wooden easel — *Songs of Thanksgiving for Imaginary Unicorns.*

Crystal Magick was a commercialized chaos of solid body perfumes, healing oils, herbal tinctures, wish candles, goddess candles, angel cards, angel posters, rain sticks, dream catchers, Chinese jade hangings, crystal pendants, pendulums, tarot decks, Wicca and feng shui paraphernalia, fairy chimes, Celtic runes, Tantric spells, Kama Sutra pocket charts, menopausal nostrums and slender, magically propertied wands. A dozen or so card tables, dressed in fringed purple cloths, were strategically placed, like stops along a game board, a female medium, much like a game piece, presiding at each one. To one side of each table, a bright yellow poster on a flimsy easel featured a blurred "glamour" shot of the medium followed by a menu of her singular talents: runes, stones, crystals, tarot cards, palm readings, fairy readings, numerology, aura gazing, astrology, etc. One table was conspicuously empty; its poster, minus any "glamour" shot, simply said *Misty Rains! Intuitive, Clairvoyant, Clairaudient, Past-Life Counselor.* Behind the table drooped a yellow silk banner declaring in bubbled, iridescent script: *Aura*

Photography for People and Pets! Snagged by bulldog clips to the hem of the herniaed banner were Polaroid snapshots of customers with garish, auric bursts of pink, orange, Vishnu blue and lime green flaring from their heads as they held up panicked, frantic-looking pets — poodles, rabbits, cats, ferrets, even snakes — to the omniscient probing eye of the auric camera. On Misty Rains' table, two slick red hands on a plastic blue clock indicated the psychic's return in ten minutes. Elsewhere, at other tables, busy mediums counseled, whispered, raised a fussy, oracular drone. Prudence hovered near one of the tables, pretending to examine miniature bottles of aromatherapy oil, leafing idly through a book called *The Yeast Connection*, reading the back of a Feng Shui Ceremonial Kit, kneeling to examine a row of soapstone Buddhas, absently stroking the wooden head — a Hong Kong import — of a Native American shaman. She was eavesdropping on other women's troubles, distraction from her own, which seemed overly familiar and therefore boring.

What is it that bothers you?

Emotions I can't describe. Jealousy?

Yes, I'd say for you there's definitely a past-life influence in that regard.

Do you think he's infatuated with me? Be-cause every single year, two or three times a year . . .

Yes, yes. Yes! I see he is definitely beginning to wake up to you in a spiritual sense.

He's on the rebound from this Las Vegas show dancer with blond hair extensions, and deep down I understand he's simply dealing with abandonment issues, anger toward past wives, I just don't want any more surprises, I'm tired of surprises.

I must tell you this, please don't be alarmed. Your mother is here with you, right now she is with you in spirit, she wants you to know this. Don't cry. Have a Kleenex. No, this is not in-terference. This is a good thing. Your mother wants to help, from the Other Side.

Not a man in the place. Only inquisitive women, seeking the perspective of ghosts, nudging at uncooperative spirits or moping over living men, childish, cheating men. Prudence narrowly missed drifting smack into a tall, doughy woman wearing a sky blue dress splotted with cumulus clouds, a giant pillowcase shift, with holes snipped for the neck and arms. Her feet were like unbaked dinner rolls, strapped into black Mary Janes, her dry vermilion hair was twisted into numerous florets around her head, reddish orange pot scrubbers.

Huffing and hewing, the woman puddled herself into a lawn chair behind the Misty Rains table, jerked a metal cashbox from under the table, and began stripping paper off various rolls of coins, clattering them into the metal box with all the expertise of a casino worker. Her sign advertised thirty dollars for twenty minutes of spiritual advisement. Prudence, who could easily resist Aura Soma, Remote Viewing, Akashic Records and Pet Photography, was tempted by the shimmery fix of seeing her future snapped down by plump, pillowy Misty Rains. No, she admonished herself, stepping up to the sales counter where she caught a grainy, inadvertent glimpse of herself in the four-way TV monitor, looking agitated and shiny-nosed. She heard the client who complained she was tired of surprises honk her nose hard, then snuffle . . . *do you suppose I'm not here, that I'm actually asleep right now, dreaming about a past life?* She could not hear the medium's reply.

Tarot of the Cat People, Santa Fe Tarot, Rock Art II, Baseball Tarot, Goddess Tarot, Ancestral Path Tarot, Russian Tarot, Chinese Tarot, Fairy Tarot, The Hermetic Tarot, based on the Esoteric Workings of the Secret Order of the Golden Dawn. How could she decide what to get Trish for her birthday? Prudence glanced through the CD display. *Tigers of the Raj (rich interlocking rhythmic textures of tabla, dhol, douffli, ankle bells, manjiva and dholak with the haunting sounds of Indian voices, swaramandala, santoor, sarangi, flute, sitar and modern keyboards), Temples in the Forest: Inner Harmony New Age Music (synthesized temple bell sound, finger cymbals and an "om" vibration combined with the sounds of forest birds and a gently flowing stream, the peaceful meditative environment of a beautiful forest), You are the Ocean (celestial water music for relaxation, an unfolding of joy composed for flute, harp, zither and cello), Sorcerer: Mask of Seduction, with Laughing Hawk, the didgeridoo and the Tibetan thighbone.* Holding a *Mask of Seduction* CD, waiting for her credit card to clear, Prudence overheard the store manager, a cross woman with fretful, darting eyes, hiss into the phone . . . *No, I can't, I've got to move all these tables out. I have to have space ready for Psychics Onstage and get the smoothies table set up by six o'clock. I've got a complete migraine. There's a woman who's been waiting over an hour for her reading, now she's upset. I'm telling you, we need to follow store policy. No, that woman you saw in the corner by the potted plants,*

84

which by the way are in desperate need of water, no, she can't come back tomorrow. Look, if I go up to a customer and say something like that, it's going to backfire . . . hang on a sec. May I help you? No, I'm sorry, Wanda's completely booked, so is Starr Wonder, I can get you an immediate reading with Misty Rains. The customer ahead of Prudence didn't want a reading with Misty Rains, so in limp capitulation, Prudence held up her hand, reserving the twenty-minute slot with Misty, who, panting behind her flimsy table, stared at Prudence, no doubt employing mind-control tactics.

Forty minutes later, Prudence lunged into the parking lot, her wallet lighter, her future oppressed by predictions. Misty Rains, having cast an assortment of polished divining stones, had begun with an impressively detailed description of Prudence's living room, right down to the two white sofas with violet and burgundy sateen pillows, had then seen her eating a hot dog in a tropical climate with an older woman (she and Deleanor at the medical clinic?). Prudence, she said, would soon meet a man on her travels, a much younger man with silver streaks in his dark hair. This man is your soul mate. I see you will meet this young man (*Young, how young?*)

soon. He has visited you once already, in the etheric realm. (Etheric realm? Prudence recalled a dream she'd had the night before she'd left for Hawaii, a slender man she didn't recognize, with long black hair, walking into her bedroom and flopping down on top of her as if she were a mattress . . . could that have been him?)

Temples throbbing, Prudence sped over to Fashion Square, parked underground, dashed inside, stepped into the mall's glass elevator, and shot upward, like a deposit in a bank tube, to Victoria's Secret, where she found Trish drifting one slender, French-manicured hand through a rack of air-filled brassieres while a chignoned, black-smocked clerk named Hermione, wearing a necklace of yellow measuring tape around her neck, snatched a collection of hipster panties — zebra, cheetah, leopard and reptile prints — from Trish's other hand, whisking them off into a nearby dressing room.

"C'mon, Prue. Try this. Before we're eighty and gumming baby food."

Prudence stooped to retrieve the teddy tossed in her direction, a white undergarment with the loose, open texture of beef tripe. Prudence's underwear came from the carousel racks at Target and Mervyn's,

86

and her mother, Deleanor, had sighed more than once over her daughter's dismal fashion sense (*Heaven knows you've inherited no shopping gene of mine, Prunie, none at all*). Prudence actually liked accompanying Trish as she blazed through malls, entering and exiting stores, glowing and guiltless, accumulating a rustling bouquet of name-brand bags: pink-and-black-striped from Victoria's Secret, pale yellow from Banana Republic, navy blue from Anne Taylor, pale gray Aveda bags. Trish Yazzie, a Navajo woman from the Bitter Water clan in northern Arizona, a published poet and professor of Native American Studies, was petite, shapely and, unlike Prudence, deliberately fashionable. She wore her dark brown hair in long, glossy layers, and enjoyed the exotic perfumes, designer clothes and expensive jewelry given to her by a string of admirers. Adored and pampered, Trish Yazzie exuded an innate feminine confidence Prudence completely lacked. They had met two years before at an English Department social (attendance mandatory) and become friends, sharing indignation over their low salaries, interest in tarot readings, and a chronic, experiential frustration with men. At the moment, Trish was shopping for a weekend's tryst in

87

Santa Monica. On a flight from Cedar Rapids the week before, she had met a handsome Swiss oboist on his way to Los Angeles to compose a movie soundtrack. According to Trish, Heimlich (no, Prudence corrected herself, Heimlich was a maneuver, not a name, she'd gotten it wrong, the oboist's name) did fabulous phone sex in three languages.

Waiting for Trish, the white teddy bunched on her lap like a giant lace hankie, Prudence licked her index finger (a habit of Deleanor's) and paged through the store's late summer catalog. Pages 1–5: the three clicks bra, the push-up bra, the balconette bra, the bralette camisole, the unlined seamless demi bra, the surplice no-wire, the seamless hidden-wire, the T-shirt bra and — the catalog's featured showpiece — a black leather bustier. She licked again. Pages 6–10: signature panties, classic panties, string bikini, Rio brief, thong, classic bikini, high-leg brief, tummy control, rear lift . . .

"Forget the teddy, Prue. I'm starting you off with a black water bra and classic bikini. We need to play up your hair. I love it!"

"You do? My mom bought the wrong box of hair color and couldn't return it, so she talked me into trying it."

"I like it, Prue. You look five years younger. Definitely more fun."

Trish flitted off. Prudence slouched deeper into the oyster sateen-striped chair, sucking on a strand of her lightened hair, watching a three-minute hosiery video that looped over and over on the small television set in front of her. Giraffe-legged models named Wilhelmina, Yasmin and Naomi mused in steamy, kittenish voices about which hosiery they preferred for what occasion, sheer, opaque, demi opaque, seamed, unseamed, fishnet, thigh-high, knee-high, ankle-high . . . all of it left Prudence unable to recall what mismatched bra and panties she had extricated from her underwear drawer that morning.

"Bet you don't have one of these."

Prudence caught a negligee in her hands, slinky, truncated, sleekly black.

"Plus a water bra and matching thong." The bra landed first on Prudence's lap, its satin cups like polished black begging bowls, followed by the panties.

Hermione briskly unlocked dressing rooms 6 and 7. In cubicle 7, Prudence hooked on the water bra and clicked three times (like Dorothy's ruby slippers), watching her cleavage lift and lower. Her beige Target bra, its underwire sprung, lay like a dingy bandage near her bare, unmanicured feet. Trish's silvery voice floated over from cubicle 6.

"I'd love to buy this leather bustier for Heinrich. How are you doing, Prue?"

In the slippery black baby-doll negligee, Prudence stared at this new, disorienting version of herself. "I'm OK." Moments later, she slipped out of cubicle 7, comfortably back in her old clothes and serviceable underwear, clutching the water bra and panties.

"I'm not getting any of these." Trish dumped a jumble of silks and laces onto the counter.

"Why not?"

"Because I'm buying this!" Swinging the leather bustier up and onto the counter, Trish dropped her charge card like a modern-day plastic cameo between the two eternally stiffened breasts.

Over a second Belvedere martini, Trish unwrapped her birthday gift, the *Mask of Seduction* CD. Prudence, sipping ginger ale, did a tarot reading for each of them using Trish's Arthur Waite deck, the cards so worn they would barely shuffle. The first spread of cards spelled romantic failure for Trish. The second, Prudence's, pointed to the imminent arrival of a young man. "Bass ackwards," scoffed Prudence, scooping up the cards, reshuffling.

"Maybe my martini is blocking the vibes."

"Maybe."

But the next two spreads repeated their previous messages. Romantic disappointment (three of swords) for Trish, a young man (knight of cups) for Prudence.

Trish shrugged, who cared anyway, men were like streetcars, a new one chugged by every ten minutes. Prudence tapped the cards into shape and returned them to Trish, who tucked them, with fey, irritable resignation, into her new chestnut Coach handbag.

Floating face-up in the chlorinated water of her swimming pool, the water black as ink and warm as broth, Prudence saw a bat swoop past, quite small, the size of a cocktail napkin. Later, when she climbed out and patted herself off, she decided to celebrate her sexy underwear purchase (the black water bra and thong panties) by going into the kitchen and fixing herself a Pimm's and Coke. The dark green bottle

Trish had given her last Christmas still had the price tag on its smooth glass neck, $18.95. *Created in 1840, Pimm's is still made to James Pimm's original recipe, a closely guarded secret known only to six people. It is a light, refreshing spirit carefully blended from fine liqueurs and fruit extracts.*

Just one more pim-pim. Pim-pam. Nude except for her white rubber swim cap (*What am I? A Q-tip!*), Prudence wavered a second time into the hot-as-hellfire house (*Just a wee nipper of ye old pim-pim*), wombled back out, plunged down into her chaise lounge beside the pool. No swimming, Prunis. No immersion, Prudential. No watery extinction like that old Shakespeare professor who'd drowned himself in his backyard pool during Prudence's first year teaching at the community college, a staged retribution, some said, on his wife's birthday. While Mrs. Shakespeare was out getting her eyebrows tinted, he'd lashed cement construction blocks to his long, yellowing feet and toppled, nose-first, into the deep end. Unacquainted with either the man or his wife, Prudence interpreted the bizarre tragedy as clear warning of the hidden dangers of academic life.

And now, heedless of what the Dutch hydrologist thought, what the dour parade of widows thought, what anyone short of the neighborhood bat thought, Prudence, on the backside of her third Pimm and Coke, pushed her pool-soaked head against the yielding plastic of the chaise lounge and bayed at the little, pale cuticle snip of moon. Bayed, wept, blew her lonely nose into her beach towel, and passed out.

Hours later, blinking awake, Prudence was no longer beside the pool on her chaise lounge, but inside, on the living room rug, beneath the picture window. She rose to her knees and peered out the window into a pinkish gray dawn, a dawn she very much confused with sunset, then bobbled outside, head splitting, to stare at this peculiar sunset, its shades of rare meat, the sun itself plainly on the wrong end of the sky. She heard Mt. Carmel's automated church bells peal, just as they did each morning at 7 a.m. In her bedroom, which Prudence managed to visit next, her suitcase gaped on the bed, nothing in its cavernous interior except her Victoria's Secret water bra and panties, flirty pink tags still on, the store's emptied bag and pink tissue strewn across the floor. Suddenly her doorbell dinged. Tiptoeing across the room, she peeked through a slat in the wooden shutters. In the driveway squatted

an ugly truck the color of rust. POLARS*
BEARS* KLIMATES* KONTROLS*. Tossing
on Fiona's thrift-store kimono (where did
that come from?), snugging the belt tight,
Prudence stubbed the ruinously empty
bottle of Pimm's back into the cupboard
above the oven, scruffled her hair with her
fingers, unlocked the door.

Two hours later, with her air conditioning fixed, Prudence True Parker,
wearing tight jeans, a white Wrangler
blouse and high-heeled bright red cowboy
boots, stood on the sidewalk outside her
house flagging down a slow-approaching
taxi. In her suitcase, bundled in newspaper
and tucked between her broomstick skirts,
bits of ochre red dirt still clinging to their
soles, were Walt's canvas garden shoes.
Along with the shoes, she had packed
Bagust's *Dictionary of Horticultural Terms*, a
plastic name tag from one of her father's
old roses, Madame de Bugnet, marking his
last place. Under her father's shoes and
book she tucked in a journal, still mostly
blank. This trip to Oklahoma was now
both charity excursion and research jaunt.
Prudence desperately needed money. As
she'd scrawled a check out to Polar Bear
Klimate Kontrol for two thousand dollars,
her resolve never to write a romance novel,

never to stoop to such drivel, evaporated and, like divine afflatus, melted away. Couldn't this trip, she reasoned, sliding into the taxi, be a perfect opportunity to research live Indians, to find a model or models for Digby Deeds' fabricated characters? She would not mention this to Sam. She would not tell anyone. She might be broke, aesthetically compromised, but she wasn't, she hoped, a fool.

Anadarko, Oklahoma

Prudence peeled eight buttons of pepperoni off her slice of airport pizza, rolled them into a greasy horseshoe of meaty red flutes. Fifty-five minutes and no Sam, no diminutive hourglass figure with waist-length black hair, no heavily mascaraed sea blue eyes, no eye-popping breasts beneath which stubbornly beat a damaged heart, no twangy Texas voice sassy and sharp as firecrackers, no Sam with her careening curves in fancy cowgirl getup, completely impossible to miss. Dabbing grease off her uneaten pizza with a paper napkin, Prudence was beginning to panic (having forgotten Sam's phone number) when Sam Hill sashayed, grand as some western empress or dance-hall queen, through the airport's front doors wearing an ankle-length denim skirt so tight it puckered across her crotch, a rhinestone-encrusted western denim shirt with shoulder pads and hot pink lizard-skin cowboy boots. A little to the left of Sam lurked a gigantic man, a dead ringer, down to the shoulder-length wavy chestnut hair, chiseled jaw and manly bulk, for Dr. Quinn Medicine Woman's frontier boyfriend, whose name Prudence could not for the life of her recall. As the two of them bore down on her, Prudence thought they looked like Disney characters, McDonald's action figures, biblical cartoons, or most aptly, like one of those steamy, overblown couples locked in a torrid embrace on the cover of a romance novel. Before she could wipe the grease from her fingertips, Prudence found herself caught up in Sam's peach-scented, bosomy embrace.

"Whoee! Girlfriend! Look at you! We got stalled up in freeway traffic, and would you believe that old goober from the fair forgot to bring us our release papers for the booth space, so we had to wait while he puttered all the way back into Oklahoma City to get them. It's been one giant cotton-pickin' nightmare. What do you think, baby?" Sam reached behind her to tug Holt forward by his license-plate-sized belt buckle. "Holt honey, this is Professor Prudence Parker, my angel sister and NPC's new codirector."

"Mighty pleasure, Professor."

Obscenely handsome, Holt Able was craggy, overdone, and loomed over her in a Paul Bunyanesque way, his handshake firm as a surgeon's, his voice plangent, deep as a canyon. Prudence nearly toppled into his massive tree-trunk arms, bleating. Instead she managed to nod modestly, mumble something Deleanor might have said: *Pleasure to meet you.*

As soon as Holt had tossed Prudence's overstuffed suitcase as if it were an empty shoe box into the gaping hot trunk of Sam's car, gallantly swinging open the door for Prudence to scoot into the capacious backseat, the three of them were out of the airport parking lot and onto the highway. During the forty-five-minute ride to Anadarko, all Prudence glimpsed on either side of the road were parched pastures lumpy as unmade beds and a few occasional groves of low-spreading trees the color of overboiled Swiss chard.

"How do you like our official Native People's Circle limo, a '67 Caddie paid for by sweet little old Episcopalian ladies back in Pennsylvania? Daddy, bless his sweet heart, found it junked in a soybean field outside Lubbock, towed it to his shop, worked on it, put in a new engine, tranny, whatnot." NPC's official car was dark blue with high-lustred trout blue upholstery interior and the distinct potatoey underwhiff of French fries.

"Runs like a champ," boomed Holt, who went on to never say much else except agree with Sam, who yakked, nonstop and loquacious, the way she always did. Holt ratcheted his head up and down at whatever Sam said, occasionally bursting forth with a Praise the Lord or Praise Our Heavenly Father. A hulking Disney prince, he huddled with Sam in the front seat, the two of them entwining and untwining hands, pecking and gobbling up and down one another's necks, until Prudence nearly wept for her own poor, solitary, third-wheel self in the tauntingly wide, musty-smelling backseat, her only companion a paperback romance, *Savage Arrow*, its cover image a half-naked muscular Indian in a breechclout clutching a luxe-maned blonde in a blouse ripped open to reveal magnificent breasts, on the floor by Prudence's boots. She leaned down, picked up the book, opened it. *Savannah could hear his guttural groans of pleasure as with eager, maddening thrusts of his loins, he almost lifted her from the rabbit-fur blanket each time he shoved into her. "En-ha-wettsa," Savage*

Arrow whispered. "I love you." One of Digby's (a.k.a. Mildred Crawley's) books! Good god. Prudence dropped the paperback to the floor where it belonged, firmly placing her boot over the couple's bared chests. Was finding Savage Arrow in Sam's car a sign? A portent? Was she meant to see Digby's offer as some cosmic lottery prize? Maybe, as Deleanor believed, her father was busy "up there" pulling holy strings to help her.

"Let me catch you up, Prue. It's hotter than Hades, the fair's been going since this morning, it's hot as blazes in the exhibition hall, even with the fan going full blast, the blades are just spinning hot air. We've got Bernice at the booth holding things together. And God help us, she's got her latest beau with her, though he is a cutie-pie, I grant you that."

"Really? Bernice has a boyfriend? How nice." Bernice was an attractive Kiowa woman in her early thirties whose birth defects had been caused, Sam told Prudence, by her mother's exposure to toxic factory chemicals. Bernice's torso was normal, but her arms and legs were as small and undeveloped as a four-year-old child's. She had to be bathed, dressed, undressed, taken to the bathroom, lifted, carried and pushed everywhere in her wheelchair. A college graduate, she worked for the Oklahoma State Legislature, and according to Sam, because she came from an important Kiowa family, Bernice had contacts and clout within the Indian community, making her invaluable to NPC. Prudence had met Bernice, briefly, the summer before, when Sam had used NPC's few funds to fly Prudence in for the Red Earth Pow-Wow, to sit with her in NPC's very first booth.

Prudence occasionally wondered at her taste in friends, questioned why peculiar specimens so appealed to her. This was mainly harmless and likely due to genetics; after all, prior to her father's passion for roses, he had gone through a long period of being obsessed with bizarre graftings and horticultural mutants. So perhaps instead of plants, it was Prudence's inadvertent hobby to attract — and collect — weird, unusual people.

"Yeah, well, Holt and I can't tell for sure. One minute she insists he's just a friend she met at the Gathering of Nations in Albuquerque, next she's calling him her 'pretty boy.' Personally, I think Miss Bernice has got her hopes jacked up sky-high again, just like last year with Enrique,

101

who, by the way, flew in late last night from Hollywood and is already managing to be a complete pain in the ass."

"How's that?"

"Being his usual prima donna self. Whining about how tired he is, gee, does he have to sign all those autographs and does he have to go to every single event on the program? Pete's sake! He's Indian of the Year, thanks to me. What does the man think he's here for? Miniature golf?"

"I think he's gay myself," offered Holt, reaching with his giant's paw to swat at a fly creeping along the dash. Whap. "Not Enrique. Bernice's new friend."

"Now we can't know that, honey." Sam whirled around to wink at Prudence while massaging the back of Holt's tree-trunk neck with one tiny bejeweled hand. "Though Bernice's friend is a little . . ."

"E-feminent."

"Well, yes, Holt honey, I'll grant you he is a little on the pretty side. He does have superlong beautiful fingernails." Sam waggled her own nails, scarlet, sharpened shovels. "Way longer than mine, and then some of his mannerisms and that soft way he talks, when he talks — well, you'll see, Prudence. They're sharing a motel room, paid for, I might add, by Bernice."

"My theory is he's one of them boy-girl Indians you hear about sometimes."

Holt might be a gorgeous cover, but it suddenly seemed to Prudence as if a few explanatory pages were missing. She wondered too, and not for the first time, about Native People's Circle, an organization existing mainly in Sam's intricately tiered imagination. How well did she know Sam Hill, when she actually thought about it? Walt Parker had cautioned his daughter about shysters and con artists, scammers and fly-by-nighters — he saw a thief under every rock — until Prudence concluded her father was suspicious to a fault, that it was unfair to so consistently presume the worst of people. Sam, for example, was hardworking and brilliant at fund-raising. Consider the Cadillac they were riding in, though it was a fact that in the one short year Prudence had barely known her, Sam's organization, aside from several hundred brochures and business cards printed by Kinko's, along with a book-sized set of bylaws, didn't much exist. Prudence based her presumption of Sam's honesty largely on her friend's Christian fervor. Beyond that, her lifelong backlash reaction to Walt had resulted in a boundless, naive willingness to give other human beings the benefit of the doubt, to trust before trust had been earned, a reactive trait Prudence had cultivated until it erupted into a backward, sometimes dangerous, virtue.

The silver-finned steel blue Cadillac plunged like a shark onto the Caddo Fairgrounds. Gray chalky dust boiled up around the broken electric windows. When Sam or Holt pushed buttons, trying to open them, they chirred and buzzed like summer locusts but stayed stuck. The Cadillac shot past shaded camping areas where dozens of families had set up tents and teepees, pitched and wallowed into a dirt parking lot right outside the huge exposition hall. As Holt towered politely beside the opened rear door, waiting for her to emerge, Prudence poked one red cowboy boot, then the other, out of the Cadillac, stood up, stretched a little, and inhaled. The air, singed, fissured with heat, smelled like charred beef and fry bread. She was starving.

"Here we are, girlfriend. Hear that? Sounds like the gourd dances, doesn't it, Holt honey? Dullest dance on earth. Stomp stomp, shuffle shuffle. Here comes Bernice, Toy Boy in tow."

Grimy, hungry, filmed in sweat, Prudence leaned over the wheelchair to give Bernice a hug made awkward by reflexive pity, smoothed over by admiration. "Hey. How's it going?"

"Going fine. Ray, this is Professor Parker from Phoenix. My friend Ray Chasing Hawk."

Prudence straightened up, nearly bumping noses with the narrow oval face of a young Native American man wearing round wire-rim dark glasses, blue jean shorts, hiking boots and a light beige T-shirt that simply said *Comanches, Lords of the Southern Plains*. She shook the young man's extended hand, cool in comparison to her own, noting the long, almond-shaped fingernails with their clear polish, the slender, smooth fingers. She noticed the startling contrast between his boyish, unlined face and the rough, arrowing streaks of silver in his long black hair. He didn't smile, his face impassive, expressionless, as he greeted her. Cinching her concho belt even tighter as if to coax attention back to herself by way of her impossibly tiny waist, Sam spoke up.

"Y'all hungry? We need to get our board meeting out of the way, so I say we head over to what the heck's the name of that place . . ."

"Talk of the Town," offered Bernice.

"Talk of the Town, that's it. Ray, take Bernice in your van, and we'll meet y'all over there. Prudence honey, ride with Holt and me. You just got here and I'm not about to take my eyes off your precious face for one single second."

Prudence gripped the laminated menu with its hand-typed fading entries — Meat Loaf, Chicken Fried Steak with White or Brown Gravy, Stuffed Bell Peppers, 24-Hour Breakfasts with 99-cent seconds of biscuits and gravy or grits and gravy, all too aware of the light but distinct pressure of Ray Chasing Hawk's thigh against her own. He'd ordered nothing, a simple glass of water sat on his otherwise empty paper place mat. When her breakfast — scrambled eggs, sausage, hash browns and wheat toast arrived, just as Prudence was thinking *salt,* she heard his soft drawl, *This what you're looking for?* as he handed her the saltshaker. Seconds later, thinking *jelly,* a square jelly packet slipped quietly from his hand into hers. She thanked him, opened it, smeared her toast.

The second annual NPC board meeting consisted of Sam twanging aloud every

106

single bylaw she and Holt had labored over that summer, while the rest of them, Bernice, with Ray helping, Holt and Prudence, sipped, swallowed, chewed, wiped their mouths with paper napkins. As Sam read from her bylaws, Ray read Prudence's mind, passing along the coffee carafe, a tin pitcher of cream, a spoon, packets of sugar, each at the exact moment she wished for these things. When Sam stopped a moment to lavishly credit Prudence for writing NPC's mission statement, "Healing Through Art," Ray's breath suddenly grazed Prudence's left earlobe . . . *I'm an artist, too. I spend a lot of time alone. I understand loneliness.* His presence began to scald her entire left side, clean down into her bright red boots, where her feet started tingling. Excusing herself to go to the ladies' room, Prudence felt the heat of his gaze follow her out of the dining room. Breathless and slightly dizzy, she found a pay phone, left a message for Fiona, then went into the bathroom, where she peered over a stopped-up sink into the mirror. Who was that? A woman with a parched tumbleweed for hair, a face shiny and exhausted-looking, a crumb of jellied toast hanging from her bottom lip. Why was he reading her mind? To entertain himself? To mock her? Did he do this to everyone? She couldn't go back out there. She absolutely could not go back out there. When she emerged, Sam, Holt and Bernice were jammed into the restaurant's small foyer watching Ray pull his van up to the entrance for Bernice, who waited in her wheelchair. With Sam and Holt snuzzling and smooching by the giant gumball machine, shamelessly devouring one another from the neck up, Prudence tried to recall the last time she had been sexually desired. Kissed even. Oh right. Barry, the crime journalist from Edinburgh, a self-confessed sex addict with a horsy overbite and jalapeño breath. She'd had to hoist him up off her couch, point him toward the front door, eject him from her house, tuck one breast back into her Mervyn's brassiere. That had been two years ago. Prudence's last contact with a man.

"Prudence honey, we were just talkin' how you were the only one who didn't get to be at the smoke ceremony last night, over at Bernice's uncle's place. So Ray has offered to smudge you himself. We can all just head over to the motel room, do a quick ceremony, and make certain this week starts out with the same blessings for us all."

108

Holt, neck flushed, hair sexily mussed, belched long and reverently. "Praise Jesus," he grinned, staring with hunger and greedy hope into Sam's bountiful, peach-scented cleavage.

With her stomach churning like an old washer, Prudence, made anxious by the imminent prospect of a Native American ritual performed solely for her benefit, perched on the flabby lip of the motel's twin bed. Holt crouched tailor-fashion behind her, a shaggy bulwark of amiability. In her wheelchair, Bernice sat sandwiched between the two beds, Sam beside her, while Ray Chasing Hawk, standing opposite Prudence, snapped open the brass latch of a narrow cedar box he had brought out from somewhere and placed neatly on the bed. With precise, graceful motions, he lifted an eagle-feather fan out of the cedar box, its handle wrapped with strips of leather and red trade cloth, a dried bundle of grayish green sage, a beaded leather bag of loose tobacco, a bloodstone pipe wrapped in soft white fringed deerskin. With careful exactness, he laid each item on the bed, calmly unwrapping the pipe, filling its bowl with tobacco, setting a match flame to the sage, and blowing steadily until a single, sharp tendril of smoke furled and split into white, dissolving wisps. As the clean astringent scent of sage began to permeate the motel room, Ray began talking, softly, rapidly. He was not a holy man, he said, not a shaman, not a medicine man, but he had been taught some things he felt moved to share. And though he was Comanche by blood, not Sioux, he considered himself to be what the Lakota people called *winktes*, a man who held masculine and feminine energies equally. Prudence felt strangely better hearing this. Perhaps this man, like herself, lived in sexual limbo. Suddenly he stopped talking and motioned for Prudence to stand up and face him, arms at her sides, palms facing upward. With the sage in one hand and eagle fan in the other, Ray, with light, firm pushes of his fingers, turned her in four directions, using his fan to purify her, brushing white sage smoke all around her. Prudence kept her eyes trustingly shut, felt the wing's mild whooshing breeze as it beat around her. When it was over, she ploffed down on the limp edge of the bed and opened her eyes. Ray set down the fan, laid the sage to burn in the open half of an abalone shell, and began to pray aloud, thanking Creator for all the gifts and opportunities of his life, then praying for members of his family, living and dead. Lulled by the dreamy, cadenced rise and fall of his voice, she scarcely noticed as, praying aloud in turn for Holt, Bernice, Sam, herself, Ray lit his bloodstone pipe, blew tobacco smoke in the four directions, then passed the pipe to Holt, who drew on its stem deeply, then exhaled, using one hand to brush white smoke over his head and around his heart before touching the bowl of the pipe to his forehead and beginning a long, strenuous prayer of his own, ending with praise for the power and glory of Almighty Jesus. He tapped Prudence on the shoulder, passing the pipe to her. She accepted, sucked, sucked harder, saw no smoke emerging from the bowl, mumbled thanks, and hurriedly passed the pipe, like a hot potato, over to Sam, who held it for Bernice to smoke. Nodding at Ray, asking him to relight the pipe for her, Bernice drew in with reverent, lengthy expertise, blowing smoke in four directions, praying with fervent ease. Then it was Sam's turn. Sam prayed in a style similar to Holt's, passionate and full of Christian reference, though she turned the pipe this way and that, in complicated, baton-like directions. As the pipe moved in a circle, passing from

Ray to Holt to Prudence to Bernice to Sam and back to Ray, it needed frequent relighting. Prudence kept her head bowed, and except for one or two furtive peeks to gauge how soon her turn was coming, kept her eyes shut. Suddenly Ray was praying audibly, distinctly — *Creator, I pray for this woman opposite me, this woman who has traveled a long distance. I pray for her loneliness. She has been scorned by men.* He might as well have stuck a red-hot poker against her chest, stamped a hot branding iron on her forehead. How did he know? She scarcely heard the fourth, final round of prayers, entreaties for the success of Native People's Circle, for Sam's health, for family and friends, for Mother Earth and her creatures, for the two-legged, the four-legged, the winged ones. She glanced up and caught Ray Chasing Hawk staring, as if transfixed, at her red cowboy boots.

When everyone's prayers were finished, Ray, who appeared to be an extremely orderly person, stood up, rewrapped and placed the pipe, shell, sage, eagle fan and tobacco back into the cedar box, all with the same finical, precise movements he had used to bring them out.

Prudence rode home with Sam and

Holt. In Sam's office, on the wall above her computer station, were dozens of black and white publicity shots, mostly autographed, of male Indian celebrities, all handsome, long-haired, bare-chested, frequently stoic-looking, and straddling the bare backs of horses. In the hallway leading to the guest bedroom, Sam had hung a photographic timeline of her only son, Eugene. Stocking-capped Eugene at birth, as a toddler, preschooler, grade schooler, preteen, right up to an awkward, deadpan portrait of fifteen-year-old acned Eugene, currently asleep in his bedroom, adjacent to the guest room. In this room, now Prudence's, all four mint green walls displayed Christian and Native American posters, embroidered sayings, feathered souvenirs, dream catchers, burden baskets and crucifixes, nailed up and thumbtacked at apparent random. Prudence unpacked her toothbrush, went into Eugene's bathroom, scrubbed her teeth, said a quick good night to Sam and Holt, who sat on top of one another in the living room. Back in her soothing green room, Prudence switched the light out and climbed into bed. Up to now, she had justified her celibacy, thinking it awarded her some vague spiritual benefit. Consider Mother Teresa,

Prudence would remind herself — think of that, lying on hard floors every night, wearing the same piece of drapery, the same tea towel on your head, every minute of your life. Still, one day with Holt and Sam, so passionately, wantonly, *fleshily* adoring one another (she could hear them even now, moaning at the other end of the too-small house), had begun to undermine the already suspect virtue of a sexless life. *I pray for this woman in her loneliness. She has been scorned by men.* Why had Ray Chasing Hawk — young/old, male/female — offered to purify and pray over her in a motel room? Why had he stared so intently at her red boots, identified her loneliness, breached her defenses, so that now, hours later, her heart felt bruised even as her mind raced, alert to sexual danger, wary.

Expected to proceed at noon down the forlorn, glaring main street of heat-stricken Anadarko, pop. 6,783, the Sixty-eighth Annual Indian Parade was off to a dismally late start. Scheduled to lead the parade on horseback, Enrique Paz, Indian of the Year, celebrity spokesperson for NPC, was still in his motel room at 11 a.m., lolling about in his underwear, watching Road Runner cartoons. After rousing Enrique,

Sam, along with Prudence and Bernice, had left an amiable Holt manning the booth in the exposition hall, while Sam took the car, nosing the dust-caked, blunt-finned Cadillac into town. All three had promised Enrique they would wait along the parade route and cheer as he trotted by on his borrowed horse. Now Prudence and Sam took turns pushing Bernice in her wheelchair, the sun blazing above their heads like an acetylene torch. Prudence, in a black lace broomstick skirt, long-sleeved denim blouse and black cowboy boots, veered and bumped the wheelchair up and down curbs and around broken places in the sidewalk as Bernice and Sam sniped about Enrique's latest girlfriend, a tall, horse-faced Kiowa girl named Crystal who wore miniskirts, purple lip liner and a set of complicated braids pinned like drapery ropes, like fancy gimping, to her mostly empty though beautiful head. Bernice's cousin Maxine claimed Crystal had four children, all cared for by Crystal's invalid mother, and that Crystal was so stupid she wanted four more. Prudence, only half listening, worried about her skin, her vitiligo. She'd doused her face in sunblock, covered her entire body, leaving only her hands exposed. Both Bernice and Sam had long, thick dark hair to protect their scalps; Prudence's hair shot like a sere yellow weed, like dry celosia, from her pale, cooked scalp. She tipped the wheelchair, rolled Bernice backward, up over a curb, and set the brake, parking her under the last unclaimed three-inch border of shade along Main Street, beneath the rusted metal awning of Dickie's Play Lounge. Though she had scarfed down two blueberry and yogurt protein bars earlier that morning, Prudence was still hungry. Her allergy kit, an amber plastic tube containing a tourniquet, alcohol swabs and a syringe of epinephrine, was shoved down into her left boot in case she was stung by bees.

Finally, one hour late and less than a block from where they waited under the metal awning, the parade began. There were car horns, feebly blatting, the anxious nickerings and whinnying of horses, a flatulent tooting of French horns. Presiding over this mild cacophony was the voice of the parade master, authoritative, indistinct, rumbling through a bullhorn. Families, mostly Indian, spottily lined both sides of Main Street, adults in plastic lawn chairs surrounded by peevish children, listless and tired of waiting in the big-wave, monstrous heat.

"Not much of a turnout compared to last year," said Sam. "The sidewalks aren't even two deep, probably this heat wave kept a lot of folks home. Yesterday was Oklahoma's hottest day on record in over ninety years. Sure enough, we're right on Indian time." Sam checked her watch, tapping her tiny foot, snapping and blowing on her lime-flavored bubblegum.

Confined to her wheelchair, fanning herself with a parade flyer, Bernice began talking a blue streak. Even the heat didn't appear to bother her much as she waved air around with the stepped-on flyer Sam had picked up off the street. "Enrique wanted Ray to ride with him in the parade. That man's scared shitless of horses. Ray turned him down, even though they've been in a couple of Indian flicks together. I'm not stealing anybody's thunder, he told me."

"I checked out his actor's bio," said Sam, whipping a comb through her long, shiny hair, "on the back of those publicity photos of his. It says professional bareback rider, expert in archery, canoeing, martial arts, I forget what all."

Bernice scoffed. "Enrique? If that man's ridden anything besides a merry-go-round and a bunch of stupid, starstruck groupies, you can shoot me in the right and left foot simultaneously."

"But in his movies he rides —"

"The trainer's off-camera, coaching him the whole time. That man couldn't ride a three-legged prairie dog. On the other hand, my boy can ride bareback at a dead gallop, and shoot a bow and arrow at the same time."

"Didn't you say Ray lives on a horse ranch?" Sam was combing Bernice's hair for her, braiding it.

"Yeah, his parents own a ranch outside Houston. Arabians. He's grown up around horses."

Throughout her childhood, Prudence had prayed for a horse. With less hope each Christmas, she'd printed *horse* at the top of her list, never getting her dearest wish, not even close, not even riding lessons. Sam handed her a piece of bubblegum. Plugging the lime green square into her mouth, keeping her eyes clamped shut against a razored brightness so intense her sunglasses hardly worked, shifting the tart cube of gum around in her mouth, salivating a little, Prudence daydreamed of horses.

A male voice soaked into her right ear, smooth as syrup, a familiar drawl.

"Your makeup is melting. Thought you might want to know."

When she opened her eyes, he was gone, and Bernice sat grinning and giddy, clutching the can of Mr. Pibb Ray had delivered especially for her.

Goaded on by French horns, snare drum rolls, the tooting of car horns, revving of engines and the loose whinnying of horses, the Anadarko Indian parade, like some sluggish, determined beast, crept forward. Enrique, waving his right arm, rode at the head of the parade, looking fastidious and strangely regal in Plains-style fringed leggings, buckskin shirt and feathered war bonnet. His horse, a too-small mean-jawed, walleyed pinto, kept skittering sideways, menacing families packed and wilting along the parade route. Bernice sniggered. "That horse wants to shoot right out from under him." Still, Sam, Prudence and Bernice waved, squinting into the sun, cheering and hollering, frying on the sidewalk, looking like diehard fans, like polygamists' wives, as Enrique passed by, jerking hard on his horse's mouth, his smile a tight, joyless grimace beneath his long-feathered bonnet. Though nearly blinded by the sun's glare, Prudence had to admit Enrique looked handsome, this

119

tall, lean emissary from Hollywood dropped down, an indigenous godling, into the lowly populace of Anadarko, Oklahoma, this man of the world, sophisticated and glamorous, star of stage and screen. Hah! All three of them (hands dropping, voices going silent the instant he'd passed by) knew Enrique's true situation — that he was an unemployed, penniless actor reduced to painting house exteriors and mowing lawns to pay rent on his shabby apartment, driving to audition after audition in his broken-down van, hoping for a role, any role, no matter how small, stereotyped or demeaning — any part in a movie, play, commercial, or late night infomercial. He was, he'd confessed to Sam, an inch from homelessness. Yet leading Anadarko's annual parade as Indian of the Year, Enrique Paz was suddenly, in this context at least, a prince, a Hollywood star, one of the world's more classically eligible, elusive bachelors. And visually, Prudence mused, he was a more handsome model for Lone Eagle than Ray Chasing Hawk. After Enrique had side-danced by, his too-small horse bucking and kicking, a dozen convertibles rolled wearily past, cloaked in prairie dust and swagged with streamers, studded with toilet paper carnations in mint greens, pale pinks and soft yellows, like so much fancy cake decor, cars overflowing with Indians from numerous tribes and organizations, all waving and smiling, followed by a tight, glittering phalanx of local high school girls marching in white fringed boots, spinning white-knobbed batons, then the high school marching band in maroon suits festooned with gold braid, faces pale and sweating under stiff, bucket-like hats, forced to march under white-hot skies, their partially tuned instruments honking and blatting, wheezing and piping, to some terrible, predetermined music.

As the palest person in Anadarko, Prudence stood out like a sore thumb. A white thumb. A thumb with vitiligo. Even Sam, with her ivory skin, managed to blend in; her long, glossy black hair gave her a near-Native look, a look she took pains to accentuate. But Prudence's hair was a dry, frizzled Tropical Blonde, and her vitiligo gave her a kind of double-whiteness, zinc white on regular white. In a self-conscious, overheated misery that had increased ever since Ray had whispered in her ear that her makeup was melting, Prudence endured the small-town parade, her splotched hands sweating against the wheelchair's gray plastic handles. After less than an hour, the parade had trickled down to a straggling, wayward, strangely silent end, and Sam hustled off, full of purpose even in the sweltering midafternoon heat, to arrange for a radio interview promoting NPC. Chomping gum, Prudence rolled Bernice along the glary sidewalk, her head bent to better hear the story of how Bernice had met Ray at the Gathering of Nations in Albuquerque, how she could tell from his eyes he liked her, he was just a little shy. "He'll get over it. My boy will jump that fence. I've got three days and nights to wear him down." Prudence commiserated with Bernice about the ongoing perils and peculiar tendencies of men, heard herself say aloud and with conviction that she was through with men, thank you very much. Bernice said she knew exactly what Prudence meant. After last summer, when Enrique had broken her heart at Red Earth in Oklahoma City, she had sworn the exact same thing. Never again. But this time, with Ray Chasing Hawk, she had some new, fragile hope.

"So what's next?" In the backseat of the car, Prudence checked her face in her round pocket mirror. It reflected one eye at a time, half her nose, most of her small mouth. She was trying to sound like an able-bodied, confident codirector as, with Sam and Bernice, she headed back to the fairgrounds. Sam answered.

"Get back to the booth, sell raffle tickets for the Pendleton blanket, Ray's art print and that movie poster of Enrique. Finish folding another hundred NPC brochures, do my fifteen-minute radio interview with those folks from Stillwater. Then there's a banquet honoring all the Indian princesses — we have to go to that — come back to the booth, work till ten. Enrique's supposed to lead Grand Entry into the arena tonight, but before he does that, I need him to sit in our booth, sign autographs, and flirt his gorgeous, unemployed ass off."

Bernice stared plaintively out the passenger window. "I wonder what happened to my sweetie? He brought me my soda, like I asked, then took off."

"He's probably busy helping Enrique down off that plug-ugly horse. That man is really starting to chap my hide. We get him all this free publicity, and what does he do? Whine like some great big Baby Huey, hide in his room, and watch TV. He had the nerve to complain this morning that a bunch of girls serenaded him outside his motel room last night, so he couldn't get his beauty sleep. What does he expect? He's a goddamn movie star to these poor people. Who cares if back in Hollywood he's leaf-blowing sidewalks? They don't know that. So what if he's an out-of-work actor, who cares if the last part he played was three years ago in *Cheyenne Warrior*? These people don't know that. To them he's a celebrity, the biggest thing to come to town since Wes Studi, last year, and Rodney Grant, the year before that." Sam sighed, checking her lipstick in the rear-view mirror. "God, that Rodney was a total babe."

Prudence wondered why Sam's makeup didn't melt. She also noted how gossiping about Enrique had become a pastime for Sam and Bernice, a sort of hard-nosed knitting, with Sam purling one snide row, Bernice picking up the next. Listening to their mean craft, Prudence almost sympathized with Enrique.

Bernice purls one row: "Have you noticed how people are only buying that one photograph of Enrique when he was in his twenties? When he was pretty enough to pass for a beautiful girl? Nobody's buying his new photographs, even though he

124

keeps shoving them to the front of the table. Nope, they reach right over those ones and grab his pretty-boy picture."

Sam purls the next row down: "That's because those new head shots are awful. The man looks like a mobster, a Colombian drug dealer, frowning like that, wearing that god-awful plaid sport coat."

When they got back to the Caddo Fairgrounds, Prudence settled Bernice behind NPC's display table, then rushed off to ladies', a block structure with wet cement floors, soggy blooms of balled-up paper towels littering the floor, and a rectangle of aluminum along one wall, substitute for a mirror. She peered into its gray, pitted, smeary surface, trying to fix her sliding makeup, dabbing the oily patches around her nose and chin with a square of harsh toilet paper, rubber-banding her hair into a scorched, brassy knob at the back of her head. So what if she was no celebrity like Enrique, no sexpot like Sam, no person of tribal influence, like Bernice. She knew who she was, a middle-aged schoolteacher trying to make a small difference in Anadarko, Oklahoma. Since they had met the year before at a bed-and-breakfast in Albuquerque, Sam had acted as if Prudence were an intrinsic part of her mission,

God's mission. And Prudence, not one to argue with God or the possibility of God's hand, was trying her best to help, to do some small, awkward good.

At the Indian Princess Banquet, Ray Chasing Hawk chose a corner seat beside Bernice so he could hold her glass of water as she ducked her head, grabbing the straw with her mouth, so he could cut up her food, bring pieces of chicken and bits of vegetable, balanced on a spoon, to her open mouth. He wore a white T-shirt with a black-ink drawing of Christopher Columbus, and printed beneath Columbus's image — *Wanted: For Grand Theft, Genocide, Racism, Initiating the Destruction of a Culture, Rape, Torture and Maiming of Indigenous People, Instigation of the Big Lie*. Sitting at the same table, Prudence picked listlessly at her food. Tribal princesses from each of Oklahoma's seventeen tribes, Arapaho, Caddo, Apache, Kiowa, Comanche, Ponca, Pawnee, Osage — Prudence lost track of the others — were asked to step up individually to the microphone and give a short speech of thanks. After all seventeen princesses had spoken, the grandfathers and grandmothers came up, one at a time, one after the other, taking the microphone, talking in their native tongue, crying or telling jokes, talk that went on and on and on, like mild weather, like clouds passing by. When the speeches were finally over, Ray got up from the table to talk to someone across the room (she could read the back of his T-shirt now — *500 Years of Indian Resistance to Colonization in the Americas 1492–1992*), and Prudence stood up then too, offering to push Bernice's wheelchair toward the exit doors. But everyone at the banquet knew Bernice, wanted to say hello, so they were stopped constantly. Still, Prudence felt safe behind a wheelchair. She felt useful. Invisible.

"Your skirt's all hiked up in back" . . . his soft Texas drawl.

Prudence craned her neck to look. It was true. The bottom half of her long black lace skirt was hitched up into the waistband of her underpants, exposing her skinny white legs in their high-heeled black cowboy boots.

"Want me to fix that?" Deft as a valet, he tugged at the black lace until it swept back down, concealing her underpants, her naked legs.

Beet-faced, she tried rushing Bernice off in her wheelchair, but was stopped in her tracks by an old Kiowa grandmother who wanted to talk.

Prudence longed to be in a small, quiet room buried in the safety of books and refuge of papers! Instead, with the banquet over, she was back in the Cadillac, Sam speeding and gossiping all the way to the fairgrounds, Bernice up front, pouting, because Prudence was in back with Ray, who had drawn a large black comb out of his back jeans pocket and begun, ever so languidly, to groom his long, lustrous hair. Suddenly he turned to Prudence, asking if he could comb her hair, too. As he tugged, unknotted, and attempted to smooth down her bushy hair, she tried to think of something clever to say.

"It's never this bad back home."

"Humidity," he said. "It's the heat and humidity."

Back in Phoenix, Prudence spoke confidently before her community college classes. She enjoyed giving talks and lectures on subjects she had chosen and knew something about. But with Ray's slender, beringed hands moving through her hair, she had gone aphasic, as dumb as any rural fence post passing by outside the Cadillac's stuck-shut, grimy windows.

They sat in matching green-webbed aluminum chairs, she and Sam, talking with the women who slowed down to glance at the literature offered by their little booth, patiently explaining Native People's Circle's dream of building shelters for victims of domestic violence. (Prudence talked less. Deleanor had spanked her on the bottom two or three times when she was little, and once, years before, during an argument, Powell had placed his hands around her neck as if to choke her, then roughly shoved her away, more disgusted with himself than her, an incident which had horrified them both, so they never discussed it and went on to act as if it had never occurred. Her experience with violence was that minimal. Sam, on the other hand, had escaped from a ten-year abusive marriage, then fallen, straight afterward, into an engagement that had turned violent, until she had broken that off, too, and fled Lubbock for good.) They sold raffle tickets, a dollar apiece, one coffee can for Pendleton blanket tickets, a second for the movie poster of Enrique, a third for Ray's ink sketch of a Comanche warrior on horseback, raising his painted warshield to the sun. The Pendleton can was bursting with red paper tickets, while Ray's and

Enrique's were practically empty. Watching the women who stopped at the table, Prudence especially noticed the ones shyly brushing their fingers over the pamphlets, betraying their desperation (*Go ahead,* she would urge, *take one, take several, they're free, pass them along to your friends*). Reservation statistics were staggering, domestic violence part of a deeply entrenched cycle of poverty, alcoholism, drug abuse, homelessness, divorce, murder. She watched their hands literally reach for help, take a pamphlet, tuck it quickly away in a purse.

During a lull in the long evening, when no one had stopped by their booth for some time, Prudence told Sam she was going to step outside the exhibition hall for a few minutes. She passed aisles of booths, jewelry, crafts, T-shirts, artwork, herbs, leatherwork, other nonprofit organizations, and pushing open one of the main exit doors, ran smack into Ray and a pretty, giggling Kiowa girl named Beebee. They insisted Prudence join them, stroll past the food vendors and amusement rides, stop to listen to a three-piece country western band playing on a forlorn stage, a warped plywood platform that looked as if a single flashlight with a dying battery was its sole source of light. Folding her long skirt around her, the same black lace skirt Ray had unhitched for her at the Indian Princess Banquet, Prudence sat on the dry, dusty grass. She had brought her journal with her and sat moving her pen in near darkness, warding off, with scribbled observation, the surprising pain of hearing Ray and Beebee laughing together, seeing them huddled, shoulders touching. Later, as the three of them headed back to the exhibition hall, Beebee stopped to talk to a friend and Ray moved in, walking close beside her. "I want you to know I'd much rather have spent time with you, she's just a kid who needs attention. It was you I really wanted to talk to, get to know."

Oh right, Prudence thought, ignoring Ray as he gallantly swung open the door for her. She stepped inside the cool hall, her journal tight in her hand, prop, refuge, defense.

The next morning, she reared up in bed, hammered awake by a loneliness that had gathered some nocturnal strength, acquired ominous voice: *I can't stand this anymore.* She could hear Sam and Holt, in the kitchen, laughing, probably calling one another Babes, Sweetie, Gorgeous, Snookums, Poochie, god knows what. Prudence dabbed at her damp eyes with the bedsheet, got up, peered nearsightedly into the mirror. Three days before she could go home. It wasn't their fault. She wished them well, she truly did. Certainly it was in the nature of that sort of love, wasn't it, to be oblivious, insensitive, everyone expected to bask in, draw near, soak up stray, leftover bits of warmth.

They drove to the fairgrounds, Holt parking the Cadillac next to a burrito vendor, so Sam and Prudence could begin lifting boxes from the trunk, hundreds of freshly printed NPC brochures, hundreds of plain blue government issue pamphlets titled *Ten Steps to Escape Domestic Violence*. As Prudence used her back to push open one of the heavy doors into the exhibition hall, Ray stood waiting on the other side. He lifted the box from her arms, and in that intimate-sounding drawl of his wished her good morning. From that moment on, Ray Chasing Hawk began to openly court Prudence True Parker. Unaccustomed to such pointed attentions, Prudence seemed hardly to respond. Only later that day, as they sat side by side on an empty table in one corner of the exhibition hall, only when an older Indian woman came up asking about NPC's raffle tickets, saying she wanted that Pendleton blanket for her niece, only after Ray threw one arm around Prudence's waist, pulled her close, and said, *And all I want is this woman here, she's my Comanche captive,* as he and the old woman laughed heartily over this — only then, as she felt Ray's arm tighten around her waist, did it occur to Prudence that she was, in fact, desired.

"So, Professor Parker." It was evening, and they were sitting on a bench outside the hall, eating fry bread. "Tell me. What is it you like about Indian men?"

The question stung Prudence. "I'm here for the women and children. For NPC. If there wasn't one man here, if you weren't here, I'd still be doing exactly what I'm doing." (What is it you like about older white schoolteachers? she nearly asked.)

He reached with his napkin, dabbed at one corner of her mouth, then asked how she would feel about staying overnight in his motel room? Taking care of Bernice was harder than he had thought. Could she stay over for one night, help him out? He'd already checked with Sam, who'd offered to bring a change of clothes into town for Prudence the next morning.

Prudence wanted to be alone. She also

wanted to go to the motel with Ray. She heard herself say yes, she supposed she could help him out.

After the exhibition hall closed for the night, Sam and Holt, Ray and Prudence, went to Pizza Hut for a late dinner. Ray sat close, seemingly fascinated by her every word, though in truth Prudence didn't say much. It felt like high school with popular Sam and handsome Holt across the table, nuzzling one another, teasing Ray about his obvious interest in geeky Prudence. In the bathroom, Sam yelled from inside her cubicle, over the sound of the toilet flushing.

"Watch out, girl. That wild young Comanche is all over you."

"Isn't he Bernice's boyfriend?"

"All in that poor girl's head. He likes her as a friend, that's it. He's taken her aside three times and told her that, but she keeps hoping, keeps seeing things the way she wants. No, angel sister. That man's hot for you. You sure you want to stay at the motel? You don't have to. You can come on home with Holt and me, honey, if you want to."

Prudence imagined another night of hearing Holt and Sam down the hall, "doing the nasty" as Holt called it. She'd never met two people so full of lust for one another and praise for the Lord at the exact same time. Besides, going to the motel might provide valuable research for the romance novel she still couldn't believe she was actually going to sit down and write.

"No, I'll go. Help with Bernice."

"Well, you watch out. Don't let that Comanche boy take advantage of you, you're just too precious. Holt says you're much smarter than you look. Ever since his first wife, that bitch, he has a color prejudice against blondes, but I told him your hair is more naturally reddish, you're not a real blonde. We feel real protective of you, honey."

"Mom and Pop?"

"That's right. You're our precious baby girl."

In the parking lot outside Pizza Hut, Ray offered to drive Prudence to the motel. Sam winked and blew extravagant kisses before climbing into the fat-finned Cadillac, with Holt roaring off like a teenager, spinning gravel and tootling the horn. On the short drive to the motel, Ray played a CD he had spent five minutes hunting around for on the floor of his van —

135

chanting baritone monks mixed in with a woman whispering *de Sade* in a sultry French accent. He asked what she thought of it. Prudence mumbled "interesting." He asked what kind of writing she did, and not waiting for an answer, went on to say he wrote, too, kept a little notebook called The Pessimist, though mostly he painted. Sex and anger inspired his art. Anger, he said, was the one emotion he allowed himself. The Frenchwoman moaned orgasmically, the body of monks chanted. His notebook, The Pessimist, maybe she could take a look at it, tell him if it was any good? They were at the motel now, he was opening the door for her, placing his hand in an old-fashioned, gentlemanly way on the small of her back, guiding her to his room on the ground floor.

Of course, she answered, believing him, stepping across the threshold. She'd be happy to look at his writing.

Bernice, he said calmly, flipping on the lights, was visiting her family. He had to pick her up around twelve-thirty. What time is it, Prudence asked. Ten-thirty, he answered, and with that, Prudence started pulling at her thumbs, a nervous childhood habit, and chattering on about Bernice, how she felt badly because she knew for a fact Bernice liked Ray a lot and thought of him as her boyfriend. She felt guilty, she confessed, being alone with him. As she talked, Prudence realized she was in the exact same spot on the twin bed where she had sat the first night, when Ray had purified her with sage and prayed for her loneliness, announced she had been scorned by men.

"I know that," he said, sitting beside her, reaching for her hand. "I feel badly too, but I've talked to Bernice, I've told her the truth, more than once. I admire her, we're good friends, but I am just not interested in anything more. Maybe it's selfish, I've never claimed to be noble, but I like a whole woman in my arms. Does that make me a bad person?"

"I guess not," Prudence answered, watching her original, nobler impression of him fade. From what he told her, Ray Chasing Hawk was angry, politically negative, pessimistic. Not exactly the stuff of heroes for a Savage Passion plot.

"Hey, it's been a long day. Want to take a bath or something? You can borrow some of Bernice's things to wear to bed tonight, she's got a ton of clothes in there." Ray nodded at the dresser in front of him, got up, pulled open one of the drawers, and handed her a pair of beige pajama bottoms and a beige T-shirt.

"A bath would be nice." As Prudence rose primly to her feet, Ray stood suddenly very close.

"May I kiss you?"

Within moments of being pressed against the motel wall and aggressively kissed, Prudence was on her back on the twin bed, Bernice's bed, Ray reaching beneath her long black lace skirt with one manicured hand, lightly scratching the inside of her bare thighs with long polished nails, unbuttoning her denim blouse with his other hand, kissing her breasts. The top of her head was on fire, her feet felt miles away.

"I want to bite you. May I bite you?"

Prudence had been bitten twice in her life, once in the knee by a Mexican fighting cock, once in the ankle by a feral half-Chihuahua, so when he took her astonished silence for yes, turning her onto her stomach, pushing her blouse above her shoulders, and sinking his front teeth into the soft pads of flesh just beneath her shoulder blades, Prudence was shocked to feel pleasure rush up under the initial stinging. He bit up and down her back, sharp tuggings, quick nips, asking over and over did she like it, did she like what he was doing? She nodded, more shocked than certain. Then he was turning her back over, shoving up her bra, biting her nipples and breasts so hard that Prudence, eyes closed, pictured blood. She heard a warning voice suspiciously like her mother's, like Deleanor's — *Silly girl, blind lamb, you have fallen into the clutches of a sexual maniac. He has lured you here, you are about to die, be disposed of, a future episode on* Unsolved Mysteries, the nightly crime show she and Fiona used to watch, a form of mother-daughter bonding, when Fiona was ten. Abruptly he stopped biting, sat up, and with one swift, practiced motion, stripped off his Christopher Columbus T-shirt, then lay down next to her, pushing her head down against his smooth brown chest. *Your turn.* She bit daintily into the soft flesh near his nipple. He was slender, it was hard to get a purchase with her teeth. *Harder,* he whispered. *Bite harder.* She did, tasting the salt and sweet of him, hearing him, *Oh, that's good, god, that makes me feel alive.* He was a madman. Was he going to strangle her next? Then, suddenly, it was over. She lay safe, the taste of his firm, good flesh ripe in her mouth.

He raised his wrist to his face, checked

the time on his watch. "Quarter past. I've got to go get Bernice. Why don't you take your bath? Here" — he reached down, retrieved the limp pajama bottoms and oversized T-shirt from the floor. He sounded calm, as if nothing he had just done or said had even happened. "Wear these. Bernice won't care."

Floating in hot, greenish bathwater, her breasts marked by the red fretwork of his teeth, Prudence heard them come in, heard the television switch on. She stepped out of the bath, dried herself with a thin, rough motel towel, pulled on Bernice's baggy pajama bottoms, Bernice's enormous, flaccid T-shirt. She felt exhausted, wildly awake. She wanted to be bitten some more. Instead she unlocked the bathroom door and stepped out from the steamy bathroom, casually saying hi to Bernice, who sat on the same bed she and Ray had just lain on, propped against a raft of pillows. Stretched prone on the other bed, hands laced behind his head, Ray watched the History Channel, *Battle Secrets of Hitler's Army.* He didn't look at her. For the next hour, Prudence helped Bernice get her clothes off, seesawed a black baby-doll nightie over her head, lifted her on and off the toilet, brushed her long hair, rolled her out of her wheelchair and onto the bed, tucked her in, fixed her pillow, comfortably wedging it under her neck. Ray, who hadn't moved a single muscle to help, turned off the TV, flung a blanket in the aisle between the two beds, turned off the nightstand lamp, and without a word, wearing only his blue jeans, lay down on the blanket. In the dark motel room, the three of them said cordial, weirdly formal good nights. As Bernice's breathing quieted, fell into the rise and fall of sleep, Prudence felt Ray's hand reach up from where he lay on the floor, find hers, squeeze her fingers hard. She fell asleep like that, her hand awkward in his, unwilling to let go.

The night before Prudence was to fly home to Phoenix, she locked herself into Eugene's minuscule blue bathroom, turned on the bathwater, and stripped naked. Peeking into the medicine cabinet, she nabbed Eugene's black razor and Gillette shaving cream. Stepping into the blue, filling tub, she dragged the dull razor over her white-foamed legs once, then twice. She felt fat, her stomach looked bloated, a pinkish beach ball, god, like Deleanor's. She was growing her mother's stomach.

Getting out and drying off, she brushed her teeth, plaited her damp hair, tugged on an ankle-length cotton gauze slip from India and a billowing-sleeved muslin poet's shirt, all she had brought to sleep in. Down the hall, in the living room, she could hear Ray, who had somehow managed to invite himself home with them, talking to Sam and Holt, his words blurred, indistinct, but opinionated-sounding. Before her bath, as she sat next to Ray on the couch, he had pulled her close, whispering in her ear, *sexy thing, you,* a phrase normally offensive to Prudence. *Sexy thing, you,* please. Such a cheeseball line! Still, his arm had felt protective, and no one, when she thought about it, had protected her in years. Capable, self-reliant Prudence Parker, with Ray Chasing Hawk's arm around her, whispering, *Sexy thing, you,* lost her bearings. She sat mute, her moral compass spinning, a blinkard blinking, bovine and flopped, undone by a man's touch, a man's cheesy murmur in her ear.

Where should I sleep, he'd whispered next, *here on the couch or in your room? My room,* she'd breathed, and red-cheeked with embarrassment, excused herself to go down the hall, bathe, scrub her teeth, change into her bulky nightclothes, fuss with the bed, arrange herself this way and that, scramble back out of the bed to search for matches, which she located in a drawer, setting the small matchbox beside the scarlet stub of candle on the shelf behind the bed, then climbing back in again. She was a wreck. Now he was in Eugene's bathroom, taking a shower. She nipped out of bed again, went to her suitcase, hunting out her father's gardening shoes and horticultural dictionary, pressing them to her chest, asking for good luck, advice, protection, guidance, then putting them back and closing the lid of the suitcase. Slipping back into bed, she poked her reading glasses on, slid them off, polished them, hooked them on again, arranged books and papers around her like a scholarly fussbudget intent on researching a subject she could never admit to. The shower cut off, followed by a shudder of pipes. The sink taps went on, off, she heard him brush his teeth, spit in the sink, turn on the water, turn off the water. The toilet flushed. Flushed again. Prudence had an overwhelming urge to yank the covers over her head, leave a tidy note of clarification on top of the blanket: She was a schoolteacher, a celibate schoolmarm, a neutered old bolster in reading glasses, not a sexy

143

thing, not a sexy thing at all! Then the door opened softly, like a sigh, and he was in the room, crossing the room, climbing into her bed, casual and kindly as an old friend, except Ray Chasing Hawk was naked and young and gorgeous, with satiny brown skin, long black hair, full lips and black, glittering vulpine eyes, ravenous eyes that did not match his calm, soft-spoken manner. He sat as patient as one of her textbooks, silent as she rattled on about her students, her ideas, her theories of this and that, until she ran out of things to say and sat humid and moist inside her gauzy bandage of nightclothes, a rabbit, panicked, wild-eyed, motionless.

He switched off the lamp, struck a match, lit the red candle, blew the match flame out, lifted her glasses from her face. Patted the mattress, nestled her down beside him, one bare arm sweet as sugar around her. Had she been mistaken? Perhaps he wanted nothing more than to cuddle, to listen to her ramble on about the healing power of stories. She had deliberately chosen classroom words, school words, using them like bricks to erect one last barricade. But that barricade had begun to crumble under his silence. It was rubble. Fearful, fragile, her extremities icy with panic, Prudence resumed talking, her own voice making her drowsy, relaxed, the danger past, nearly asleep. He struck then, tense, agile, ardent, waiting until she was so sleepy, so defenseless, she fell at his touch. In one flicker of motion, he'd stripped off the billowing poet's blouse, the long gauzy slip, had her on her back, nude, arched, halfway off the bed, hair grazing the carpet, getting fucked, the only possible word, fucked (hardly a romance word) again and again by a young, slender, silent man whose long rush of black hair veiled her face, streamed like water over her belly, brushed like silk down her thighs. All night she endured his rapacious attacks, all night she was buffeted, rent, splayed, surrendered, gouged and bitten. He drove her on and on, without mercy or rest, until they lay awash on the bed together, the sheets like stilled, choppy waves, until he started up again, calling her body a playground, saying little else. Brutal, untender, yet not unwelcome, his greed, ripping into her, smashing down defenses. A witness (as it turned out, there was one) might assume she was being assaulted. Violated. Yet she was pliant, did not resist his holding open her thighs, biting her breasts, her stomach, fucking with hard, violent energy, forcing her by his greed, his lust, into one single, harsh, backward bloom.

She couldn't begin to describe it.

The hot, glary light in the room suggested late morning, even noon. He was completely dressed, brushing his long hair, swiftly braiding it, as she watched from the bed. He said good-bye, detached, impersonal, swift, courteous. He needed, he said, to drive three hours south to Lawton, there was a woman he had to meet at a bookstore at one o'clock. He leaned over the bed, gave her a quick, sweet kiss, then was gone, closing the door softly behind him.

Good. Fine. Last night had not been about divine intervention, love or permanence. She knew that. Prudence dressed slowly, her body aching and tender (*When you leave, when you go to the airport tomorrow, I want to have fucked you so hard you'll barely be able to walk* — had he actually said that? Try putting that in a Savage Passion romance, hah!). She tried not to limp into the kitchen, where she found Sam and Holt sitting at their island counter drinking coffee, and Eugene, Sam's fifteen-year-old son, rattling Sugar

146

Pops into a giant plastic salad bowl. When he saw her, he nearly dropped the box. Suddenly Prudence recalled the sound of someone getting up in the middle of the night to use the bathroom, a vague memory of the door being ajar, leaving a few black inches of space. God in heaven. Had this shy, acned boy witnessed her splayed half off the bed, legs open as a schoolroom scissors? Act normal. Deny everything.

"Hey Sam, Holt. Morning, Eugene. Nice to finally meet you."

Eugene dove headfirst into the refrigerator, mumbling something about milk, while Sam, wearing a short emerald satin kimono, winked at Prudence. Holt, barechested, wearing only tight blue jeans, stretched out his long legs, crossed his big shapely hands behind his head, and grinned. Eugene shut the refrigerator door, left his salad bowl of Pops untouched, and fled, flame-faced, from the kitchen.

"We're sure happy for you, darlin'. Holt agrees, he seems like a pretty nice guy."

"Yup. I stand modified and corrected. Those girlie fingernails and silver ear hoops had me fooled."

"We just hope he treats you the way you deserve. He said he'd call, didn't he?"

"No." At Holt's shocked look, Prudence

amended, "He did say he'd like to drive out to Arizona sometime." Holt sighed, morally soothed.

"Well, sure he will, honey. And we know he'll call. Holt and I believe you are just too fine a woman and too intelligent of a woman to ignore. Do you mind if we pray for you all this morning?"

So Prudence stood in a small, tidy kitchen in Anadarko, Oklahoma, with Holt Able and Sam Hill wrapping their arms around her, calling on the Lord to protect and watch over her, to open Ray Chasing Hawk's eyes and heart to see what a precious jewel their Prudence was. As they prayed for her, Prudence opened her eyes just wide enough to catch a glimpse of red-faced, lustful Eugene, flitting by like a sick calf.

An hour later, Eugene sat in the backseat of the Cadillac sneaking hot, lustful glances at Prudence, who sat nearby, probably reeking of sex, though she'd showered until the water ran cool. At the airport, after hugging Holt and Sam good-bye (Eugene opted to stay in the car) and checking her suitcase, she hobbled gingerly in her red cowboy boots (*I'll fuck you so hard and so long, you won't be able to walk straight to-*

148

morrow) to a newsstand, selected and bought a postcard showing grass dancers at a pow-wow in Caddo, Oklahoma. After printing neatly on the back, *Greetings Digby, Have been in the field. Accept your offer. Sincerely, Prudence T. Parker,* she dug his address out of her wallet, wrote it on the postcard, purchased a stamp, mailed it, limped over to the gate, and with a sense of scorched convalescence, sat down. Three different businessmen failed to strike up flirtations with her. On the plane to Phoenix, a Jell-O salesman from Mexico City, bolder than the rest, asked her out. Prudence's refusal was scarcely audible; she was busy thinking how easily she had dropped into Ray Chasing Hawk's girlie-nailed clutches, fulfilling Misty Rains' thirty-dollar, twenty-minute prediction and surprising, if not thoroughly appalling, herself.

Tempe, Arizona

At last! Restored to the cool solace and chaste privacy, the safety and refuge of her home, with her father's shoes and dictionary placed reverently away in a keepsake box along with photographs and other mementos, among them an old Ping-Pong paddle and dented ball from the one game with him she'd ever won, a deck of authors cards he had given her once, one of the old white cotton handkerchiefs she used to iron for him as a kid, earning ten cents apiece, a few letters he had written her when she was in college, always with a small check enclosed — on her way out to the laundry room that evening, a basket of clothes from her Anadarko trip perched on one hip, Prudence counseled herself. You did what people do. A one-night stand, a two-night stand. So what? Who cares? And if he never calls, which he won't, why should he, Miss Easy Pants, so what? At your age, you had a first and last adventure. Get over it. Stepping back into the house, she halted in the doorway, paralyzed, listening to the voice message. *Hey, it's me. Ray. Whatcha doing? Call when you get a chance, I'm back here in Houston at the ranch. Talk to you later. Bye.*

Prudence set down her laundry basket and replayed the message, alert to subtext, emotion, signs of love, lust, infatuation. She had no idea why he would call. Two days later when he called again, she forced herself, in slow motion, to lift the receiver. As he talked, Prudence loosened her blouse, then confessed about the bruises, like sickly roses, yellow-green and wild, fading across her breasts.

"Be honest. You like it, my mark on you."

At her own soft admission, *yes,* Prudence began to fall into the place he had prepared for her — the keepsake box of her father's things, memories, talismans, totems, bits of her childhood — unable to prevent her own descent into darkness, the unnamed place and path she was to take next.

Exactly as she had for seven Christmases, Easters, Thanksgivings and summer vacations since divorcing Powell and moving to Arizona, Prudence hovered, watching strangers disembark from planes, disregarding every reunion that wasn't hers, peering like mad into the sleeve, the covered ramp, whatever it was called, pitched forward, weight on her toes, anxious for a glimpse of her fast-growing child. Why was Fiona last, or nearly last, off every plane, with Prudence stiff as a puzzle piece by the time she finally saw her daughter, the sight of whom caused her body to flood with unimaginable relief, a warm, endorphic rush of pleasure. Seeing Fiona, kissing her warm freckled cheeks, patting her curly auburn hair, brought pure, biologic peace to Prudence. Since birth, Fiona True Parker had possessed the ability to calm her mother, to soothe Prudence's galloping, skittish heart. They were compatible in temperament, metabolism, aesthetic, in perfect accord. As a toddler, Fiona had puddled contentedly between her mother's feet in the shower; it took languid hours for the two of them to leave the house for an outing or set of errands, content in one another's company, moving in matched, sedate rhythm, unhurried, pacific. Often Prudence and little Fiona would not set foot outside the house until midafternoon, and then, the longing to return home would overcome them at the exact same moment. Prudence had never understood the complaints of other mothers about their unruly, disobedient, tiresome children. Fiona was the best friend she had ever had, and the more she cherished her daughter's companionship, the more she began to dread its eventual loss. Children were destined to grow beyond a parent's influence, though everyone knew an occasional son or daughter, impeded, self-obstructed, retrograde, growing gray in the cradle, a sad being who never left home. Prudence didn't want that for Fiona. She didn't want her to be like whey-faced, pitiful Sybil Hink, in her fifties, unmarried and eager for doom, still living with her ancient mother and unwholesome ghost of a father. She would have to find the strength to let Fiona go. Until then, Prudence sipped rich marrow from each hour of her daughter's childhood. Even now they sometimes still huddled like hens on the white couch in the living room, tucked under soft green cotton blankets, propped against opposite armrests, bare feet intertwined, sipping cocoa or tea or iced sodas, reading books together. Prudence especially missed the years when Fiona had been ten and eleven, missed their nightly bike rides through the neighborhood, ending, in warmer weather, with a skinny-dip in the pool, or in cooler weather, with a bowl of popcorn and mugs of hot cider. She missed their breakfasts at the local pancake house, missed watching *Emergency 911* and *Unsolved Mysteries* together as they dug with twin spoons into the same bowl of Kraft's macaroni and cheese or mint chip ice cream. Beginning in junior high and even more so in high school, Fiona disappeared, as was to be expected, into her room, distancing herself from her mother. Prudence heard her whispering on the phone, watched her dress up and go out with friends. This was predictable, healthy, the way of things, and Prudence hated it.

Darling, adorable Fiona! Restorer of worlds! Harbinger of companionship! Waiting at the airport gate, Prudence's hand shot up, making little whoops and dips of pleasure before she saw Fiona wave back distractedly, talking to someone following close behind her, her attention divided between her mother and a short, apple-cheeked young man in a baseball cap.

"Mooler! your hair, blond, I love it!" Fiona kissed her mother, gripping the boy's arm as if to keep him from bolting. "This is Kirby."

Wasn't that a vacuum? Prudence dimly recalled Fiona, before she'd left that summer, talking about a Kirby — an older boy she'd met downtown on Mill Avenue. Prudence also recalled hoping a summer away might cure Fiona. Geographical distance, that classically cold dash of water. Apparently she had been wrong.

"Yes, but, how . . . ?"

"When I got to Albuquerque, there he was, holding a dozen red roses, waiting to fly back to Phoenix with me! Isn't that cool?"

The boy's romantic gesture, the sheer waste of it, nearly toppled Prudence. She wondered about the dozen roses, where had they gone?

"A pleasure." Prudence shook his pink, dumpy hand. A timorous, sweatish youth, shrugging and modestly ducking his face, no doubt with a car waiting to whisk Fiona off into his seedy patch of underworld, leaving Prudence to drive home in an empty car. She was buckling under that scenario as the three of them, Prudence, Fiona, Kirby, in Three Musketeerish fashion, strode along toward baggage claim.

"We gave my roses to this poor lady whose husband died last year. We sat next to her on the plane. Moolet, would you mind giving Kirby a ride home? I told him you wouldn't mind."

How on earth was she to respond? Magnanimity? Nonchalance? She didn't want to lose Fiona before she had even gotten her home. "Sure," Prudence boomed, sounding false, feeling boxed in. "Not a problem." She heard herself, masochistically, go further. "In fact, Kirby, why don't you join Fiona and me for dinner . . . we have a little tradition of going out to eat whenever she returns home from her father's."

"Ooooh, Moo!" Fiona nudged Kirby. "What did I tell you? Islands, right?" Infatuation turned Fiona's face into a vacuous tipsy-pudding, raisins for eyes, as she watched Kirby manfully haul her only luggage, a long, dark green canvas duffel bag, oofing it off the carousel, knocking his baseball cap askew. Prudence watched, uncharmed, as Fiona slipped her arm around her mother's waist. "Ooooh, Mommy! So happy! My two favewit peeples!" Hmmph, thought Prudence, but Fiona's touch, as always, softened, soothed, reassured her.

At the Islands, a dim, tropically themed

hamburger place, Prudence ordered the Wave, Fiona the Kahuna, while Kirby, Prudence noted, ordered the most expensive hamburger, the Great White Shark. She listened to Fiona's report on Powell, his second wife, Wanda Mae, their eight-year-old daughter, Yoshi, who ran around all day in fake tiger skins and never smiled. The inflamed glances passing between Kirby and her daughter did not escape Prudence, the intertwining of fingers, the intimate dipping into one another's baskets of fries. A table's width from her daughter, Prudence concluded, without any proof other than her own saddened gut, that Fiona was no longer a virgin. Fate had assigned this spoon-chested, wilting sprig, named after a vacuum, as Prudence's love replacement. The single impartial observation she was able to make about Kirby and Fiona was how alike they looked. Brother and sister, down to hair color, skin tone, eyes, chin dimples. Prudence used to think lovers or spouses who looked alike stayed together longest, but time and her own relationships (Powell, mainly. People had regularly mistaken them for siblings) had proved her theory wrong.

Kirby stood up from the table, waggling his fingers. "He wants to go wash his hands," Fiona beamed. "He washes them more than most people, because of his profession."

"Oh, what's that? His profession?"

"He's the manager at Gumby's Pizza, he's working there until he can save enough money to start school. He wants to pay for it all himself, not owe anybody. Isn't that so smart?"

Prudence winced, thinking of her own debt, that bleak, ponderous mammoth plodding behind her, thonk, thonk, thonk, of tonight's dinner, charged to Visa. Digby Deeds' offer was taking on increasingly seductive shapes. Perhaps their meeting in the library bathroom had been fated. Destined. Ray Chasing Hawk a further sign, a green light to proceed down the lucrative avenue of a Savage Passion romance or two. Since their last brief phone call, she hadn't called Ray back; since then he had left three messages. Fiona! She couldn't let Fiona know about her one-night stand with a Comanche Indian young enough to be her son.

"Kirby had another job this summer. In a nursing home."

"Yup, that's correct." Kirby slipped back into their booth, snatched up Fiona's hand, kissed and held it between his own freshly washed hands. "Doing CRN training, seven bucks an hour. They started us off toe tagging."

"Toe tagging?" Now he had Prudence's full, marveling attention.

"Yup, just what you're thinking. Like little sales tags. After that, my buddy and me had to help a bunch of old ladies get undressed, lift them on and off toilets, wipe their asses and stuff . . ."

"Kirby, yuck!"

Fiona's shrieks only cranked up his enthusiasm. "What did it, the day I walked, was when they made me give this old geezer a suppository, made me stick this laxative, it looked exactly like a little white bullet, up his ass. That's the day I walked, man. I couldn't take that shit. So to speak." He ducked his head into his newly arrived hamburger, his Great White Shark.

"So now he makes pizzas!" Fiona looked at him with gloppy awe.

Prudence knifed her hamburger, plain, just meat and bread, in half. "Well," she said. "Well," she repeated. "That must have been quite a trial. The suppository, I mean."

"Shock treatment, man. I couldn't deal."

"Kirby's really a musician."

Aren't they all, Prudence thought. Now

159

I'm going to have to ask what instrument he plays, and he's probably going to say bass.

"What instrument, Kirby?"

"Oh, nothing really. I noodle a little. Bass. Electric bass."

"He's sooh great, Marmoset. You should hear him. He and his friends are recording their own CD. They call themselves the Undertakers, because of the one week Kirby and his friend Zeke attended mortuary school."

"Another story," Kirby snorted.

"Wonderful. You kids want dessert? They have that killer triple fudge thing, remember, Fee?" (Remember, Fee, when it was just the two of us, best friends, jokers, an era of bliss?)

She dropped the boyfriend off at his apartment complex, the Jolly Roger, in Mesa, waited in the car while Fiona walked him to his door, watched as Kirby and Fiona stood, clinging to one another, the agony of separation clearly upon them. Prudence sighed, remembering how swiftly Ray had left her that next morning, driving halfway across the state of Oklahoma to meet someone else. When Fiona returned, she slid into the front seat, stayed silent a good five minutes. Finally, she spoke.

"Isn't Kirby great, Mommy? He thinks you're really cute."

Cute? I'm nearly fifty, Prudence thought. "You really like my hair this color?"

"Yeah, you look about ten years younger, not that you didn't look good before."

"Thanks, honey. You look great, too. I love that shirt." Fiona was wearing a red T-shirt with leather lacings up both open sides. Was she too thin? Were those shadows or her ribs?

When they finally got home, it took two of them to heft the long green duffel bag, with its weight of ten dead men, out of the trunk, wrestle it through the kitchen and down the hall into Fiona's room. As they heaved and strained like sailors, Prudence thought, I should have made use of that boy's measly brawn, let him prove his love, wrench his back, drag this in.

Fiona stood at the message machine, popping through the voice mail, replaying the newest one, before turning, wide-eyed, to Prudence.

"Mah, who is THAT?" She replayed it again. They stood listening to Ray's soft, harmless-sounding drawl. Another theory shot down, that you could determine a man's intentions by his voice. *Hey Pru-*

dence, it's me. Call when you get a chance. Same number here in Houston. Hope you're well.

"Who IS that?"

"Someone I met in Oklahoma. A friend."

"No way. Mooler's got a boyfriend!"

Later that night, having arranged a space for Fiona on the couch, gotten their soft green blankets and mugs of Irish tea ready, Prudence waited, then went down the hall to tell Fiona the tea was getting cold. She found her daughter twisted into a pale, ectopic pretzel, ankles crossed, talking on the phone, twirling the cord. Knock, knock, who's there, Prudence thought bitterly. Suppository boy.

"Five minutes, Mom. Promise."

Hooded and broody under both blankets, Prudence hunched on the couch, drank first her tea, then Fiona's. Fiona was in love, loyalties were shifting. An hour later, convinced it would be futile to restrain biology (Fiona, still on the phone, was taking her first seven-league-booted step down the snake-ridden path of men), Prudence decided she, too, would take one bold red-cowboy-booted step of her own, would return a certain long-distance phone call, would not be left behind.

Should you be judged by your worst or your best deeds?
You have six months to live and un-limited funds. What will you do?
Would you rather be whole or good?
　　　　　　　　　　— Carl Jung

Compose your own obituary. Include a snapshot.

On various blackboards in assigned classrooms, Prudence liked to chalk down ethical teasers, moral slipknots. Creativity, like truth or a morally authentic life, had to be hunted, stalked, waited for, flushed out of its shy hiding. Though she was a disappointed idealist, Prudence had escaped cynicism, hedging herself in and bucking herself up with three safe choices: Chastity, Charity and Teaching. Her students, passed over, rejected by other faculty as ungifted, linguistically deaf, thematic dopes, were advised to register for Professor Parker's Advanced Personal Journey class. Prudence reached out and took them all in, her muddled masses, semester by semester proving her point — that a faint eloquence could be coaxed out of the humblest turnip. Several years back, similar convictions had carried her into a number of charitable, short-lived pursuits — teaching journal writing to women in prison, poetry writing to young girls at risk, tape-recording the life stories of homeless men lining up to be fed at the Andre House in Phoenix. Everyone had a story, and every story held dignity. But when her own story, with its triune strands of loneliness, a poisonous, low-level contempt from her colleagues, and mounting financial woe threatened to overwhelm her, Prudence had pulled back, reluctantly (temporarily she hoped), from saving the world.

Typically, on her first day of class at the community college, wearing one of her several tent dresses (for years now, she had cloaked herself in large dowdy shifts, beige, oyster-colored shrouds of natural cotton, linen or raw silk blends), Prudence would declare to her new students: *Unlike Buddha, I* am *attached to outcome. I am attached to the outcome of each and every one of your stories. In my class, you will learn to tell truths, not Truth. You will honor your life as a work of art, as a kind of sand painting or mandala, temporal, precise, worthy of respect, even reverence. You will learn to take yourselves seriously while understanding, paradoxi-*

cally, we are as nothing. Since drama was frowned on in academic life, Prudence was intentionally dramatic — switching off overhead lighting, snapping flame to patchouli- or vanilla- or pumpkin-scented candles, playing exotic CDs, inviting students to sit with blank paper and idle pen until a word, phrase or image begged to be written down. *Learn to listen and eschew judgment,* she wrote at the top of one student's paper. Write your first authentic word, even if that word is *shit.* Especially if that word is *shit,* and you have never allowed yourself to say or to write the word *shit.* Prudence's approach was therapeutic, her pedagogy spontaneous, her students mainly adults, washing back into school via community college, their average age forty-five. Many were divorced or newly separated, freshly hatched out of a long-standing codependence, unfurling damp, tissue-thin wings, woozy with freedom, unbalanced and fragile. Typically, on that first day, Prudence would waft about the front of her classroom in a pupa-like shroud of, say, white slubbed linen, inviting students to pull their chairs into a circle, introduce themselves by way of a word or an image written down and read aloud. At least half of them left the page blank, eyeing her with gimlet suspicion. Eventually, she won them over, and by mid-semester they were bringing small gifts, CDs of their favorite music, flower seeds from their gardens, small talismanic objects, a purple heart covered with Milagros, a sketch of an Athenian goddess, a shell necklace from India, a marble egg, medicinal roots, twig teas.

But Prudence had doubts. What if she was merely eccentric, eclectic, shallow? An intellectual marshmallow? Was she mainly liked because her methods (half-baked therapies?) were too easy? One or two students invariably dropped the course, individuals who equated education with rigid, empirical curriculums, with pedantic, humorless manuals of instruction. The grid-thinkers bailed, leaving their small, scornful residue of judgment to dissipate, slowly, in their absence. By the end of the first week, there might be fifteen out of an original twenty students, by the end of the second week, nine. Once in a while, a grid-thinker stayed on, scowling and truculent, wreaking revenge at semester's end with a mean, needling evaluation: Professor Parker's "class" was too touchy-feely, too New Agey, it reeked of self-helpism. What, scrawled across one form, in heavy-leaded pencil, does emotion have to do with art? (Everything, Prudence lectured the handwriting, which she recognized as Morton Wrecker's cursive brawl, a paunchy spoilsport of a man. No, Morton, art IS emotion, the creative act a wound healing itself and turning, as the painter Georges Braque said, to light.)

Years before, Prudence became convinced that some conspiracy of higher education demanded a warlike ugliness of its classrooms, a rigmarole of dust, ashy fluorescence, filthy linoleum, begrimed windows with thin, dingy splints for blinds (and once, a dying pigeon, lavender and plump, fluttering and flopping against the window as she tried to elucidate narrative conflict — eventually, given permission, the students just spun their desks around to watch the bird's final moments, a horrific, superior, upstaging commentary). Was the price of education a synthetic, meager, colorless setting? The worst classroom Prudence had ever been made to teach in was an ROTC meeting room, a balding beige square of the universe, its walls aggressively papered with gigantic posters of military bluster, trimmed in lurid recruitment slogans — in that room,

Prudence had responded with insurrectional eloquence. MYS★ ENEMYS★ DEFINESS★ MES★, she'd written on the board in giant block letters the first day, leaving it there the entire semester.

College policy did not permit room requests, so Prudence was placed in drab boxes, chambers leached of color, stale tombs of thought. To counteract the poor atmosphere, Prudence would arrive early, light a dark cone of Satya Sai Baba incense, set up her music, pull the blue-legged chairs with their kidney-shaped desktops into a circle, write an ethical challenge or inspirational quote on the board. And just as there was always a student, like Morton Wrecker, who hated her class yet dug in, as if entrenched (MYS★ ENEMYS★ DEFINESS★ MES★), so there was always one student who developed a crush, an excrescence, a damp-eyed infatuation, sidling crabwise up to Prudence after class and lingering, asking transparent questions about eros, soul mates, and might she ever consider going out with one of her students? Never, Prudence answered. Absolutely never. The firmness of her reply, the depth of her conviction, was based on the single errant occasion she had dated a student, traveled to San Francisco with him in fact, and slept chastely beside him on a broken-springed bed in an inexpensive hotel on the edge of the sex district, a six-block walk from the book fair she had invited him to, stretched beside him in white velour pajamas in a shabby room, an orangy red light from a *Live Nude Dancers* sign blinking across the sheets all night long. What had saved Prudence from this near-disastrous liaison had been the young man's sexual ambivalence — he had finally made up his mind, he later told her, because of that weekend. Thanks to two sexless nights in bed with Prudence, he was, he realized, unequivocally gay.

Exactly one week after her encounter with Ray Chasing Hawk, Comanche Indian and Lord of the Southern Plains, on the first day of the fall semester, ten students shambled into her latest ugly classroom, choosing their seats as super-stitiously as lottery numbers. With her lambs huddled in a cautious, dingy circle, Prudence switched off the lights, lit a cinnamon-scented candle, and began to play the music of Joan the Mad, a tormented, poetic queen of the fourteenth-century Spanish court. She let the Moorish music, the

169

candle flame, the semidarkness, do its work for several minutes. Then, standing before her class, poised on the precipice, the edge of pilgrimage, she spoke. *Over the next fifteen weeks, you will shape yourselves into mandalas, sacred circles, die to old perceptions, be given over to fresh consciousness and renewed life. Our lives are grains of sand, leaves of grass. Our lives are infinite in scope.* Her circle of strangers, faces softened by candlelight, shyly introduced themselves. Afterward, Prudence switched the lights back on so they could write and read aloud spontaneous self-portraits. As they read, Prudence scribbled notes in the mar- gins of her green and white attendance roster, shorthand descriptions to help her, in the coming weeks, match names to faces:

Sheldon Pettipiece: pink, rotund, girlish voice, red suspenders, loves to bake

Heywood Marsh: black, scowling unibrow, grid-thinker, Morton Wrecker's clone?

Elaine Durrell: bitter ex-wife of famous poet, pink sneakers, more than one ax to grind

Dwayne Bird: tall blond aeronautics engineer, too upbeat, Prozac?

Flo Wafer: massage therapist, passing petition against breast implants, beeper going off in class

Jimmy Flores: unemployed actor, vegan, taking the lead from Flo Wafer, passing around flyers offering half-price colonics at a newly opened health spa

Maxine Bell: wintry twig, second place in high school alumnae contest for poem "Death, Life's Everlasting Song"

Joe Harlinger: Santa Claus minus red suit, Xerox repairman, insists literature died with the Russians, specifically Dostoyevsky

Happi Tuite (pronounced tweet): tumbly red hair, freckles, hospice worker, has to skip class when clients dying

Waconda Short: nude artist's model, obvious breast implants, traveled through Tibet on a Vespa, passes Flo Wafer's petition without signing

All of them divorced. On each of them, Prudence could smell their bitterness, lonely. Grains of sand, leaves of grass.

★ ★ ★

For the past seven nights, Fiona had hollered *Phone!* and Prudence had borne the receiver, like a lit torch, into the hot, claustral, oil-stinking garage, hunkering on the cement step, bare feet on the sisal welcome mat, talking for two, three, sometimes four hours, Ray's voice so low-pitched and murmurous, the garage the one place she could hear him. Inside, Fiona had the TV on or her CD player, or else the dishwasher was sloshing and grinding while the air conditioner whooshed automatically on and off. Sitting in the unlit, suffocating garage gave Prudence some measure of privacy. She didn't want Fiona overhearing her dizzy, asinine giggles, the vulnerable, husky timbre edging into her voice when she talked to him. Still, Fiona cracked open the door every night, flipping on the garage light, waving various scrawled messages in front of her mother, *Mom! How many more minutes? I'm expecting a call from one of my friends. I need to make a call, it's 10 p.m.! Do you know how late it is? Mom! Do you have any idea how long you've been on the phone?* Prudence would raise her free hand, press the mouthpiece of the phone into her

172

stomach and whisper, *Just a couple more minutes, sweetie, promise. I'll let you know when I'm off,* then fall back into the latest meandering, mysterious artery of conversation with Ray Chasing Hawk. She could hardly remember, by the time she hung up, what it was they had talked about, as she'd sat hunched on the concrete step, her bottom numb, sweat trickling down her back, neck, both sides of her face, puddling between her breasts. She was aware of Ray saying he was writing erotic poems about her (ha! with her fishy belly, prickly unshaven legs and a new vitiligo patch spilling like milk along her calf?), *I'll mail them to you.* Prudence hoped his poems weren't corny, because if they were, she couldn't love him. When she was sixteen, Dexter Leipzig had written her such sappy, ludicrous verses she had fallen straight out of puppy love with him. Hanging up from these nightly phone binges, Prudence would stumble back into the brightly lit, air-conditioned house, dazed and intoxicated. She would stand in the kitchen cramming fistfuls of orange fish crackers in her mouth, or opening a carton of Ben & Jerry's, grabbing the biggest spoon in the drawer, plying up fudge chunk marshmallow. Sometimes Fiona was still awake, fuming, tapping her watch or her toe like an exasperated parent. Or she might have gone to bed defeated, without having talked to her friends or even to Kirby, since her mother had hogged the phone all night long, yapping to some Comanche Indian, some Native American from god-awful Texas, Jesus H. Chrysler! (Prudence overheard this standing outside Fiona's door late one night, a carton of melting chocolate chunk ice cream in one hand, a cracked wooden spoon in the other.)

His erotic poems were faintly penciled on pale green lined paper, a ragged fringe along the margined side where he had ripped them from a spiral notebook. Prudence arranged them, like assignments, along her bed, beside the photograph he had enclosed, an eight-by-ten black and white head shot taken during his two-year acting stint in Hollywood — he looked charming, chubby-cheeked, slightly goofy, somebody's cute kid brother. He had printed diagonally, in black marker, across the top left-hand corner, *Maa Paewatsi, Kwabaru Paewatsi Muhraru — Kultseena Peeka.* What was that? Comanche? *Paewatsi,* what was *Paewatsi?* It must be important, it was mentioned twice. How frustrating, his inscription could mean anything. Prudence breathed deep, picked up the first poem in her lineup of four. If she frowned upon numerous misspellings, winced at grammatical blunders, the rest of her was scared witless. In high school and once in college, boyfriends had penned corny bleatings of praise to her, a ham-fisted rhyme or two, insulting to her literary sensibility. Here, in Ray's penciled, misspelled phrases was wild-bloodedness, a forewarning of how he would exhaust and conquer her. She held the pale green papers to her chest, tried to catch her breath. The poems made her want him, they made her pray he would never appear.

At some point in every phone call, he asked what she wanted from him *in a sexual manner*, what excited her. Whenever he asked, she simply sat on the concrete step, hot, silent, embarrassed. Then one night, after downing three glasses of cheap spaghetti wine, Prudence dashed off her desire, and before she could reread it or lose her nerve, she folded the shocking, inebriated admission into an envelope and mailed it. Something about black satin, white skin, a crime of blood, his teeth and tongue, pain and pleasure, something extremely weird, nothing like the self she

175

knew. He never mentioned it.

One night they decided, or Ray decided and Prudence said fine, what day he would drive out for a visit. He had an art show in Oklahoma, he could drive straight out afterward, arrive on September 6, a day, she told him, she would not get home from school until seven or so, but still, she could leave a key.

"Have you talked to your daughter about me? I want her to be comfortable, to feel OK about me being there. I'm fine with sleeping in the living room. If it's OK, I might stop by when I get into town, drop off a few things, but then I'll stay away until I know you're home. I don't want your daughter to come home from school and find a complete stranger in her house."

"Fee, can we talk?"

"What did I do?"

"Why would you think that? I just want to ask you something."

"Is he coming here? That Indian guy?"

"Will you just sit outside with me a minute?"

"Mah, I'm waiting for Kirby to call. He needs a ride to Gumby's."

"This will just take a sec. Remember I told you about Ray, how we met in

Oklahoma, how we've been talking on the phone and all, well, he's driving out to visit next week, and I was just wondering, I was wondering if . . . I was just thinking . . ."

"Fine with me if he stays in your room."

"What makes you think I was going to ask a thing like that?"

"Mah, some man you're gagas over is driving out to visit you? Hel-lo. I don't care. I honestly don't. Frankly, I'm happy you met somebody. I've been kind of worried about you."

"He wants you to feel comfortable about him coming here."

"Fine. I'm happy for you, Mom. Really."

"It's pretty scary."

"Scary? Normal, I'd say. You've been by yourself way too long. You were getting weird. And as long as we're talking, I need to get some birth control pills. Just in case I decide to have sex, though it still seems pretty disgusting to me. Can you take me to see your gynecologist?"

Whoa. What was this? Blackmail? Still, Prudence didn't want to be one of those parents whose head stayed in the sand, who didn't know which end was up. Apparently, she'd been way off about Fiona's virginity. And why did her daughter think sex was disgusting? Was that Prudence's fault? The next day, she called Dr. Van Wie for Fiona and booked a fifteen-minute psychic consultation for herself at Crystal Magick.

Tapping one black-painted fingernail on Ray Chasing Hawk's glossy head shot, right on his nose, tap, tap, tap, Raven Wonder pronounced him Prudence's soul mate. In past lives, he'd been a chief on horseback, a Kurdish tribesman, a Jewish rabbi. His creativity was prodigious, they were numerologically compatible and had experienced much past-life karma together. Then Raven closed her eyes, scribbled frantically across two sheets of paper, handed them across the card table to Prudence. Spirit messages, she explained. Free of charge. When it happens, it happens. Prudence carried the messages to her car, where she sat trying to decipher them: *Go mob places pane oboe is ire across released Newark. Soul's iris rise sued ion Ree. Lads are all erect. Evil is aura. Icecap is melting. Snee is across!* Prudence drove next to Victoria's Secret, where she tried on a white fleece robe with a hood, a long beaded ivory gown, and a short black negligee with a floppy candy-box satin bow, charging all three to her credit card. On the way home, she stopped at a Dairy Queen, ordered a banana split, and took three bites before throwing it out. At Fry's grocery, she located a dollar copy of *Cheyenne Warrior*, rented it, went home, microwaved two bags of popcorn, and sat on the couch, winding and rewinding the film to the ten-second shot of Ray, naked except for buckskin leggings and a breechclout, making a bold flying leap onto the back of a galloping palomino. When the doorbell rang, Prudence pressed stop on the VCR, put down the bowl of popcorn, and opened the front door. A UPS man in brown shorts and shirt awaited her signature on his clipboard, a large box at his feet. Lugging the box inside, opening it with a dull kitchen knife, she found a legal notice informing her of Digby Deeds' demise, of his willed gift to her. With *Cheyenne Warrior* coming to its sentimental end in the background, Prudence upended Digby's forty plots from the box onto her carpet, each bound in a trim black casing. *Savage Wind*, *Savage Fire*, *Savage Love*, *Savage Persuasion*, *Savage Tears*, forty types of Savagery in all. Poor Digby was dead, and like a modern-day Rapunzel, Prudence, it seemed, would have to find a way to spin dead man's straw (*Savage Straw!*) into gold.

★ ★ ★

On the morning of Ray Chasing Hawk's anticipated arrival, September 6, Prudence blazed awake with one thought — tomorrow at this same time, a naked man would be in her bed. Young, handsome, sexually rapacious. Impossible. Who could believe it? She had fallen asleep with Ray's Hollywood photo under one pillow, his poems under another, all of Digby's forty plots at her feet. Yawning, Prudence slid eight-by-ten Ray out from under her pillow, carried him to her face, pressed his voluptuous, full lips against hers. Smack. Just then Fiona's clock, a Garfield head, the same timepiece Fiona had awoken to since third grade, started bing-binging down the hall. Seven o'clock. Prudence's peaceful domain on La Diosa, street of *la diosa,* the goddess — all her serene, solitary civilization was about to end. The night before, she had slipped on the babydoll nightie with its black lace flaps like insect wings, its sad, slippery bow. She'd even dropped over her head the ivory silk floor-length gown with beaded edging — reminding herself of a calla lily, or a smooth-hipped vase. She'd wrapped herself in the white robe, drawn the hood up

180

around her face — a wan initiate in some medieval religious order. What did one wear first? Who knew these things? In further jittery preparation, Prudence bought Sacred Fire massage oil, a fat oval bar of soap scented with almond, lavender body lotion, age- retardant makeup. She had scrubbed her bathroom, changed the sheets, shot the vacuum around. She considered painting her fingernails and toenails but that was too far outside standard upkeep. Having spent hundreds of dollars preparing for his arrival, Prudence grew increasingly convinced he wasn't showing up. Any derailment could occur between Houston and Phoenix. She began to have doubts he was real. The more she fussed, battened down, as if for a hurricane, a tornado, a monsoon, El Niño, for some extreme weather or other, the more she suspected he was a mirage, a teasing phantasm configured from her own prolonged loneliness and sexual deprivation.

Down the hall, Fiona bellowed with laughter, great barks of hilarity. Pillow talk. Mr. Tattoo, last thing at night, first thing in the morning, either squalling or laughing, nothing moderate or in between. Yesterday she had taken Fiona to the gynecologist for birth control pills, unsure if her own easy compliance demonstrated positive or defeated parenting skills. Fiona was, of course, happy. She had a job, a car, a boyfriend, birth control pills and a new cell phone. Not yet eighteen, she was rushing pell-mell into adulthood while Prudence was being sucked back into an adolescence she had never had, struggling to achieve a late-blooming femininity, to accept being the subject of a younger man's erotic desire. She wasn't thirty, she wasn't forty, she was a year away from fifty! True, on a good day, people guessed she was much younger, late thirties, early forties, but they were never, ever surprised to learn she was a schoolteacher. On her last trip to Fry's, besides renting *Cheyenne Warrior*, Prudence had poked the newest issue of Cosmo under her English muffins, then sat on the edge of her bed in the black negligee, its pink tags still on, reading sexual how-to articles — *The perineum, his passion patch! Practice the mind-blowing scrotum stroke!* — wincing, trying to picture herself doing such a thing to anyone. Hopeless! By the time she left for school that morning, with her house immaculate and her stomach in knots, Prudence was convinced, no, actively hoping, he'd changed his mind, met someone between here and

Gallup, a beautiful Native American woman, a much younger woman, any woman at all. She prayed for some obstacle, like a great biblical impediment, to roll across the far too easy pathway to her door. All day kept busy, she held office hours, counseled students, attended a curriculum review committee meeting, taught class, found various excuses to slip into the women's lavatory and anxiously regard herself in the full-length mirror. She had chosen to wear a shapeless ankle-length ivory silk blend shift, a matching, equally shapeless jacket and flat, round-toed black shoes. In class, she arranged the men on one side of the room, women on the other, and had them write down, spontaneously, all the rules they had grown up with, familial, societal, gendered, spoken, unspoken, self-inflicted. She had them stand, men facing women, and shout their rules aloud, simultaneously. Then she handed out long strips of red cloth, asking them to tie one strip around each part of their body that had suffered an injury. Physically or psychologically? Flo Wafer asked. Whichever, Prudence replied. By way of demonstrating, she tied strips around her forehead, heart, genitals, both knees, her left ankle, her right thumb. Puzzled but trusting, her adult students tied strip after strip until the classroom fluttered with red. From these places, Prudence said, from the memory of these wounds, will emerge your truest stories.

Driving home, ravenous and panicky, Prudence stopped at Wendy's, ordered a double patty cheeseburger, chomped it down, and fretted afterward about beef breath. At a snail's pace, she turned her faded Nash Rambler onto La Diosa. Her beloved little street had never looked so dear as it did now, on the verge of invasion. Ah, good. No silver-blue van with Texas plates in front of her house. Fiona was home, that was all. Prudence parked in the garage, set her briefcase down in her office, walked through the kitchen, stopped short in the doorway of her neat, orderly bedroom. A pair of black cowboy boots sat to one side of her dressing table. A feathered war bonnet sat atop her bedside lamp. On one wall dangled a war shield, aggressively painted. A rectangular cedar box, the one from Anadarko, with its tobacco, sage, eagle-feather fan and pipe, sat neatly on the floor beside the cowboy boots; behind the box slumped a black duffel bag and two lumpy, maroon-cased pillows. Ray Chasing Hawk had walked straight into the privacy of her bedroom and planted his belongings as firmly as flags of conquest on the moon. Fiona snuck up, plunked her chin on her mother's shoulder.

"Mah. What is that thing on the lamp?"

"A dance bustle. Part of what he wears when he dances. Oh Fee. I'm ill. Is anybody here?"

"Nobody but us."

"My gosh. I can't do this."

"Mah, all those hours on the phone? Your three-hundred-dollar phone bill? Just go into the living room, relax, watch the news like you always do. But comb your hair first, it's kind of whacked."

Prudence batted her hair with a brush, then sat on the couch watching a commercial for diarrhea, a woman smiling beatifically before swan-diving into a pristine, pine-fringed lake. In the midst of a heartburn commercial featuring a tap-dancing pink esophageal tube, the doorbell rang. Prudence dashed back to the bathroom, mussed her hair a little, walked to her small, saltillo-tiled foyer, took a deep breath, and opened the front door.

Waiting beneath the amber porch light was a slender young man, gleaming black hair flowing down over his shoulders. He wore a black cowboy hat with a beaded

185

band, a jean jacket (hanging it up in her hall closet, Prudence would see the back, three Sioux Indians wearing sunglasses, *FBI* printed at the top, *Full-Blooded Indian* at the bottom), a plain black T-shirt, a belt with a large buffalo-head buckle, very tight jeans, cowboy boots. Prudence stood before him in her shapeless ivory shift, little thoughts skating up and down, skidding up and down, some smooth slope of panic. *One little two little three little . . .*

"Hey."

"Hey." With that, Ray Chasing Hawk stole across her threshold, and Prudence Parker's life, its whole neat, lonely edifice, tottered briefly, resisted slightly, then collapsed.

"I made it. I'm here."

Part Two

Tempe, Arizona

If asked, Prudence Parker would probably say she liked her breasts. Pink and white, she'd say. Two little birthday cakes. Her legs were nice, too. Slim, well-shaped. Her skin had forever embarrassed her. Ghost white, pale as horsepaste, and her milky butt, whitest of all, flat as a poor man's wallet, deflated, she supposed, from years of sitting. And now, the random islands, the slow-floating archipelagoes of skin weirdly splashed as if with bleach. Her health was otherwise excellent, her body healthy, though subtle signs of erosion, of loosening slope, were upon her.

Prudence would not remember exactly how it happened, the precise manner by which she wound up in her bedroom with Ray, the door locked. Whatever she had feared and fantasized, dreaded and hoped for, occurred in such rush, such blur, all she could recall was the disorienting, heady sense of trying to keep up with what was happening. And how had she forgotten his beauty? Lithe-limbed, graceful, aggressive, he was the most confident, gorgeously naked man she had ever seen. She'd forgotten it all, that he'd lived in Hollywood for ten years, been in movies, commercials, MTV videos, been a bass player touring with name rock bands. Now here he was, naked and far too young-looking, a mini-movie/rock star unshucked in her bedroom, devouring her like a lump of soft white sugar. Coming inside her the first time, he growled, low, rough, feral *grr*-ings that ended on a bark — she had never heard anything like it and worried about Fiona's hearing him, even over the considerable noise and constant blow of her repaired air conditioner. For her part, Prudence lay silent afterward, the way chickens did, the way hens lay post- copulation, necks crinked sideways, eyes blank and blinking.

After the second time, her vagina burned; by the third, it ached, floated apart from the rest of her, a turgid bloom. When at last he fell asleep, sprawled on his gorgeous stomach, one arm draped across her midsection, Prudence lay paralyzed, eyes wide, alert to his breathing, afraid to stir in case he woke and pounced again. Three thousand or more miles away in Texas, Ray's claim that he liked sex three times a day had seemed harmless, a young man's boast. She'd pictured those three times spread evenly throughout the day, like square meals. Meals. Food. Groceries. Bills. Mortgage. She lay under the weight of his arm, thinking of the stack of Crawley romances, the forty Savage Passion plots, all in her spare room, stowed under her childhood bed. Soon, she needed to seal herself in, churn out her first romance. Prudence turned her head a little. By the light of her bedside candle, she regarded his smooth copper skin, glossy black hair to the middle of his back, his proud, arrogant, chiseled features — the man sleeping beside her inspired a whole slippery avalanche of clichés. Why had this exotic creature, so visually perfect for the cover of a Savage Passion novel, driven thousands of miles and picked her schoolteacher's bed to land in? Surely there were beds in Houston and more than enough women. And why had Digby Deeds selected her to inherit his lucrative plots when, initially, she had made it plain as day she didn't want them? Truly, Prudence marveled, the most remarkable events in one's life, the most astonishing people, arrived mysteriously, with little logic or planning — as if some larger, more complex fate overrode the small, decent destinies most people planned for themselves. Prudence flattened herself out from under Ray's arm, tiptoed down the hall to Fiona's bathroom, plonked onto the cool toilet seat, which swerved from her sudden weight. Peeing, she suddenly remembered another thing he had casually mentioned about his music career in Los Angeles. To keep from being homeless, he had composed soundtracks for porno films. How disturbing was that? Padding down the hall, past Fiona's darkened room, past the spare room, back into her bedroom, she blew out her Ecuadoran bark candle and slipped back under the sheet as quietly as she could (though his arm shot out, found her, pulled her close). She didn't really know who he was, did she? He could be anyone. He was an artist, she knew that. Had he driven three thousand miles just to lie in her bed? Why not also to get into new art galleries? When a man kisses you, his spirit enters you through his breath — who had told her this? Her mother? Her friend Trish? Some psychic? When a man comes inside you, his soul stays, a spirit-lodger, for seven years. Prudence lay calculating. After just one night, Ray's soul would be lodged inside her, festering, for twenty-eight years. Correction. Fifty-six, if she counted the night in Anadarko. Dogs didn't live so long.

The hearts of the dead haunt us! Drawn to the hot flames of love, we flee life's cooler powers, thus sealing our doom!

Bah. Honk. What Prudence had just come up with for the opening lines of *Savage Heat* sounded like preposterously bad Goethe or the worst of the worst George Sand. The difficulty was, Prudence recognized and appreciated good writing. Ten years before, she'd even written a book, *The Solace of Guilt,* a slim fastidious volume of literary stories that had won a national prize, securing her a series of teaching jobs at community colleges. She had published several more stories in small literary journals, signed on with the first agent who courted her, Verlin Vink, a man partial to night golf and dismal prognostications about contemporary literature. He hated her work. He hated his. To this day, Prudence still had a defeated-looking manuscript of stories no one, including herself, cared about anymore; she had stopped sending it out, forbidden Verlin to send it out. She had ceased talking to Verlin on a monthly or even a bimonthly basis. She couldn't remember when she had last talked with him. For all she knew, he could, like Digby Deeds, be dead. For the last six years, Prudence had ceased writing altogether, preferring to throw her energies into helping others write their life stories, make sense and pattern of their too-modest lives. Sometimes, though, if she saw a powerful movie or read a sublimely written book, the ache to write leapt up, briefly sickening her blood, a virus triggered, assertive but short-lived. Now, with Ray Chasing Hawk in one bedroom and Digby's torrid books and steamy plots in another, Prudence, frustrated, snatched up one of the Crawley romances and studied it not for inspiration — that was impossible — but for example:

Tears blurred her vision as Long Lance stood silently, untying the leather thong that held his brief garment around his waist. Amanda tried not to faint. One glimpse, and she knew she could never survive what he intended to do to her.

In less than two weeks, Prudence

Parker's nocturnal life had become thoroughly muddled. In one bedroom, a tireless youth chased her around, spinning her into this position and that, shaking back his long, vainglorious hair after each orgasmic triumph. Whenever he fell mercifully asleep, she would tiptoe down the hall to her Romance Chamber (as she now thought of it) to convert whatever Ray had just done to her into silken intimacy, loving tenderness. At first, she hoped to survive such arduous conversions by keeping a small book of her own, a journal commenting on the conventions of romance: *Beauty, it appears, must capture Beast, must defang and drag the wild man into the woman's house and domesticate him, for it is his very wildness, genetically favored, that dooms the man. In romance, children are conspicuously absent. In romance, woman always triumphs, though pregnancy is not allowed. Romance proves a man's cock only briefly his. Visit any shopping mall. Dispirited young fathers push strollers, the wildness drained from them, the mothers in charge, the bobble-headed infant an innocent despot. In mall light, the full torment of biology is exposed. Were theologies invented and wars fought to provide distraction, bold routes of escape for the domestically terrorized male?* Such speculations depressed her, so Prudence abandoned them to concentrate on the moneymaking possibilities of her new clandestine work.

How synchronous — a Comanche lover landing on her doorstep, snoring in her bed, muse for Digby's plot (which involved the Sioux, not the Comanche, but that could be remedied). Secrecy was key. If Ray learned he was research material, he might become inhibited. He might refuse. Object. Leave. No one must know, not even Fiona or Deleanor. No one. Shuttling sleeplessly between rooms at night, Prudence hoped to survive Ray's bedroom gymnastics long enough to add a new, lucrative volume to the Savage Passion series, and thus ward off bankruptcy. Like anyone with a secret life, Prudence, at first, flourished. In the beginning, at least, she positively bloomed.

Chaste, flame-haired Rebeccah, knowing it was wrong to meet the powerful Sioux (Comanche?) warrior, Blazing Eagle, went to him anyway as the (summer? winter? autumn?) sky darkened. When he pulled her into his massive (slender?) bronze arms, as he held her rosebud (full? trembling?) mouth captive beneath his own, she knew they'd never separate — even though their two worlds, warring cultures (white and Co-manche? civilized and wild?), would try to tear them apart!

Cordoned off, this division of sex from romance took its toll. Each night, Prudence diligently hobbled, quasi-exhilarated and naked under her long ivory robe with its monk's hood, out from her bedroom and down the hall to her Chamber of Romance, which smelled increasingly of ink and mental torment. The passage between rooms became lengthier, harder to traverse. Working to bridge the gulf, Prudence's ability to imitate Mildred Crawley grew easier. Words flowed from her pen, as if the script were akashically written and she its mere scribe, as if Digby himself floated her pen, his spectral energies dictating the words: *With his sleek bronzed stature and jet black hair, Blazing Eagle was all petite, fiery-haired Rebeccah had ever desired. She had disobeyed her widowed mother and scorned society to savor the searing rapture she found in her red-skinned warrior's arms. A defiant, intelligent beauty, Rebeccah swore to stand by his side forever — as beloved — never as slave, never as captive, always free!*

Prudence acquiesced because she was curious, because she possessed the pa-

tience to lie still, because his aggressive-
ness roused something in her, a surprising,
primal submission reminiscent of dogs,
chickens, cows, horses, giraffes, cats, ot-
ters, a whole specific menagerie she could
claim to have seen, at various times and lo-
cations, having sex. His was a humorless
urge, a brutal quickness, a conquering instinct, no endearments, no tender wit, no
emotion. Swift, physical sex, male domi-
nant, female compliant, deeply unsatis-
fying, yet its near violence oddly excited
her. In the beginning, at least, the shock of
it made her want him constantly. Eventually their sex took on a bitter tinge, a
suppressed anger. Ray Chasing Hawk was
sexually practiced but not skillful, acro-
batic but in a hurry. Beyond that first night
in Anadarko, in the motel, when he had
asked permission, he'd never kissed her
again. He didn't understand kissing, he
told her, had never liked it, not with
anyone, ever. (*His mouth closed over hers,
with tantalizing gentleness.*) He favored
taking her from behind. Other women, he
insinuated, had been satisfied, had kept up,
been wilder, rougher than Prudence, but
she wondered if they hadn't been like her,
giving up, playing false. Something fragile,
almost childish, lived beneath his aggres-

sion. When he slept, he clung to the two pillows he had brought with him from Texas, hard lumpy pillows in maroon cases, refusing to explain his nightly attachment to them. And still, sometimes he read her mind — times when her unsatisfied body kept her fretful and awake, he would, as if sensing her distress, wrap an arm around her, pull her tight, call her baby or some Comanche word, then she would calm down, fall asleep against his stone-smooth, warm flesh. While Ray curled around his ancient, overwashed pillows, his "huggie pillows," she, Prudence, held on to him.

Prudence dressed, went to school, taught her classes. She felt languorous, vague, fragrant with sexual moisture and a slow, humid exhaustion. Ray waited for her, watching television, painting or doing beadwork, petulant if left alone too long, jealous of her time if she brought student papers home. Comanche men don't cook, he announced, a ludicrous statement he went on to prove by fixing a single dinner for her, a plate of watery, flaccid spaghetti with lukewarm canned sauce. In the mornings, she fixed pancakes, omelettes, hashed brown potatoes with melted cheese, while he sat at the kitchen table telling her she looked sexy, cooking for him. After they ate, he washed the dishes, a meticulous, subtle resentment in his movements. On days she didn't teach, they used her car to drive south to Tucson or north to Flagstaff or Sedona or Prescott to visit art galleries, browse through record stores and second-hand bookshops. A passenger in her own car (Ray drove), Prudence felt anesthetized, pinned beneath his decisions, his behavior, as if her sexual passivity had leaked into everything they did together. He decided the hour they left the house, the hour they returned. Like some pale, sickening leaf, Prudence felt herself weaken. Like most new lovers, she mistook their bed for her life's sole defining surface.

How had a man, in such short order, become the arbiter of her days? Didn't she possess will, strength, discernment? It was as if she were in some state of waking paralysis, unable to speak or to choose. Ray wore black, jokingly called himself No-Heart. Each night, as he slept in her bed, she tiptoed down the hall, entered the one room untouched by him, and labored away at *Savage Heat*, haunted by a German story she had once read in translation — a nameless man, bound with rope from head to toe, coming to consciousness, discovers flies buzzing, crawling over him. He transforms his bound condition into entertainment, a popular act in a small traveling circus. One day, the circus owner's wife, who pities and perhaps loves him, cuts the man's ropes. But it is too late. His captivity defines him, he has grown attached, self-enslaved, self-charmed. Using his teeth and his hands, he rebinds himself, making sure this time the rope cuts even deeper.

ROMANCES* READERS* SURVEY

Which of the following do you feel should *never* be included in a romance? Please select three and rank them by placing a number 1 next to the most distasteful element, a number 2 next to the second most distasteful, and so on.

_____ a. rape
_____ b. explicit sex
_____ c. sad ending
_____ d. physical torture of the heroine or the hero
_____ e. an ordinary heroine
_____ f. bed-hopping
_____ g. premarital sex

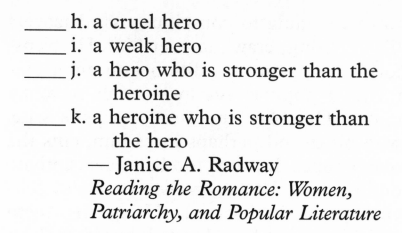

— Janice A. Radway
Reading the Romance: Women, Patriarchy, and Popular Literature

a. Fiona is down the hall, music on, the door of her room closed. In the bedroom, the windows are open, a soft, light rain falls on the rose leaves as he unbuttons, pushes down her jeans and underwear, leaves her sweater, the gray one, on, and pushes her backward onto the cool white surface of the bed. He pushes his own jeans partway down and, already erect, roughly enters her. She begins to shudder, not from pleasure, but because — she does not know how to describe this — inside her, his sex has voice: *I own you, you are mine.* On a Sunday in late September, a light rain falling, this lasts two, perhaps three seconds, her hearing of this *voice.* In her core flesh, he has taken possession. In a single, swift assault a bond is forged between her soul and his. She wants him to acknowledge this, to ask if he felt it, too, but he laughs, pulls her to her feet, leaves the room, a petty conqueror, leaves her to enjoy washing between her legs, pulling her clothes back on. In a motel room in Anadarko, during the smoke ceremony, when he had stared and stared at her, in a way no other man had ever regarded her, what was it he had seen? *Will you let me do whatever I want to you?* he had once asked. *Yes,* she had whispered, her body on sudden fire with the longing to lose herself. To be bound. She glances at her face in the mirror, sees cool silver rain reflected from the window, sees she is that. Bound. His.

b. He tells her to lie down on the bed, on her stomach, lights several candles, and, naked, begins to massage her. Tenderly, he lavishes his smooth, slender hands over every part of her body, spending the longest time on those parts of herself she is self-conscious about and secretly hates. He seeks these places out, kneels over her, massaging her belly, quaggy from childbirth, an ugly place she has long been ashamed of, his black hair falling on either side of his narrow face, she is amazed to see his expression, devoted, radiant, tender. Angelic. *Like an angel.* Then he brushes the black silk of his hair up and down her body, lightly sweeping her skin with the soft curving lengths of his hair. Without warning, then, he drags her up to her knees, enters her brutally, from behind.

c. Naked, companionable, they sit in bed sharing a cheap cigar and the single glass of red wine she will ever see him drink. He puffs on the plastic-tipped Swisher Sweet, then in an altered voice, and a heavy accent not his, identifies himself as Nathaniel T., a rural southern black man. Nathaniel smokes, talks, tells her about young Ray's boyhood, a folksy, eidetic tale of abuse, beatings, rape, a childhood of such numbing violence Nathaniel has offered to speak for young Ray. *And Missy, you have only heard the beginning,* Nathaniel blows a thready stream of smoke, *so many terrible, unspeakable things happened to that boy. Things a soul would scarcely believe.* Then Nathaniel is gone and Ray, uncharacteristically, kisses her on the lips, calling her *waipu,* sweetheart, *tuurapu,* dear. She notices his front teeth are filed, slightly pointed, how stealthily he moves, though other times he walks rapidly, with a slapping sound, as if he had big, peanut-shaped feet. She is wakened some nights by him yanking her against him, biting her shoulder and growling, a gutteral, bestial sound. A bird of prey, he locates the future with his hands, long brown fingers, oval nails, talons. His paintings, full of movement, are of hawks, ravens, eagles, crows. In Oklahoma, he had spotted her, singled her out, swooped down, a man dead to mercy. *I am nobody's husband, nobody's boyfriend. No one holds a place in my heart.*

d. The mattress a white-sheeted stage, the bedroom a black-box theater, the musty, dark inside of an old camera. Holding a pale lit candle, his long hair framing purely indifferent, androgynous features, kneeling above her he drips hot gouts of wax over her naked breasts and stomach, impartially observing her cries, her shudders. Afterward, in the shower, a small white-tiled cubicle, an up-ended pencil box, she stands vague and still, the wax a hardened ivory spatter over her breasts, as he kneels on the tile ledge, using a black-handled razor on her, until her vagina/cunt/pussy is smooth, glabrous, a pearl, exposed, shell pink, and gleaming. She feels a shock of forgotten childhood, a nostalgia for her body before it grew sexed. Surprised by the sly, erotic charge, she entrusts this part of herself to him as he works carefully, deftly working the razor, spreading open her lips, using the back of his hand and wrist to nudge her thighs wider, a controlled, neutral grace to his actions. Standing inside the warm, white throat of water, her genitals exposed, she is embarrassed by her pouchy belly, by the runic scar from her ectopic surgery, by the small veins on her legs, by the patches of unpigmented white skin. She finds the harsh exposure, his unhurried inspection of her arousing. She finds humiliation exquisite, this shaving of her genitals, and later, the blindfold, the cuff restraints for her wrists and ankles, his cruel, overriding curiosity and emotionless *examination* of pain. His one instruction, the one she cannot obey, is to feel no emotion — *Good girl, that's it, keep your legs open, relax, that's it, that's it* — afterward she will lie there, desire pooled between her legs as he sleeps heavily, his smooth, slender, ringed hand on her damp thigh or slack breast, his touch impersonal, peremptory, a master's. Heart starving, she will go quietly down the hall to translate what has just occurred, turning out a few more pages of the kind of love silly, sentimental women long for. Emotions, he says, are stupid. Emotions are the enemy. She thinks of all the drab, colorless women escaping into romance. Like them, she has become half-dead, a lustreless sparrow.

e. To help her, he studies her clothing, puts together new combinations that are, she has to admit, much nicer. He grooms her, blow-dries and brushes her hair. He is an artist, he says, his eye easily offended. *You have a gorgeous body. Women half your age would die for a body like yours.* No more wearing white, it washes you out. Earth colors. Dark colors. You should color your hair darker, dark brown would be great. (He is drawn to slender women with long dark hair, olive skin.) She is a gorgeous woman and doesn't know it, this makes her sexy to him. She is intelligent, this excites him, too. She loses weight, though he warns her not too much — a bag of bones is not sexy. Glasses on a woman can be very sexy-looking, he says, so she wears hers. They're nice, he says, but the wrong shape for her face, so she takes them off, puts them away. In a matter of weeks she has become a small, slender woman with newly dyed brown hair, wearing a tight black sweater, jeans and boots, dressing in the duller colors and tighter sizes he approves of. Her pussy/cunt/vagina is shaved, because that makes a woman sexy as well. Black sweaters, jeans, boots, long dark hair? Is he shaping her into himself? Yet she can scarcely wait for each ordinary day, its hours dull as clocks, to be over.

Will you let me do whatever I want to you?

Yes.

Slips out from under him, moves in her own cold skin through the house, to his easel and paints, to the pine table where he does leather- and beadwork, to his shelves of Native American history and art books, his CD collection, the room she has somehow given over to him. Studies his paintings, his books, his moccasins, touches everything, trying to read him, to understand, as in her old childhood ritual, wandering her father's house at night, looking through his things, so inaccessible, who was he, what is the secret here? She returns to her bedroom, stands over his body, slender, firm, still boyish, his long black hair with its rough arrowings of silver, his narrow face, straight nose, thick, sensual lips, closed eyes. Silver earrings, a small hoop in one ear, a matching hoop and a second earring with a long silver drop in the other. Asleep, he looks eighteen, not thirty-five. She has also seen him look cadaverous, old, his body a slim, tight coffin, his gestures mean, the voice glinting, a scythe.

She believes no one should pity her, she is free to undo the spell. On days she goes to school, dressed in the clothing he has chosen for her, her darkened hair combed straight the way he likes, she feels panicky, incomplete, deprived of air.

f. In class, she reads an essay aloud, a

brief essay challenging the myth of the consistent self. The author, a British Freudian named Adam Phillips, claims human beings are a broth of composite selves and contradictory voices. Environment and companions have much to do with which self dominates, which identity prevails, which voice speaks, which self sleeps with what other self in another person. Terrifying concept! She looks up when she is done reading. Her students are blank-faced, clearly hostile to the ideas of the British Freudian. They hold stubbornly — wrongly, she thinks — to the notion of one congruent, integrated self mating with another congruent, integrated self.

**MIRACLE DEAD BABY LIVES*!
UNITES DAD AND MOM*!**

**BURGLAR*'S SKELETON
FOUND IN CHIMNEY*!**

RATS DREAM OF MAZES*!

**FRIED CHICKEN HEAD
FOUND IN*** McNuggets!

She has asked them to cut articles from the newspaper, bring in bizarre stories, odd facts. To survive trauma, she says, humans forget. The adult task then becomes to unearth repressed memories, to understand, release and heal. The articles, the bizarre stories and facts are oblique ways, she thinks, to help break open secrets, forgotten truths. Bizarre articles, because they amuse and distract, do not threaten. Away from him, sometimes, she feels herself again. Her former self.

g&h&i. *You want some? You want it? You know you do. You have a great body. Open your legs. Wider. Put it in. Move your hips. That's it. Did you come? Wicked woman.* Done mostly in the dark now, plain, unadorned, no games, sex reduced to Anyone. He never looks at her, never speaks her name, never says a tender word.

"I don't do Hallmark sex. I don't do white-boy sex. It's a physical act."

"I could be anyone?"

"Anyone. So could I. It means nothing, it's a physical act. I've told you before — don't ask if you don't want the truth."

On television, this pimp orders his two women to walk behind him at all times, heads down. They are not allowed to speak. They are his, he boasts. He can do anything with them he likes. Watching the documentary, Ray says he doesn't understand those women. She understands. Per-

210

fectly. She keeps her own head down now, barely speaks. His anger can be triggered by the smallest comment. Something she says can be fine one day, an insult the next. His anger is unpredictable, an icy adrenaline giving him life. Hadn't he warned her, been honest from the beginning? Anger and sex, he'd said, were the driving force of his art. *Anger is the one emotion I allow myself. I like my anger. It keeps me from doing anything stupid.* She has tried weeping, speaking softly, placating, reasoning, arguing, shouting back. Nothing works, she is beginning to learn. Nothing.

"If I'm so mean and nasty, why don't you throw me out?"

"Because you're not always like this. I don't recognize you like this. You're a different person. A whole different personality. Two people."

(If it wasn't for her and her stupid emotions, if she'd remember to turn out the light like he'd asked, if she'd ever listen to him, if she'd ever get it through her thick head, if she wasn't so stupid as to ask him to wash dishes when he was trying to paint, how dare she ask such a thing, if it wasn't for her, her stupidity . . .)

j. You like women with dark skin and long dark hair, why are you with me? Because things with you go deeper than looks. Why are you here, you're free to go, the door is open. Why don't you go? Because. I haven't broken you yet.

What binds her? Sex, his beauty, a certain cultural allure, his long hair, dumb as that sounds, or dumber still, the Native American "mystique"? Trish once said white women will put up with shit from Native American men that no Native woman would ever put up with. They're notorious, she added, for using white women. Is it the way he calls her *sweet thing?* The way, occasionally, he still reads her mind? The way he can seem fragile and aggressive at the same time? Is it the artistic potential she sees in him? The pair of earrings he's promised to make for her out of shell and leather and bone? The deerskin moccasins with elaborate Comanche-style beadwork? Is it those rare times he says he loves her?

k. *I only tell you what you can handle. The day you trust me is the day I will be truthful.* How can you trust somebody who doesn't tell the truth? He tells her he won't sleep with anyone else as long as he is with her. She believes that because he is fastidious, alert to disease, insistent on cleanliness. (*Go wash, are you clean down there? Did you wash? Go wash up.*) She has never thought of her body as dirty or unclean, but now she is self-conscious about her taste, her smell. There are so many deterrents to her pleasure, she grows irritable, tired, nearly sick of him. She leaves sleeping, goes to her room, her world of impossible romance and savage heat.

He taunted her with torrid kisses under a fiery Texas sky. Hours later, when Blazing Eagle climbed into her teepee, Rebeccah saw he was pure Comanche from the feather in his hair to the fringed moccasins on his feet. His muscled body, stripped naked except for a breechcloth, oiled to a copper sheen, smelled of rich leather . . .

Rich leather! Prudence flung down her pen. He sounded like a purse. Maybe she should consult Digby's ghost for inspiration, or run to the library to see if they carried a compendium, some world treasury of clichés. He smelled of . . . what? . . . bear fat, sage, sweet grass, grandma's home cooking, a slab of Spam . . . her male muse down the hall, asleep in her bed, smells like the peanut-butter-flavor Hot-Glo lotion they'd bought at the Castle Boutique. (Handing the bottle to the clerk, a clean-shaven young man who looked like one of her former students, she tried looking casual, as if she were buying cat food at Wal-

Mart. What if she bumped into one of her current students among the hot dongs, pocket vibrators, simulator pussies, butt plugs, glow in the dark dildos, things she had never heard of, much less seen before? Turning toward a rhythmic, cracking sound behind her, she had seen a young man, pink and round as a jawbreaker, hair shorn to stubble, studded tongue poked out, uncurling a black whip in repetitive, calculated snaps. The trance-like, violent whap of his arm, his tongue poking out, pulsing with red, greedy life, unnerved her. Crack. Holding the little brown bag of Hot-Glo, she searched for Ray, found him bent over the magazine rack, paging through a local issue of *Swinger's Hotline*.)

A smoldering tale of revenge and passion as only Mildred Crawley can write! Her latest tale has all the ingredients the first lady of Indian romance is justly famous for — torrid passion, cruel villains, raw and savage tension. Another Crawley triumph!

— Romantic Times

Prudence keeps the quote taped above her desk. Torrid passion, cruel villains, raw and savage tension. She has all three now. So is her life a romance? She doesn't think so. Adult love, difficult love, seemed to fall somewhere between the fantasies of hardcore sex and soft-focused romance. Was it wrong to want that kind of love, the kind you worked on, the kind that pushed past simple yearning, simple wanting, and sought to fully accept and be accepted by another? The kind of love she and Ray had — fire, crucible, test? She picked up her pen. *He taunted her with torrid kisses under a fiery Texas sky. Hours later, when Blazing Eagle climbed into her tepee, Rebeccah saw he was pure Comanche, from the feather in his hair to the fringed moccasins on his feet. His muscled body, stripped naked except for a breechclout, oiled to a copper sheen, smelled of the world he lived in, the prairies and plains he hunted in, smelled of bison and woodsmoke, of bear grease and deer hide, of sweet river water and rough winter grass.*

There, Prudence thought, deriving a sudden, surprising satisfaction from her task. That's more like it.

Houston, Texas

An hour before sunrise, armed with a Rand McNally road atlas, family-size bottle of pee-colored Listerine, his two "huggie pillows" and a small black leather bag lumpy with change, Ray stood over Prudence's sleeping form. *Rise and shine, my little Mini-Wheat!* Dragging on her jeans and sweatshirt in the dark bedroom, stumbling out of the house in fuzzy slippers like a recalcitrant child hugging her pillow, poked and prodded toward the van, Prudence assumed there must be some urgency, some reason for the pre-dawn rush. There wasn't. *Hit the sack, hit the road,* was just the way Ray traveled. Yawning, Prudence hoisted herself into the passenger seat of the van, having somehow agreed to cross three thousand dead-as-a-stump, flat-as-a-skillet miles to southeast Texas where Ray's parents lived, to spend Christmas with them. With Deleanor in Hawaii and Fiona in New Mexico, there really was nothing to hold her.

Denny's, Kountry Kupboard, the Iron Skillet — wherever he stopped, Prudence was slow to order. It all looked the same, she thought, forcing herself to point to one of the bright plastic pictures, the number 3 breakfast, or the Monday Early Bird Special, or the Grand Slam. In the van, when he offered a choice — stop now or farther up the road — Prudence kept silent, unable to think through such a big decision. *Too late. Better learn to speak up.* And no matter how tired he was from driving, in whatever night's cheap motel room he'd picked, Ray would tell her to spread her legs for him, then fall asleep, *'Night sweetie,* arm slung, heavy as a post, across her hip. *Happiness is what you do for meeee.* Prudence used to laugh, it had sounded so funny. *Even when I'm wrong, I'm right.*

Ray's stepfather, Joe Flores, and his mother, Empara, had cleared the land themselves; in the green heart of their acreage they had constructed a modest one-story home of tawny yellow brick with hyacinth blue louvered shutters. Bermuda grass collared the house, and a four-foot link fence protected the lawn from their dozen or so Arabian horses. The house fronted a wooded, semiwild acre, fenced with round pipe painted the limpid blue of morning glories. Empara had named this deeply shaded wooded place Paradise Park. Inside was a redwood picnic table painted the same startling blue as the fence, a half-barrel barbecue and a home-made wood and rope swing. The swing, which hung low from one of the sturdier limbs of a massive oak, moved slightly from time to time, as if stirred by the weak aftermath of warm hurricane winds blowing up from the Gulf, or by a spirit perched, childlike and curious, on its broad seat. North of the house stood two barns built by Empara and Joe, one for mares, one for geldings and stallions, and nearby a hot-walker, a round training corral and two concrete bathing pads shaded by corrugated green plastic roof-ing. Across ten acres of pastured land grew china grove trees, with silvery, mottled bark, and oaks, with dark, leathery thumbs of leaf. Here and there, neither lush nor sparse, grew tall rusted green spires of cedar. And everywhere was evidence of the earthy elegant presence of horses.

Prudence would see none of this until daylight. In the deep rural darkness, she could only sense the land, the rich, raw smell of horses and manure, as Ray got down from his van to unlock and scrape back the long chain-link gate, drive slowly inside, get back down, close and relock the gate, guide the van up a straight concrete driveway into an open-sided carport beside the house. Tiny white Christmas lights sagged in thin lines, like barbed wire lit up, over the shorn tops of evergreen shrubs. Walking up the curved path to a narrow front porch crowded with potted plants and muddied pairs of work boots, Prudence stood waiting as Ray rang the bell once, then a second time.

"Ready, sweetie? To meet my folks?" Ray leaned down, gave Prudence a kiss on the cheek. "You'll love my mom. Everyone does. And remember, if Joe starts to tease you and show you his karate moves, that means he likes you."

When the door opened, Prudence saw, on the cream-colored wall in front of her, glossy photographs of Joe and Empara with their prizewinning Arabians, framed by dozens of show ribbons, satin bursts of red, blue, yellow, pink and white. A second impression would form more gradually as she moved through the rooms of the neatly kept home, likenesses of Ray at every turn — oil and pastel portraits, publicity photographs, calendar shots, modeling

219

shots, family photographs, even a life-size marble bust. Aside from the front hallway's photographs of Arabian horses framed by show ribbons, two figures, two holy images, competed for wall space in this house, that of Mary's son, Jesus, and Empara's son, Ray.

Ray's mother, who had opened the door with a genuine cry of welcome, had a lovely, open face, high, broad cheekbones, large hazel eyes and long thick white hair caught up in a ponytail. She reminded Prudence of those kindhearted kindergarten teachers children fashion small, worshipful gifts for out of yarn and Popsicle sticks, glue, lace doilies and red paper hearts. Empara's husband and Ray's stepfather, Joe, was a former karate instructor and full-blooded Apache, stocky and strongly built, given either to silence or to long, complex stories that ended abruptly in a small, baffling joke. Standing in the small foyer, Prudence noted, in the dining room to her immediate right, a miniature artificial Christmas tree set on a card table, its diamond lights winking on and off, holiday cards carefully arranged on the dining room table around an old-fashioned crèche, artificial pine boughs and faded sprays of red poinsettia wreathing a pair of polished brass candlesticks, Christmas decorations set out year after year in customary, habitual spots.

Cheerfully, Empara showed Prudence the guest bathroom, Ray's workroom, his old bedroom where she was to sleep. She and Joe, Empara explained, were up before sunrise each day, feeding the horses, turning them out to pasture, raking out the barns — *We work every day, even on Christmas, caring for our babies. This is your vacation, dear, and we want you to thoroughly enjoy yourself. If you decide to ride the horses, if you and Ray want to go riding together, you're welcome to do that, too. If you want to help out in the barns or just relax and sleep in, get your rest, whatever you want, dear, is fine with us. We're just so glad you're both here.*

She'd intended to wake early, go outside and help with the horses, yet she woke near noon, stayed in bed a long while, wandered down the hall to the kitchen to pour a cup of still-warm coffee. She found Ray in his workroom drawing, sat and watched awhile, then went back into his bedroom and sat on the bed stroking the black-brown coarse hair of the buffalo hide, the spiny honey brown hair of elk hide, coverings that stretched heavy and stiff over brown-and-beige-striped sheets.

Ray told her he did not, as a rule, bring women home to meet his parents. Prudence could almost imagine herself a girlfriend or fiancée from the eager way he went through his closets and bureau drawers, showing her his old black motorcycle jacket, his dozens of sketchbooks from high school, his shelves of books on Native American history. Once, while he was in the shower, Prudence snooped through a black file cabinet next to the bed and found photographs of his ex-wife and former girlfriends, one perched on the hood of a car, another smiling up from a toy car in Disneyland, a third posed with Empara beside one of the white Arabians. All pretty, all dark-haired. Where had they gone? She found a file folder full of identical publicity head shots, the same photograph he had sent her, pre-inscribed exactly as hers had been — *Maa Paewatsi Kwabaru, Paewatsi Muhraru* — *Kultseena Peeka.* How many women had received this same photograph, this same exotic untranslatable message?

Most days, by noon, Prudence, wearing jeans, a warm sweater, heavy socks and work boots, would wander out to the barns, help Empara muck out stalls, watch

222

Joe training a new colt abused by its former owner. Joe worked to cure the young horse of its kicking and biting, its fear, patiently breaking down its terrified defenses. *You can't do that with humans,* Joe would talk to Prudence as he worked the colt, *you can't teach a human to trust again. Maybe with a psychotherapist, but the person would have to want help, ask for help, and most people won't.* Prudence leaned on the rails of the corral, the winter sun's faint warmth on her back. *Gentling a horse is like gentling a woman, by touch, by soft voice.*

If it wasn't raining or too windy, Prudence might stand motionless in the fenced winter fields watching the Arabians, floating saddles of sunlight slipping down their creamy backs, their pale, milky necks curving down like the stamens of wildflowers, their velvety ash black muzzles nursing tough little crops of sparse December grass, some with one front leg elegantly canted forward. She stood still as they approached, three or four at a time, curious, nuzzling, nudging at her, stood motionless as they broke into a run, tossing a white thundering lariat around her, their hooves drumming the earth, their power, the rushing wind of them, bringing her to tears, sensing how honestly

223

they lived, how clean in their skins.

Heck, I grew up with them, Ray shrugged when she tried to tell him. *Horses mean two things to me. Glue and leather.*

Sometimes his left eye developed an uncontrollable tic, an involuntary winking. Sometimes he might stutter slightly, or stammer. Ray loved books and bookstores, yet words snarled and tangled across the page whenever he tried to read. Words, he said, wouldn't hold still for him. He liked her to read aloud to him, read from the dozens of books he'd collected on Native American history. He had trouble with numbers, too, and couldn't type, so Prudence wrote his artist's statement, his biography, updated his gallery and price listings, read aloud from books until her voice grew hoarse (read her way across Phoenix, New Mexico and on into Texas, right up to the gate of his parents' ranch), read tirelessly over the noise of traffic or by candlelight, sitting up in bed, glancing down to see if his eyes were open, gazing at her, listening, or if he had fallen asleep, lulled like a child, his head nestled against her bare thigh. Reading aloud, Prudence began to learn the history of the Comanche people, his people, facts she was tempted to plug, like sticks of dynamite, into the working chapters of *Savage Heat*, chapters she had smuggled to Texas in her suitcase, hidden beneath layers of clothing. Comanche men, with notorious vanity, dressing their long hair with buffalo dung. Comanche men, free to enjoy as many wives as they could support, often marrying a dead brother's wife or wives, a wife's sister or sisters. Adultery in Comanche women, on the other hand, was brutally punished — it would not be uncommon for the wronged husband to slice off his wife's nose, making her unappealing to other men. Most mornings at the ranch, Prudence would wake under the warm, weirdly flat weight of the elk and buffalo hides and listen to the rich, stoical silence coming from the next room, where she knew Ray was quietly painting. Then one morning, she decided to take her journal and go through Joe and Empara's small house, describing each room, cataloging objects within rooms. In Bachelard's essays, he alluded to the speech of objects, to the memories, secrets and reminiscences held within objects such as boxes, drawers, wardrobes; he wrote about the speech of houses themselves, from attics to cellars. He wrote about the nest and the shell as homes with an esoteric language. Perhaps she could interpret Ray, understand him, his moods, his anger and sexual coldness, through objects he'd lived with, in the house he'd grown up in. She would listen for the honest confessions of objects and rooms. She would begin here, in the room she slept in.

Ray's Bedroom

The carpet a dense, Aegean blue, the walls sandy beige. By the door, a square beveled mirror and plain light switch; above the switch, a brass crucifix. Two windows, curtained with a rough-textured oatmeal material flecked with dark, wormy slubs of brown. Closed blinds behind the curtains dim and filter the light. A double bed, sheets striped in tan and brown, like a man's dress shirt, and for blankets, buffalo and elk hides. Brought from Phoenix, Ray's two "huggie pillows," in their faded, overwashed maroon cases, pillows he claimed he could not sleep without but would never explain why. Beside the bed, on top of a black metal file cabinet, a lamp, its base made of shining gouts of orange and yellow glass that lit up from the inside. A set of men's weights on the floor. On the wall between two walk-in closets, a framed poster of a wolf, entitled *Spirit of the Sacred Forest*. On a second wall, a badly done oil portrait of Ray, seated sideways, looking bloated and bored, grasping an eagle-claw staff. On a third, a reproduced painting of Jesus, seated sideways against a moribund background of hard, somber blue, his bowed head nimbused in a mossy gold. On the same wall, a photograph of Ray and his deceased twin brother, Erroll, Empara standing behind them, smiling and proud, a loving hand on each boy's shoulder, the last picture taken of Erroll before he died, when both boys were eighteen, close to Fiona's age. In the two walk-in closets, Native American books, old music videos, Ray's clothes, including the black leather jacket, a buffalo skull wrapped in a white sheet, a jar of tiger teeth, cougar, bear and wolf hides, boxes of hawk, eagle, crow and owl feathers. *Wildness,* she wrote. *Strength, death, God.*

Hallway

Blue stem of carpet, sandy beige walls. On one wall, a large velvet painting, five bulldogs sitting around a poker table, one wearing a green visor and dealing the cards. On the opposite wall, a Bruce Lee calendar, a glow-in-the-dark crucifix, a 3-D holographic picture of the Crucifixion, the three sorrowing figures at Christ's feet seeming to move slightly as you passed by them. *Strength,* she wrote. *Martyrdom and chance.*

Ray's Bathroom

Baby blue tile, a single window looking out on the horse barns, a homemade curtain of darker blue toweling, the window's bottom half insulated by a square of aluminum foil. A photograph of four horses on one blue wall, an Appaloosa, a quarter horse, an Arabian and a paint. On a wooden plaque above the sink, the Prayer of St. Francis (*God grant me the serenity to accept the things I cannot change, the courage to change the things I can, and the wisdom to know the difference*); on the back of the toilet, a red nail brush, a can of Glade air freshener (Strawberries and Cream scent). On the blue-tiled countertop, a hunk of orangy, cheddar-colored soap set in a crystal dish, a maroon fingertip towel tri-folded beside the dish. A bright yellow ribbed plastic drinking cup. Towels, light blue, worn thin, washed clean, hang on chrome towel bars by the toilet and on the sliding shower door of opaque glass. *Utility, practical function, horse-worship.*

Ray's Studio

A white drafting table, a black stereo system on top of a pine chest of drawers, a twin bed with a striped Mexican blanket, a stamped tin mirror hanging above the bed, a chrome and vinyl stool, a small black metal file cabinet; three bass guitars leaning against one wall. A painted teepee lamp, a tiny bulb illuminating the inside of the teepee. A poster, an Edward Curtis photograph, of Black Elk. *Vanished world, lost dreams.*

Living Room

Two plush blue velvet couches with circular ruffled blue pillows set in an L shape, a round table between. Two clocks ticking, a soft, murmurous duet. A coffee table, nut brown, bare of magazine or ornament. Two recliners, a large brown plaid "pappa chair," a small dark brown "mamma chair," each with an oval braided foot rug, like a lily pad, in front of it. The recliners face a giant TV screen. To the right of the

TV, a set of bookshelves holding books on horses, horse breeding, horse care, training manuals. Photographs of Ray and Erroll as babies, as children, as teenagers, and the same photograph of Ray, Erroll and Empara that hangs in every room of the house, because it is the last picture of Erroll. Ceramic figurines of horses, clowns and one off-white Buddha. On all four walls, Ray's artwork, pastels of horses, crows, buffalo, a large oil portrait of Ray, young and serenely androgynous, in Plains-style regalia. To the left of the TV, a four-foot Greek-style statue, a marble naiad in a toga, flanked by two gray vases resembling crematory urns. In one corner of the room, a black exercise machine Joe calls Black Beauty. On one of the couches, a black massage pad with a complicated set of dials and settings (pulse, zigzag, random, wave), and on the floor beneath it, a foot massager that glows red under Empara's aching feet as she and Joe watch Spanish soap operas and *Wheel of Fortune*. Above one couch, a gigantic black sombrero, silver braid around its brim and crown; beside the sombrero, a poster-sized photograph of a white stallion, mane and tail streaming, galloping in gold-lit pastures. The curtains in this room are sheer, nondescript, faintly floral. *Comfort, sorrow, pride, horse-worship, memorial for Erroll, gallery for Ray. Conventional, tragic, sorrowful, mundane.*

Kitchen

An expanding wooden rack holds a knobby cluster of baseball caps. Overhead, a seashell wind chime hangs motionless. A double aluminum sink, a window above the sink; on the windowsill, a row of small wooden tulips painted red and green. The gray countertops are synthetic marble/plastic, the floor is white linoleum with tiny blue diamonds, the curtains the same oatmeal worm-slubbed texture as in Ray's bedroom, every window insulated, like the bathroom window, with square leaves of foil. A round wood table with matching captain's chairs, where Joe and Empara sit for coffee, sweets, meals. Above the table, a light fixture combined with a ceiling fan. On one wall, a portrait of the Last Supper; on the adjacent wall, three Native American wall calendars, each with a photograph of Ray. The cream-colored refrig-erator door holds a scattering of magnets: a Texas boot, an Indian warrior, various advertisements for plumbers, insurance salesmen, chiropractors, the operating hours of the nearby library in Alvin. Above the stove, a pass-through opens into the living room, facing the TV. On its surface sits a Jesus pencil-and-pen holder, Jesus opening a white robe to reveal his red heart, a monkey with stick-on feet hanging upside down beside Jesus, a sign *Hang in There* on his little brown chest, various pads, message pads, vague heaps of household clutter. *Jesus and Ray, knicknacks and clutter. Ray and Jesus.*

Foyer

Over the front door, a blessing in Spanish. To the left of the front door, two large green rubber trays, one for mud boots, one for cowboy boots.

Dining Room

Photographs of Ray, artwork of Ray's, oil portraits of Ray, sheer Barbie-pink curtains, pink mini-blinds behind the curtains shutting out the west light. A large table and chairs, seldom used. A display table of ringleted Victorian dolls wearing stiff lace hats, suggesting a time when Empara might have enjoyed other, more feminine

232

pastimes — her world now the prize-winning Arabians, her husband and only surviving son. *Oppressive, Victorian ideal of beauty, pressure on Ray, the surviving son.*

Empara's Office

Above the door, a feathered Indian shield and painted cow skull. Beside that, a small arrow quiver. Over the large window with its shut blinds, the same sheer Barbie-pink curtains. A cluttered desk and card table, a brown-and-orange-plaid couch paved over with back issues of *Ladies' Home Journal*s. All along one wall, black and white modeling photographs of Ray in Native American poses and costumes, looking years younger, his hair luxuriant and thick, his face unlined and smooth, his expression haughty, vulnerable, sly, sexy, victimized. A photo of Ray and Erroll, blown up to poster size. A tea towel calendar, hung by a pencil-slim dowel, a transferred photograph of someone's child, smiling above the linen months and square days. The family's financial center. *Argument between Empara's Catholic faith and Ray's Native American beliefs. A secret, shaming disappointment over which son* died?

Conclusion

A house cluttered with shrines — to Ray, to Ray and Erroll, to Arabian horses, to the life of Jesus, to Bruce Lee, to Native Americans, to a secular smattering of clowns and dolls, the odd Greek naiad, the solitary, fat-bellied Buddha in his white fold of contemplation. A modest exterior of mild yellow brick, an interior of passionate tributes, overlapping devotions. The house is comforting in its aesthetic lawlessness. Still, after her painstaking inventory, Prudence feels no closer to solving the riddle of Ray's stony defenses, his flarings of anger, no closer to the reason for the name he has given himself. No-Heart. *Tragedy. Sacrifice. Wildness. Death at every turn.*

Squatting down in coarse, stubbled winter grass, he prays over the dead hawk, over the two wrapped bundles he'd taken from his mother's freezer, thawed now, a crow, a second redtail. Pinching moist, shredded tobacco from a blue Bugler's package, he presses some on the hawk's chest, more beneath each wing, beneath the tail, on the head between the eyes, then wraps the hawk with long two-inch strips from a white T-shirt, crossing, crisscrossing, fastening, binding the strips with a length of clothesline, his dark hands moving with customary, practiced grace, his dark hands reminding her of smooth brown talons, their clean, ovaled nails more predaceous than human.

He picks up the thawed bundle closest to him, wrapped in newspaper and bound, like the redtail, with clothesline.

"It's going to smell a little. The crow." He looks up, his long hair an ebony frame around his oval face, his eyes slick, richly black, gleaming. As it always does, the pure, feral beauty of his face weakens her.

"Sure you want to stay?"

She nods. The crow lies between them, nested in its newsprint bundle.

"OK then." Like a mother unswaddling her newborn, Ray unwraps the large, heavy-bodied crow. It is as long as her forearm. A sweet stink floods her nostrils. The mild, warm Texas wind shifts, takes the smell. Exposed to the winter sun in its damp bed of cold, blurred news, packed in a white detergent powder mixed with bits of cedar, the crow lies on its back, neck twisted, the taffetaed blue-black head cocked, empty-eyed. Ray grasps the tail feathers with one hand, tugs. "These should pull right off, just like this, here they come." He hands the fan of black glossy feathers to Prudence, picks up the game shears she bought for him the day before, neatly snipping off first one wing, then the other. Prudence winces at the quick, piercing sound, the snap of pliant cartilage, the moist-breaking bone.

"What do you do with the rest?"

He nods toward the pasture. "Bury it out there or else put it up high in a tree branch. I'll bury the head next to an ant-hill." Still squatting on his haunches, Ray reaches for the last bundle, a second redtail.

"This is a young one, smaller, male." Prudence sits on the damp grass, sunlight square on her back, the rich black-green iridescence of crow feathers gleaming against her pale, narrow hand. Ray unwraps the hawk, prays in Comanche.

"This one's perfect. See his winter coat?" He uses the game shears, expertly cutting each thick golden talon off. "I hate cutting a perfect hawk." He snips each wing at the shoulder, tugs out the tail feathers, absorbed, methodical, silent. Watching him, Prudence feels proud of her own calmness. Ray would never say so, but the way in which he presumes her help is, she understands, a form of praise. *Sorry, I don't do white-boy shit. I care for you in my own way. If you don't like it, go find yourself some white boy to say corny shit to you. That's not my way.* She doubts another woman had walked out into this pasture with him holding the remains of a crow, saying nothing as he took the bird from her hands, placing it high in the silvered branches of a leafless china grove tree, uttering a prayer. She doubts another woman had watched him carry the bodies of two hawks further out into the field and bury them. Today's happiness had nothing to do with his physical beauty, with their sexual chemistry or his sometimes brutal manner of speaking, a way he called honest. This was some other magnetism, something Prudence had never experienced before, holding her to him, compelling her to endure anything, a capitulation of will that was at best ecstatic, at worst terrifying.

She helps him carry the hawk and crow wings, loosely wrapped in the inked, pulpy nest of newsprint, into the warm house.

"What do we do with these?"

"Clean them. Have you had enough? Still want to help?"

As the air in the tiny blue-tiled bathroom thickens and turns humid with a wild, gamy odor, they work side by side, dipping and washing each wing in a sinkful of soapy warm water, loosening, then tugging individual feathers out from the three sets of wings. They work without speaking, then he shows her where the shoulder bone is hollow, how it can be fashioned into a whistle, shows her the layers and types of feathers, primary, secondary, fluffs, spikes, the slight bits of down, traditionally used for pillows or to stuff the cloth figures of dolls. He puts one of the quills in his mouth, draws it hard between his slightly sharpened front teeth.

"I do that to get the gristle, the bits of flesh off."

She waits for him to spit out the gristle, bits of meat.

"You ate that? Did you just eat that? Raw gristle?"

"Why not? Want to try? It's the old way of cleaning quills."

She tugs a feather out from the hawk wing she's been working on, turns its quill end, the ivory nib of gristle, a bit of rosy meat still attached, sets it between her teeth. The little knob of flesh and gristle sits, a slight foreign pressure, on her tongue. She draws the quill out between her teeth. Swallows.

"How was it?" He is, she can tell, impressed.

"Not bad." She tugs out another feather, sets its quill end between her teeth, pulls, swallows, her expression neutral. She goes faster, pulling bits of gristle and meat off, quill after quill, bits of hawk going down into her stomach, a creature once skimming the sky vanishing inside her. They continue to wash and rinse feathers, arranging them by size and type on an outstretched blue bath towel. With her fingers, she lightly coats each feather with hair conditioner, hands it to him to dry lightly with a hair blower. The crow's feathers, spatulate, bluish black, hold a bold, hard gleam. The hawk's are striped, subtly mottled in shades of russet, black, cream, tan. Prudence remembered how Ray had unwrapped the hawk, opened the damp, crackling newsprint, how vivid the splash of nut brown was across its curved snowy breast. They finish by placing the cleaned, glossy feathers in a handmade cedar box, and Prudence feels it again, the basic pleasure of doing useful work. She wishes it could always be like this, exactly like this, their existence together.

At a Chinese all-you-can-eat buffet, Ray

asked for a plastic fork. He had always loathed the taste of metal in his mouth, even as a kid. Prudence watched as he twirled and poked the pebbled pinky beige flesh of a baby octopus into his mouth, shaking its rubbery eyestalks at her, wriggling it around in his mouth so it looked still alive.

"Ugh. I'm not kissing you for at least twenty-four hours. Yeesh! You're eating its eyeballs."

"I eat you and you have eyes."

"Oh my god, Ray! Shh."

But his crude comment pleased her, and he knew it.

Three fully loaded trays of Chinese food later, Ray shifted a toothpick in his mouth, pulled his T-shirt up, pooched out his smooth brown belly, smacked it, groaned.

"Prue, why didn't you stop me? You were supposed to stop me."

"Maybe I like watching you make a pig of yourself."

"Why would you like that?"

"I don't know. Because normally you exhibit such self-control." Feeling her hair, Prudence made a small *tchh* sound.

"Maybe if you'd comb it once in a while." He burped.

"I do. Five or six times a day."

"Come off it. I have never seen you comb your hair."

"That is not true. I comb my hair five, six, maybe seven times a day, it just doesn't look like it."

Before they left Phoenix, she'd colored it again, this time reddish blond. She couldn't control her hair's reactions to weather — how it went flat, bumpy, frizzy, wavy or full-blown tumbleweed, according to dew point and humidity. Her shoulder-length hair acted like a weather barometer, while Ray's always looked satiny and gorgeous, even when he'd just woken up. It wasn't fair.

"Whatcha thinking?" He pinched the little roll of fat around her middle. "Golly, my gut hurts. If there's no sex tonight, it's your fault for not stopping me. You should have stopped me." Another groan, followed by a pursy belch. He stood up to leave, pocketing a handful of fortune cookies. "What do you want to do now? It's early, not even eight o'clock."

Prudence shrugged. "Go home, I guess, or stop and get some groceries to take home to your mom." Sometimes they had nothing in common at all, could think of nothing to do together. Maybe it was just sex, maybe that was their only glue, the

241

other pieces wrong, lost, barely together.

Pillow time! Empara called cheerfully each night as she and Joe headed into their bedroom after the ten o'clock news. Prudence and Ray would answer good night, pretend to be going to bed, too, Ray in his sleeping bag with his "huggie pillows" on the living room floor, Prudence in the bedroom down the hall. After waiting an hour or so, she would tiptoe past Empara and Joe's bedroom, nudge herself down into the sleeping bag so she and Ray could have nearly motionless, sweet sex, Ray hugging her close afterward, whispering she was gorgeous, sexy, so good to him. Afterward, she slipped out, gliding like some revenant lodger through the cold air of the house to climb back under the buffalo and elk hides, their doubled weight like a lying down under the earth's crust, as if she were face-up, scarcely breathing, in her grave. From the first night, Prudence felt Erroll hovering, curious, nearby. She knew he entered her through Ray because their sex felt so entirely different, Ray's hands more the hands of an eighteen-year-old, bold, tender, awed. She wondered if his young spirit traveled between the multiple photographs of Ray and Erroll, Empara

242

standing behind her dark-haired handsome twins, one hand proudly resting on each boy's shoulder. Erroll, confident and popular, wearing a red plaid western shirt with pearl buttons. Ray, skinny in a black Kiss T-shirt, picked-on-looking, defensive, the one, if you had to predict, who wouldn't last in this world. But life had ended for Erroll, not Ray. With his right shoulder sprained from roping practice, he'd insisted on bull riding — wanting, he told Ray, to surprise his mother with the two-hundred-dollar cash prize. Thrown sideways out of the chute, his right leg hung up in the rope, his head kicked open, Erroll was in a coma seventeen days, then gone. In the choking dust of the arena, in the powdery, hoof-ringed, bloodied dirt, Ray held Erroll in his arms, waiting for the ambulance. In the ambulance, he held his brother's hands and cried. It was Ray who would learn a boy with a grudge had rigged the bull pick, an argument over a girl, a rival who made sure Erroll got a fiery, unpredictable Brahma, half blind and out for murder. Ray, calling his mother with the news. Ray, picking his brother's burial clothes, calling relatives, arranging a service, then driving Empara to the grave site every day, watching her hair go from reddish brown to white in a matter of weeks, watching the first silver strands show up in his own. Then Erroll's girlfriend, Luisa, wanted to marry Ray in sorrowing tribute to his brother, but she ran off on their wedding day and would eventually marry instead the boy who had picked the bull, who had, in effect and through a mistreated animal, murdered Erroll. She would marry him, have two children, two little girls, then get divorced. Years later, when she called, Ray agreed to meet her at a nearby mall. She wanted to apologize, she said, maybe get back with him, try again, she had been so young, stupid. Ray had laughed, a new, hard, merciless laugh, called her pathetic and walked away.

In Empara's kitchen Prudence cooked lasagna, pot roast, spaghetti, scones, chocolate chip cookies, breads, meat loaf, soup. She made extra batches of lasagna especially for Joe, bought exotic flavored coffees for Empara. She stopped thinking, stopped reading; she preferred feeling plain, vacant, useful. Around his parents, Ray treated her with exceptional consideration, drawing back a chair for her at the kitchen table, bringing her a glass of water, complimenting her cooking, helping with the dishes after supper, massaging her shoulders as the four of them sat watching TV at night. Every two days or so, they left the ranch to drive the hour into Houston, to eat at his favorite Chinese buffet or at Popeye's Chicken, go to discount record stores, Half-Price bookstores. At the house, Ray mostly stayed in his room, painting. When he came out, it was to eat, watch TV, sleep.

One afternoon, visiting the Houston Art Museum at Prudence's request, moving rapidly from one gallery space to the next, Ray kept up a stream of bitter invective about white culture, white people. Prudence tried to understand, though she privately thought he sounded reductive and small-minded. She defended the principles of art collection, though she had never given those principles much thought, had simply accepted museums as valuable places of cultural preservation. Ray called them halls of death, vehicles of white appropriation and mass violation. Exasperated and finally out of patience, she flung out her lowest card. Called him a racist.

"Of course I am." He sounded absurdly cheerful. "I hate white people."

"Well, what in the world are you doing with me?"

"I like you as a person."

"You always say I look dead."

"You do. All white people look dead to me."

"What if I said I think my oh-so-white skin turns you on?"

"I never said it didn't."

"Well, if I look dead to you, then you're sleeping with a dead person. That makes you a necrophiliac."

"If you say so. Think about it. I sleep with a white woman in a white bed in a white room in a white house with white furniture and white appliances in an all-white neighborhood, I live with a white woman by the Puritan name of Prudence who drives a white car, wears white, and honey, don't take it wrong, I'm not trying to be mean or nasty, but you are so white you glow in the dark. You are cellophane. When you sit on that white couch of yours, all I see are two green eyes. So yes, white people look dead to me. Even you."

They were moving through a chambered maze of period reconstructions — French rococo, French baroque, Puritan, Spanish Colonial, Italian Renaissance — an intricate, eerie, ornate catacomb. Ray denounced everything as European white crap, evidence of death, disease, genocide. Could he not see one thing of value or beauty in European culture? she asked. Could he admire nothing? Perhaps if he went to Europe?

"I have no desire to go to Europe. Why? To see a bunch of square buildings with points on top? I can see those here."

By the time they left the museum, Ray seemed invigorated, juiced up by his own culturally assaultive energy. Sooner or later, everything with him soured into political diatribe, an attack on white people, white culture, and Prudence was suddenly sick of it. Then, during the hour's drive back to the ranch, they stopped arguing, their hostile energy exhausted. They began, instead, to discuss the motives behind acquisition and collection, Prudence continuing to defend the intentions of museum enterprise, Ray continuing to call it glorified theft. They still disagreed, but this time the friction of their opposition was playful, more debate, a spirited competition, not accusation and attack. Things with Ray were like that, mercurial, capricious, swift-changing.

On the afternoon before Christmas, with his parents spending their day no differently from any other, working with their horses, Ray drove Prudence two hours across town to the poorest side of Houston, near the oil refineries. He wanted to show her where he had lived his first ten years, the small blue house, the wooden porch he had spent nights crouched under, terrified, hoping to avoid another beating by his father. She remembered what the imaginary character of Nathaniel had told her about Ray's childhood, how he had been punched, slapped, whacked with boards and baseball bats, made to sleep in the dirt under the porch. They sat looking at the house where all this had taken place, the spot on earth where his spirit had been broken. The house itself looked faded, hunched in on itself, as if slightly shamed.

"Did he hit your mother?"

"No."

"Erroll?"

"No. It was me he hated."

"Why?"

"I was scrawny, I liked to draw, I was quiet and hated sports. Erroll was the all-American boy, the athlete, the champion cowboy. When he was drinking, my father would always start yelling how I should never have been born. I was born only half Erroll's size, not even breathing. Born dead, basically. They threw me in some kind of box and started yelling through a bullhorn, to shock me, I guess. When she brought us home, Mom kept Erroll in the crib and me in a sock drawer, I was that tiny. Small as a sock, well, a pair of socks. So my father would always get worked up on how I should have stayed dead, I wasn't a son he could ever be proud of. Basically, I wasn't Erroll."

They had driven a few blocks past Ray's childhood house, parked outside an old-fashioned corner store. Ray walked inside, he hadn't been there, in that market, he told Prudence, since he was ten. Nothing had changed. The same sweet smell of over-ripening fruit, bananas, cantaloupe, muskmelon, of wilting produce, lettuce, kale, cilantro, the decaying scent of meats laid out in white enamel pans inside the butcher's glass cooling case, the softened bundles of bread in their plastic packaging. Above their heads, neatly pinned on a plastic clothesline, hung bandannas, triangular flags of navy, yellow, red, black, labeled $1.50 each. "I can't get over it. The food looks exactly the same, the place smells exactly the same." Ray bought a package of round cookies with yellow icing, the kind his mom had brought home when they were kids, him and Erroll. Sitting on the counter by the cash register was a glass barrel of whole, wart-skinned pickles, suspended like turgid, eyeless fish in murky green brine. "My mom used to give Erroll and me a dime between us to buy two pickles. Five cents apiece. I bought my first pack of bad-boy cigarettes here, too. Lucky Strikes." They took the yellow-iced cookies and left the dark, cramped, ripe-smelling market, driving past shabby, broken-down houses, unpaved streets with no sidewalks, no plants or trees. "Nothing's changed, Prudence . . . all Mexican families . . . though my one friend, Eddie, he was white, I wonder what happened to him, Eddie Costanzo, we used to build these forts in vacant lots. Let's go see my brother."

Erroll was buried in a Catholic cemetery, an enormous, immaculate cemetery covering several city blocks. Mature trees cast dense patches of cool thick shade over pale purblind acres of markers, stones, statuary. Ray parked beside a curve in the white-curbed road, got out and walked over to his brother's grave. Twin cedars, taken from the ranch, were planted on either side of Erroll's black granite stone. Wind chimes and Christmas ornaments hung from both cedars, as well as garlands of silver tinsel. At the foot of Erroll's stone stood a wooden reindeer planter, brightened by a burst of red silk poinsettias. *I have fought a good fight, I have finished my course, I have kept the faith: Henceforth there is laid up for me a crown of righteousness. Timothy 2 Chapter 4.*

"Mom comes here a lot. Joe brings her every Sunday."

"Where was your father . . ."

"He walked out on Christmas morning, when Erroll and me were eight years old. Said our big present was him going away and never coming back. I haven't seen him since. Know something funny? Six days after Mom and I buried Erroll, I tried to get a job here. Filled out an application form, everything."

"A job as?"

"A gravedigger. Didn't get it, though."

The wind chimes tinkled, a forlorn, toobright sound. Prudence kept her hands in her jacket pockets, her head down. A matching black stone stood to the right of Erroll's, with Empara's name and birth date inscribed. To the left stood a third burial marker, Ray's, its black, shining surface blank.

On Christmas morning, Ray came into the bedroom bringing a cup of cinnamon coffee for her. The night before, after his parents had come home from mass, they'd given Joe and Empara gifts they had picked out — a boxed video set, *The History of Christianity*, an assortment of Starbucks holiday coffees, a tin of homemade Christmas cookies, and a large coffee table book on Arabian horses. Ray and Prudence had agreed not to give one another presents, but Ray had a surprise for her, a pair of turquoise, coral and shell earrings, and Prudence gave Ray a signed book on the art of Howard Terpning, a western artist Ray had once modeled for and admired.

"Where are your parents?"

"Like every other morning, sweet thing, outside. A horse doesn't know it's Christmas." While she sipped her coffee, Ray nuzzled his head into her lap, looked sweetly up and, with a childlike expression of mischief, suckled one of Prudence's breasts.

Powell refused to celebrate holidays. Every Christmas morning, when Prudence called, Fiona answered, unhappy.

"Merry Christmas, sweetie."

"Moo-la-lah! Merry Xmas yourself. It sucks here."

"Why?"

"For starters, Yoshi got about sixty presents, which I was expected to sit and watch her open one at a time."

"Well, what did you get, honey?"

"A book of photographs. It's pretty cool, actually. Different families from around the world put all their possessions, their worldly belongings, out in front of their houses, then a picture is taken of them standing there, surrounded by their stuff."

"That's it?"

"Well, yeah. Wanda Mae probably figures I'm too old. For presents, I mean. And you know how Dad is. This afternoon we're all going skiing."

"Do they have a tree or anything?"

"Dad threw a string of lights over a dead cactus in their living room."

"That's typical. Did he like his cookies?" Every year, Prudence sent Fiona off with a tin of Powell's favorite homemade cookies, powdery white crescents made of sugar, butter and walnuts. A sentimental vestige of their marriage.

"Gone in one day."

"Still a tradition then. What'd you guys do last night?"

"The usual. I stayed home while they headed off to that bonfire thingamabob at the pueblo. Wanda Mae fixed a big vegetarian dinner, and the usual gumbo of oddballs came to the house, Bird Man, Dweeb, plus some new guy from Perth, Australia, who played a didgeridoo while Dad accompanied him with drums. Totally embarrassing." Fiona sighed. "I miss you, Mom."

"Miss you, too, sweetie."

"I miss our old Christmases. When I was little."

Fiona meant the beautifully decorated tree, the gorgeous music, the days of baking holiday cookies and breads to give as gifts, going to church at midnight on Christmas Eve. Fiona meant when Powell and Prudence were still married, when they were all under one roof, as real a family as they would ever be. Prudence suddenly felt terribly sad, heavy. That dream had died so long ago.

"Hey, me, too. I miss that, too."

"What's it like out there? It's so weird, thinking of you blowing around Texas."

"Well, I'm on a horse ranch, the weather's mostly warm and windy, and Ray's parents are very nice."

"Nicer than the Grinch?" Fiona didn't much like Ray, so Prudence could hardly expect her to be bowled over by the people who'd raised him.

"Actually, Joe and Empara have been

great. I rode one of their horses yesterday, a pregnant mare named Allegra." Prudence didn't add how terrified she'd been, how short the ride had proved to be, less than twenty minutes, how sore she'd been afterward. "Maybe I'll ride again today, after I help Ray haul some bales of hay into the barn." She had no intention of riding, but for some reason wanted Fiona to picture her pitching hay, riding horses, doing happy things of a ranchlike nature.

Prudence heard Powell in the background, joking around. Pictured him leaning against the counter, in a kitchen she knew well. After all, it had been hers. Hearing a noise in the doorway, she glanced up from the phone. Ray stood zipping up his black windbreaker, saying he was going out to help in the barn. Here was her past, leaking through the telephone, colliding with her new life, with a Comanche man fourteen years younger than she was. Prudence had on one of Empara's old plaid bathrobes, and a pair of Ray's heavy gray socks. Her eyes were probably smudged with old mascara, her nose felt greasy. He came over, kissed the top of her head, ruffled her sleep-knotted hair, then was gone.

"I'd better let you go, sweetie pie. Call

me anytime. I miss you a lot."

"Me, too, Moomers. Uh, say hi to Ray," Fiona added uneasily. "Merry Xmas, all that."

"Sure will, hon. Same to your dad, Wanda Mae and Yoshi. I'll see you in ten more days, baby girl."

She'd forgotten to ask about Kirby. Funny, Fiona hadn't mentioned him either. Prudence stood up, went to the window, and, opening a crack in the blinds, watched Ray walk toward the barns. The skies were raw, weepy, oysterish. Prudence turned away, narrowed her gaze at the phone. She'd given Deleanor the number, had mailed it to her in the Christmas card she'd sent, but her mother hadn't called.

"Mom? It's me. I called to wish you a Merry Christmas."

"Why bother?"

Moments of silence passed. Prudence thought her mother had hung up.

"Oh, Merry What All to you, too. Sorry, but it just doesn't feel like Christmas." Her mother was crying.

"Oh my gosh, Mom, I'm so sorry." Prudence felt selfish and horrible. She tried to think of something. "Remember those Christmases you and Dad were in Europe,

South America, Vietnam? All those years you guys lived out of the country? I was the one missing you those Christmases. I'm so sorry. I just needed to get away, I really did. And I believed you, I honestly thought you were serious when you said this would be no different from any other day, that you didn't want to celebrate Christmas without Dad, that you were going to ignore the whole thing. In case you're wondering, I am getting lots of rest. I've been so exhausted lately."

"Well, good." Deleanor sniffed. "What's it like there?"

"It's OK. His parents have this little place they built themselves. Their horses are gorgeous. White Arabians. I've been helping rake out stalls and stuff. Cooking a little, too."

"What are you, their slave? Cooking, raking out stalls? What kind of holiday is that?"

"No, Mom. I want to. They said I could do whatever I wanted."

"How nice of them."

This was impossible.

"I went out for my walk this morning, and ever since, my throat feels like I swallowed a razor. There's some kind of Chinese flu going around . . . I may as well just lie down and wait for my ambulance."

"Mom, quit it. Has Fiona called?"

"No. Not a word from my only grand-child."

Prudence had forgotten to remind Fiona to call her grandmother. "You know how it is at Christmas, Mom, how the lines get all tied up. Everybody calling home."

"I wouldn't know." Silence.

. . . eight potato, nine potato, ten potato . . .

"Well, I'm sorry you're not feeling well."

"This could well be my last Christmas here on this earth. I don't see why you and Fiona couldn't have flown over and stayed here with me. Powell has her at his place every single year, and from what Fiona says, Christmas there is no great shakes."

"Are you going out to dinner or any-thing?"

"I'm going to Shirlee Wu's around noon. She's having a family get-together, and when she heard I was all alone, insisted I come over. Her older brother's visiting, he's a retired acupuncturist, Shirlee says he's thinking of moving here." Shirlee was Deleanor's yoga instructor. "You having a big Christmas shindig over there?"

"Not really." She didn't dare say she'd volunteered to make the whole Christmas dinner, turkey, mashed potatoes, pumpkin pie. "Ray's mother is just throwing together some leftovers." She lowered her voice. "She's not much of a cook, Mom. She's awful, in fact. Everything's fried to death."

For the first time in the conversation, Deleanor sounded pleased. "Well, that's hardly healthy."

"Pray that I live through the next few days."

"She probably uses canola oil. That stuff's an industrial lubricant."

"Worse. She uses lard. Snowcap lard."

"Oh my heavens, Prudence. Don't eat one bite."

"I'm trying not to, I really am."

"And make sure you get out for a walk every day, get fresh air. Breathing all that manure can't be good for you."

"I'll walk. Listen, I'd better go. I'll call again or you can call me."

"Oh, don't bother. I've got your father's favorite Christmas album on. *Christmas with Conniff.*" Deleanor started to cry again, so Prudence promised to be there next Christmas with Fiona. *If there is one,* Deleanor sniffed, blew her nose. *If there is another Christmas.*

There will be, Mom, I promise. There will be.

★ ★ ★

259

Done. Phone calls. Merry Christmases. Lies and half lies. Prudence felt flat as a pancake. She wandered through the quiet, empty house into the kitchen, found her own recently baked chocolate chip cookies, ate three in a row — no Ray pinching her stomach, no mother clucking over fat grams, no Fiona wrinkling up her nose at the dairy in the cookies, the butter and eggs, no one to make her feel unlovely, unhealthy or criminal. Christmas Day. Looking out the window, Prudence ate two more cookies to push the guilt over Deleanor and sadness over her father's death and Fiona's being unhappy further back, then caught her breath at the abrupt sight of six white horses galloping straight toward her, flying across the pale winter pasture, manes and tails streaming, stopping short at the fence, before turning to gallop far beyond the house, out of Prudence's sight. Under a stand of oak trees, in the same pasture, a second cluster of horses stood motionless, heavy, shade-dappled.

She let herself into Paradise Park, bringing her journal, thinking to write, but sat instead on the wooden swing, facing the untrafficked, tree-lined road, pushing herself a little on the swing, dropping her head forward, closing her eyes, holding to the ropes of the swing, letting the rounded toes of her workboots furrow the dirt. She was always so tired now. And always, she longed for him. (*All I want is this woman here, she's my Comanche captive.*) She could fault Ray, but not blame him. She had chosen this stagnant water, this dark silence and unmoving air. The binding rope was hers.

Then she heard him in the distance, calling, saw him standing in front of his parents' house, shading his eyes, calling for her. The wind whipped his long hair across his eyes as he pulled open the blue gate, motioning her toward him.

"What are you doing out here? You don't even have a jacket on. Come inside before you get sick or something. Besides, I'm hungry." He put his arm around her, turned her in the direction of the house. "Remember, happiness is what you do for meeee."

Empara had given them foil-wrapped empanadas, homemade pastries filled with fruit, to take on the road with them. Ray had mapped out every last mile to Phoenix; in Dallas, Fort Worth, Amarillo, they stopped at seven, eight, ten Half-Price bookstores, where Prudence bought a dozen or more books from the Erotica section. She had decided to focus on sexuality in her next class, have her students explore their sexual histories, write erotic memoirs, draw sexual maps of their bodies. Sexual anatomies. In large part because she wanted to understand what was happening, sexually, to her.

In cheap highway motels, rooms lit by outside mercury lights (*You know the rules, no clothes in the bed*), he would grab her breasts, tug hard, twist the nipples, fuck her from behind, never looking at her, never speaking except for an occasional gruff command. Partially aggressive, half idle, thrusting away as if bored, while she, on hands and knees, listened to a forensic detective on television named Chesterine, a large haunch of a woman with eyes like pocketknife slits, say every human being on earth carries unique *debris*, a map of *debris* on them, distinct as a fingerprint. When you are *intimate* with another person, you mix *debris*. Hair, skin flakes, fibers, fluids. On their way back to Phoenix, in half-star motels with names like Silver Saddle and Cactus Inn, Ray fucked her as he watched reenactments of murders, watched detectives search for clues in forest preserves, on bedroom carpets, in the backseats of cars, fucked her as prisoners were led shackled, and mainly unrepentant, to their deaths, fucked her — mixing *debris* — as he watched a death row inmate order his last meal on earth, a double cheeseburger, fries and a vanilla shake, fucked her as three lethal injections were administered, one to sedate, two to stop the lungs, three to stop the heart. On her hands and knees, her own heart stopping, she saw the execution chamber, the overlit theater with plastic aqua drapes, the audience behind bulletproof glass watching the murderer, strapped to his turquoise upholstered cross, hearing his final words, *Jesus, dear God, I'm coming home,* just as Ray came inside her, feeling little other than an appreciation for the fine congruence of events.

Though sometimes, like at the Silver Saddle Motel, number 12, the Annie Oakley Room (*The Peerless Lady Wing-Shot teamed up with Buffalo Bill Cody sometime during the 1880s at the St. James Hotel in Cimarron, New Mexico, to plan his Wild West Show, Buffalo Bill's Wild West Congress and Rough Riders of the World, where she would be one of his featured acts for the next seven-*

teen years, shooting, at thirty paces, dimes tossed in the air, shattering cigarettes held between the lips, slicing playing cards in half, the thin edge held toward her), Ray would pay her a sudden, fierce attention, asking had she come yet, an event, which, if it happened, was never the lovely pitch and swell she remembered from other lovers, even from Powell, but a hard-edged, localized sensation she would feel relieved at having accomplished, like work or a reprieve from work, proof presented not of her pleasure but of his masculinity. Dissatisfying as her sexual labor was, she craved more. At his parents' ranch, Ray had been a respectful, tender lover. Had that been Erroll? The farther west they traveled — she noticed this — the more emotionally cool and sexually rapacious he became.

A few hours outside the unimpressive town of Clovis, New Mexico, Ray stopped at a convenience store, started to walk inside to pay for gas, then hurried back. He stood outside Prudence's rolled-down window, his face blanched, stricken.

"My pillows."

264

"What?"

"My huggie pillows. I left them back at the motel."

"Well, do you think —"

"No. We have to go back. I have to go back. I can't leave my pillows."

"Couldn't we just call the motel and —"

"It's only three hours back. I have to, Prudence. You don't understand." Clearly, she thought, she didn't. Ray looked ready to cry.

As he drove, Ray explained, haltingly. "Erroll and me, those were our pillows when we were little, when we used to sleep together in one bed. I've never been without those pillows."

"Since . . ."

"Yeah. Since he died."

"How many years?"

He looked over at her. "Crazy, huh. You think I'm crazy."

"No, I don't."

He took the Kleenex Prudence handed him from the glove box, pulled off the road, turned off the engine, and talked without looking at her, staring out at the empty fields and rainless gray skies. "I knew my brother was going to die. I had always seen it, I didn't understand how I saw it, or how he was going to die, and I tried telling my mom when I was around ten, tried telling her about the nightmares I kept having where my brother was dead. The day Erroll died, I knew about the fight he'd gotten into at the rodeo the day before, I knew about his shoulder, that he'd been hurt. I thought about stopping him. Not letting him go. But I didn't. I didn't speak up, just watched him cross the yard, climb up into that big old Dodge truck he loved so much, and take off. I let him go, like something I couldn't change. That's what I told myself."

"Ray. He wouldn't have listened."

"No. He wouldn't have listened."

"So it's not your fault."

"No? Think about it. Erroll was my father's favorite. Smack Ray, hug Erroll. My mom's gone on vacation with Joe, my stepdad. For the first time she's not around. Erroll gets in a fight over a girl who's two-timing him. I've had premonitions for years, dreams he's going to die. Now he's wanting to go to the rodeo on Sunday, compete with a bad shoulder. I don't even tell him to watch out, be careful. To this day, my mom believes I didn't know about Erroll, going to the rodeo, hurt like that. 'Ray,' she says, 'you would have stopped your brother, if you'd known. You wouldn't have let him go like that, you would have made him stay home. You just didn't know.' I can't tell her the truth. I can't tell my own mother the truth. I can't tell anyone. Except you. I guess I just told you."

Tempe, Arizona

Ray pumped his right arm in an upward direction. "Crank up the volume, Prue, you're fading." She'd been reading *The Little Big Horn Remembered* for the past hour, reading out loud, as they drove toward Albuquerque. *They came upon us like a thunderbolt. We retreated until our men got all together, and then we charged upon them. I called to my men, "This is a good day to die; follow me." We massed our men, and that no man should fall back, every man whipped another man's horse and we rushed right upon them.* — Low Dog, Oglala . . . The lulling motion of the van, the morning sun on the side of her face, the rhythm of the words had more than once caused Prudence to drop asleep, head falling forward, then startle awake. Pulling herself out of the thick mud of sleep, she would refind her place on the page, read on. Ray loved her to read aloud; her voice mollified, soothed, softened him. For Prudence, it felt motherly, reminiscent of reading to Fiona when she was small. Everywhere our warriors began yelling: *"Hoka Hey! Hurry! Hurry!" Then we all went up and it got dark with dust and smoke. I could see warriors flying all around me like shadows and the noise was so loud it seemed quiet in there and the voices seemed to be on top of the clouds. It was like a bad dream.* — Standing Bear, Miniconjou Lakota . . .

From Albuquerque to Phoenix, Prudence finished reading *The Little Big Horn Remembered*, then started in on a craft book about how to clean and preserve feathers, a book so dull she swore she was reading aloud in her sleep. When they got home late that afternoon, Ray lugged in their things, including the buffalo robe he'd insisted on bringing back from Texas (*It'll keep you warm, sugar britches*), and Prudence's box of Half-Price books, before falling, face-up and groaning, across the bed.

"I have to sleep, I'm burnt, my little Mini-Wheat, my saucer of milk. Tomorrow, first thing, I've got to find a job. My paintings aren't selling, Prue. I'm broke."

She tried to imagine Ray clocking in somewhere, wearing a tie, a dishwasher's apron, a Wal-Mart vest, a man who had barely finished high school, could not use a computer or cash register, a proud man who was highly intelligent and highly dyslexic. She held a bundle of laundry in her arms. "What sort of job?"

"What I used to do in Houston. Model. No sex tonight, hon. I'm dead tired."

"That's fine." She tried not to sound relieved.

"What are you going to do now?"

"Start a load of laundry. Call Fiona at Kirby's, let her know I'm back, check messages, go through my mail, pay bills, finish unpacking."

"No you're not. You're not doing any of that. Come over here and lay down with me. You need rest. You're tired, too."

She dropped the laundry and lay down, Ray wrapping his arms tight around her, pulling her so close her face felt squashed, almost puddled, against his warm chest. So seductive, always draining her. She lay weak, unmoving, until he fell asleep, then slid out from under his arms, and went padding restlessly about the house, checking the mail, opening Christmas cards, rereading the note Fiona had propped up against the coffeemaker: *Welcome Home, Mooser . . . missed you! Guess what? Kirby gave me a diamond necklace (don't worry, it's small)!!!* Promise you won't scream when you see my hair! She played her voice messages, the last one a shocker from Bernice in Oklahoma City. She played it twice, and later for Ray, who would laugh out loud, slapping his knee with cynical delight. *Hey, you guys, two big pieces of news you might be interested in. Enrique went home right after Anadarko, and now he's a big soap opera star in Bolivia, a hotshot, riding around in limos, mobbed by women, and I can't tell if he's joking or not, but he says he's thinking of running for president. Then, last Friday, Sam and Holt skipped town with twelve thousand dollars, two big NPC donations that had just come in. They left a note saying they couldn't live a godly life in America anymore and were headed down to Panama to become missionaries for Christ. Turns out Holt's wanted in three states for embezzlement, and Sam served time for fraud back in Lubbock. It's all over the local news, the local papers, everywhere. The cops have already questioned me twice, and they've got Sam's boy staying in Oklahoma City with his grandma. Those two royally scammed everybody. Speaking of scamming, Ray, how are things with your white sugar mamma? I'm on legislature time here, just thought I'd pass along the news. Oh, and tell Prudence Sam never got around to*

271

putting her name on any NPC papers, so she's safe, no one'll be coming after her. There's a friend for you. Bye.

Pushing his profile up close to the medicine cabinet's mirror, Ray regarded his face, painstakingly, from every possible angle. Every morning now, he stood damp from his shower, stark naked, brushing his long black hair, flipping it this way and that, his motions charged with languid, complacent narcissism. Since he'd begun modeling, he'd started patting Prudence's drugstore wrinkle cream under his eyes. He sat on the toilet, Natural Man's Purest Black hair dye dripping down his temples, as Prudence, wearing plastic gloves, reread the directions. He shaved his testicles and trimmed his pubic hair. He agonized over every hair prematurely loosening from his head and falling to the bathroom floor, fretted over his belly, its slight overhang, like a small pot lid above his boyishly slender legs. He located his image in every sort of reflective surface, even car windows. Once, when he was showering, Prudence stood on the dry side of the shower door marveling at how erotically, how caressingly, he soaped his body, tilting back his head to rinse and shake his supple wet hair. She had seen his modeling portfolio, flicked through photographs of Ray in numberless Native outfits and poses, looking haughty, magnificent, breathtaking. He had modeled for a number of world famous western artists; one painting even hung in the Smithsonian. Ray had achieved a sidereal, minor sort of fame. With a tad more muscle and thicker chest, Prudence thought, he could easily be Native America's answer to Fabio. Even now, watching him pee into her toilet and leave the seat up, Prudence could picture Ray Chasing Hawk gracing the luxe, glittering cover of P. T. Parker's astonishing new romance, *Savage Heat*.

It had been her idea to check the bulletin board outside the community college's Art Department. Twenty-four hours later, Ray had called the Models Wanted ad, driven to the Scottsdale Art School for an interview, and found himself immediately employed. Exotic-looking, a fresh face, he was much requested, wearing his Comanche leggings and a bone choker, or bare-chested in an open black leather vest, tight jeans, black cowboy boots, his hair flowing around his coppery shoulders. He left her house looking gorgeous; he returned puffed as pastry, pleased and ever more vain. Women began calling Ray for advice on what sort of paints to use, what brand of canvas. Women called to meet him for coffee or lunch, asking to see his portfolios, his artwork. He began to disappear for hours at a time, helping his new friends get started in the art world, or trying to sell a painting to a potential client. Prudence pretended to stay calm but she imagined the other models, lush, careless female nudes, or worse, the art school's students, affluent middle-aged women, hobbyists, Sunday painters, taking him out for intimate lunches, or to their homes for private modeling sessions — her imagination became a torturous bed of nails, every nail a predatory woman. After weeks of such torment, she decided to ask Ray if she could stop by one of the Saturday morning sculpture classes. She chose Saturday because one of the students, Harleen, kept calling the house. When Prudence tried to ask about Harleen, Ray said she was an African-American ex-model, divorced from her husband, "a wonderful lady going through a hard time." Hard time, my blind eyeball, Prudence thought.

So on the chosen Saturday, over the egg, ham and potato omelette Prudence split between them, giving Ray the larger half, she asked, how do you do it? Sit in a pose for hours and hours, people gawking. Don't you get bored, or horribly stiff?

Mmm, he smiled across the table, mouth full, chewing. He loved her Big Ray Breakfasts. Since he'd moved in, Prudence had never cooked so many breakfasts in her life. She felt like a short-order cook. When he was still in Houston and calling her every other night, he'd told her Comanche men didn't cook, and that nothing in his world was sexier than watching a woman cook. So here she was, months into this cooking business, thick as oatmeal in her rumply pink fleece robe, feet sweating inside wool slippers, hair askew, wielding a spatula, plodding between sink and stove, a regular kitchen Wilma, while Ray sat at her table, cool, collected, handsome, his hair braided, wrapped in strips of red trade cloth, wearing a dark blue vest with brass tackwork, a crisp white shirt, tight faded jeans and a pair of elaborately beaded elk-hide moccasins he had made himself (another thing that caused women to swoon, his handmade moccasins, leggings, war shirts, buffalo headdress, bone and leather chokers). Except for the slight, purplish crescents under his eyes, Ray looked closer to nineteen than forty. Prudence, on the other hand, had begun to feel like a sitcom grandma. A worn-out Rubbermaid.

"Don't you get deathly bored? Or self-conscious? What in the world do you think about, sitting for hours like a rock? I'd faint, twitch, something." She scowled at the smudge of raspberry jam she'd gotten on the sleeve of her robe just as Ray reached across the table to pluck, with tender reprimand, a bit of egg crumb from her lip. Now she was a messy child as well as a walking pot holder. She'd been so busy cooking for Ray, thinking about Harleen, who had called again last night, leaving no message, only a digital name trace on the caller ID, she'd eaten absently, distractedly. Thus the bit of crumb.

"I dunno, Prudence. People ask me that all the time. I look at people. Study features. I've basically trained myself, over years of practice, not to blink or to move."

"The women there at the school must love the chance to paint such an exotic, handsome Indian man."

"What are you getting at, Prudence? Yes, I am a good model, yes, I'm sure they see me as exotic, yes, there are some bored, spoiled women there, yes, I sometimes flirt my ass off, especially if I think it might be a good business connection for my art, yes, some of them are attractive, I can't help that. This is old, I'm tired of it."

"What's old?" She tried sounding innocent. "Tired of what?"

"Your insecurity, jealousy, whatever it is that makes you not trust me."

Prudence got up, moved toward the refrigerator. "Did you take your vitamin?"

"No."

She set one vitamin, oval and beige, next to his glass of orange juice. He took it, swallowed it down with the juice.

"Thanks for breakfast, that was great, sweetie. That'll get me through a long morning. Today I find out if the school's new director will let models accept cash for having our photographs taken."

Ray sometimes came home with dollars in his pocket, tips from students taking photographs of him. According to recent rumor, the school's new director wasn't going to allow models to accept extra money.

"What if she says you can't take tips?"

"Then no one takes my picture. If I lose the job, so what? I'm exploited enough. Artists sell paintings of me for thousands of dollars, and I get ten bucks an hour. So I'm supposed to let rich students who pay plenty for art classes take pictures of me for nothing? No way."

Prudence saw his point. She also saw that if he was fired, he would have even less money than he had now. She liked it when he came home with an extra twenty dollars to treat her to a Mexican restaurant or to a dollar movie. The less money he had, the more she wound up paying for things and the more they argued. A friend at the school, a model named Jade, had told Ray he'd make twice as much money if he'd strip, pose nude, like she and her husband did. He'd be busy every day. Ray refused, though, and Prudence was secretly glad — one less thing to worry about, all those women seeing how gorgeous he was naked. And Prudence wasn't worried about Jade's calling the house, about Ray's frequent lunches with her. After all, she was married. The husband's name was Fred. Then one day Ray mentioned he had gone over to Jade's new place to help her move some things. "Oh?" Prudence had asked. "Did they buy a new house?"

"No," Ray answered casually, "she and Fred have separated. She's got her own place, a little studio near the school."

"Have you been there?"

"Yeah, a couple of times. She wanted my advice on decorating and stuff."

Ray had described Jade as "funny, mannish and sun-damaged." But Prudence didn't trust Ray's cagey descriptions . . . married, old, round, stout, fat, short, wrinkled, big-rumped, pear-shaped, sun-damaged, jowly, all exaggerated negatives calculated to ward off her jealousy. On the rare occasions Prudence met any of these women, his description of them, even stretched thin as gum, rarely fit. I didn't say they weren't attractive, he would reply to her observation that the women she saw versus Ray's descriptions of them were at a wide variance. She decided now was the moment to ask.

"Ray, would it be OK if I stopped by your class today, just for a couple of minutes? I'm thinking of adding drawing to my own class this semester, and if I dropped by the studio, I could get a better idea of how an art class works. I'd just sit quietly in the back, take a few notes, and then leave."

"Sure, that's fine. That'd be nice. Are you coming with me now, or stopping by later?"

She gestured to her robe and slippers, the dirty frying pan she was carrying to the sink.

He slipped behind her, grabbed at her little sog of belly, rolled it around. Her mommy pouch, he called it. He nuzzled her neck.

"You know, you'd make a great model, Prune. You've got an unusual look. They're not looking for runway types so much as an original look." Gallantly, he lifted the frying pan from her hand. "Here, let me do that, then I've got to go. And to answer your first question, how do I do it, sit there for hours, it kind of depends on the instructor — some classes, nobody talks, everyone holds their paintbrush just so, it's deadly serious and deadly dull. Other classes are fun, everybody talking, joking around, makes the time go by faster. Here's your pan, clean as a whistle." He gave her a kiss on the forehead and was gone, out the garage door. Seconds later, he was back, a sheepish look on his handsome face.

"Do you have a coupla extra dollars I could borrow, sweetie? My gas tank's empty."

She padded over to her purse, rummaged out a twenty.

A second kiss, this one, light, near the lips. "Thanks, babe." The door closed. Gone.

Prudence stood next to her purse holding her emptied wallet, wondering how often he forgot to repay her, how often she didn't bother to ask for her money back, five dollars, ten, not wanting to sound greedy or petty? After all, he had cut the lawn, trimmed the hedges, front and back. A month ago. Still. Hadn't she told him in the beginning that she believed in him as an artist, wanted to give him a chance to make it? Why? he asked. What did she want in return? Nothing, she'd insisted. Six months later, to say she still wanted nothing was a lie.

In the shower, Prudence stood under the lukewarm spray of water (Ray had used up the hot) staring at a long swirl of black hair pasted to the white tile wall, at gray stains near the drain from his Natural Man hair dye. She was trying to remember what it had been like, months ago, when her bed, her bathroom, her wallet, her car keys, her days and nights, had been hers, hers alone.

The Scottsdale Art School, a 1920s Spanish mission–style building, L-shaped, with a red-tiled roof, sat on a huge corner lot in the Scottsdale arts district, amid velvety green manicured lawns and sweeping, graceful rows of palm trees. Internationally renowned artists, booked years in advance, flew in for short residencies; the parking lot glittered with Mercedes, Lexuses, Jaguars and SUVs, the drivers mostly women, women of leisure, women with time on their hands, women of affluence toying with art, with artists; it did not take much for Prudence to imagine at least one of them toying with Ray, who sat posed, exotic and underpaid, in their aesthetically overstimulated midst.

Nosing her little rust-spotted Nash between a gold Lexus and a hearse-sized Cadillac, Prudence, armed with a red spiral notebook and pencil, entered the art school, walking down a spacious tiled corridor where student still lifes, portraits and desert landscapes hung crowded along a white wall opposite a wall of floor-to-ceiling windows. She slipped into the sculpting studio, hoping to be inconspicuous, but Ray, elevated on his model's platform, spotted her, and motioned to a tall, rangy woman in a white butcher's apron who turned, waved her right arm at Prudence like a windshield wiper, a metal sculpting implement in her hand.

"Howdy! You must be Ray's friend. I'm Susan, the instructor. C'mon in. Feel free to walk around, ask questions. Don't be shy."

Prudence managed to wave her own arm back and forth a little before dropping into a tan metal chair at the back of the room, cracking open her notebook and pretending to sketch out the dimensions and placement of people and objects in the room. Peeking up from her clumsy rendering of a sink and series of wall cabinets, she saw Ray, off his model's perch, standing close beside an elegant-looking African-American woman. When he rested his hand on the woman's sleeveless (bare) shoulder, Prudence's pencil point snapped off.

"Word's out you're a teacher." A man in a green-and-black-checkered lumberjack shirt blocked her view, extending a chunky, clay-speckled hand. "Charles."

"Prudence. Yes, I'm doing a bit of research for one of my classes."

"Fire away, I'll do my best. My wife is the real artist in the family, I tag along for the ride."

Prudence leaned to one side, trying to see around Charles' checkerboard girth. Harleen — that had to be Harleen — had exited the studio with Ray. Prudence's face blazed, her body hummed wildly as a diminutive, attractive woman wearing oversized tortoiseshell glasses, her body lost inside a loosely tied clay-smeared apron, came up to her. This turned out to be Charles' wife, Yvette.

"Ray's an absolutely divine model. We all adore him. And he's so knowledgeable about his culture. Is he a student of yours?"

"No. Ray lives with me."

"Really?" Yvette seemed mildly stunned. Silently, they both watched Charles lumber off in the direction of an opened box of Dunkin' Donuts.

"Yes, really." Prudence set the record straight. "We've been living together since we met seven months ago."

"How odd," murmured Yvette. "He never said a word. Well, I've got to get back to my work. I'm sorry, your name is?"

"Prudence. Prudence Parker."

"What an old-fashioned name! So Puritan. Well, Prudence, as my husband said, feel free to ask anything you like. We all feel honored to have someone like Ray modeling for us."

Ask anything you like? Prudence wanted to ask Yvette if she was the woman who kept calling the house and hanging up without leaving any message. She wanted to ask Ray why he hadn't told anyone about her. How did he present himself?

Bachelor? Man about town? Unattached? Available? Who was she, then? A prim, old-fashioned Puritan who stood around flipping eggs?

Prudence scrabbled around in the scratchy bowels of her purse until she came upon a novelty pen, a gift from a student, its purple ink mixed with bits of glitter to mock her dour mood. Ray was back on his model's stand, his back to Prudence, still talking to Harleen (what a name — darling spliced with harlot). As if reading her thoughts, Ray spun on his model's wheel, threw her a dazzling wink, a rare, beatific smile. Prudence frowned, ducked her head, feigned sketching. Her wounded, tender imagination had turned livid. Harleen was clearly smitten, Yvette's perplexity a dead giveaway. *Horrible. Horribilus. Horribilo.* Prudence soothed herself with fake conjugations. A childhood habit. *Meato, Meati, Meathead.*

Setting the Styrofoam cup of boiled bitter coffee, an offering from Charles along with a stale Bismark, beneath her chair, she spent the next ten minutes taking notes, drawing purple diagrams, mastering her seizure of jealousy with the dry, measured discipline of observation.

Studio: a rectangular (Charles guesstimated seventy by thirty), white linoleum flooring, oversized Palladian windows with blinds along the west wall, the opposite east wall taken up with large square mirrors. Narrow, icy beds of fluorescent light overhead. In one corner, a capacious moth green sink and counter with a clay-spattered microwave. In the opposite corner, a slack-mouthed plastic bag full of gray clay, dumped beside a human skeleton, its jaundiced, dejected-looking bones dangling from a metal stand. *Does all human drama begin with flesh and end with a skeleton?* Directly behind Prudence, a flat green blackboard. To her left, corralled into a third corner, a gaggle of spindle-legged easels. In the middle of the room, two model stands, square boxes, each with black iron piping along one side. In the center of each stand, an armchair sat on a wooden disk, enabling the models to spin in any direction. The sculpting students, eight women and two men, all wearing white aprons, sat at small adjustable work platforms, laboring with rapt intensity, spinning their gray busts, ten variants of Ray's head emerging, knob-like, from ashen lumps of clay. Yvette waved Prudence over, explaining as she rethumbed one of Ray's ears, that this particular clay was water-based, and to keep it moist, malleable, students took their busts home, wrapped in damp towels or T-shirts. Yvette's sculpting table held a plastic spray bottle and a scattering of sculpting tools that reminded Prudence of dental implements, except these were gunked up with clay. When Prudence touched it, Yvette's bust felt cool, fleshy, plantlike; the profile looked remarkably like Ray's. While Charles blodgered about the room, jovial, ignoring the slick knob of clay on his stand, a gloomy, unworked shape rife with failed possibilities, Prudence watched Yvette deftly pinch and smudge with agile thumbs and fingers . . . *The clay is forgiving, thank god. I don't know about the others, but for me the hardest part is learning to think three-dimensionally.* As Yvette spun her platform to inspect Ray's opposite ear, the damp head wobbled dangerously. Across the room, Yvette's subject sat motionless and shirtless, a bone and leather choker around his neck, a coyote headdress on his head, its dry, bristled snout and cavernous eye sockets pointing forward, its limp pelt and lifeless legs draped against his satin-smooth brown back.

"I feel so sorry for that animal," Yvette whispered. "To think it once ran wild and free."

An exotic zoo of perished wildlife existed in Prudence's house now, whole skins and hides of elk, buffalo, otter, beaver, deer, wolf, coyote, snake, ermine, bones and feathers of crow, owl, hawk, eagle. Skins, skulls, beaks, bones.

Surveying this gray botany, this bulbous flora of Ray-heads dotting the studio, Prudence thought of the hundreds of likenesses of Ray Chasing Hawk, paintings, busts, photographs, calendars, hung on walls in galleries, government buildings, banks, auto dealerships and ordinary homes, perhaps even tucked away in closets.

"What do you think?" Ray came up behind her. He had removed his headdress, leaving a faint red line across his forehead.

"You're right," she whispered. "They do sculpt themselves."

"What'd I tell you? Same thing with portraits. It's supposed to be me, but if you look closely, they're remaking themselves. Want to see one of the painting studios?"

Waiting for Ray to collect his things, Prudence overheard the instructor, Susan, talking to Harleen about progesterone, recommending a book called *What Your Mother May Not Have Told You About Menopause*. Harleen looked older than she had appeared from across the room. She looked tired and sweet-natured. She looked as if she had health problems. Prudence felt shamed over her previous jealousy, her wild assumptions. Maybe Ray was right. He admitted to being secretive, but did that mean he was dishonest? Maybe she was ruining everything, like he said she was, with her insecurity, her jealousy. But why would a man be secretive if he didn't have something to hide? Her moment of shame turned itself into a tiny, drilling headache.

The unlit painting studio was a claustrophobic room, heavily curtained, the model's stand was a square black dais with a plain wooden chair. A single panel of black velvet hung behind the chair, a portable electric heater sat on the floor. Ten or so easels, heron-legged and paint-spattered, stood about the room. The room felt chilly, shadowy, faintly erotic. Prudence imagined a female model riding the chair backward, head thrown back, neck arched and exposed, the creamy white expanse of her flesh startling against the black drape. Most of the models, Ray had told her, walked casually around the school, smoking cigarettes, wearing nothing but lightly cinched terry robes. They were, he said, rarely beautiful or perfectly shaped.

More often, they had unusual body types or markings, like the ex-stripper with hairy armpits, or the biker with tattoos mapping her body, or the seventy-year-old grandmother who had given birth five times, a heavily petaled artichoke of a woman, or like his friend Jade, breastless, reed-thin, lithe. She had called last night, Prudence had heard Ray laughing, talking in those same low, intimate tones she remembered from his long-distance calls to her months ago. Her jealousy, a ravenous flea, hopped from Harleen to Jade.

"Jade around, Ray? Maybe the three of us could get some lunch."

His friend was in her office, working up monthly model schedules. Whittled thin as a pencil, with razor-cropped black hair, puckish features and awkward, jerky movements, Jade was dressed in baggy khakis and a man's white broadcloth shirt, cell phone singing in her loose pants pocket (*Sorry, just Tom the contractor calling, about to tear down a wall in my new apartment*). She had recently had liposuction done around her waist, and had an upcoming appointment to get the wrinkles around her eyes lasered. Jade told them this as they walked down the sidewalk. Ray, silent, kept his dark glasses on even in the Mexican restaurant, which had a seafood motif, fishing nets with glass balls, a stuffed silver-blue marlin nailed to the wall — decor left over from the previous restaurant.

Prudence ordered nachos with vegetarian refried beans.

"A bean is a vegetable. How do you order a vegetarian bean?" Ray sounded irritated.

"A bean is not, technically, a vegetable." Jade blew a stream of cigarette smoke at him. "A bean is a legume. And refried beans are usually made with lard. Vegetarian means no lard."

"Lard? I didn't need to know that." Ray's face pinched up in disgust.

"Yeah, well, that's why I'm thin. Food makes me sick. I'll have a martini, dry, please, with a double twist of lemon."

Their food arrived. Prudence stared down at the bright yellow sombrero-shaped platter, poking at her vegetarian bean nachos while Jade complained about the latest screwup in the model schedule, then started in on her failing marriage, her rapid-eye therapy, a best-selling book she was reading on how to become a surrendered wife, how the author had been interviewed on *20/20* the night before. Her own

291

marriage, the author claimed, had been a mess. Desperate to save it, she had begun saying yes, *cheerfully,* to everything her husband did, whatever he wanted, surrendering her will, her opinion, her sexual desire, her taste in clothes, yes, even her paycheck, to her husband (and what a tubby walrus he was, Jade snorted). Within two weeks their marriage shot straight off the rocks — they were like newlyweds again, everything revived in that department. Zealous to impart her method to a world of miserable wives, the woman had dashed off a simple how-to book that was selling like hotcakes. Wives who had formerly nagged, rolled their eyes and reminded their husbands for the umpteenth time to pick up their socks from the floor and a quart of milk at the store (no, not that milk, dummy, the other kind, the kind we always drink, haven't you even noticed *that,* what sort of moron are you? etc.), these wives were advised to reverse tactics; act meek, submissive, grateful and demure — restoring their husbands to lost power and potency. Ray said it's true, this liberation shit's wrecked everything, women don't behave like ladies anymore, they all wear men's pants underneath their damn dresses.

"Tell you what. I'm ready to try anything to save my marriage. Fred is handsome, childlike, vain, and I love him to pieces. What do you think, Prudence?"

Prudence's mouth was mushy with bean dip. "About?"

"Surrendering to your husband. I know you don't have one. I mean the concept."

Ray answered for her. "She thinks it's a heap of cowdoody. And Prudence hates my two biggest male fantasies."

Prudence wiped her mouth, curious. "What are those?"

"Finding a woman who knows how to obey, and having sex with two women at once." He shrugged. "I'm no more original than most guys. I just have the balls to be honest."

"Aha, I knew it." Jade winked at Prudence. "Beneath that exotic, smoldering Comanche exterior, we find one more hard-boiled, hee-haw Texas redneck! She" — Jade nodded at Prudence — "is a saint to put up with you."

Saint, Prudence thought. Try fool.

Ray laughed. "I said I was honest. I never claimed to be nice."

Were she forced to pinpoint the origin of her snooping, Prudence would have to say it had started in her father's upstairs "den," that mysteriously male space opposite little Prudence's bedroom, where as a bored, inquisitive, perpetually anxious child, she would sneak, riffle through boxes, files, desk drawers, sleuth, uncover aspects of Walter Parker, the mysterious *man* she might not otherwise have known. College poetry, a deck of playing cards, pictures of half-naked women, various boyhood mementos. Not much, boiled down, but naughty enough to thrill and torture little Prudence with the notion that there were secrets locked away inside men, and unless you snooped, peeked, how could you begin to know the other, hidden dimensions of the man? Didn't the full measure of a man lie in what he kept hidden? Either you loved him more because of what you found, or you unveiled a devious monster and could, in the nick of time, spare yourself. Prudence was after ManTruth, and this justified her snooping, engaging in low acts for a higher good.

Powell, for instance. A week after meeting him and two days after sleeping with him, Prudence sneaked his journal from under his flat, dirty pillow and hastily scanned its yucky, rumpled pages, pouncing on an overwrought description of a woman named Brandi, her incredible beauty, his despair over Brandi's ever noticing a poor sod like himself, etc. Stepping out of the shower, Powell had caught Prudence, and from that day forward, through all ten years of their marriage, he never wrote another incriminating thought for his wife to find. She was beautiful too, Powell assured Prudence at the exhausted end of their first fight over Brandi, but in a different way. Why did men always say Prudence was beautiful, but in a different way? Maddening, weaselly praise that could mean anything. Ten years into the kind of marriage she figured was as good/bad as anybody else's, she'd found (not snooping this time, just cleaning house) a handwritten love poem written to someone Not Prudence. Someone blond, perpetually smiling. This turned out to be Wanda Mae, Powell's current wife.

Uncovering the secret lives of men had begun with her father, with Walter, and the sorry truth was: Prudence *always* found things. Betrayals. If she had never stumbled across anything, the story might be different, the urge to snoop might have withered, like an appendix, from sheer uselessness. The cost of snooping was high; ingesting filched particles of evidence

made her furious, crabby and snappish —
and secret trespass denied honest confrontation. She was left to fume, to construct
paranoid scenarios in the grim theater of
her imagination. But if she didn't snoop,
she might walk around hobbled, enfeebled,
lied to. Was she doing one thing Ray
couldn't know about? No. She was boring
as a brick, predictable as the Christian and
Roman calendars combined. Maybe that
was her problem. Should she date other
men, sneak about? Date whom? The guy
she'd met once in the airport while waiting
for Fiona, a packaging manufacturer, bald,
tubby and softhearted? She'd accepted his
business card, come home, flicked it in the
trash. A little too bald and far too nice.

Times when she couldn't stand Ray anymore, when she saw right through him,
plain as day, when he began to look
scrawny and old, he turned seductive, oily,
attentive, reeling her, like some great stu-
pefied fish, right back in. Around the
house, he thought nothing of wearing
baggy gray shorts, funny black nylon slippers, his hair clipped up in one of Prudence's tortoise claws, a yellow bandanna
folded around his forehead, a goofy, slipping crown. But heading out to the art
school, or to meet someone, he dressed in

elegant black, dropped his gleaming hair down, grew some electric, sensual aura. Prudence had seen for herself how women tried not to gape, their mouths opening like grouper fish, *You're so beautiful,* scribbling home numbers on the backs of business cards. Ray had a collection of such business cards, the real business on the back. In the middle of the night, with Ray asleep, Prudence would sometimes shuffle through them, stare at the numbers, scrutinize the handwriting, Kirsten, Carlissa, Gaia, Susan, Victoria, Tara, Heidi. Who were all these women, calling, leaving their numbers? Ray spoke to them in such low, intimate tones, she could hardly make out what he was saying. Edging barefoot up to the kitchen door, hyperalert, ears straining like pink teacups off the sides of her head — *I love you, too, but I know my place. We'll have one of our little talks soon. You're jealous? Why? When I get over there, want to hang together?* She heard him describe places *they* had driven to — in her car! — using her gas! — trips Prudence had paid for, talking as though he traveled solo, free as a brightly plumaged male bird. He told each one what he wanted her to know, and they kept calling. One morning he confronted Prudence, in her monk's bathrobe, ear to the door. Furious, he began to wait until she was in the shower or out of the house to call the women, whoever they were, back.

Another night, after he'd caught Prudence sleuthing about in his van at 2 a.m., his anger lasted two weeks, two long, sex-deprived weeks when he slept in his underpants, his back to her, until one night, when she was sound asleep, he dived on top of her, bit her neck, and they clung to one another, gasping and desperate. Was this love? The next morning, they were sweet and halting, with Prudence promising not to snoop, and Ray promising never to lose his temper ever again. They would, they promised, touching noses, nuzzling like ponies, be very, very good.

February. Pink, heart-shaped, raining valentines, the month of February found Prudence rustling through his things in the middle of the night, drawn especially to his multipocketed black wallet and the many-zippered black canvas bag he called his portfolio. Here she seized upon many possible clues, pizza receipts, movie stubs, addresses, directions to homes, a handful of photographs of women in sexy outfits and seductive poses, one in a Renaissance getup, a cone of rigid emerald cloth on her head, long, fluffy red ringlets, hands primly clasped, an Effanbee doll in the fairy tale series Prudence used to buy Fiona each Christmas, but an old doll, eerie, wrinkly and overeager-looking. Prudence plucked damning evidence out of the air, out of the water, and more successfully, out of the trash barrel and recycling bin, a vague confetti of half proofs. Of what? Of a cagey life? Ray was hygienically scrupled, so she doubted he slept with any of these women, but he was ethically unprincipled, compelled to hide their existence from her. This year's February, neither heart-shaped nor sweet, this sixth month of Ray's living with Prudence, died in an ugly showdown. On a Friday evening, with Ray beading a moccasin and refusing to look at her, sitting at his worktable, stabbing beads into deerskin with methodical accuracy, punishing her latest transgression with cold silence (hours earlier, he had caught her searching through his jean pockets in the closet), Prudence, since he refused to hear her miserable, fabricated explanation, summoned up a full-scale theatrical faint, toppling, eyes rolled back, onto the unvacuumed, mushroom- colored carpet near his feet. Trick fainting was a technique she had been taught in a college acting class but never practiced, so the result was phony and mortifying. She lay, head near his tennis shoe, eyes squeezed shut. He didn't even laugh. *That's it,* he said, putting down his needle and sinew thread, and stepping over her prone form. *I've had it with your crazy, boring emotions, with your suspicions and accusations, with being blamed for things I've never done. Yes, I have a secret life. Yes, I only tell you what you need to know, what I think you can handle. I have never done a thing to hurt you, there is no "other woman" like you seem to think there is, I haven't had sex with another woman like you seem to think I have, though yes, my friends are mostly women, it's always been that way, I don't know why, so yes, I'm sick of your stupid jealousy, your little girl's insecurity. You've pushed me to where I don't care anymore. I'm leaving. I'm getting out of here.* And picking up his black canvas portfolio bag, the very bag Prudence had rifled through the night before, locating three new phone numbers and addresses (Kim, Dawn, Lori), he did just that. Got into his van, where she had recently found, under the driver's seat, two movie stubs and a receipt for two lunches, buzzed open the garage door with her electric opener, and drove off.

Still on the floor, Prudence didn't move.

She lay awhile, then finally sat up, picking moccasin beads off her cheek, three orange and one blue. She had no trust in him, he had no trust in her. Yet lodged like a chip of granite, a splinter of flint, something still pulsed in the vicinity of her chest, something sore and aching, a sensation that felt, peculiarly, like love.

Opening the front door, answering the bell, Prudence saw a man in a brown shirt and brown shorts, earphones on, humming the Bee Gees' "Tragedy" song, and holding a package from New York. The galley pages of *Savage Heat*, hers to proofread and send back. While holding the UPS man's clipboard and signing her name, Prudence heard the phone ring. She closed the front door, heard a feminine, slightly slurred female voice. *Ray, it's Eela, how are ya? Listen, got your call, I'd love to get together, but only for coffee and only during the day — I'm newly married, wasn't sure you knew that. Call if you'd still like to get together, though. Bye now. Have a great day!*

Eela! Who was that? Clutching her *Savage Passion* manuscript, Prudence, as dramatic and despairing as her own nineteenth-century heroine, Rebeccah, burst into a noisy, graceless torrent of tears.

★ ★ ★

They sat in Trish's car, dolled up in tight black minidresses, Prudence's filched from Fiona's closet, Trish's her own, from Nordstrom's.

"Nervous?"

"Kind of."

"Trish, look. Over by that Dumpster."

"Mattresses!"

"*Used* mattresses. Just tossed out the windows and piled on top of one another."

"Like a trashed wedding cake."

"Remember the ad — *look for our blue light?* Well, there it is."

"We're in the blue-light district."

"What's our code again? If things get weird?"

"Professora. If either one of us says professora, we're out of there."

"Not many cars."

"Still early. Not even nine o'clock."

"Tell me one of your potato jokes."

"OK. What do you call potatoes that wear glasses?"

"Seeing-eye potatoes?"

"Spec-taters."

"That is so completely dumb, I love it. Look, a guy, going in by himself . . ."

"White shoes, he's wearing marshmallow shoes! What do you call potatoes three and under?"

"Tater-tots?"

"Right. Let's go."

"What's the code again?"

"Professora."

Hours earlier, before they had pulled into the parking lot of a sex club in downtown Phoenix, Prudence, sobbing, had called Trish.

"Ray's gone. He drove off. We had this huge fight. Huge."

"Worse than that time you hurled one of his paintings onto the lawn?"

"Much worse. I fainted at his feet. I was trying to get his attention."

"He'll be back. The man has no money, where would he go? Hey, want to go out? It's Friday night."

"Dinner?"

"No. All we'd do is sit and analyze Ray. Let's do something wild."

"Like what?"

"I don't know. What's something we would never normally do?"

Which is how they wound up inside Bare Encounters, a sex club, perched on chrome barstools, sipping bottled water and listening to the confessions of a Lutheran counselor in white suede shoes.

Minutes before, they had been met at the entrance by a gruff slab in her seventies, gray hair in a greasy, slipping bun, rocking a rubber stamp (*Ladies Free*) across the backs of their hands. Trish asked if it would be possible to get some kind of tour, as this was their first time, while Prudence stared at a frieze of black rental whips arranged above the woman's head. "Yaller!" the woman bellowed to a second woman, squat as a gourd, hair in a coarse brown shingle, plodding out from a back room. "Yaller, throw these two a tour, will you?"

Yaller insisted on the superiority of Bare Encounters compared to the other two local, competing clubs. "Here we have our own mini-boutique. There's a strict no-pants rule for the ladies, so we have a rack of little dresses, real cheap, nothing over ten dollars. That way, if a woman shows up in jeans or slacks, she can purchase one of these dresses on the spot, change, and head right on in. Our Spa Room's real popular." Prudence and Trish peered into a steamy, heavily mirrored room, ajumble with dark green plastic palms (pothos, bamboo, dieffenbachia) and a marbleized, sunken double Jacuzzi. The unoccupied room had all the ambience of a dank, neglected herpetarium. "It's nothing to see ten or fifteen folks squeezing in, naked as jaybirds, having fun, if you know what I mean. You girls say this is your first time?"

"We're here to look around. You know, curious."

"Oh, you'll love it, I guarantee you that. Things really heat up as the night goes on. Attractive as you two are, you'll be beating the guys off with sticks. Don't be afraid to get aggressive, let the men know you're not interested, they'll back off. We have bouncers, so there's no trouble in that direction."

They traipsed behind Yaller as she whisked them through a gloomily lit buffet area, its purple carpet littered with morts of lettuce and cheese shreds, its cloth-covered tables dotted with platters of limp celery and carrot sticks, rubbery cheese cubes with dry, shrinking edges, flat tiles of saltine crackers and a row of brushed-aluminum tubs stocked with mini-cans of apple and orange juice, sodas and plastic bottles of water, lying belly up, labels peeling, in sloshy, melting ice. "We allow no alcohol on the premises; so if somebody wants a drink, we tell them to get with a bottle in the parking lot." They walked past a stage with a mirrored floor and three brass dance poles. Nearby, angled from a ceiling corner like a small shoplifting monitor was a TV, looping a soundless video of a gaunt, pie-eyed woman giving rote, uninspired blow jobs to a series of sprung-kneed, faceless men. Yaller winged open a door so Prudence and Trish could step through to a cement patio narrow as an aisle, backed by a stockade fence made of thick pointed posts, like a row of ominous dark pencils. "Out here gets completely overrun with folks doing their thing," Yaller boasted, ushering them past a large outdoor Jacuzzi, "our second most popular spot." Back inside, they dutifully trailed Yaller's gourd-like rump up a dingy flight of red-carpeted stairs. "Here's the Orgy Room. You girls go on, take a peek through our spectator window. This place gets pret-ty hairy, it's nothing to see thirty, forty folks in here all at one time, butt naked and bouncing off the walls." Prudence pressed one eye against the glass peephole. A gigantic bed, round as an Olympic exercise trampoline, dark aqua walls, fish-tank lighting. "Better let Humberto through. *Bwaynos nacho,* Humberto." A good-looking, sullen kid trundled an empty, industrial-sized laundry cart past them. "Sheets are changed and washed after each bare encounter, we take pride in everything's being completely sanitary." On the heels of Humberto rolling by with his laundry cart, a statuesque black man passed by, naked, his gait serene and unhurried. "Leonard's harmless, he's here every night, rain or shine, walks around, takes a shower, that's it. A place like this attracts its 'regulars,' the guys with fetishes, oddball turn-ons. If they're harmless, we let 'em stay. Here's our Couples Only Room, same peephole arrangement, and over across the hall, our Swinging Couples Room." Yaller led them through a kind of anteroom where seven men, fully dressed and silent, sat on twin black vinyl couches. Ignoring them, Trish inquired about fire safety.

"Safest place for a gal to be on a Saturday night. We've got three bouncers, Jimbo, Jumbo and Wags, making sure nobody gets away with anything and everybody has fun. People come here to have a good time, and it's our business to make sure they do just that."

"What time does it start getting . . . busy?"

"Midnight, one o'clock. People come here after shows, movies, other parties, so it's real crazy by two or so. Fridays, Saturdays, we get the youngsters, the college crowd. If you don't mind my asking, what do you gals do?"

Trish waved one impeccably groomed hand. "Manicurists."

"Well, you're both real pretty and dressed nice, so you'll be fresh meat in the lion's den. We're open till four a.m., all the food you can eat, all the fun you can have. I've seen everything you can possibly imagine, there's not a thing left in this world that shocks me, I've seen it all and then some."

They followed Yaller's broad, gold-smocked back downstairs. Sitting by the mirrored stage, two young women, amply fleshed and pasty white, wearing matching fuchsia negligees, twirled idly in club chairs, sipping Cokes. Lurking in his own chair behind them, neck craned up to the nearest TV, a miniature mustachioed man in checkered pants sat rub-a-dubbing the tiny bump of his crotch. Unnerved, Trish and Prudence hustled into the buffet area, emerging moments later, with two water bottles. Settling themselves at one of a dozen or so little round bar tables, they watched the white-shoed man glide toward them with a soft, predatory approach. He introduced himself as Lew Sagness, Lutheran family counselor by day, sex addict by night. Nudging one another under the table, Prudence and Trish carried on their conversation, ignoring Lew, perched on the stool between them.

"Their names are mostly Hispanic. Silvas, Romero, Mendoza."

"So?"

"Dark eyes, dark hair? That's what he likes."

"Not necessarily. Look at you."

"Raquel Welch? Demi Moore? Jackie Kennedy? His goddesses? I'm so far from that, it's pathetic."

Lew, who had made a second effort to ingratiate himself by presenting each of them with a can of ginger ale and packet of peanuts, turned to Prudence. "Young lady, you are the spitting image of that movie star, what's her name, she was in that terrible, terrible movie, can't think of the name. Anyway, you could be her sister. Heather Locklear. That's it. Heather Locklear. Sure you girls aren't up for a little experimenting? I can show you a good time, absolutely no pressure, it'll be great."

"No, we are not interested. You may sit with us, if you want. You may eavesdrop. That's all." Prudence felt irritated by this slimy so-called Lutheran creeping about in dorky white shoes. She felt scornful of his business card, which she now used as a coaster.

"Jeez. You might look like Heather Locklear, but you sure sound like a school-teacher."

Prudence didn't answer. She was busy watching an athletic-looking woman in a silver spandex bodysuit hook one muscled thigh around the center brass pole, arch backward and begin to writhe like a sinuous, glittering serpent. Twirling languidly in their club chairs, the two hefty girls in transparent fuchsia nighties sipped their drinks, as the woman stripped off her bodysuit and entwined herself, nude, around the shiny pole. Prudence resumed talking.

"He compartmentalizes. The man totally loves boxes. The way most guys watch sports or have a hobby like woodworking or golf, Ray moves things from one box to another. Constantly."

"Obsessive-compulsive."

"In and out of boxes, in and out of boxes. We'll be doing errands, ordinary stuff at some little mall, and he just has to stop behind Sweet Tomatoes or Outback Steakhouse to check if they have any of those black rubber boxes, those ugly milk carton things? He already has at least twenty stacked up in the backyard. You know those bathtub-sized plastic bins and tubs they sell at Kmart? He has those, too. His van is a big metal box on wheels. I swear, if you opened up Ray's head, you'd find one big tackle box inside."

"At least he's tidy, Prue. Most men are slobs."

"And he's constantly paring back, re-arranging. I could wind him up, point him toward a mess, and in ten minutes he'd have everything sorted, stacked, organized or tossed out. The man is a human sorter."

"Want to go back upstairs?" In order to ditch white-footed Lew, staring without invitation or ceremony into her cleavage, Trish meaningfully bumped Prudence's ankle under the table. "Maybe we'll see something."

"You girls let me know if you change your minds. I'm going nowhere." Lew toasted them with his can of ginger ale.

"Thanks, but no thanks," Trish muttered as they edged their way past the mirrored stage, the naked woman, like a Velcroed monkey, still clinging upside down to her pole.

As they headed upstairs, Trish leading, Prudence close behind, two swarthy men in white shirts and dark pants rose from their chairs and followed, gaining three stairs, then two, then one behind Prudence, who now heard a lust-thickened whisper near her left ear, "You two ready for action?"

"Nope," Prudence snapped. "We're schoolteachers." The two men melted back into the shadows.

Almost immediately, they came upon Leonard navigating the dim-lit hall with a steely flagpole erection, followed by the laundry cart trundling past, stacked perilously high with clean folded sheets, a poker-faced Humberto at its burdened helm. In the Swinging Couples Room, two sets of couples sat perched on the edge of a floral-patterned sofa, boygirlboygirl, dressed like Mormons in dark suits, plain ties and severely tailored party dresses. A rattan swing, like a gigantic plant basket, dangled in one corner of the room next to a king-size bed with a floral trapunto bedspread and seventies-style teakwood headboard.

"Hi," Trish spoke from the doorway. "You guys gonna do anything?"

Boy One spoke. "We're kinda thinking about it. Care to join us?"

"No thanks."

Prudence, marveling at how Trish managed the same panache in a sex club as she did in a shopping mall, was suddenly smacked with an uprush of paranoia. "What if one of our students sees us here?" she whispered.

"You worry too much, Prue. I want to see strangers having sex. I've never seen that before."

They went back down to their old table. Nothing had been happening upstairs, though Lew had made progress in their absence. Wedged between the two fat girls in their hot-pink nighties, he winked at Trish and Prudence, one shoe dangling like a long white kayak off one black-socked foot. A second pole dancer had joined the first, an orangy tan woman, oiled and tattooed.

"Trish. Do you think you could actually do something in this place?"

"Have sex with strangers, you mean?"

"With other people watching, joining in? I mean could you do that?"

"Part of me likes to think I could, especially if the guys were attractive enough. That tattooed lady, for instance, she's so gorgeous — what would I do if she asked me for sex? I have fantasies about women."

"You do?"

"Sure, I've fantasized sex with strangers, too. But I don't know if I could actually do what all these people" — Trish indicated a new group coming in — "are apparently here to do. Why? Could you?"

"Good god, no. I'm a wreck around someone I know, much less strangers. Plus, I'm terrified of diseases, AIDS and stuff. Though if I had her body" — indicating the newest pole dancer, winding sideways around the pole — "I might turn into a total exhibitionist. Ray jokes about going to orgies, having threesomes, he says sex with the same woman gets boring."

"He's talking about sex. Love is never boring."

"He says he could have sex with anybody, that it's just an act."

"Sounds like he'd fit right in."

"No, he's too cheap to pay the thirty dollars they'd charge for him to get in here."

Trish yawned. "It's past my bedtime. Want to go upstairs one last time, see if anything's going on yet?"

"Gad, look at all those college kids coming in." Convinced one of her students was about to wander in and spot her (how many hundreds of students had she taught over the years?), Prudence panicked. "Professora, professora!" she hissed.

Grabbing their purses, Trish and Prudence slipped off their barstools. Emboldened by the fact that she was leaving, Prudence paused to poke her head into a small side room, catching sight of first the porno flick on TV, then the fat, naked Jellyroll Man tugging away at his rubbery pink dick. She paused in the doorway of the damp, rotty-smelling Jacuzzi Room, where a lanky man wearing only his cowboy hat bucked around in the white bridal froth of the hot tub while a woman with breasts long and white as baguettes rode him at a watery gallop. Catching Prudence, along with Trish, gawking in the doorway, the man plucked off his hat and yelled, *Yee-haw!*

It was past midnight when they left Bare Encounters, and things were just heating up, cars waiting for parking spots, people streaming inside (*We get a young crowd on the weekends, mostly older folks on Sundays and weekdays. Fridays and Saturdays are plenty rowdy, we see a whole lot of downright nasty stuff*).

On the freeway, Trish spoke first. "Know what? I'm glad I didn't see anyone having sex. The picture would just be stuck in my head forever. Wasn't that like Dante's hell? The rung of lust? I'm taking a shower the minute I get home."

Home. The word pointed to the sad absence of Ray. By the time Trish pulled the car up in front of her house, Prudence felt horrible.

"The van's still gone."

"He needs more time to cool off."

"He can be so mean, Trish."

"I know. I've seen it all my life. On the reservation, off the reservation, same damned thing."

"What?" Prudence was taken aback by the bitterness in her friend's voice.

"Indian men, using white women. Doing stuff Native women wouldn't let them get away with. Ray has his good points, from what you say about him, but I think he's hurting you, too. No man's worth that, though god knows I'm no inspiration." Trish was referring to the Navajo security guard, Slim Begay, who'd lied about not being married, taken the thousand dollars she'd loaned him, and vanished.

They sat a minute.

"Fiona's at Kirby's. I don't like how much time she spends there."

"How old is she?"

"Almost eighteen. It's sad, Trish. We used to be so close, now we've drifted apart because of men."

"Same reason most women drift apart.

Hey, can you believe it's past one? I'd better get home. I have a stack of papers to grade tomorrow. One more joke?"

"OK. What did the zero say to the eight?"

"Where'd you get that figure?"

"Nice belt."

In the kitchen, Prudence slid Fiona's thrift-shop stilettos off her aching, swollen feet, and jabbed the blinking message button. *Hey babe. I'm up here in Flagstaff. I ran into an old friend, Rita Bragswolf, from my music days in L.A. Remember me telling you about her? She's living here with her boyfriend now, so I'm at their house for the night. I'll give you a call tomorrow.* (Slight pause, his voice soft, reluctant) *Hey babe, love you.*

Taking a long, hot shower, then toweling off, Prudence wept. *I can't do this. I can't.* She needed to blind herself to his beauty, plug her ears to his honeyed apologies. Pulling on baggy sweats and a big T-shirt, running a comb through her wet hair, Prudence snuffled, blew her nose, then fell into bed, making a decision. It was over. Ended. Fin. Fini. Finito.

Fiona stood over her mother, black minidress in one hand, a single black stiletto in the other. A pair of sheer black panty hose dangled off one shoulder, like a gutted snake.

"Have fun, Mah?"

"Wah?"

"It's one. You slept until one." Fiona plunked on the edge of the bed, dress and shoe in her lap, and jerked her chin toward Ray's side of the bed. "Where's La Indio?"

Prudence sat up, fell back again. Her eyes felt like bathtub stoppers. She sniffed. Bacon.

"I made breakfast. Poachers and bacon. Want me to bring you coffee?"

"Sure. Wow, Fee. One o'clock? I haven't slept this late since high school." Prudence still couldn't open her eyes. She tried again, succeeded, only to find Fiona hovering over her, red hair shorn, and dyed in the most extraordinary checkerboard pattern all over her head, maroon squares, bleached white squares. Her daughter's head, half bowling ball, half game board. "Fee, your —"

"You hate it."

"No, no, sweetie, I don't hate it. It's just very . . . bold."

"Well, I hate it. Kirby keeps balancing red and black checkers on my head. He says he's going to glue them on one night when I'm asleep."

As she laughed, Prudence realized this was the first time she had seen Fiona "Kirbyless" in weeks. It was also the first time she had slept alone since Ray had materialized on her doorstep months ago. She and Fiona were by themselves; this felt odd, freeing, and faintly glorious.

Fiona served her mother coffee in her own favorite china cup, the pink child's teacup her grandmother, Deleanor, used to serve her "coffee" in, hot sugared milk with barely enough coffee to turn the milk a light beige.

"Oooh, fancy." Prudence took a sip. "Thanks, Bunky." A painful awareness stirred. Some unpleasantness.

Fiona scooped the stilettos and black minidress off the floor, plucked the vaporous trail of stockings off the bed.

"Where's Kirby?"

"We broke up." Said casually, as Fiona slipped out the door to add the black dress to the numerous termite mounds of laundry on the floor of her room, as Prudence, hunched in bed like a convalescent, sipped her coffee. On her way to the kitchen Fiona stopped, poked her head in the doorway.

"Where is he? You didn't say. La Indio?"

Aware of the ammunition she was

handing Fiona, realizing, too, that if she said it aloud, it might well be true, Prudence hesitated. "I think we broke up. And please don't call him that, Fee. La Indio." She raised her teacup. "Excellent."

"Hey, we axed two worthless men on the same night? Awesome. You want your breakfast in bed or the dining room?"

"Dining room, sweetie. I really should get up. Any calls?"

"Haven't checked. I dropped Kirby at work — he started his new job at Papa Johns — and stopped by here to do laundry and stuff. Honestly, Mah, I thought you were dead. You never sleep late."

"Sorry. Trish and I went out last night, to dinner and a . . . a club."

"Because he wasn't here, and you could finally have some fun? Breakfast is ready. English muffins, bacon, poached eggs, orange juice, just like our old Sunday breakfasts, remember?"

So easy, to be shed of difficult men. Tears of relief sprang to Prudence's eyes. Of course she remembered her old breakfasts with Fiona. She had loved them.

"Sure do, hon. Need help?"

"Nope, I got it. It's more brunch than breakfast, kind of a postbrunch."

★ ★ ★

They lingered in the sunny dining room amidst a cheerful litter of emptied cups and glasses, muffin plates dotted with crusts, egg bits and dabs of jam.

"What happened with Kirby?"

"Oh, he's an idiot. I am so sick of taking care of him, he whines about everything, he's one big Baby Huey. This morning he got all mad at me for setting his work pants on fire. So I dropped him at Papa Johns and told him I didn't want one thing more to do with his sorry ass. Oops." The first of Prudence's two house rules involved no foul language. The second, less precisely defined, had to do with honesty.

"You set Kirby's pants on fire?"

"Accidentally. They were hanging off the back of a chair in his kitchen, I spilled coffee on one of the legs, tried to wash the spot out really quick in the kitchen sink, then thought I'd dry them on one of the burners, just for a second. Dumb, I know. I scrubbed the spot out, had the front burner on low, and was kind of waving the pant leg over the burner when Kirby yelled from the shower that he needed a towel. I got the towel, threw it in the bathroom, came back, and by then the leg was in flames. His only pair of work pants. First day on the job."

"Ouch."

"He started hopping around in his towel, yelling, Whadya do that for, whadya do that for, so I shot a few things back, then it got ugly, and now we're split up."

"For good?"

"For good. And you? Where's Ray? The house is so quiet without the hair dryer." Ray's method of drying fresh paint on his canvas by using a hair blower, a harsh whirring that shot on and off every ten minutes, drove Fiona crazy.

"I accused him of cheating on me."

"He probably is cheating on you. He's a sneakpuss. Everybody sees it but you. And I hate his Indian shit everywhere."

"Wait a minute, Fee, that's harsh. I didn't jump all over Kirby, I didn't get personal, I could have said how's the Pizza Boy who dangles from fishhooks for fun, but did you hear me say that? I've been trying to let you figure out for yourself what a loser he is — that wasn't fair, Fiona." Was their time together to be spoiled, arguing over two men they had just broken up with? "Look, let's not —"

From under a dirty heap of laundry slung by the back door, Fiona's cell phone rang.

"Leave the dishes, Mah." Fiona went to the laundry pile, dug her phone out from under a pair of jeans, saying "I'm sorry" before disappearing down the hall toward her bedroom. Prudence started clearing the dishes. She washed them, swept the kitchen, put Fiona's darks in the washer, was fully dressed by the time Fiona emerged from her room, thrift-store purse over one shoulder. She laced her arms around her mother's neck, touched her forehead to her mother's nose.

"Sorry, Moozie. I try to like him but I think he's sneaky."

"He is sneaky."

"You admit it?"

"I make him sneaky because I'm so snoopy."

Fiona drew back. "You don't believe that, do you? If he wasn't sneaky in the first place, you'd trust him."

"Maybe you're right."

"Of course I'm right. He's not telling the truth, so you look through his stuff, then he gets mad at you? C'mon, Mom, you can do so much better than him."

"So can you."

"Yeah, but I'm not spending the rest of my life with Kirby. I'm worried you'll put up with this guy forever. He lives off you and goes out with other women. Even if he's not sleeping with them, he's seeing them on the sly. It's not right, Mom. I try, I do, but I don't trust him. Plus I hate his cheesy artwork. His art sucks."

Fiona followed her mother's stare. Ray stood listening in the doorway.

"Well," Fiona sounded bright as a newly forged penny, "looks like I'd better make like a banana and split." She pecked her mother on the cheek. "I'm meeting Kirby for lunch. He's treating. Hey" — awkward, brushing past Ray. "Love you, Mom," Fiona's voice drifted back as Prudence stood looking at Ray, heart thumping, knees buckling. He stepped into the room, grabbed her, smushing her face into his chest.

"I'm sorry, Prudence. You mean too much for me to leave you like that." He kissed her ear, spoke into it. "We need to talk. Will you come sit with me? Don't worry, it's nothing bad." He took her hand, guiding her to her own couch in the living room, where they sat together, Prudence apprehensive, Ray grave. Now he held both her hands in his. "I need you to listen, Prudence. Remember my friend Rita, from my music days in L.A.? The woman who raised wolves? I showed you pictures of me

324

with her wolves, back at Mom's ranch?"

Prudence vaguely recalled a photograph — Ray, hair in two long braids, holding a wolf cub.

"After our fight, I headed north to get away, to think. I drove up to Flagstaff, decided to stop in at the Father Wolf Gallery, see if maybe one of my paintings had sold. There was a message there, a note from Rita saying she'd moved to Flag and wanted to get in touch with me. So I called, drove over to her house . . . I told you all that on my message . . . anyway, her boyfriend is this Navajo guy, a Sun Dancer — turns out Rita's been Sun Dancing six years now, I didn't know that. When I got there, they were getting ready to head up north for a pipe ceremony. They really wanted me to go, so I went up to the Sun Dance grounds with them, ended up talking a long time with some of the leaders there, went into the sweat lodge, prayed . . . and" — here he squeezed her hands painfully hard — "I've committed to being a Sun Dancer, to doing my first Sun Dance." Ray rested his head down in her lap like a child. After a moment, he sat up, still gripping her hands, as intense, as serious, as she had ever seen him.

"I need to ask two things of you, Prudence."

"OK."

"Rita's fiancé is one of the Sun Dance chiefs, a kind of subleader under the head chief. He's offered to be my mentor, my spiritual teacher. I need your support in this."

"Of course, Ray. This is wonderful."

"The ceremony goes on for four days and four nights in July, during the solstice. It's a hard thing, Prue. Really difficult."

She could barely hear her own voice. "I'll support you."

"I have to start preparing right away. Starting tomorrow, I'm going to fast. No food or water for four days and nights, just like I'll be doing up at the Sun Dance. I've fasted before, on my own, but only for a day or two, and always with water. I'll probably slow way down, I won't be able to do much. I'll need you."

Prudence suddenly remembered copying a sentence into her journal a year or two before, words that had, in some vaguely charming, grand way, deeply moved her:

"O, Mrs. Cadwallader, I don't think it can be nice to marry a man with a great soul."

Now, like idealistic Dorothea in Eliot's *Middlemarch*, she, too, loved a man spiritually driven, cut deep with faults. In the space of a few moments, Prudence felt as if, without vows or ceremony, she had just wed herself to a man struggling to lay hold of, and to claim, his soul's great mystery.

Two days later, nibbling as quietly as possible on half a tuna sandwich in her kitchen, Prudence watched Fiona's little gray car, Mouse, bounder into the driveway. Prudence had not seen her daughter since their manless breakfast together.

Fiona gave her mother a hug, cocked one arched, unpenciled brow toward the garage. Her wiry hair, still patched with squares of dyed maroon and bleached white, was bristly, lawnlike, growing out now.

"I see the van's back."

"Yes, he's here, Fiona."

"Why are you whispering?"

"Come outside a moment. Ray's asleep in the living room."

They walked around the block as Prudence explained. Fiona was skeptical. She knew her mother's weakness for men with spiritual leanings.

"I don't buy it."

"Buy what?"

"His spiritual shit. It's an easy way to get back in your good graces. He doesn't want to leave here. Where would he go? The man has no money. He'd be homeless. Don't get mad, Mom, but I think that guy would say or do anything to stay in his current situation. Heck, who can blame him?"

"I can't get you to think otherwise?"

"I bet he's in there sneaking a peanut butter sandwich right now."

"That's enough, Fiona. You may not agree, but please show some respect. Restraint, anyway. I haven't breathed a negative word about Kirby. I expect the same from you."

"OK, but Kirby doesn't live in my house. Ray does. Why's he fasting anyway? Trying to flatten the old spare tire?"

Without offering too much grist for Fiona's mill of ridicule, Prudence explained the Sun Dance briefly. She ended by defining Ray's part in the ceremony. "He's becoming a kind of spiritual warrior."

Fiona snorted. "Sorry, I don't buy it. But for your sake, I'll try."

"That's all I ask. He's pretty weak right now, he's got two days of fasting left.

Mainly he just sleeps and watches TV."

"And that's different? Sorry."

But when they came back into the house and Fiona saw Ray at his worktable, beading, when she actually saw how weak he was, how haggard-looking, she said hi, softly, and asked how he was doing.

He glanced up. "OK. How about you?"

"I'm OK, too. The thrift store's shutting down, so I've been out looking for a new job, something I can do after school."

"Good luck."

"Thanks. Good luck with your fast. Mom says you've got two days to go?"

"Yeah." Ray's voice was raspy, parched.

The second night, in bed beside him, Prudence felt heat rise off Ray's parched flesh. His breath was carious, his cheeks hollow, there were purple trenches under his eyes, and his energy had diminished to barely moving, not speaking. By the third day, he was dizzy, weak, nauseous, only able to lie in bed or on the couch, barely awake, his breathing shallow. On the fourth morning, at sunrise, he surprised her by coming in from the backyard, looking for her. Prudence, sitting up in bed, was grading student papers.

"Come outside," he whispered. In the

backyard, he pointed up to a telephone wire in the alley behind the house. Prudence didn't have her glasses on, so even squinting, all she could see was a dark, indistinct shape.

"A hawk. Redtail. It's circled me twice now."

She peered up into the glare as the hawk left its perch, winging in a large, slow wheel directly above Ray before it flew west, vanishing.

"Three times." His voice rasped, cracked slightly.

"I've been here ten years, Ray. I've never seen a hawk before this morning."

"They don't live around here. Too many people."

By five o'clock that afternoon, Ray broke his fast with sips of water mixed with apple juice. Then, saying he felt fine, a little weak but fine, he drove over to an older Comanche man's house to visit. When he came back home several hours later, he said the man's wife had served him three plates of food. In bed that night, Ray pulled her to him, and Prudence skimmed her hands over his flesh, feeling the ribs, the gaunt hipbones. He kissed her then, a rare kiss, and Prudence was glad she had not complained about another woman feeding him. She honestly wanted to change, to understand him, to become a better person. She wanted to walk this path with him. Be more spiritual. Which meant, among other things, she had to be honest about something.

"I did something while you were gone."

"Something naughty?"

"Kind of. Well, not really."

"What?"

"Trish and I went to one of those sex clubs."

"You did not! Really? Did you guys —"

"No. We just kind of walked around, drank water, left."

"Not much amazes me, Prudence, but this does. You? A sex club?"

"I knew you wouldn't believe me."

"Hey, don't get me wrong. I'm jealous."

"Ho, Mr. Spiritual —"

"Quit it. Just tell me."

So Prudence described their experience at Bare Encounters, beginning with the heap of used mattresses by the Dumpster to Yaller's "tour," to the pole dancers and Lew, the Lutheran sex addict.

"That's wild."

"Mundo bizarro."

"How much did it cost?"

"Ladies free, men pay thirty dollars."

"Does Fiona know?"

"No, and don't you ever tell her. I borrowed one of her dresses and said I'd gone dancing."

"I bet you looked hot."

"The Lutheran guy said I looked like Heather Locklear. Know something, Ray? I've never dressed up like that in my life. In a tight little dress and high heels."

"How 'bout one more time, for me?"

"Maybe. Right now I'm in your sweatpants."

"Oh joy. Now I'm turned on."

"You should be. They're your favorite color." Prudence got up, went into the bathroom, popped out her contact lenses, rinsed them, and came back into the bedroom.

"That's right. Black. Now come back over here so I can manhandle you." Grabbing her sweatpants by both knees, "Grrr. Sexy woman, you."

"Aren't you supposed to be celibate?"

"That's only for a few days before and after Sun Dance. Right now you're mine." Toppling Prudence backward onto the shaggy buffalo hide, Ray fell next to her.

Blazing Eagle removed his moccasins, dropped them to the floor beside the bed of fur upon which Rebeccah lay. "Love me, my woman," he whispered as she clasped her snow white arms around his dark, strong neck. His midnight black eyes burned with fiery passion as he brushed her ruby lips with his.

"Make the sun rise in my heart, woman."

"There is only you, Blazing Eagle. Only you. Forever."

They were quarreling again. This time, because he had refused to speak to her mother on the phone.

"I don't do family. I told you that."

"I've never even asked you before. But she knows about you, knows you've been living with me almost a year, I thought you should —"

"I don't do shoulds. Your mother thinks I'm a gigolo, your daughter thinks I'm a freeloader. So what? You seem to forget the ethnic difference . . ."

Her family wasn't good enough because they were white? Prudence ignited, went up like dry tinder. "Skin color isn't everything."

"Try telling that to somebody who isn't white. You're doing it again, Prudence. Using your emotions. Driving me away with your goddamn emotions."

She had risked asking a favor, hoping to improve the impression Ray had made on her mother thus far. She had to credit Deleanor, who had asked tactful, interested questions about Ray's artwork (typical white-people questions, Prudence could already hear him), only asking once (a question left unanswered) — *Does he help with the bills?* Since her mother clearly conveyed what she thus far thought of him (horse apples and ptooey) by calling Ray What's His Name or Wild Feathers, Prudence mentioned him less and less, until he was nearly erased from her phone conversations with Deleanor, as if he did not live with her, sleep in her bed, quarrel with her, love her. But they were on a new spiritual path now, and Prudence had hoped he would talk with her mother, reverse the long-distance damage, dispel Deleanor's opinion of Prudence (in this regard, anyway) as foolish, duped, a Miss Weak-in-the-Knees. Old as Prudence was, she still wanted her mother's blessing.

"What's wrong now, Prudence? Why are you standing there all mopey? Cheer up. I'm bored with this subject. We've gone over it again and again. Nothing's changed. I'm nobody's husband, father, son-in-law, boyfriend. Get it through your head. This is reality."

"Your reality."

"That's right, and that's the way I like it. Black and white. It keeps my nose clean."

"Life isn't black and white, Ray. It's far messier and more colorful than that."

"No. In my reality, which I control, things *are* that simple."

"You'll never talk to my mother?"

"My answer will never change."

"Oh, you make me so mad!"

"Your choice."

"It's selfish, what you're saying."

"I said I was honest, remember? I take care of me first. I'm not a doormat like you, letting people walk all over me . . ."

"A *doormat!* Who invited you to stay here, who encouraged you to paint, to succeed as an artist, to pursue your goals and dreams? You are so ungrateful!"

"You want me out? I'll leave right now."

"I didn't say that. I'm just saying I gave you a gift — and you're not even thankful."

"I knew it. You wanted something out of this. You're as full of bullshit as everybody else."

"I wanted your friendship, your love."

"Don't use that stupid word."

"OK, relationship. I thought we had a good relationship."

"I hate that word. Relationship. It's a negative word."

"Fuck. I give up."

"You want me to leave? Say the word. I can be out of here, out of your life, in a minute. I've done it before. Unlike you seem to think, there is no other woman in my life. There is no other place to go to. I'll go sleep in my van somewhere, I've done it before."

"Please. Let me get out my miniature violin."

"Don't think you're the first woman who's tried this kind of shit on me. You're only one in a long line . . ."

"Oh, now I feel special. One in a long line . . ."

"Yes, you are one in a long line. Sorry to burst your bubble, Prudence, but you're no different from the next woman, the next person I see on the street corner."

"How can you say that? I love you!"

"Why? Give me a good reason."

"Because . . . I don't know . . . we get along?"

"We get along? What the hell kind of reason is that? Why do you want me here — are you that afraid to be alone?"

"I was alone for years before I met you."

"Let me ask you something. If I'm so mean and nasty, so terrible, why do you want me here? Your daughter doesn't like me, your mother doesn't like me, why would you want someone like me in your life?"

"Because you're not usually like this. I don't understand what is happening when you get like this."

"Get like what? Honest? You told me you wanted honesty, what you don't get from anyone else in your life, certainly not from those so-called Christian con artist friends of yours in Anadarko."

"Honesty is not the same as cruelty."

"I'm bored with this discussion. It's the same old same old. You want more from me, admit it, you want marriage and the white picket fence, you're just too chickenshit to admit it. You can't even be honest with yourself, much less me."

"I don't want marriage, I've been married. What are you doing?"

"Getting my stuff. I can't stay here anymore. I've gotten to the point where I don't care. Once I reach the point of not caring, it's over." He was in a rush, lifting his canvases, his paintings, off the walls, stacking them up, carrying them out to the

337

garage. Prudence ran up behind him and started pummeling his back and shoulders — *"You can't do this, you can't do this!"* — he drew back and looked coldly at her. "Leave me the fuck alone. Just go away. If you can't accept me the way I am, then I need to leave here."

Having fled to her writing room, Prudence could hear him moving around in the bedroom, in the bathroom, packing his few things. How lightly he had lived in her house! She moved down the hallway, stood in the kitchen, watching him pack up his art supplies, his music, his clothing, carrying everything swiftly out to his van. After all his talk of needing her support, after all she had done for him, shared with him, given him.

"Some Sun Dancer! Some spiritual being! You're stupid and fucked up, you're just a scared little boy hiding behind his anger. You're a joke."

Horrified by the near-murderous force of her words, she ran back to her writing room and slid down one wall, tucking her knees in close to her chest. How many women had he lived with and left the moment he'd felt his freedom, his precarious identity, threatened? He was right, she wasn't special. Coiled tight, she crouched,

338

listening to the sounds of his imminent departure, feet slapping from one room to another, yanking up objects like weeds, lifting things down from her walls, shields, war shirts, moccasins, paintings. Now she really was free to enter a monastery, become some sort of old nun. Disappear. No one to stop her. She still had the literature, pamphlets and brochures in a drawer somewhere, about various women's cloisters. Oh, wouldn't that shock the pants off her mother, throw Fiona for a loop, plus all the other people she'd tried to placate and please, adapt to, cut herself down to size for, of course he wouldn't care, he wouldn't even know, how many times had he told her that when he left a person, removed himself from a situation, he never looked back? She could simply recede into her newfound cloister, live out her remaining days under a wimple, while he waltzed in and out of other women's houses . . . a hard black stone skipping across the lonely surfaces of vulnerable female hearts.

He stood over her, touching her shoulder. Disoriented, already a nun, she looked up. He knelt down, put his arms around her. "I'm sorry. I'm sorry. I'm just so scared, so lost. I don't know what I'm doing."

(**Fiona:** Sure you do, you just need a place to stay, admit it. Mom makes it completely easy for you. You don't have to work, you don't have to do a thing. She spoils you rotten. Besides, Mr. Moocher, you wouldn't last one night in your van, and you know it.

Deleanor: Beauty is as beauty does. The man's a gigolo, a con man, using his looks, which aren't any great shakes, if you want my opinion of those pictures you sent, to entice lonely, gullible women. Pull yourself together, Prudence. Throw him out. Marry a banker. Get yourself provided for. Your poor father would be spinning in his grave, if he had one.

Trish: A lot of Indian men are messed up, Prudence, I've grown up with them, remember? I just don't want you to be hurt. I'm worried about you.)

In the kitchen, the phone rang and rang, followed by a woman's voice, boisterous, booming.

"Hey, little brother! It's me. Rita Bragswolf. Up here in Flag! Anybody hooome?"

"Let me get that. Be right back, sweetie, OK?"

He returned with the receiver, helped her stand, kissing the top of her head, her eyes, her cheeks, her mouth. Prudence soaked up the balm of Ray's oily, sweet contrition, while Rita Bragswolf's voice boomed on and on, like a muffled cannon.

He positioned the phone so they could both listen.

"The Phoenix job starts Monday, my boss promises a cool seventy thou after one month's work . . . Jasper and I are thinking of moving down there. He can teach ceramics, he does that now anyway in Tuba City. My boss has promised to help me find a place to live, though it might take a week, two weeks tops, meanwhile I'm without a place to stay . . ."

Tell her she can stay here.

Ray raised his eyebrows. *You sure?*

Prudence nodded vehemently, *Yes . . . tell her she can stay here.*

"Rita? Prudence says to come here, you can stay here with us until your boss finds you a place."

"REALLY? You guys mean that? Wow, that's so darn nice! Tell your girlfriend thanks a million. I'll just bring a coupla changes of clothes, my hair dryer, maybe an iron. That is so cool of you guys. Jasper can come down one weekend, and we'll all hang together. Let me tell him."

Rita's voice faded, then came booming back. "Jasper says great. He thanks you guys a whole lot. Also, since Prudence is a teacher, he wants to know if she happens to know of any teaching jobs in the area . . . art, mainly ceramics. Wait a sec . . ." Ray stroked Prudence, hugged her, kissed her forehead, nose, cheeks, lips, nibbled her ear.

"Jasper wants to know if it would be OK if Boss came down, too?"

"Boss?" Ray asked.

"My German shepherd. My big fat harmless boy. 'Member, Ray, you met him when you were up here?"

"Oh right. I remember. Big dog. Better ask Prudence, since it's her house." Ray handed the receiver over.

"Hi, this is Rita, hey listen, thanks a ton for letting me stay with you guys."

"No problem."

"Listen, I have this dog, he's huge, about as big as they come, pure white and outrageously gorgeous. He's a German shepherd from Germany, the real thing, a celebrity dog. He was originally trained for Barbra Streisand, who changed her mind at the last minute, so I bought him at half price from my trainer friend. Boss is the world's

342

biggest, most obedient dog, he just lays there, never moves at all. You have a backyard? You do? Great. Well, he can stay right out in the yard there and not cause a bit of trouble."

"Does your dog, I mean, does Boss normally live in the house?"

"Oh sure, he sleeps in bed with us, the big galoot. But listen, he'll be fine not coming into your house. He'll be perfect in the yard. He's so beautifully trained, he won't move a muscle. A dog like that normally costs thousands."

"Well, that should work. Go ahead and bring him."

"That is so awesome of you. Now he'll have a place to stay while I'm at work. Jasper's not much for dogs, which is probably why he asked. Hey, whaddya think about my little brother's becoming a Sun Dancer? Ray and I are old friends from back in our music days in L.A., I tell you, I'm still blown away, going into that gallery in Flag and seeing his artwork like that, now my little brother is becoming a Sun Dancer, with Jasper as his teacher. It's a total trip."

Rita's dense, thickety talk made Prudence feel tired. She passed the phone back. Ray and Rita arranged what time she would show up, what day, and Ray gave directions from the I-17 to Prudence's house. Prudence marveled, as she went into the kitchen to get a drink of water, how far and wide Rita's voice carried. Ray came into the kitchen and, after giving her another kiss, hung up the phone.

"Thanks, sweetie. Rita's an old friend, and like she said, it will only be a short time till she gets her own place. A week, two at most."

"It'll be nice to have company. Hey, plus a celebrity dog. The closest I'll ever get to Barbra Streisand."

"I have to warn you, though — Rita's a character. She wears all kinds of crazy getups, leopard-print combat boots, for instance, and she's got a ton of energy."

"And Jasper, her boyfriend, is a Sun Dance chief?"

"More like a subchief. He and this other guy are the two main leaders of the Mountain Sun Dance run by Stanley Young Dog. Young Dog is subchief under the head chief of the Sioux Nation out in South Dakota, Edward Standing Elk."

"My gosh, Ray! Do you remember me telling you how I got invited to the first Sun Dance they held up there in Pinon by an ex-student of mine, Ken Tsosie, whose family has a lot of land up there? I think I know who Stanley Yong Dog is, I mean I saw him anyway. I remember thinking he was amazing, and I definitely remember two other guys, subchiefs or whatever, out in the arena. That means I've probably seen Jasper."

"Well, he'll be here soon, staying in your house."

Prudence felt genuinely thrilled. A Native American holy man in her house! She watched Ray unpack his things from the van, put his clothes and boots back in the closet. And she did not resist when he pulled her into the bedroom, closed the door and locked it, when it felt like the first night he had come to her house all over again, but this time she was ready, this time her passion, her emotions, her I'm sorry, matched his.

Deleanor called to remind Prudence to get a DEXA Scan, a bone density test for calcium loss. Lately her calls relayed medical advice, advice meant to remind Prudence of her age (middle) — with senescence and debility, the two wicked fairies of geriatrics, lying in wait around the corner. DEXA Scan, colon cancer tests, LASIK eye surgery, blood marker tests for ovarian cancer, updates on the mammogram debate, hot flash management, newly unveiled dangers of hormone replacement. When she called Deleanor back to reassure her, yes, she would look into getting a DEXA Scan and a test for colon cancer, Prudence also mentioned the Sun Dance, how Ray had made a commitment to a spiritual life, to a good, honest, inspiring life. That a Sun Dance chief and his fiancée would soon be guests in Prudence's home, what an honor that would be.

Hmph. Deleanor sounded skeptical, costive, unimpressed. *Hmph.*

And Fiona, briefly home from Kirby's, pouring herself a glass of iced tea, only said, *That's nice, Mom,* as she floated out to the living room to watch a rerun of *ER.* Prudence was stumped. Why was her family so unimpressed by something so interesting? Why were they so indifferent to her new spiritual undertaking? Were they completely prosaic? Culturally impoverished? Swiping down the kitchen counters with orange-scented cleaner, Prudence chided herself. Though their indifference hurt her feelings, she should try not to judge them.

Hoo whoosh. Ray, who had begun a new

painting of an Apache man that morning, the second in a series depicting the eighteen Arizona tribes, brandished his hair dryer in Prudence's general direction. He was always happiest at the beginning of a new painting, at the beginning of anything.

In the living room, Fiona was attempting to swallow a bite of her overly dry peanut butter sandwich, staring at, but not hearing, an old episode of *ER*. *Jesus H. Chrysler*. Her mother was losing her mind. Her mother thought she was an Indian. Now she was inviting other Indians into the house, his friends, not bothering to ask if Fiona cared, if Fiona minded, what Fiona thought of the whole thing. It's a pueblo, she would tell Kirby later, her mother was turning their house into a fucking pueblo. *Plus she's dressing different. Tight jeans, tight sweaters. She looks nice, I guess, but it's not my MOM.* (Kirby's own mother had run off with his father's younger brother, so Kirby hardly knew anything normal about mothers, though if he stopped and thought about it, he had noticed a definite change in Fiona's mother. She looked a lot less frumpy, and walked in a way his friend Art kept pointing out in other women, educating him as to the telltale manner in which women walked who were getting laid a lot. So Kirby figured, in his admittedly dumb-guy way, that Fiona's mom must be getting plenty of sex from her Indian boyfriend, a sneaky womanizer, according to Fiona, which Kirby didn't dig, given his history with his own mother. He just wished he could persuade Fiona to do something other than cuddle and kiss. He was sick of cuddling. He loved Fiona, but she was driving him nuts with her virginity philosophy, her *I'm sublimating my erotic energies into my art* bullshit. That Indian dude was some kind of sexual Schwarzenegger, if Mrs. Parker's walk was any kind of give-away. With Kirby, it was the one-handed monster all the way. Lately he'd taken to, no, been pathetically driven to, jerking off inside his gorilla suit as he shambled and shuffled around in front of several apart-ment complexes advertising free utilities and free move-in specials. A perverse and isolated performance, that's what Fiona's celibacy-as-art was driving him, miserably reducing him, to.)

Fiona

In between Scrabble words, Kirby and I agree on how fucked up parents are, how we're the ones raising them half the time. Fuck adults. Adults suck. Yada yada hoo.

"Is a drake a male swan or a male duck?"

"Duck."

"Ai is not a word."

"Ai is too a word. It's a type of sloth. Ten points."

"Cheater!"

Waiting for Kirby to patch out a word with smooth, saltine-pale tiles, I switch on our little orange TV, the one I heisted from Thrift Outlet. A roaring doomsday of animals is on fire in Europe. Pigs, sheep, cows, horses, all ablaze, an auto-da-fé, animal crackers in a charring soup, craggy hills of slaughtered animals, a British farm couple in front of their flaming cattle, the woman weeping, the man's face crumpled as a stack of pancaked cars on a flatbed. I turn the sound off so Kirby can concentrate. We've talked it to death, talked it to a pulp and a wound, mainly me, mostly nights when I can't sleep, but c'mon, buddy-up, the world's ending. It's the Romans all over again, so arrogant we can't see our cities on high, holy fire, animals turning to ash, skies withered, the water heavy with filth, the dirt toxic, sex equals HIV equals death, we yakkety-yak on cell phones, go see movies, Hollywood dreams that hypnotize us, eat what we want, consume what we want, go anywhere, we're drowning in poisoned honey. Dying of greed. We're like a man whose foot is on fire but he's not paying attention, he's not even watching it burn, he's not even feeling it, he's too busy, he's got a lot to do, he's earning a living, he's in insane, fucking denial. A beautiful day in the neighborhood! I see it — who doesn't — Kirby gets depressed about it, possibly suicidal, so I try not to bring it up much, even though I think about it constantly. Incessantly. I worry. Does everyone have a murderer in their family? A pedophile? A thief? A fucking crack hound? Everyone with their dirty bit of tragedy. The skeletons are out of the closet, running the show. Everyone a fucking Hamlet. Do I attract these types? Is it my school? I go to this charter school, a fine arts school, in downtown Phoenix, but it's more like a joke. The other day, some kid went into his high school in San Diego and wasted a couple of kids and a teacher. The cops found him on the floor of the boys' bathroom with his dad's gun, and some of us talked at lunch, saying, yeah, it could happen here, the majority of us are screwups, though we're supposed to be cool, artistic, enough of us are messed up on various substances and experiences, it doesn't take a rocket scientist (boy, do I hate that phrase, my dad is forever using it) to figure how any one of us could charge in, guns blazing, call it performance art, a collaborative installation piece, then we'd all be interviewed on *60 Minutes*, *20/20*, *48 Hours*, CNN, poked under television's microscope, America's Children: Killers or Victims? We're sick cells, symptoms of a bigger disease. Kids smoke heroin in the bathroom, though that's recently changed since one kid turned silent witness, ratted, so now a policeman patrols the hall for crikey's sake, poor dude, sweats it, our token pig, we give him a hard time. He hates that we're nice to him. Kids blow off homework, sit in class, say they don't have to learn a thing, much less freakin' history. All they have to do is express themselves, so what if nobody understands, it's not about understanding, communicating, it's past that. It's about making enough noise to convince yourself you exist. Art's not healing either, art should be disturbing, it should make your mind puke. Angelina, our lesbian social history teacher, I love her, she has hair the color of blue sleeping pills and dreams about buying this old broken-down villa in Italy, Angelina says there's a perfect word for us. Solipsistic. Good Scrabble word. I'm so ready to leave, three more months, June 1. The kids coming in are so much stupider than I was, the school's turned into a playpen, public schools dumping their trash kids into ours. We're funded by the state so there has to be a quota so that means let anybody in, no audition, no talent. The first couple of years were cool, the kids all came from another art school that had shut down, they were serious about their music, their dance, their art, but now they're gone, and these new dumb-butts stream through the doors, doing weird shit on our First Friday Art Night such as rolling around on the floor to incredibly bad heavy metal music, wearing a prom dress and vomiting marsh-mallows into a green rubber trash barrel, standing half naked in back of a see-through shower curtain, rubbing bodies with a sponge dipped in dyed water to look like blood. Angst shit. The poor confused parents actually smile and clap a little.

The world's ending, SpongeBob SquarePants.

The other night, waiting for Kirby to get back from Domino's, I saw this documentary about a generic British family, husband, wife, three girls and a boy, who volunteered to live in a row house in London, as if it were 1900. For three months they agreed to live like it was one hundred years ago, wear the clothes, cook, eat the food, clean house, do wash, all of it. The first month, they had to go outdoors and use an earth toilet, an outhouse, then they got indoor plumbing, which hardly worked . . . the wife tried taking a bath in half an inch of cold water, the water turning to black grime from her body, and on camera, nude, she burst into tears. Man-bub went off to work every a.m., all cheery, glad to break out of that *dour* house with everything smoking and breaking down, while the wiff, good wiff, had to stay home, *scrub, wash, iron and sew* the livelong day. Brutish work, British work, so hard, she broke down on camera, disintegrated again, her mind a nubbin, her hands raw and ruined, she hated her husband since he got to leave every day, go out because he was a man. She was what, she whispered into the hidden closet camera, a hunk of inefficient cleaning equipment? Her mind turned to cheese, to jelly, her mind went foul on her. She was a twenty-first-century educated woman, with freedoms and rights, she said, swollen-nosed and blinking up into the camera, installed there for private confession. She was ferociously unhappy, she twitched all over with misery. I felt sorry for her. Things brightened up considerably when she hired a maid (a social inferior) to do all the hands-and-knees, elbow-grease sort of work, flip mattresses, get at the fluff everywhere, she called dirt fluff, her hands still red and chafed and raw from a week's laundry, while her daughters gave up on the little boy's homemade birthday cake, which looked more like a greasy puddle, and instead made a hand cream of whale fat and almond oil from a recipe in *Mrs. Beeton's Book of Household Management.* With the poor, skinny-kneed maid vigorously whacking at carpets with a wooden paddle, scrubbing at floors on her hands and knees, our wiff cheered considerably, chucked on her 1900 bonnet, and with a basket on her arm, hands slicked with her daughter's lotion and smelling like a whale, popped off to market to buy legumes, potatoes, a sausage, whatever was authentically available during that time. I tried to think what era I would most like to pretend to live in. Before Mom and Dad's divorce is what I came up with. That era of history when my mother, my father and I all lived together.

Kirby says humans can't stand being human, being conscious they're going to die. It makes people crazy. I disagree. Greed, in my celibate opinion, is the failure of humanity. *But what's behind greed?* he asks. *A desire for comfort,* I answer. *What's behind the desire for comfort? Think, Fiona. A dream of heaven? Paradise? Eternity? What's behind that? A deeper dream? A wish? To never, ever die? To be immortal? I win,* he says.

"Carp's a fish. A bottom-feeder."

"To carp means to nag at someone."

"Oh, like you nag at me."

"I do not. I do not carp."

"Nah, you don't. Just kidding, Fiona. Carp is a bottom-feeder, though. Fifteen points. Sorry. I win by ten."

"Change one letter and it spells crap."
"Still five points, no good."

My best friend, Stevie Ray Vap, is smart and classy down to her cat's-eye rhinestone glasses. She says people relate selectively, see what they want to see. For example, say I build a secret perception around a person. A dream. The more I like him, the more dreamlike the perception, and the dream can be all that keeps me going each day, thinking things with that person will turn out just the way I dream. Everything that validates my dream, my version of how things should be, brings me closer to that person. Everything that argues against it infuriates me, depresses me, makes me fight like hell with that person. Like last night, on our way to another dollar movie which, as usual, I pay for, I got so pissed at Kirby, we were screaming at each other in the car. I was wearing my pink satin jeans, a lime green tank top and black combat boots, and I jumped right out of my own damned car, which, out of the lunacy of my heart and the stupidity of my mind, I had let him drive. Fighting is exhilarating. We got high from it, the adrenaline made us see all over again how much we loved each other. But, as Stevie would surely point out, the fight started with Kirby messing up my dream, my secret, rosy picture of *Us* that holds me to him, even when it all stinks, even when I know he still carries that stupid picture of Deneen Boyd in his wallet, I know because I peeked. I'm a snoop, he's a sneak, it's a volatile combination. The worst.

A latte with a cinnamon rugelach from Goldbar's? A plate of chocolate pancakes at IHOP? Something to prop me up through another Saturday at Thrift Outlet, Arizona's fashion gutter, sociological museum, poor-taste emporium, never-ending garage sale, fire sale, a place that smells, stinks of human sweat, grime, loss. A warehouse of rejection. Every single thing in this store, probably even the customers, arrived here through rejection. Being so unwanted as to be shunned and cast out. That's quite an energy field. Everything shrugged off, shelved, priced, marked down, picked over, discarded. A plant or an animal has the good sense to organically dissolve into something else, to not be redundant, but this crap's not going anywhere, it just circulates and recirculates. Right over there, in Furniture, is my mom's old green-and-white-striped couch.

It's been there two months. Right now two little kids are quashed down on it, holding hands. Sweet. No, not sweet, they're flogging one another with a grimy pink clown. My mom bought new living room furniture. Two white couches. Coordinated. Clean. Now our living room looks like something from a magazine, but we have a hard time relaxing on objects so white. It's more like we perch. Our old couch looks all saggy-bottomed, pouched and dingy, the white stripes dirtied into the color of weak tea. It has a red price tag sticking out of it, and the two kids are still knuckling one another. Our couch had its little history, it was familiar and ours, the place Mom and I plunked down every night to eat dinner, watch *911* or *Unsolved Mysteries*, read, rub feet, take naps. Now it's a pound dog, waiting for a home. A dog gets two weeks to look cute and pathetic enough to find a home before it's gassed. After once seeing a dump truck unload a mountain of stiffened dogs and cats, thousands of them (raining cats and dogs, one more of Dad's famous phrases), into a landfill, I did a research paper. But, hey, a couch can wait till kingdom come, it's in no danger at all.

A lot of Mexican families come into the

store, so all our signs are in Spanish, too. Then there's homeless people, a lot of them living under the oleander shrubs by the freeway, like this one guy, his whole life bundled into a cardboard box on the back of his rickety black bike, who wears a stack of maybe fifteen baseball caps on his head, the brims all going in different directions. Or Rodney, the dim-witted guy who stares at me and the other girls while pretending to look at stuff. Queenie says he's harmless, a bulb loose is all. Or high school kids setting trends, buying weird combinations of stuff. The occasional transvestite who heads straight to Lingerie, limp see-through sleaze which I, for one, would not touch with a ten-foot pole. A lot of times I feel sorry for the Spanish-speaking mom who has five or six kids, plus a mean or really worn-out-looking man with her, and she's in full, pitiful charge, counting dimes and pennies out of a torn wallet. I give her everything for free, just shove it along into the bags. What's the point, chiseling an extra twenty-five cents from people like that? The smiles I get are worth getting fired over, shy, beautiful smiles, the mothers so grateful for anything extra, for a small break of some kind, it fucking hurts. Fuck, take the store, clean the place out, give this shit a home. My friend Stevie calls Thrift Outlet a cultural museum. History mopes here, sullen, melancholic, its unwanted objects arranged into categories, fads, trends, decades. A lineup of old popcorn poppers, a shelf of fondue pots, miles of beige outdated computers, terrible belts, pure horrors of shoes. It can be politically radicalizing.

I read how in Japan, kids like us are called *freetas, fleetas,* something like that, kids drifting from menial job to menial job. One guy, eighteen, started to work for a new company that planned to make a fortune importing beetles from Indonesia, but the beetles died en masse the second day, and the kid was out of another job. There's a crisis in Japan, thousands of these kids, the system failing them, the article said, they had no future and didn't care. Maybe there's a crisis like that in America, but since nobody's come up with a catchy name, it doesn't officially exist. I've had two spectacular jobs so far, Cinnabon's in Fiesta Mall, a nightmare during the short course of which I managed to pack on fifteen pounds of cinnamon-bun lard, and now, whoo-hoo, Thrift Outlet. Kirby's more of a *freeta* than me, he's had tons of jobs. He's washed dogs in a pet grooming salon, undressed old people in a nursing home, managed first a Gumby's, then a Domino's, stuck in his little pizza cage between a Fancy Nails salon and a Chinese buffet (indefinitely shut down since the health inspector cited evidence of cockroaches, including one that strutted boldly across the chopping board as if it were in vaudeville, Kirby knew all about it because the inspector staggered into Domino's afterward, all white and woozy. He and the wife never ate out anymore, he confessed, he'd seen too much, he was ruined for anything but his wife's cooking and eating in his own home off his own plates, eating with his own sterilized knife and fork). Kirby's worked as a telemarketer, selling first-aid kits to small businesses — the place a holding tank for ex-convicts, thiefs, thugs, drug addicts and pimps, Kirby began to figure he was the only one there who hadn't done time in the slammer, though he did appreciate the dress code, people wearing whatever they wanted, mostly sweatpants and T-shirts, so they all looked the same, like they had all just tumbled out of the same bed. And that one Christmas, when every kid in America was screaming for a Teletubby, Kirby worked in a Toys "R" Us, wearing a red-and-white-striped jacket too big for him, wishing everyone on the way in and out an obnoxious Merry Christmas, though he was really supposed to be checking for strange bulges and jutting corners under coats and jackets. Hired to spy on customers, to nab shoplifters, Kirby was, in turn, spied on by other Toys "R" Us employees, dressed up as customers, so it drove him crazy, not knowing if the person he was greeting was a shopper or a hired goon, some poor clapper like him. He'd worked in a resort in Scottsdale, the Princess, cleaning toilets, hand-rolling velvety beige fingertip towels, arranging them in giant baskets on marble countertops, dumping used towels into the hotel's laundry bins, swabbing squadrons of taupe toilets, dumping ice cubes down each one's porcelain throat. Rich piss, poor piss, women's piss, grandpop's piss. Guess what, Kirby said, it's all piss, saying it gross me out on purpose. I am not a relaxed person when it comes to bodily functions. I think people should be etherous vapors, colorless, odorless. Since he got fired from Domino's for talking to me on the phone instead of taking delivery orders, Kirby's started working as a sidewalk gorilla for the Buena Vista apartment complex, shambling up and down the street in a shaggy suit, waving a little sign, *Free Utilities First Three Months*. People in passing cars stare or throw trash — one guy drove around the block twice just to pitch grapefruits at him — or yell obscenities, though sometimes little kids wave and look excited, like they want to take him home and play with him. I happen to know Kirby fantasizes about being abducted, taken to some million-dollar home in Happy Valley or Cave Creek, a Frank Lloyd Wright trilevel home that looks like a smaller version of the Princess resort, where, kept as a household pet, he would lumber around in his suit, only crawling out of it at night, when the children, a boy and girl, were asleep. The little girl would grow up, fall in love with and marry him, then Kirby would be lord of the trilevel resort house, a powerful man with hairy beginnings. He's never told me that fantasy, I know it because I peeked in his journal, and there it was.

Lately he's weirding me out, wanting to wear his gorilla suit out in public, or wear it to bed. It's too hard to snuggle with a gorilla, I told him last night, much worse than fucking (though we didn't) a duck. His first job, he'd been the Ugly Duckling at an Ugly Duckling used car lot in Gilbert, slapping around in a white terry cloth duck suit with webbed orange vinyl feet. When he got fired, the day after we met at Thrift Outlet, he'd stolen the suit and, wanting to impress me, tried wearing it to bed. He was a two-week Santa once, too, a sandwich board strapped on him, pacing on a street corner near a busy intersection, advertising cut-rate jewelry. So far he likes being the gorilla best, likes smelling of artificial fur and sweat and Big Chief chewing gum, which he snaps and grinds between his molars. He's worked up a gruff simian voice for the people lucky enough to walk, ride bikes, or zip past him on electric scooters. At least half those people ignore him, snobs, noses-in-the-air. He hates those people, nurses an inner cartoon of tackling them from behind, galumphing up, then hurling himself onto their ignorant backsides, knocking them to the spit-riddled combat gray sidewalk. I read that in his journal, too.

(Fiona had two semiboyfriends before Kirby, Jeremy, a pasty, overweight kid with particolored hair, orange and brown, who drove a Cream-of-Wheat-colored Cadillac and talked incessantly about computers and being a dystopian. What's a dystopian?

Fiona had asked. Opposite of a utopian, he'd answered. She looked up utopian and decided she was one. He'd tried to kiss her once, halfheartedly, out of weak social pressure to kiss someone, but Fiona had averted her face, told him she couldn't do that, wasn't ready and didn't know if she ever would be, so he'd driven them to Denny's, where they'd ordered chocolate chip pancakes with chocolate whipped cream. Jeremy and his father had moved to a commune outside Dallas after Jeremy's mother, admitting her preference, ran off with his father's youngest sister. Every once in a while Jeremy called and left a message on Fiona's answering machine that sounded like he was trying to imitate a black street person, saying things like Yo and Whazzup. The second boyfriend, Nicholas, a fey, anorexic boy, had shoulder-length shiny caramel-colored hair. Nick constantly wore a long black stained trenchcoat and spiked dog collar. The one time Fiona had brought him home, Prudence thought he was one of Fiona's girlfriends, since he was wearing a vintage fifties black taffeta sheath, sheer black stockings, slingback heels, makeup and a rhinestone hair band. Where are you two girls going, all dolled up? Fiona and Nicholas had laughed over that for days. They had kissed on two separate occasions, parked in his car, kisses like dry little pinches. The second time, Nicholas, with cool gynecological aplomb, had palpated her breasts while Fiona rested her hand, as lightly as if taking a temperature, on his crotch, a place which felt quite flat to her, going against everything she had ever heard and read about that dangerous male triangle. She really didn't like being touched, unless it was to have her shoulders massaged or her feet rubbed. She wasn't into sex the way most kids her age seemed to be, and oral sex, which was supposed to be healthier, truly disgusted her. One reason she was good friends with Stevie Ray was because Stevie had sworn to remain a virgin until she got married or turned twenty-five, whichever came first. Carrah Stanley was Fiona's other good friend, and Carrah's father had died of AIDS. Fiona had met him once at Carrah's sixteenth birthday party, where he was holding a piece of white angel food cake on a white paper plate on his lap, his bare legs skinny as two white straws. Mr. Stanley was the thinnest man Fiona had ever seen, and anyone could see he had once been truly handsome, but now he was all teeth and empty skin. Still, he'd had the sweetest, slowest, most loving smile Fiona had ever seen. He died two weeks after Carrah's sixteenth birthday, and one day, after letting a skateboarder with nit-infested dreadlocks feel her up one night in the community park near her house, Carrah, too, swore off sex, and went every July with her mom and five brothers to a camp for families who had lost a relative to AIDS. What do you guys do up there for three weeks, Fiona had asked. Talk. Cry, swim, have relay canoe races, play team sports, sing songs, stuff like that.)

Well, rock my shorts. Queenie breathed hard, coppery curls bouncing all over her bitty head, hairpins quivering. In a phoof of righteousness, Thrift Outlet's manager, Flo "Queenie" Wafer, standing a full head shorter than Fiona, wearing a turquoise Mexican fiesta dress and hopping like a canary on a hot sidewalk, totaled the day's profits one more time, slapping bills down, greased strips, ones, fives, tens, twenties, ones, fives, tens, twenties. Queenie usually favored housecoats with tropical prints. Red hibiscus. Yellow ginger. Purple orchids. She squinted up at Fiona, on her last exhausted leg, having had a long day at school, then barreled straight to work past three freeway accidents, and now it was ten in the goddamn p.m., as Queenie would say, and all Fiona wanted was to go home and sleep, except home had turned into the Pueblo, where her mom was letting some Indian take over the house, hang his war shields and feathered bonnets, play music from the eighties, blast a damn blow dryer every five minutes over his canvas to make the paint dry faster. Just that morning, Fiona had picked out another of his long black hairs, this time off her sprouted wheat toast. His hair was everywhere. And she couldn't stay at Kirby's, they weren't speaking, not since she had confronted him about the picture of Deneen Boyd in his wallet. And now Queenie, barking up her leg like a demented Chihuahua — something small and begging to be kicked. *Rock my shorts,* what kind of thing was that for a sixty-year-old Bible-thumping woman to say? In truth, Queenie thumped her beloved *National Enquirers* a lot more than she thumped any Bible, but still. *Forty dollars short, we're forty dollars short, Fiona, and either we've been robbed or someone's been care-*

less with the register again. Queenie slewed her eyes toward Fiona, who was literally swaying from exhaustion. *The store can't afford this, hon.* Queenie scooped all the bills together and held them like a green ostrich duster. This was the second time the store had come up short in a month, both times with poor math-addled Fiona at the register. *I see two ways to fix this. No, three. Either I fire you, which is out of the question, or I pinch the money out of your paycheck, or we jack prices in the store for a couple of weeks, until we make up the difference.* Queenie had managed Thrift Outlet for over ten years, she was the store, was just like it, worn down, tacky, strangely vital, complete with a colorful history of having once been married to a Greek immigrant in the Mafia. Queenie was one of the main reasons Fiona stayed on at the store. That and Queenie didn't seem to notice or care how much Fiona filched, ripped off, stuffed in her backpack, clothes, plates, cups, napkins, clocks, even the orange TV. Kirby's apartment was completely furnished by Thrift Outlet, the poor man's Target, they called it. Queenie might blow a gasket from a shortfall at the register, but she didn't seem to mind the slow pilfering, the leakage, of goods from her store. *OK, I'm a* *beat pup. I want to get home to my crime shows, then hit the hay. We'll make it up tomorrow, we'll jerk up prices in Furniture, Housewares and Shoes.* As Queenie dragged on her coat and slugged her fake leather purse over her tiny shoulder, Fiona noticed her fuzzy green heel-less slippers, the sort of thing Fiona adored, a boss who wore fuzzy slippers on the job. She got her own purse, a clear vinyl bag with dyed blue water, plastic seaweed and a fake goldfish belly-up along one side, said good night, and walked out to a parking lot devoid of cars except for Queenie's gold and white Impala and her own charcoal gray Suzuki. What was on the hood of her car, illuminated by the parking lot lights? White rocks, landscaping chips, quarter-sized, that spelled out across her hood: 2 GOODS* 2 BES* 4 GOTTENS*. This had to be Kirby. Suddenly Queenie appeared beside her, Fiona smelled her Tic Tac breath.

A nutcase did this. I hope it's not Rodney, that poor guy with the brain of a chipmunk. Queenie looked around at her Impala. *Nope. Just yours, sweet beet.* Maybe that Deneen Boyd picture was old, maybe, like he'd said, he'd forgotten it was even in his wallet. Maybe she had been jealous for no reason. Still, it was upsetting, an upsetting picture, Deneen, lying on her side, head propped in one hand, long brown hair sweeping down to the carpet, gazing seductively into the camera, wearing a giant Red Cross T-shirt and nothing else, judging from the look of her long, slim brown legs poking out from the hem of the shirt. Even though she was tempted to forgive Kirby, now that he had done such a cute, dumb thing, she couldn't let him get off that easy. She'd go home and sleep in her own room. Parking her car in the driveway (another sore point among many since Ray parked his Texas van in the garage beside her mother's car, somehow landing Fiona out in the driveway, ousted, it irked her no end), Fiona made plenty of noise to warn her mother she was home, slamming the car door, rattling her keys before inserting the house key into the front door's lock. As she stepped over the threshold, something crunched and rolled away beneath her foot. More little white rocks. She knelt down, reading them with her finger. IS⋆'M SORRYS⋆, the O shaped like a heart. Leaving the rocks undisturbed, she stepped into the dark, silent house. *Mah, I'm home,* she called in the general vicinity of her mother's bedroom. *Hi, honey,* she heard a weak, distracted-sounding reply.

She tiptoed past her mother's closed door, scooted down the hall toward her room. What if Kirby was in there, lying on her futon, an apology spelled out across his chest? She yanked on her Barbie doll light cord. No Kirby. Should she call? No. She'd make him sweat a little, teach him a lesson. No more carrying sexy photographs of old girlfriends. He didn't have a single photograph of Fiona, sexy or otherwise, anywhere in his wallet, anywhere in his apartment for that matter, though it was true, as he'd pointed out, she'd refused to have her picture taken since she was *twelve*. Fiona flung herself onto her futon, scrunched her favorite pillow under her head, closed her eyes, turned her radio on so she couldn't possibly hear anything obscene going on down the hall. It had been a day from hell. When the phone rang, waking her, she waited to the count of ten before picking up the beige receiver of her Thrift Outlet phone. *Hey.* His voice, apologetic and so sweet, it nearly made her cry.

When she looked into Fiona's room the next morning, Prudence would discover her daughter, fully dressed, asleep, mouth gaping, the phone against her ear, the Garfield clock irritably cheeping under the muffled weight of her pillow.

On the day Rita Bragswolf was expected down from Flagstaff, Ray, wearing gray jersey shorts and black hightopped sneakers, left Prudence's house toting a canvas backpack humpy with river rocks on his back. Hefting an additional large rock in each hand, he took off jogging across the front lawn and down the street, nearly naked, black hair to his waist, lugging rocks, trotting backward down the middle of the street to build up his calves, then forward to build up his ankles.

Half an hour later, sweat-glazed and panting, Ray dumped his pack of rocks by the back door and was already in the shower when an electric blue Honda Civic slunk, as if defeated, into the driveway. Prudence, who had been in the front yard watering her pots of red geranium (plush with vulgar blooms, overrunning the delicate Crystal Palace lobelia and suffocating the yellow pansies) and holding a just-yanked weed in her hand, looked up to see a round-nosed blue runt of a car, stuffed to the gills, riding low, every window jammed with something, the darkness of objects pressing against glass, the trunk open and lashed with sisal rope, the end of an ironing board jutting out like a long silver thumbnail. What appeared to be a burly polar bear at the wheel was, in actuality, the enormity of Boss's head, hanging like a great shaggy globe over Rita's shoulder, the rest of him inhabiting the whole length and breadth of the backseat. (*He just loves watching the road, and I am his own personal chin rest,* Rita would add, blithely indicating the trail of dog-slobber darkening her turquoise-fringed T-shirt.) Prudence squeaked off the garden hose. The pipes, old and precariously jointed, gave a great, shuddering clank inside the walls of the house. Rubbing her hands down the sides of her jeans to clean them, Prudence walked over to the car.

Rita cranked the window down. "Hey, this place is great!"

A few moments later, as Ray opened the front door and stepped out, wearing nothing but skin-tight jeans, his hair whelked up in a pink towel turban, Prudence passed by him, hissing *Help* and staggering under an armload of clothing, Rita's leopard-print cowboy hat angled lopsidedly on her head. Languid, in no discernible rush, Ray crossed the unmown, shaggy lawn and hugged Rita before reaching into her jumbled, bursting toy box of a car and pulling out random items, a steam iron, a set of plaid hatboxes, a Mr. Coffee coffeepot, various mismatched cowboy boots, belts, jewelry boxes, photo albums, a stainless steel dog bowl the size of a satellite dish, a pillow-sized bag of dog food ripped open and dribbling kibble, and carton after carton of Natural American Spirit cigarettes. It took all three of them, Rita, Prudence and Ray, an hour to clear out the contents. (All that STUFF, Prudence thought ungraciously, in MY house. UGH.) Installed in the backyard and true to Rita's word, Boss sat eerily motionless, a snowy behemoth, the largest dog Prudence had ever seen, surpassing in height her neighbor's now deceased Great Dane, who years earlier had reared up on its hind legs one night, ready to seize Prudence's small skull in its jaws before the dog's amused owner stepped outside shouting, *Quit it, Ned, quit being a pest.* Now Boss quashed his rubbery black dial of a nose against the floor-to-ceiling window of Prudence's dining room, his small, beady eyes darting right to left, left to right, tracking Rita's blurred progression through the house. Prudence, who thought of herself as a contemplative sort, was unable to contemplate or gain perspective from the well-worn philosophical perch in her mind. Ray, on the other hand, seemed amused by his old friend, now sprawled in one of Prudence's poolside chairs, chain-smoking American Spirits, hacking and describing her break-neck drive from Flagstaff, during which she'd encountered the wreckage of a small plane, run out of gas, her cell had rung at least twenty times, and a pack of wan-dering llamas had blocked the road outside Payson. Rita was a monologuer, someone who left no room for response, no space in which to wedge a compressed observation, a sliver of memory, any modest recollec-tion of one's own. Taller than Prudence, Rita had waist-length dyed black hair of a coarse, rough texture that matched her voice. Beneath a tarred shingle of bangs, her features were pointy, her skin leathery, creased and tanned to dull mahogany. In youthful days, Rita would have possessed a certain saucy, scoundrelly beauty. An ex-otic huntress. A female pirate, perhaps. Now she had a face like an aging Italian actress, ravaged but striking, more lovely than not, a strong-boned face that could carry off the most virulent red lipstick, the gaudiest, dangliest, clankiest earrings. Rita had changed out of her turquoise, slobbered-on T-shirt into a black T-shirt with a giant wolf's head on the front and a pack of wolves on the back. She'd kept on her turquoise broomstick skirt and leopard combat boots. Her figure looked dumpy and bumpish, and as if reading Prudence's thoughts, she ruefully slapped her belly.

"I've put on twenty-five fucking pounds since I've been with Jasper. Don't ask me why, but Navajo men like their women big. I have never been this HUGE in my entire life, and it's from all the dang meat and potatoes I have to cook for Jasper every night. Left to myself, I'd live on sushi."

Back inside the house, as Rita sat on the carpet in Prudence's former writing room (now a temporary guestroom) flipping through leather photo albums crammed with pictures of her daughter's wedding to a meek-faced Irish entrepreneur from County Cork, along with shots of her Andalusian stallions, pet ostriches, llamas, goats, geese, and Rita herself mugging with Native American actors, singers and activists — during this, Prudence managed to indicate the direction of the guest bathroom, the extra wire hangers in the hall closet, additional sheets and towels in the linen closet. Two weeks, she soothed herself. Two swift weeks.

Fiona was unsoothed. *Invasion* was her first and most lasting impression of Rita Bragsworth. Hairs from Rita's head, black and long as horsetail hairs, nested in Fiona's bathroom sink. Long, thin punctuations of hair scribbled across the pink tile countertop, stuck to the sides of the bathtub. A tube of Gleam, squished and ugly, a purple toothbrush, bristles splayed and broken, dozens of cheap lipsticks, nauseating perfumes, a gaudy hill of jewelry, a slew of amber pill bottles — Nu-Life pills for energy, pills for women's bones, capsules of fish oil and evening primrose — a bath towel, ugly-striped, discolored and crumpled on her bathroom floor every morning, a bouquet of super-sized Tampax roughly bursting from its ripped box next to the toilet — Fiona tried, she honestly did try, she complained to Kirby, but having to share her bathroom with a woman who overspilled and slopped like a muddy spring flood into Fiona's idea of things was, in a word, Gross. (And though it hadn't yet happened, the *Invasion* would precipitate Fiona's move into Kirby's squirrel-sized one-room studio. This wouldn't occur until Jasper, Rita's fiancé, a Navajo holy man and Fiona's last straw, showed up.) Rita was horribly ensconced between Fiona's and Prudence's bedrooms, and Fiona would not believe her ears that next morning — the clanging 6 a.m. alarm, followed by a radio booming at earsplitting volume, then swatted down presumably by Rita's hand, followed by a strung-out series of zoolike yawnings. (Fiona would offer this to Kirby: *The woman roars out of bed yawning, ravenous . . . clonks into the kitchen in her godawful giant bathrobe with mooseheads all over it, slam-bangs around fixing coffee in her Mr. Coffee maker, then goes and sits outside, this fat fog of smoke, this nicotine smog all around her, and then there's her polar bear of a dog, and even if she's not saying one word, even if she's just breathing, even if she's not even there, it's still loud. I can't explain it. She's a hurricane, always coming or going. Hurricane Rita. She could wipe out the state of Florida.*

How did she get there? In your house?

That's the crazy part. She's a friend of his. Mom was being nice. Trying to be hospitable. My god, you just want to locate a dial on the woman and turn her down, down, down, off. I can't even tell if I like her or not, I'm too busy fighting all the noise she makes.)

From her bed, Prudence, too, heard the clanging alarm, the booming radio, the great, masculine, roaring yawns. "She sounds like my grandfather," Prudence whispered, spooning up close to Ray. "I'm surprised she doesn't bang her fists on her chest. Belch and fart."

"Give her time. She's still being polite."

That first morning, as Prudence crept into the kitchen to make her own coffee, Rita strode in, dressed for work.

"Whaddya think? My friend Adele, an ex–Ford model in L.A., used to take me to the most amazing boutiques — we'd get stuff off the fire sale racks — I picked this skirt up for a hundred bucks, marked down from — get this — seventeen hundred!! Italian designer, the label still on it — whaddya think? Does it go with the boots?"

The Italian miniskirt had little square patches sewn all over it. Dangling from each of the patches were miniature forks, knives, spoons, plates, cups, saucers. Over Rita's left knee bobbed a miniature copper teapot. Prudence was so intrigued, she barely noticed what else Rita had on other than razor-toed purple cowboy boots and a slash of blue-red lipstick screaming across her incessantly moving lips. "Mmm." Prudence took a sip of coffee. "You look . . . amazing."

"You think?" Rita gave her hair a little shake, sweet as a pony tossing its mane (though after seeing it dozens of times a day, for dozens of days, Prudence would reassess the shake as a nervous tic, right up there with Rita's habit, when she heard or saw something she didn't like, of performing a rapid chiropractic self- adjustment, a quick swivel-pop-crack to her neck).

"I look pretty damn hot today. I wish Jasper could see me. You don't think it's too much for my first day of work, do you?"

Of course it was. And a braver soul might have admitted such an unwieldy truth. But Prudence's chronic dread of confrontation conspired with her polite upbringing to render her mum on the topic of Rita's outlandish getup.

"I gave Boss his morning kibble, so he's good to go. He'll just sit in your yard all day, good as gold. I should be home by six. Wish me luck. Two weeks tops, says my boss, and I'll be raking in forty-five to fifty thou."

"Wow. What is it you do again?"

"Book radio shows. Nationally syndicated. I call people off a list and convince

381

them what they know is valuable and interesting enough to buy airtime. A radio show producer or glorified telemarketer, depending on your perspective. Where's little brother?"

"Asleep."

"I'm stopping at the store after work to pick up sushi, want some?"

"No thanks."

Prudence stood in her house, a foreign-seeming place now, watching Rita's little blue car bomb off down La Diosa. She savored the silence, the miracle of an uninterrupted cycle of breath, inhale-exhale. She wondered what she should wear to school that day, wondered when she would hear from the Zebra publishers about *Savage Heat*, their reaction to the copyedits, the proofing changes she had made.

The phone jingled. Glancing at the caller ID, Prudence picked up. "Morning, Mom." She listened as Deleanor nattered on about new bloodwork tests, a something-something radical sediment count. Since Walt's sudden death, her mother monitored the world according to medical news updates, FDA warnings and Dr. Sinatra's sensible, no-cost recommendations. As Prudence drank her coffee and listened to her mother, she saw Rita's little blue Civic zip down the street and shoot back into her driveway. Deleanor had just finished quoting Dr. Wayne Dyer and gone on to complain about the impossibility of finding just the right Ferragamo shoe width when Rita, looking soaked and distraught, started pounding on the front door.

"Hang on a sec, Mom."

"What? What's wrong?"

"Nothing. I need to unlock the front door."

Rita blasted into the house, the miniature copper teapot on the hem of her miniskirt swinging, lidless.

"God Almighty! I stopped to get gas and an entire fucking *wave* of gasoline shot all over me. Look at me! Drenched! I've got to take a shower, change clothes, I called work, told them I'd be late. Fuck! My skirt! I just hope I can get it dry-cleaned. Fuck!" She shot down the hall. Prudence returned to the phone.

"Prune . . ." Her mother's voice came through crabbed, peevish. "Who was that? What's going on over there?"

"I have a houseguest." Prudence felt dizzy from gasoline fumes.

"Oh, that's nice. Who is it? An old

school chum?"

"A friend of Ray's. Rita Bragswolf."

Silence.

"Mom?"

"Another Indian?"

"As a matter of fact, yes. She's part Chickasaw, part Maori."

A large, pained sigh. "I don't know what's going on over there, Prudence, but you're not the same girl."

"I'm not a girl, Mom. I'm practically fifty."

"Quit that. Stop rushing. I just mean you've lost your . . . *oomph*."

"*Oomph?* What are you talking about?"

"I don't know. Your joie de vivre, your sparkle. You always sound so serious now. It's happened ever since that Wild Feathers moved in. I'm worried you've gone Indian."

"Oh for god's sake, Mother," Prudence rolled her eyes and reached for her secret stash of M&M's in a Tupperware container in the freezer hidden behind Ray's two frozen hawks, "I have not *gone Indian*, whatever that means." Just then, Rita reappeared in a turquoise shirtwaist dress and red slingback high heels. The dress had giant cowboy boots flying all over it. Freshly lipsticked, Rita tossed her long hair, popped her neck and grinned.

"OK, back in the old saddle. See yah!"

Prudence waggled good-bye with her fingers, her mouth crammed, pacified by the click and dissolve of candy-shelled chocolate buttons.

"I heard that woman swearing. What kind of person uses foul language so early in the morning? I don't think this is right, Prudence. What about Fiona? What kind of atmosphere have you got going over there?"

"Fiona's dandy, Mom. She's hardly even here."

"Why do you suppose that is?"

"Because she's turning eighteen. She's got a boyfriend."

"Eighteen is not as grown up as you think."

"I wasn't even living at home at eighteen. You didn't know half of what I was up to." A pause, followed by "And I'm not about to tell you now," collided with Deleanor's "Well, don't start telling me now. I don't want to hear it."

"Sorry, Mom, I gotta go. I have to teach today, and I'm late. Rita was swearing because she stopped to get gas on her way to work and got hit by a wave of gasoline."

"Now why would that sort of thing

happen to someone? I'm really concerned, Prune, about what's going on over there."

"Nothing's going on. It was an accident, the gasoline. It could have happened to me, to you, to anyone. It happened to happen to Rita."

"According to Wayne Dyer and Louise Hay, there are no accidents. The universe is clearly trying to tell her something. She didn't get the subtle messages, so she got whacked with a wave of gasoline."

"Maybe so, but that's not our business, what the universe is trying to tell someone else. You going to yoga today?"

"Already went. That new teacher is hung up in Downward Dog, made us do it half a dozen times. My hamstrings hurt."

"I love you, Mom. You're an inspiration. And I have not, I promise, gone Indian."

"Well, I'm darn tootin' not happy about this other one moving in. Sounds like your place is being overrun."

"Not true, Mom. Fly over and see for yourself. I gotta go. Love you."

"Bye, peanut head. Love you, too. You be a good girl."

Her mother had been signing off like that for years, calling her *peanut head,* saying *You be a good girl.* It was nice, though, Prudence admitted to her bathroom mirror as she flossed, to have one person in the world who still thought tenderly and protectively of her, who remembered her as a child and not just a confused, clumsy adult.

"Hey, sexy." Ray revolved lazily in bed, stretching, waking up. He was like a teenager, sleeping late, lolling about, his pampered sensuality an irritant to certain responsible individuals with jobs, grown-up persons who had to be up early, dealing with things, getting ready for work, working to pay for things like the roof over his handsome, indolent head. "Watcha doin', sugar britches?"

"Getting ready for school. Going to *work*." Her voice, she couldn't help it, was tight, clipped.

Alerted by her tone, he turned wheedling. "Need me to do anything, sweetie? Take out the trash? I'm going to mow the lawn next week."

"Sure, that would be nice." *Be my guest, take out the trash, get around to the lawn one of these days.*

"What's wrong now?" It piqued Ray when his charm failed.

"Nothing," she lied. "Nothing's wrong."

"Well, cheer up. I don't like my women mopey or fat."

Mopey or fat! Your women! Prudence mentally flung her red cowboy boot, the one she was pulling onto her left foot, at his head.

"Rita go to work, sugar?"

"Yup."

"Who called?"

"My mom."

"Ah, Dr. Deleanor." He sauntered naked into her bathroom, languorously swooping a brush through his long, polished hair, leaning into the mirror to fret over a non-existent wrinkle under his left eye. Prudence nudged past him so she could get at her lavender estrogen pill, her pale orange progesterone pill, her *I'm an eternal girl* pills.

"Mmm, sexy this morning." He nibbled her neck. "A wery sexy wittle sawcer of milk . . . rrrrrumph," he growled, pinching her butt. "Gonna give me some of that to-night?"

With two pills dissolving in her mouth, Prudence made a resistant sound followed by an illogical, murmurous assent.

Her bright idea, hatched in Texas, to teach a course called Questing for Eros, had unleashed an erotic grenade in her classroom, blown open Pandora's naughtiest box. By mid-semester, the reading material and writing assignments had begun to produce bizarre side effects, tangled unions, suggestive possibilities, semi-dangerous liaisons. She needed to rein in her errant, aroused students, cry Whoa Nellie, throw an icy dash of intellectual analysis, of cerebral abstraction, over their newly wakened libidos. But how? she puzzled, unlocking her office door. Today was Sexual Body Map day — student presentations of erotic body maps, colored and drawn to life scale on butcher paper. The following week, they were to perform written monologues giving creative voice to their sexual organs of choice. And some weeks before, she had rashly given Dwayne Bird and Jimmy Flores permission to collaborate. Having seen a touring production of *The Vagina Monologues*, they had approached her with an idea for a parallel piece entitled *The Penis Dialogues*. Because four weeks had seemed eons away, because of who knew what other weakness or state of perpetual distraction she'd been in, she'd said yes. Prudence counted the squares on her office calendar. Seven days before she would be forced to watch Dwayne and Jimmy prance about in pink rubber penis costumes (*giant finger puppets*,

Dwayne had giggled) — the whole thing would be excruciating and her fault. How much of her life, Prudence wondered, had gone awry simply from not saying no.

Seated at her desk, with her door shut, Prudence tossed the majority of her paper mail into the trash before popping through her voice messages. Nothing of interest except Deedee Grind from Zebra Romance, saying they had received her edited manuscript and were definitely excited to publish P. T. Parker's *Savage Heat,* that Prudence would hear back from them very, very soon. Meanwhile, Deedee cooed, *have a passionate day.*

A passionate day? A knock at her office door.

Sheldon Pettipiece stood in her doorway, his sexual body map rolled into a loose, quashed tube under one pudgy arm. He offered to walk her across the quad (a depressing diamond of sere, withered grass), asking permission to present his map first since he had a dental appointment (double root canal, ugh). He had labored over his map all weekend, he told her, shifting the tube of paper from one arm to another. *All in all, a very stimulating project. Ha. Ha.*

Prudence imagined earnest, methodical Sheldon filling out his student evaluation, detailing exactly how stimulating Professor Parker's erotic class had been. She pictured prim, snide Dr. Finch, the newly appointed English Department chair, calling for an investigation of Prudence's pedagogical practices. She would be caught up in academic scandal, pilloried, cast out. As for Sheldon, who knew what kundalini serpent was coiling up and down his ass because of her assignment — Sheldon was an aging bachelor, short and tubby, a beach ball with legs and a pink, perspiring face. His glasses slipped perpetually down his small, round nose so that he was forced to constantly nudge them back up with one stubby finger. He had woodchuck brown hair, woodchuck brown eyes, and evinced the unfortunate tendency to ramble in his speech, to apologize incessantly for his poor organizational skills which caused him to overcompensate, overhighlight, over-Xerox, overexplain. And because he had confessed it so baldly in his erotic writing assignments, Prudence knew Sheldon was sexually conflicted and desperately lonely. He also loved to bake. Today he had dressed carefully in beige canvas tennis shoes, khaki Dockers and a long-sleeved Izod knit shirt with orange and blue stripes that further inflated his beach-ball physique. Beside her, Sheldon seemed to bounce, so that Prudence pictured him rolling along the moribund lawn, scudding across the smooth sidewalk and dribbling, forlorn and detumescent, into the gutter.

"Tell you what, Professor, I'm so damn nervous, I hope I don't faint." Sheldon's glasses were slipping down at twice their usual rate, his face looked radishy and slick.

"You'll be fine, Sheldon. I'm certain everyone else is just as nervous as you are. Remember, we're all on your side. We're for you, not against you." Though catching sight of chronically embittered Elaine Durrell sloping along in her signature pink sneakers, Prudence couldn't be completely convinced of that. Still, the calming effect her assurance had on Sheldon made her glad she had said it.

"All right, class. Today, as you know, each of you will present your sexual body map. Our first presenter will be Sheldon Pettipiece. Any questions before we begin?"

"Dr. Parker?" Haywood Marsh insisted on calling her Dr. Parker, an elevation in rank so amusing to Prudence she never bothered to correct him. "After our maps this week and our monologues next, what is the exact date for our end-of-class party? I have some travel arrangements I need to make, but I don't want to miss anything."

Haywood was referring to the upcoming Erotic Dinner Party to be held either at Prudence's house (less likely) or the home of a student (more likely). Everyone was to bring an erotic food dish, along with a sexy poem or prose piece to share. Another of Prudence's inspired ideas.

The students quieted as Sheldon bumbled and adenoidally chuffed his way up to the front of the classroom, carrying his map and sport water bottle, his *liquid refreshment,* as he called it. His paper sexual self furled back up the moment he'd gotten it unfurled, so Prudence suggested he thumbtack his map to the wall. This involved Dwayne's jogging down the hall to the English office for tacks and a hammer. As Sheldon pounded all four corners of himself onto the wall, Prudence feared he might wimple into a cold faint. So, when he began to display unexpected poise and confidence, as the students genuinely laughed at the story of his stimulating weekend with a certain raspberry jelly doughnut, she was enormously relieved. Sheldon's public agony, replaced by a fragile charisma, his florid tenderness and heart of oceanic proportion, locked away in a rotund, sweating, homely form, his magnificent potential as a lover measured against the remote chance of his ever being loved, a man too short, too podgy, too panting and sentimental to ever be taken seriously, this yawning chasm between his latent talent as a lover versus his erotic segregation from the world, produced a spectacle so moving, with Sheldon himself utterly transparent in his lustful revelations, that when he concluded by taking a long, noisy draft from his orange sport bottle, several of the women wiped away tears, while the remainder of the class, including Prudence, sat motionless, mute, stunned by the underground sexual glory of their own Sheldon Pettipiece. Popular for the first time in his adult life, Sheldon bowed, checked his sport watch, apologized for his early departure, prised four thumbtacks from his body map, fumbling and repeatedly dropping the rolled-up tube until Elaine Durrell and Happi Tuite rushed forward, nearly caroming into one another in their eagerness to help, and since it was break time anyway, Elaine, the more assertive of the two, walked Sheldon, her long pink sneakers flashing, to his car.

When she returned, puddling down in her chair, it was clear to Prudence that Cupid's most mischievous arrow had wandered out from Sheldon's sexual map and plunged straight into Elaine Durrell's bruised and bitter heart. (Indeed, eight months later, Prudence, along with the rest of the Questing for Eros class, would be invited to Sheldon and Elaine's sunset wedding at the local botanical garden. Wedding toasts would begin with a reference to Sheldon's love affair with jelly doughnuts and end with the bride and groom toasting Prudence for providing them with the opportunity to meet and love one another.)

Driving home from class, Prudence marveled at the disparity between Sheldon's rotund woodchuck body and the sweet, glimpsed heart of the great lover beating within. Think of the privileged ranks of gorgeous, narcissistic men in the world, fruitlessly adored, versus all the homely men, physically sidelined but aching to love. Prudence was pondering this as she opened the back door to find Ray, completely nude, headphones clamped over his ears, sunbathing on her chaise lounge.

"Hey."

Ray scrambled to a seated position, while Boss, resting his humongous head on his paws, his tongue a pink wet bathmat lolling out the side of his mouth, shifted two small eyes to glance dully at her.

"Whoa. Scared me. I thought you were Rita."

"I don't know how you can lie out here all day."

"Helps me maintain my savage manliness. Hey babe." He brushed past her (*Blazing Eagle's bronzed, muscled shoulders gleamed*), smelling of sweat and Banana Boat oil. While he was in the shower, Rita came home, barging in the front door yakking on her cell phone, sending Prudence a happy little wave, while continuing out to the backyard to plunk in a chair by the pool and, still talking, light up a cigarette. Jasper, Prudence guessed from Rita's slinky feline slouch, as she bundled up the day's bills and collection notices and shoved them all in a drawer. Everyone would just have to wait until her check arrived from Zebra Romance.

Ray and Prudence sat down to reheated frozen pizza as Rita arranged a circle of damp white petals of sushi on a glass platter, setting a small cup of brown sauce in the center, like the eye of a daisy.

"Is that raw?" Prudence hated the idea

of raw fish.

"Let's just say if you threw it back, it might swim. I live on this stuff. Here, try."

"No thanks."

"Ray?"

"Sure." He nipped up a glistening fish-petal, dipped it in soy sauce, slipped it into his mouth.

"Awesome, huh? This is so incredible, being free to eat whatever I want. Every darn night back in Tuba City, no matter how tired I was, no matter what, when we both got home from a full day of teaching at the school, I had to get busy and cook meat, potatoes, tortillas, fry bread." Rita tilted back in her chair, slapped her belly. "That's where all this comes from. I've packed on thirty pounds since leaving L.A."

"How's Jasper? You talked to him?" Ray reached for another piece of sushi.

"He's driving down for the weekend, and if you guys don't mind, bringing our bed. Little brother, can you take down that twin bed in there, it's killing my lower back. My back's wrecked from years of animal training, I've been thrown from horses more times than I have birthdays, and then there was that world-famous elephant attack at the San Diego Zoo. I'll just sleep on the floor till Jasper brings the bed. Sure you guys don't mind? My back's totally killing me, in fact could one of you walk on it after dinner? You'd be perfect, Prudence, since you don't weigh much."

With Ray supine, a screwdriver clamped between his teeth, dismantling Prudence's childhood bed, taking apart the four maple posts, carting the headboard, footboard, rails, box spring and mattress into the laundry room, Rita, facedown on the living room carpet, head facing the TV, instructed Prudence how to plant both bare feet on opposite sides of Rita's spine, and walk back and forth. More like rolling than walking, Prudence thought, her feet losing purchase on the Jell-O-y surface of Rita's flesh. Suddenly, there was the unsettling crack of something calcific, followed by Rita groaning and wheezing. Queasy from the rubbery slippage of Rita's flesh, the sharp, twiglike snap of bone, Prudence hopped clumsily off, slightly wrenching her left ankle.

"Ahhhhhh, that was SOOO GREAT. That was the exact spot, girl, did you hear that crack? You got it."

Sitting up, placing her hands on both sides of her head, Rita administered a fast, terrific twist to her neck. Prudence heard a gristly pop as Rita jerked her skull in the opposite direction. "Hear that? Much better. I'm going to head outside for a last smoke, then hit the hay. I am one beat pup. This job, I'm beginning to wonder, I mean it's total commission, and I didn't make a darn thing again today. Talked my ass off, didn't snag one client. Hope I make some dough tomorrow. Don't forget, guys, cable company's coming tomorrow to install two cable boxes, one in the living room for you two and one in my room. Got to have my true crime shows."

Coming in from the laundry room, Ray stood rubbing his strained arm muscles. "OK, Rita, floor's yours. Ready to dye hair with me?"

"I was just telling Prudence I'm pooped. But yeah, sure, let's go for it. Where do you usually do yours?"

"In the bathroom."

"I can use the kitchen sink. Actually, do you think Fiona'd mind if I used her bathroom? She's so darn cute, your daughter, she reminds me of my Erin, both of them with that same red hair and feisty spirit."

Fiona, furious, stood at the door to her bathroom, arms akimbo, surveying the freckling of black spots all over her pink wallpaper, pink tile countertop, even her mirror. She creaked open the cupboard door under the sink, yanked out the pink plastic trash can, found what she suspected, right on top, a ripped-open box of Lady Clairol. *Midnight Raven.*

She had stopped by to get her mint tooth floss, quietly passing the living room, lit by TV, *Forensic Detectives*, some guy rebuilding the skull of a murder victim. Her mom and Ray were cuddled close on one couch, while Rita lounged, with her fake DYED head, on the other.

Prudence found Fiona in the kitchen, eating peanut butter with a plastic spoon. "Hey sweetie."

"Mom," Fiona hissed. "My bathroom!"

"What's wrong, what do you mean?"

"There's hair dye everywhere. *She*" — Fiona jerked her chin toward the living room — "must have shaken her wet hair all over my bathroom, there's nasty flecks of black dye all over the place!"

"I'm sorry, honey, I'll ask her to clean it up."

"That's so rude, I can't believe she'd do that."

"You're right, honey. I promise I'll ask her. Guess what? Rita's getting us cable tomorrow."

The news had scant effect. Fiona dropped the spoon in the sink, slid the jar of peanut butter back in the refrigerator, closed the door. "That's nice. I'd better get going. I have to get over to school. Did I tell you I have an art show in six weeks, over at Metro? My performance piece won first place out of our whole class."

"Fiona, that's great . . . I'm so proud. What's the piece about?"

"Can't say. It's still . . . evolving."

"PRUUU-EE!"

"Mom, why does he do that? Bellow? How can you stand it? It's so mom-and-pop. So 1950s."

"PRUNESTER! Where's my poppy-corn?"

"My god, Mom, he's screaming for treats." Fiona looked incredulous. "Hey, I gotta go. Love you."

"Love you too, sweetie. We should spend a day together."

"Yeah, that would be nice. Maybe . . ."

"PRUE! C'mon! There's a show you'd like — something about soft face recognition to solve crimes!"

"Guess you'd better get in there . . . we'll talk, plan something later on."

On the same day Rita skipped work to

401

have a manicure, a pedicure and her upper lip waxed, Ray was running with rocks down by the canal just as Prudence retrieved the mail from its black metal box outside the front door. Carefully, she opened the black-and-white-striped envelope from Zebra Romance. Ten thousand dollars! She kissed the check, slipped it back into its envelope, and returned to preparing enchiladas for Jasper Chee, grating cheddar cheese into an orangy heap, mixing it with shredded chicken and diced onion. Life was on the upswing. She had penned a dumb romance, been paid extravagantly for it, and now a Navajo holy man was about to visit her home. Plus Ray was being kind and attentive, though they hadn't had sex in over two weeks. Things with Rita were better, too; she was gone most of the day, and Prudence was working on tolerance, adjusting her attitude. Nothing was perfect but all was well. Except for Deleanor. Still upset with Prudence for letting Ray (and now Rita) live with her, her mother rarely called, though she did use her i-Mail, an electronic letter-sending gadget she'd recently purchased in Honolulu, sending Prudence daily spiritual inspirations and health alerts from Dr. Sinatra, his latest medical alert concerning the deadly properties of canola oil, an industrial lubricant made from rapeseed and sold for human consumption. A half-empty bottle of the villainous oil sat on Prudence's counter . . . oh well, when it was used up, she'd buy something else. Her other, more immediate worry was Fiona. Fiona had left for Kirby's two nights before and Prudence hadn't seen or heard from her since. Fiona always called right back whenever Prudence phoned, within ten minutes, fifteen at most. Today her calls had been met on Fiona's end with a weird-sounding, dead noise, and all of Prudence's latent distrust of Kirby roared to the surface. Who was he? Prudence hadn't a clue. If asked, she would describe him as shiftless, spoon-chested, too-idle and hopelessly monosyllabic. Twenty-four years old and the best he could do was parade around in an ape suit in front of apartment complexes. Worse, he had become involved in suspension art, and Prudence knew a little about that. She and Ray had watched *Primetime* one night and learned of a new, disturbing fad among young people — shoving stainless steel hooks into their flesh, suspending themselves from ceilings, bridges, even freeway underpasses. Kirby lived in the Jolly Roger, a run-down apartment complex behind Taco Bell in Mesa, that much she knew. She also knew how many lithesome Persephones were daily abducted, taken into hell by scruffy modern-day Plutos. Who was this Kirby? Why was Fiona always over there? Had she lost control of her daughter? Had she had control? Prudence did not believe in controlling children so much as understanding them. Hastily rolling and tucking the last enchilada into the baking dish, she wiped her hands on a dish towel (a blue-striped cotton cloth Fiona had bought for her, *Feng shui, Moomers, you need your water element, the color blue in your kitchen, to neutralize possible hostile energy between the stove and the sink*) and tried Fiona's cell number again. Nothing. Increasingly frightened by the collage of gruesome images forming around the scenario of a kidnapped and tortured Fiona, determined to locate Kirby's phone number and go, like Demeter, in search of her lost daughter, Prudence did what she had never before done: she invaded Fiona's bedroom.

— *pull on the Barbie doll dangling from the corded end of the overhead light switch. Room a mess. Open the nightstand drawer, find the address book, feel, beside it, a little zippered cloth bag. Pick up the bag — lumpy, full of something. What? Pills? Pills! Unzip, look in. Ohmigod! Dump out pills on Fiona's bed, a scattering on the rumpled sheets. Black pills, white pills, brown ones with a yellow stripe . . . wait, that's a Midol, but the rest . . . contraband, ominous. Fiona, unconscious, lying helpless in Kirby's den of suspension horror . . . flip through the address book, find his name, a phone number. Rush back to the kitchen to call the number, ohno, the doorbell! Police? —*

"Cable, ma'am. I'm here to install two cable boxes as requested by an R. Bragswolf. Bragswolf — is that a real name?"

The technician is a refrigerator-sized black man in a white jumpsuit, methodical and patient in his movements, inured to the technological dopiness, the electronic sap-headedness, of his customers. After showing him the living room and Rita's room, Prudence rushes to the phone to try Kirby's number, hastily inked on her palm. It rings and rings. She tries Fiona for the hundredth time. Having inherited from her mother the inclination to panic (*Never forget, Prudence! For good or for bad, we Parker women are three things: late bloomers, quick panickers and petite, not short*), to awfulize, to assume the unholy worst, to plunge herself into premature mourning for everything she'd ever loved, a genetic panic she is helpless to stop once it starts, with Ray out lugging rocks, her enchiladas cloaked in foil and refrigerated, with the cable man wearing his tool pouch, slow-working and trustworthy, Prudence snatches up her car keys and dashes outside. She will drive to his apartment, locate Fiona's little gray car. She will beg the manager to open Kirby's door if need be, open the door onto what horrific tableau? Prudence's heart drills inside her chest, light as a hummingbird's. She hasn't felt this frantic since twenty-two-month-old Fiona toddled away from a lax baby-sitter named Madge Barkley and crossed two trafficked streets to a little green park, where she was discovered by a police detective two hours later, wearing a soggy diaper and making patty-cakes in the leaf-littered sandbox.

Unseeing, Prudence accelerates right past Ray, bent forward from the weight of his rock sack and walking rapidly. He looks up. Was that Prudence whizzing past? Predictable, reliable, law-abiding Prudence? Assuming he'll find a note of explanation, Ray trudges back to the house. But there is no note, no explanation, and in Prudence's place, there is only a cable TV technician.

★ ★ ★

Mouse is nowhere in the parking lot. She knocks on number 113 of the Jolly Roger complex, peers in the window, hands cupped around her eyes. An unclothed mannequin lies facedown in one corner of the living room. No one answers her frantic knocking and hallooing. Partially calmed by not seeing Fiona's car, her scenarios of murder somewhat quashed, Prudence drives back home, where she finds Ray and the cable man in front of her television, Ray gripping the black multi- buttoned remote, receiving a quick tutorial in channel surfing.

"Fiona called. She says you've left dozens of messages on her cell. She's on her way home right now."

"Oh thank god! Where was she?"

Ray shrugs, turns back to his schooling. As her eyes adjust to the living room's dim light, Prudence spies Boss stretched out, camouflaged, on her white couch.

"Ray!"

"Oh right . . . c'mon boy, outside."

"Big pup," the cable man murmurs admiringly.

"Mom, why were you calling me every

ten seconds?" At Prudence's command, they were in Fiona's bedroom.

Prudence rattled the small zippered bag of pills. "I am going to ask you something, Fiona Parker, and I don't want you telling me anything but the honest truth. What are these?"

Staring at the little embroidered bag in her mother's hand, Fiona began to laugh.

"Oh no, Mah, you think I'm a *drug addict?*"

"Of course I think that, and until a few minutes ago, I thought you were dead. You must always answer your phone when I call. Always. What are these? Black beauties?"

Fiona collapsed, hooting, on her futon. "Black beauties? Mom, those are yours! You gave them to me about a year ago, they're valerian root! Here, let me show you. This one's Motrin, these are aspirin, vitamins, more valerian root, two herbal diet pills I got from you, one painkiller left over from my dental surgery two years ago, a vitamin C, one Midol. That's it. My stash of drugs."

"Oh."

"Goofmommy. Black beauties? Where did you get that name? I'm sorry, but that is so completely hysterical."

Prudence sounded vague. "I don't know, I saw some local news show about teenagers and drugs, what to look for, the police showed all these confiscated pills lined up on a piece of felt, that's where I got black beauties I guess, so when I saw these were, well . . . black, oh, I don't know. Where were you?"

"I had a job interview, plus I stayed late after school to work on my performance. The batteries went dead on my phone, so I couldn't call you even though the light was blinking, and I knew it was you calling. Can we go to the kitchen now? I'm starving."

The cable technician loomed by the open front door, forced to shake Ray's left hand, as the TV's remote control appeared to be surgically grafted to his right.

"Wow. Cable? Cool."

"Rita's paying for the whole thing — says she can't go another night without her fix."

"I'm sorry you were so worried." Fiona hugged her mother. "See? I'm not dead, and I'm not a drug addict. And guess what? I got a job!"

"Wonderful, what —"

Fiona wrinkled her nose. "Well, it's not the greatest, but it pays pretty well, and I get to set my own hours. It's telemarketing for a singles service."

"One of those dating things?"

"Yupdup." Fiona had her head poked in the refrigerator. "Mmm, enchiladas, what's the occasion?"

"Rita's boyfriend is driving down for the weekend. I'd like you to meet him, Fee. He's Navajo and a Sun Dance chief. Good grief, I am so relieved you're alive! You have no idea how much I love you. If anything ever happened to you, I'd —"

"I know, Mom. I feel the same."

"You do?"

"Yes! Every time you go off driving somewhere, I worry until you get back. We definitely got the panic gene from Grandma."

"Can you stay for dinner? I really want you to meet Jasper."

"Can't, Mom. I have rehearsal. What if I stay over tonight and meet him in the morning?"

"That's fine. I think I need a glass of wine to calm down. I'm shaky from being so worried about you. There's a leftover bottle of Black Opal back behind the flower vases, oops . . . no, just cheap red stuff. Spaghetti wine."

"Why are you pouring wine into a coffee

410

mug?"

"Ray doesn't drink, neither does Rita — Sun Dance vows. I'm sneaking."

Fiona rolled her eyes. "For chrissakes, Mom, it's your house . . . uh-oh, here she comes." Rita's little blue Civic screeched up and shuddered to a halt in front of the house. From the window, they could see Rita's jaw working against her cell phone.

"I'm sorry, Mah, that woman drives me nuts."

Suddenly, in the workroom next to the kitchen, Ray's hair dryer shot on, speed-drying his newest canvas. As it switched off, they could hear Meat Loaf, an eighties band, blaring. "Mom," Fiona shook her bristled head, "I honest to god don't know how you stand it." She walked down the hall toward her bedroom.

Going into the living room, Prudence stared at the TV, lodged in its pine armoire, a foreign black box on top of it, various instructional pamphlets strewn over the glass surface of the coffee table. Prudence sighed. She didn't much like TV. Before Ray's arrival, she'd seriously considered doing what Powell claimed to have done years before, thrown the idiot box out, taken it to the dump. He'd been on a media fast for over a year now, no newspapers, no magazines, no TV, no radio. He claimed not to have the faintest idea what was going on in the world. A stress-free way to live, he said. Completely novel. *Imagine, hearing yourself think.* He'd stopped reading books, stopped writing in his journal. *I want to hear my own mind.* One afternoon, he'd even had Wanda take him to a mall in Albuquerque and lead him around, blindfolded. *Very hallucinogenic,* he told Fiona, who'd told Prudence, *the sounds, the textures, the smells. Very psychedelic,* reminding Prudence of why, decades before, she'd found Powell appealing. Now, four hundred channels of cable streamed into her house, into her consciousness, the culprit a small black box on top of the TV, paid for by Rita Bragswolf.

Rita bounded like a vulcanized Labrador into the house. "I have a good chance of winning my case, plus the retainer fee is a hundred dollars. Look! I went to that beauty shop you recommended to get my upper lip waxed." Ugly red blisters bubbled along Ritatop lip. "Hot wax burn."

"Ouch."

"Hurts like blazes . . . Jasper's on the 202, stuck in rush hour. Look at my lip!!

Oww."

Prudence went out to her backyard, broke off a light green stem of aloe vera, brought it in to Rita, showing her how to squeeze and daub the cool bitter-smelling gel on her singed lip.

"It's not bad, Rita. It really doesn't look that bad."

"You think? I don't know whether to sue or not, plus I'm so broke I'd have to put the retainer on my credit card. Sales sucked again this week. The acupuncturist backed out at the last minute, then my reptile specialist bailed. No sales, no commission. This job is not what it was cracked up to be. I'm even dipping into my savings now. I've still got my two boys, my Andalusians, boarded up north for eighty bucks a month, I'm still paying all Jasper's utility bills since he's so strapped from having to pay alimony to his bitch ex-wife, and to top it off, I just had to fork up seven hundred dollars for a new wolf pup. Here's my camera, Prudence. It's digital. Got a hot deal on it last week at the flea market. Take a couple of pictures of my lip, will you? For evidence? Thanks."

Prudence snapped three different angles of Rita's upper lip. "What was that you said? Wolf pup?"

"Didn't Ray tell you I used to raise wolves out in L.A.? He had one all picked out from a litter, 'member, little brother?" Rita yelled, pressing the green aloe stem like a trick mustache against the burnt space in between her nose and lip. Ray's hair dryer shot on, he couldn't hear, so Rita shrugged. "Some idiot drove by the house one night, shot it dead. Anyway, Jasper said it would be OK with him if I went ahead and bought this timberwolf, eight weeks old, one hundred percent pureblood, raised by the Nez Perce tribe. Her brothers and sisters just got released into the wild at Yellowstone, but they kept Nizhoni out for me. The breeder wants to ship her right away because her husband's tempted to keep her, she's such a little beauty. Jeez, my lip! Pipe ceremony's this weekend, we'll all drive up for that, then Nizhoni arrives on a ten o'clock flight from Akron Sunday night. Can you go to the airport with me, help me pick her up from freight? She'll be crated up, poor baby."

The TV blared, top volume, from the living room where Ray was now struggling to flip cable channels. Her panic over Fiona, the cable installation, a wolf due to arrive, a trip north to the Navajo reservation for a ceremony she knew nothing about, Rita's boyfriend, Jasper, due to arrive any minute, all these events, in close succession, plus the two coffee mugs of wine she had secretly downed, all made Prudence feel odd, as if there were two, or three or four of her, each more befuddled than the last. Rita poked bits of leftover sushi into her mouth as she halfheartedly unloaded the dishwasher.

"Smells darn good."

"Enchiladas."

"Jasper's all-time favorite. That man can eat, I tell you. Wait till you see him, he is the most gorgeous man in the world. We haven't been apart in three years, if you know what I mean." Rita winked. "Hey, you should let me come in one of these days and talk to that erotic class of yours, I bet I could make the old schoolhouse shake." Pouring soap granules into the dishwasher, she glanced up at Prudence, grinning wickedly, and whispering, "Six or seven orgasms a night. For three solid years."

"Well," said Prudence, "that about takes the cake."

"Being away from him this long has been torture, though I have dropped weight. Jasper says a little weight loss is OK so long as it's not in my tits. He can't stand droopy tits."

Is that how a holy man speaks? Prudence wondered. Oh, what would she know? What did she know indeed? Only that Jasper was late, her prized enchiladas were drying out around the edges, and Rita was back outside, smoking and pacing, on her cell, consulting a second lawyer about her singed lip, her cigarette tip glowing, a firefly in the darkened yard. Ray was soldered into his favorite spot on her couch, watching a music documentary called *One Hit Wonders.* She knew this because during the commercials he kept yelling for her, so finally Prudence sat down a moment, watching balding old rockers in their forties and fifties reminiscing about wall-to-wall groupies and endless drugs, the good old days, until she couldn't stand it (them) anymore and jumped up.

"Sweet cheeks, where you going?"

"To check the enchiladas," she fibbed, dashing back into the kitchen to tipple from a replenished mug of wine. Suddenly Prudence heard a truck, saw headlights in her driveway. Curious to meet the man who could give Rita seven orgasms a night, Prudence trailed Ray outside. She saw a dumpy middle-aged Indian man with a wide, fleshy face, black hair in a braid down his back, in blue jeans and a T-shirt, wrestling a mattress, sticking like a giant quilted tablet, out of the truck bed.

"Hey nephew." Jasper let go of the mattress to man-hug Ray. Prudence positioned herself modestly in the lean shadow of a palm tree.

"Uncle! Good to see you. Prudence, where are you? Get over here. Meet Jasper."

As they shook hands, she tried to keep her distance. What if he smelled Black Opal on her breath?

"I've made enchiladas," she murmured.

"Great," Jasper laughed. "My favorite." His dark brown eyes gazed warmly, knowingly, into hers, and because he was spiritual, Prudence fell a little in love with him.

"Baby!" Rita jetted out the front door, arms flung open, wearing a slinky black jumpsuit bisected by a wide white belt strewn with chunks of fake turquoise. She had her reddest lipstick on, her long hair brushed. Her figure was noticeably trim from her sushi and cigarette diet. She and Jasper rocked and hugged, hugged and kissed, swayed on into the house, arms strapped around one another's waists. They hung around Prudence's kitchen, nonstop kissing and cooing and patting each other on the bottom, while Prudence took up banging and fussing with pots and dishes. Ray, newly deft, poured glasses of water, set out silverware, his waiterly behavior a shock to Prudence since he normally lounged in front of the TV, waiting for her to bring his dinner, though, to be fair, he washed the dishes afterward.

Rita broke away from Jasper, she had a business call coming in, wasn't hungry, didn't want dinner. While she paced the yard with her phone, Ray and Jasper sat down at the kitchen table as Prudence flitted in a triangular pattern, stove, refrigerator, table, stove, refrigerator, table, trying gracefully, though she was a little tipsy, to serve their food. Jasper simply nodded, not looking at her as she placed a full plate before him. When he bowed his head in prayer, Ray bent his, too. Prudence stood nearby, hands clasped, while Jasper thanked Creator for his safe journey, for the good food before him, for his nephew, for his nephew's companion, Priscilla. The men fell to eating, rapidly, in heavy silence, as Prudence/Priscilla managed to salvage the last two enchiladas for Fiona. In less than fifteen minutes two men had devoured an entire pan of her gourmet enchiladas along with two stacks of warm flour tortillas.

After dinner, Rita dragged Jasper down to Applebee's for coffee and dessert while Ray and Prudence watched a Discovery show on sea anemones. Ray had helped her clean the kitchen, and now he rubbed her shoulders during the commercials. As he massaged, Prudence sat thinking how best to spend her check for *Savage Heat*. Ten thousand dollars! Curled up beside Ray, who, channel surfing with the remote — his manhood — in both hands, finally stopped at an interview with Iron Maiden, Prudence basked, replete in new happiness, Ray beside her, cash coming in, hopes high for a life on the right path — on every level, blessed.

A string of concussive thumps awakened Prudence for the sixth time that night. Squeezing her pillow around both ears, Prudence tried not to hear Rita's seventh orgasm — scream — moan — sigh — inches away, on the other side of the wall.

Fiona had come home, as promised, to spend a rare night in her room, eat breakfast the following morning with a medicine man, shaman, guru, whatever he was. She had scarcely crept beneath the covers when she heard unmistakable sounds coming through the heater vent near her bedroom floor. Vile physical touchings, inches away, bodies squishing, fluids mixing, ugh. Mercifully, the sounds stopped. Mercilessly, they started up again. That did it. If Fiona had to hear the lewd thumping groans of sexual congress one more time, she would simply die. She did not die, instead lay rigid, gnawing one corner of her pillowcase, her index fingers stopping up both ears. That was it. The final straw. After the breakfast she had promised her mother, Fiona would, temporarily at least, move out.

Beneath the stiff slippage of buffalo hide, with Ray asking if she was too hot, with Prudence answering yes, she was, with Ray sitting up to roll the heavy flap of hide back, then lying back down, with the hide, seconds later, unrolling and fwapping Prudence in the face like a leaden pie crust, Prudence gave up. Lay still, defeated and sleepless. Seconds later, Jasper and Rita started up again.

"Psst, Ray."

"Mmm?"

"Hear that?"

"What?"

"*That.*"

Ray slapped her butt, muttered something about "doing the nasty," yawned, and dropped right back to sleep.

An ectoplasmic Deleanor floated above Prudence's portion of the bed, mouth drawn tight with disapproval, finger wagging . . . *Unhealthy, what's going on over there, Prudence, your father wouldn't approve at all, I can say that for darn tootin'.*

At her end of the hall, Fiona fell at last into a sort of twilight sleep, cotton balls wadded in both ears, two pillows, weighted down by a combination thesaurus/dictionary, over her face, arms and legs sprawled in stiff, rigid protest.

Prudence stood over the blue-blanketed lump in Fiona's room. "Fry bread time!"

A thin moan seeped out from under the blanket.

"Jasper's made a marvelous breakfast."

A deeper moan, a groan really, after which the lump rolled over, the blue blanket slipping off to unveil the sweet, singular issue of Prudence's flesh, pale, freckled arms flung, hair re-dyed one shade of burgundy, sticking up in thin, whipped spikes.

"Mah. I cannot face those people. I can't

look at them."

"What do you mean, bunkie?"

Fiona sat up. Catching the blanket around her waist, looking crabbed and groggy, she fixed a sleep-deprived eye on her mother.

"Your holy breakfast-fixer was inches away from me, having sex, with Rita, all night long. All fucking, excuse me, night long. Look." Fiona pointed toward the wall. Prudence looked. A dictionary, obviously thrown, lay open, pages splayed, near the floor vent.

"Don't tell me you didn't hear them. They sounded like a porno soundtrack."

Prudence looked sharply at her daughter. What would Fiona know about porno soundtracks? "Yes, I heard them. I think the only one who slept through it all was Ray."

"That's because he can't hear. He's deaf from all that eighties music."

"I agree, it was awful, and I'm sorry, sweetie, but just do this one thing for me. Sit down to breakfast with us. Someday you'll appreciate having met a genuine medicine man."

"Big whoop. OK, I'll be up in a minute." Fiona sniffed, conciliatory. "Smells good."

"Homemade fry bread. Thanks, hon, it

means a lot, your being willing to meet people from other cultures."

"OK, but I still can't look at them."

Prudence's dining room table was loaded down with platters of food — scrambled eggs mixed with green chilies and cheddar cheese, heaps of glistening link sausage, pots of jam, dishes of butter, a glass pitcher of orange juice, and the centerpiece — Jasper's warm fry bread, stacked high, bubbled, slightly browned.

"Ah, here she is. Morning, sweetie. I'd like you to meet Jasper Chee. Jasper, this is my daughter, Fiona True Parker."

Blushing past her temples and deep into her maroon hairline, Fiona limply shook hands with Jasper, who, having pushed back his chair, rose to greet her.

Sitting down, Jasper glanced across the table. "Nephew? Do us the honor?"

Ray began by thanking Creator for the food set before them. Peeking through her fingers, Prudence thought how she hadn't heard Ray formally pray since that first night in Anadarko, in the budget motel room, when he had smoked her with sage, when she had thought *him* a holy man, even though he had come right out and said he wasn't.

After Ray's prayer, everyone except Fiona fell upon their food, lavishing compliments on Jasper, who presided at the head of Prudence's table with a mild, grandmotherly glow. Fiona picked at the dollop of egg on her plate, nibbled on a cusp of fry bread, raised her hand in a traffic "stop" gesture as the platter of sausage links passed by. True to her word, she hadn't once looked at the holy breakfast-maker or his orgasmic companion, Rita.

By contrast, Rita was waking up, gaining in volume and loquacity with each bite of food. She wore the easy bloom of someone erotically replete. She looked, Prudence thought, slightly greasy. Carrying on about her days as an animal trainer, her pioneering work with African elephants in San Diego, how her training as an EMT, a paramedic, had come in handy during the world-famous elephant attack videotaped by a Japanese tourist who happened to be Johnny-on-the-spot, a tape repeatedly shown on *Animal Stories*, one of the most requested episodes in the entire five-year history of the series . . . blahblahblah . . . Prudence had heard all of this before.

"You were a paramedic?" Folding three sausages into his fourth fry bread, Ray took a great bite. "I didn't know that."

"You bet." Thus ensued a numbing account of Rita's work on urban cadavers, including her recovery of a man decapitated in a freeway crash, how she'd had to plunge around in the shrubs until she'd found the balding head and carried it to the ambulance, tucked, like a warm soccer ball, under her right arm.

Fiona clonked her glass of juice down, her face gone white as a blanched parsnip.

"Rita, that's no subject for breakfast," Jasper admonished. "I'd rather talk with nephew a little about his preparations for Sun Dance. This year's solstice falls on July 21, so it's not far off. And Prudence, you'll want to get together with Rita, so she can instruct you, woman to woman, in the things you'll need to know."

Rita snatched the last fry bread on the plate. "First thing to know, it's a ton of work, gathering sage, cooking for all the men, taking care of the camps, then you need to know what to wear, shawls and long skirts, though if you don't have 'em, you can borrow mine. I've got scads of everything."

"And no see-through skirts." Jasper spoke up. "I remember this one Sun Dance, the brothers were all out there in the arena, fasting, dancing, suffering, and there's this one white chick, no one had ever seen her before, hanging out under the arbor, off to herself, just sitting there all quiet, except she's got her two bare legs stuck straight out, you know, open, and this one brother, because of where he's at in the arena and the way the light is shining, he sees straight up her legs to that lady's bush. Hey, brother, look there, he says to the brother next to him. Pretty soon all the brothers are getting distracted, some white lady sitting across the way, her bush airing out for all to see. Then she stands up, the sun shining right through her skirt, which is made out of this really thin white stuff, so now it's even worse, it's like she's standing there naked, a pretty big distraction for all the Sun Dance brothers out there in the arena. So you ladies have got to be real careful what you wear, how you sit, how you conduct yourself. Real modest. No bush hanging out."

Prudence was shocked. *Bush?* Maybe Indians were more at ease talking about such things? She lacked perspective in this. Glancing at Fiona, she noticed her daughter's complexion had gone from white to red, her entire face flushed to the roots of her whipped-up hair. "Uh, thanks for breakfast." Fiona scraped back her chair.

426

"I've, ah, got tons of homework."

Jasper's broad face puddled into its benign, grandmotherly look. "Nice to meet you."

Rita reached out, lightly slapping Fiona's bottom. "See ya, gal. You're the spitting image of my Erin in Dublin. You two could be twins. Hit those books, girl. Make us proud."

Normally, Prudence would insist Fiona clear dishes, help clean up, but this time she let her go. She really wished Jasper had talked about something spiritually instructive, culturally edifying. Not a woman's *bush,* for god's sake.

While Prudence politely declined Rita's invitation to go with her and Jasper to the annual Ostrich Festival in Mesa, Fiona, in her room, unbeknownst to her mother, gathered up things to take to Kirby's (that disgusting breakfast conversation the last of last straws) while Ray, in the kitchen, scrubbed a multitude of pots, pans, dishes, swept the floor, dribbled sausage grease over Boss's food, and handed the giant stainless steel dog dish to Prudence to take outside.

"Boy, does Boss's coat feel dry," Prudence said, coming back in from the yard.

"He's eyeball deep in his dog dish, sucking up sausage grease."

"Probably needs the fat." Ray lifted his T-shirt and pooched out his smooth brown belly. "Speaking of which, I need to run."

"Did you finish your talk with Jasper?"

"Yeah, he wrote down a whole list of stuff I need to get. I'll show you later, it's in the workroom. Where are you going with that?" He was looking at the dessert plate in her hand, the cold bits of egg, sausage and fry bread arranged neatly on it.

"Jasper said to take food outside, do a spirit offering."

"Oh right. That's good."

Watching him swab the sink, rinse down the dirty water, his back to her, Prudence felt a surge of tenderness toward Ray. Preparing for the Sun Dance seemed to have given him focus, a moral high ground. Their daily lives had become better, kinder, unmarked by rancor or meanness. No more cold, conquering sexuality. Come to think of it, since Rita'd moved in, there'd been very little sex. None, in fact. It was like they were brother and sister. Why was that? she wondered.

"Did you hear them, Ray? Last night?"

Wiping his hands on a red-checkered dish towel, Ray draped it neatly over the oven bar. "Yup. And it's been giving me ideas all morning." He moved behind her, grabbed her hips, started walking her toward the bedroom. "C'mon, sexy thing."

"But —"

"No buts. C'mon, sweet thing. You know you like it when I'm rough with you."

Prudence missed Fiona's leave-taking, no different from other times she'd gone over to Kirby's, except this time she'd taken her favorite stuffed bear, all her pillows and a week's supply of underwear. She'd also left a note near the phone in the kitchen, with Kirby's phone number and address, plus the number where she could be reached at her new job, Big Dreams. *I love you, Mooler, but I need time away — mainly from your Houseguests! Call me anytime. Your twin white* . . . (Twin white referred to an e-mail personality test they had once taken together, where they had each picked the other as their twin soul, in response to the color white.)

As Fiona tiptoed past, clutching her pillows, underwear and teddy bear, she couldn't hear her mother and Ray, the bedroom door was closed, but she knew they were in there. Taking a nap, fully clothed, was how she pictured them.

Hours later, when Rita and Jasper came home from the Ostrich Festival, Prudence was on the couch beside Ray, watching rock music biographies, Ozzy Osbourne, Annie Lennox, Aerosmith, Meat Loaf. Since they'd gotten cable, she'd never watched so much television about aging rock stars in her life.

"That ostrich thing was a gas, you guys. Jasper! Where are you? Jasper, show them what I bought you, baby." A small man, not much taller than Prudence, Jasper strutted into the living room wearing squeaky-new, blindingly white, razor-toed cowboy boots.

"One hundred percent pure ostrich skin! Those babies normally go for four hundred and fifty bucks, but I talked the guy down to two. Is that a deal or what? We had a great time, huh, baby? We lost money on the ostrich races, ate ostrich burgers, then they had these ostrich-feather dusters in all sizes, some as big as palm trees, gigantic hand-painted ostrich eggs, ostrich purses, all the world an ostrich — hey little brother, 'member that old band — K.C. and the Sunshine Band — remember those guys? They were there, playing live, a bunch of old farts, but still on top, weren't they, baby? Prudence, look what else I got. You can try some if you want."

Prudence read the label on the white plastic squeeze bottle Rita handed her. "Emu oil?"

"Yup. Skin cream made from ostrich oil . . . it's supposed to be miraculous. God knows my face needs something."

On Sunday, Jasper and Rita were up early, Jasper swaggering in his new, squeaky ostrich boots, both of them heading out to the Renaissance Faire, where Rita would not be able to resist buying a black blanket with white Celtic horse heads all over it. Craving respite, peace and privacy, Prudence and Ray stayed home. Prudence read, prepared for class, called Fiona's cell, left a message. Ray painted, sunbathed, jogged with his bag of rocks. Rita's ongoing presence had made confederates of them. Together they wondered how soon she would be moving out, why she and Jasper were playing around at Ostrich Festivals and Renaissance Faires, spending Rita's money like tap water instead of trying to find a place to live. Plus, Prudence added, she's flying in a seven-hundred-dollar wolf from Akron, Ohio.

"Ray. What if she never leaves?"

"Has she said anything?"

431

"Not a word. Her commissions aren't happening, her bills are huge. The woman can't afford to go anywhere."

"Well then, she should pay rent. She needs to pay you."

"What if she hasn't got any money? We can't put her on the street."

"No, Prune, we can't."

"Can we at least ask her to be quieter?"

"I'll try. I don't know about when Jasper's here."

"No kidding. I don't mean to be a cultural moron, but so far I haven't seen much about that man that's holy. He makes great fry bread, possesses the sexual stamina of a Rasputin, and lets Rita pay all his bills and parade him around like an exotic pet. A pet in ostrich boots."

"Are you comparing him to some spiritual stereotype? Some Dalai Lama in your head?"

"Maybe. Uh-oh. Here they come."

Rita shouldered her way in first, dragging the Celtic blanket she had bought at the Faire, followed by Jasper, limping and exhausted, saying his bunions were killing him and he needed to take a quick snooze before heading back to Flagstaff.

Rita disappeared into her room, flopping

alone on her mattress to watch a rerun of *Law and Order*. As if sensing his mistress's misery, Boss nose-drooled across the glass expanse of the dining room window, snuffled air along the bottom edge of the back door. Jasper was gone, and the living room, once a cool sanctuary of dappled light where Prudence used to read books, drink tea, and listen to classical music, had become an unlit cave where Ray lolled, T-shirt hiked over his protruding belly, watching music biographies of old eighties bands, moping over the mere inch by which he had missed his rock 'n' roll boat to fame. I need to get my life back, Prudence thought, but how? Where do I start?

Monday morning, toting a basket of damp, dirty bath towels out to the laundry room, Prudence stopped, staring in horror at her backyard, at the dozens of dark brown plugs dotting the grassy swath behind the pool. A large black fly landed, buzzing, on her cheek, and Prudence took one hand off the laundry basket to swat it off. Think where that insect's heavy feet and wire-thin tongue had just been! Basket on hip, Prudence turned and marched back into the house.

"Ray!" She stood in the doorway of the

workroom where he sat making a preliminary sketch for another painting that wouldn't sell. "RAY!"

He lifted an earphone from one ear, looked at her.

"There's dog poop all over my yard, and whole armies of flies!"

That night, when Rita barged in the front door lugging a marble horse head — I stopped off at a swap meet on the way home — got the guy down thirty bucks from a hundred. *I stopped after my massage — got a discount from this Korean massage therapist who did his radio show on our station promoting something called MiGun where you lie on a bed of hot wooden rollers, cures everything from arthritis to cancer. Prudence, you dig this horse head? Isn't it too fabulous? I'll just set it down in the living room . . . this room is too white, anyway, it needs some pizzazz . . .* Ray came in, interrupted her, took the horse head, placed it unceremoniously on the coffee table, and with a firm hold on Rita's left elbow, escorted her outside. Prudence saw him gesturing toward Boss's feces littering the lawn, pointing to a horde of flies blackening the sky. Rita apologized, he told Prudence later. She promised, scout's honor, to clean it all up by the very next day.

When Prudence came home from school, she found the brick patio gleaming and wet, freshly hosed off. A luminous, crime-yellow fringe of spiraling curls dangled along the entire length of the porch overhang, with humps of flies, bloated and black, freckling the strips. Wearing a leopard-print bikini, Rita sat by the pool smoking and yakking on her cell. Something at the far end of the patio caught Prudence's attention, so she cracked open the door to look and saw a plastic kiddie pool, the garden hose overfilling it, one side of the blue pool sagging, water starting to flood onto the bricks. Rita plucked the phone off her ear, pointed to the pool — *For Nizhoni — her flight's a day early, she's booked on a ten-thirty tomorrow night.* Prudence nodded and coughed. Her lungs had started to burn from a cloying, unhealthy, chlorotic smell.

"Fly spray. I bought a gigantic can, used the whole damn thing, put up fly strips, too."

Choking, Prudence backed into the house, shut the door and retreated to her bedroom, where she lay face-up on her bed, pressing an eye pillow, plump with barley hulls and lavender flowers, an aromatherapeutic Band-Aid, over her eyes. She tried to recall where Ray was, where he told her he would be. He was, she finally remembered, modeling for Tuesday night's open studio.

Waking up hungry, Prudence came out into her kitchen, where she found Rita energetically mixing garlic and soy dip for her raw tuna steak. By way of greeting Prudence, she snapped the waistband of her broom skirt. "Ten more pounds of meat and potatoes, gone."

Prudence stared groggily at the pinkish sponge-pad of tuna, at the brown sauce with white garlic bits.

"C'mon, Prue, sit with me. Live large." Rita swam a forkful across the table. Prudence reluctantly opened her mouth, scraped cold fish off the metal fork with her teeth.

"Great, *n'est-ce pas?*"

Prudence nodded.

"Told you. Here. Share half. I'm not hungry. I had a red chili burrito for lunch."

Prudence took two edgy bites. What she liked, she realized, was the soy sauce.

They sat on the freshly cleaned patio, passing a diminishing quart of Ben & Jerry's back and forth, Rita telling Prudence how her alcoholic mother had committed suicide when Rita was eight, how she'd come home from school to find her mother's body. Her father? He'd abandoned them before Rita was born, though she'd met him once, a handsome Chickasaw man whose shady dealings with the Mafia ended up getting him murdered — *There's a million dollars laid up for me in a Swiss bank somewhere, my dad's lawyer contacted me after his murder, but hey, I'd probably wind up deep-sixed if I ever tried to touch it.* She talked about her years on the road, beginning at age fifteen, traveling with rock bands, her brief marriage to a white fundamentalist Christian, her string of semi- famous Native American lovers. Rita spilled a life story of trauma, loss, near-wealth, a brush with fame, a passion for animals, and now, finally, the life she'd dreamed of, marriage to a spiritual man like Jasper Chee. Spooning down into the last, melting layer of mint chip ice cream, Prudence tried to imagine eight-year-old Rita finding her mother's body, soaking up the blood with a towel, waiting for help to arrive, imagined the gangster murder of her handsome, aloof father, and began to understand the result — an orphaned child, unforgivably wounded, terrified to be alone. All Rita's noise and self-generated whirlwind fending off her greatest enemy — silence. Still, Prudence couldn't stand living with her. Opposite temperaments. The noisy versus the quiet, the prudent versus the brash. Nobody's fault. She passed the ice cream carton. One bite left. "Hey. Your lip looks a lot better."

"I decided not to sue those women. I'm not sure they even have insurance, they're both single moms with families to raise. It's not worth it."

As they sat in the fading light of the yard, Ray stepped out the back door wearing a crisp white shirt, Pendleton vest and jeans. He looked glossy and cheerful, a side effect of modeling, Prudence supposed, of being admired for hours on end, sketched, doted on. A woman with a Navajo accent had called earlier that day, left a giddy, breathless message for him. Should she talk to Rita, confide in someone who had known Ray longer than she had? When he went inside to take a shower, when he was out of earshot, she asked.

"Ray? Hell, he's always been kind of an odd bird. Never saw him with a woman, now that I think about it. I was never attracted to him, too androgynous, too pretty. We'd hang out, ride horses, go to pow-wows, music events, stuff like that. Far as I know, he's always been kind of a loner."

Prudence told her about all the women calling.

"Mmm. He cares about you, I see that. But I don't see that he's committed to you. Like Jasper and me? It's definite, we're getting a house, getting married, we're going to grow old and die together, it's a for-sure thing. Jasper, literally, is the man of my dreams. I dreamed about him for a full year before I met him. Ray's too complicated. If I were you, I wouldn't close out my other options."

"What do you mean?"

"I mean if he's seeing other women, even if it is just for coffee, like he tells you, you should go out too. Tit for tat. Then watch his reaction."

"He says he wouldn't care, he's not the jealous type."

"Bullshit." Rita's cell phone rang. "Hi, baby, hi, peaches" — she winked at Prudence, silently mouthing *Jasper* — "yeah, baby, we're ready to come up for the ceremony. I'm leaving work early, my boss said it's cool . . ."

Prudence carried their two spoons and

the empty ice cream carton into the house. Ray was still in the shower. She turned the volume down on the voice mail. *Hey, it's me, Bonnie, I'd love to get together with you, go over my portfolio like you said, get some tips about breaking into the art world . . . I'm available any night except Wednesday . . .* Prudence pushed delete, punched old Bonnie out of Ray's world. Oh dear, that was deceitful. And useless. Bonnie, whoever she was, could just call back, *Hey, you get my message?*

"Prune?" He stood damp and naked in the bathroom, smiling at her. "Full moon tonight. Can you trim my hair for me?"

She stood behind him, running a comb through his long hair, snipping the ends. Every full moon, he asked her to do this for him. Trim his hair.

"Ray. What would you do if all of a sudden I chopped your hair off?"

"Kill you. Why?"

"Just wondering."

He shook his hair free, glanced sideways in the mirror. "Looks good, sweetie. Thanks. Anybody call for me?"

"I don't think so." Prudence stooped down, picked up black bits of hair with a dampened wad of toilet paper. "You can check the machine."

"Here, I'll do that, hon." He took the toilet paper, finished cleaning the floor. He was so much nicer after he'd been out of the house, as if attention from other women translated into some overly solicitous, guilt-ridden attention toward her.

"Mom, it's me. How are you?" Prudence had decided to call Deleanor.

"Comme ci, comme ça."

"I called to tell you I'm going up north tomorrow, but I'll be back home Sunday night."

"Going where?"

Prudence explained. Deleanor was silent. Then she asked about Fiona, was Fiona going to be all alone at the house?

"Mom, she's almost eighteen."

"Eighteen smeighteen, she's alone in a big house at night."

"She'll be fine. Her friend Stevie Ray will be staying with her." Fibber, Prudence chided herself. If anybody will be there, it'll be Kirby. "Besides, there's Boss."

"Boss? Who's Boss?" Her mother sounded suspicious, as if she were envisioning yet another Indian invading her daughter's house.

"Rita's dog . . . an enormous German shepherd. From Germany. He was trained to be Barbra Streisand's guard dog. He'd scare the pants off Godzilla."

"Oh, all right. I'll try not to worry. Did you get my last i-Mail?"

Prudence had, in fact, received the latest word from Deleanor's personal electronic pulpit, something about three old men, how you should treat them all well because who knew which one might be God in disguise. "It was nice, Mom, thanks." Suddenly Prudence felt bowled over, ambushed, by choppy waves of guilt. Guilt over Fiona's moving out, guilt over her widowed mother's hurt feelings — her mother should live with her, not Ray, not Rita, they weren't family. That was what a good daughter would do for her old, grief-stricken mother. Invite her to move in, make her mother's last years cozy, and her own virtuous. But had she and Deleanor ever really been that close? Did her mother have any idea who Prudence was, and if she did, would she still love her? Prudence felt flattened by the endless dishonesties of family life. Well, her family life.

"Sorry, Mom, gotta go, I'm trying to catch up on schoolwork."

"How's that going, peanut?"

"Fine, fine. Listen, I'll call you when I'm back, I promise." Reaching into the drawer by the phone, Prudence fumbled out a miniature Baby Ruth, bit the wrapper off, put the waddy, sticky chocolate into her mouth and chewed, nearly drooling, as Deleanor complained about how she couldn't turn around without bumping into things, the carpet smelled of onions — Prudence stripped off another wrapper, poked a second Baby Ruth in her mouth, chewing, jawing, half-listening, until Deleanor gradually wound down and sighed *bysie-bye*.

Part Three

Part Three

Northern Arizona

Mountainaire was a bedroom community outside Flagstaff, a subdivision of neat wood
cabins and A-frame homes set along the edges
of dirt and gravel roads, shaded by great
shadowy pine and fir trees. The two-hour drive
was uneventful, even peaceful, giving Prudence
time to reflect. Her Questing for Eros class was
a success, though Prudence herself had lost interest. It was like being a guide through a
country she had already discovered, mapped,
and moved on from; the hours in class now had
a slogging, walk-through-mud feel. She considered turning the remaining weeks of class over
to her students, assigning them rotating posi-
tions of leadership. She could sit in the background, hover in a benign, docent-like way, let
them cavort in their newfound carnal voices.
She'd attend the erotic feast, then close that
door with relief. Since Ray had come back from
Flagstaff, since he had committed to being a
Sun Dancer, they rarely had sex anymore. He
treated her like a best friend, a roommate, a rel-

ative, and on the rare occasions they did have sex it was perfunctory, a wordless coupling done by dark surprise, in the middle of the night. She glanced over at Ray, listening to NPR as he drove the van — something about an English diver, a woman who had just captured the world record for holding her breath underwater. His profile, framed by his long black hair, held some new dignity along with the androgynous, elusive, deerlike quality he had always had, something more spiritual in nature, definitely erotic.

The sight of Blazing Eagle's seductive black eyes, coppery skin and high, chiseled cheekbones, his long, straight nose and jaw, so powerfully set, his waist-length hair, gleaming and midnight black, stirred Rebeccah in the familiar region of her heart, boldly woke the more mysterious region below her belly.

Ray looked over at her, innocently curious. "What?"

"Nothing."

"Ready to hang with the savages?"

"I'll be OK."

"Just stick with me, do what I tell you, you'll be fine."

Prudence gazed at the rough, darkening

walls of forest on either side of the road, ponderosa pine, pinon, the occasional spired, golden flash of glittering aspen, their ghostly pale trunks and deceptively frail-looking branches. She was making decisions. One: no more erotic classes. Two: she would visit Deleanor, fly out to see her at least twice a year. Three: she would spend more time with Fiona, have a talk about things, air out problems. Four: what to do with the plush relief of ten thousand dollars in her bank account? She could hardly wait to sit down, sort through her jumbled trough of debts, pay everything off, put whatever was left in savings, maybe treat herself and Fiona to a day of shopping for new clothes. She needed to get cracking on *Savage Arms* . . . if she could manage to shut her eyes, pinch her nose, and write one more hideous romance, she'd be debt-free. That left thirty-eight more of Digby's forty plots still staring at her, but Prudence couldn't stomach writing them. On the other hand, what if she could? Thousands of dollars!

"Here's the turnoff for Mountainaire, we'll be there in a few minutes." Ray opened the windows so cool, astringent air flooded the inside of the van. "Mmm, love the smell of pine trees, don't you, sugar?"

Rita's dusty blue Honda was parked at a jaunty angle outside a woodsy-looking cabin. They climbed several open planked steps to a narrow, half-rotted wooden porch, rang the bell by the front door. "Nephew! Sister!" Jasper threw open the door, giving each of them a big hug as Rita swooped out of the kitchen. "Howdy, guys, stew for everybody, lamb and green chili stew!" Taking cover behind Ray, Prudence found herself in a dark living room lit only by fire from a small black woodstove. Rita introduced young Alistair Wackerman, spindle-limbed, white as an oyster, and draped over one of two matching homely sofas in the living room. A schoolteacher from Grey Hills, he partially unfolded from the couch, nodded at them, folded back down again. Prudence and Ray trailed Rita into the tiny cluttered kitchen and helped themselves to fry bread and bowls of stew. Sitting in the dining room, using fry bread as a scoop to eat her stew, Prudence asked Jasper about the plants, dried, bundled, and hung in uneven ranks from the ceiling.

"Navajo tea. Ever had it? I'll make some for you after dinner. It's good for colds, digestion, things like that. My people drink it all the time."

Prudence noticed a paperback open on the table. "What are you reading?"

He passed it down the table. "I read everything I can find on the war."

"Were you there, in Vietnam?"

"Two tours."

Rita had perched, a cawing buzzard, on Jasper's lap. "Jasper has Vietnam books in the bathroom, the bedroom, every room in the house. He reads three or four at a time. Vietnam movies? We rent those constantly. Ask me anything about the Vietnam War, and I can't answer you, but" — Rita's laugh sounded equally proud and put-upon — "Jasper can."

They talked about which Vietnam movies they had all seen, then Prudence asked Ray did he want more stew, yes he did, so she got up, carried his empty bowl along with hers into the kitchen, reverting to the old behaviors Deleanor had taught her, behaviors she'd rejected and run from decades ago. Cooking men food. Serving men food. Waiting on a man, attending to his needs first. Yet here, in a different cultural context, this appeared to be correct, even expected behavior. And not wanting to stand out more than she already did by being so white, Prudence followed Rita's lead, setting a fresh bowl of lamb stew in front of Ray, who, talking with Jasper, reached one hand up and, without looking at her, benevolently patted her hip.

The four of them toured Jasper's house, a poorly lit, musty warren that reminded Prudence of those stiff ramshackle houses she used to construct out of playing cards, laying the edge of one card against another, then another, constructing a labyrinth of tiny, tilting, shadowy rooms that inevitably and satisfyingly collapsed. In one of the back bedrooms, books, all Rita's, crowded onto makeshift shelves. Dozens of framed photographs crazy-quilted the walls, Rita as an animal trainer, Rita posing with rock and roll stars, Rita posing with Native American movie actors — *my wall of fame,* she brayed, *my old celebrity life,* though Prudence caught the look of boredom settling like a small pain over Jasper's face. A second tiny bedroom, a double futon taking up most of the floor, a closet imploding with all of Rita's fringed shawls, boots, blouses, velveteen broom skirts, and a more modest bookcase holding Jasper's books on Native American history, plus Rita's massive zoology texts. This bedroom, unheated, was scarcely big enough to turn around in. The four of them stood huddled in the doorway, gazing in.

"You guys get cold in here, there's a space heater you can yank out from under all those clothes in the corner, it heats up pretty well."

Back in the living room, Prudence sat on one of two broken-springed brown plaid couches, Ray's arm strapped around her, watching a special on doo-wop. Alistair Wackerman had left, and the four of them, drowsy and full from dinner, sat like stuffed owls in the dim, firelit darkness. When the doorbell rang, Rita got up to answer it. Moments later, Prudence stood shaking hands with Harold Martinez, a dark-skinned, taciturn man with a long, thick braid down the middle of his back, and his son Darren, a tall, fairer-skinned version of his father. Two white men, Lame Wing, grizzled and stooped, with a wispy gray ponytail, and Harrison, a rangy, rectangular-shaped man who looked eerily like a grown-up version of Prudence's only high school boyfriend, a Jesuit-schooled intellectual named Ludwig Von Danz. Following their subdued greetings, all six men, along with Rita and Prudence, sat evenly as bowling pins along the two couches, watching doo-wop, the synchronized dancing, no one saying a word. Tucked under Ray's arm, Prudence decided that what she most wanted was to head back to the cold futon room and go to sleep.

"Sleepy?" he whispered. Reading her mind.

Prudence nodded.

"Then let's go." Hips touching, they rose in one smooth motion from the couch. Ray spoke. "We're going to bed, everyone."

There was a general indistinct murmur topped by one of Rita's lioness yawns. "Good idea, bro. I'm beat. Big day tomorrow."

In the ice-cold tiny bathroom, Prudence brushed her teeth, noting the warped, patched area where the plywood flooring had rotted away under the peeling linoleum, and on the back of the toilet, a stack of aging paperbacks, all on the subject of Vietnam.

Bundled in black sweatpants, thermal shirt and giant woolly socks, her backside snuggled against the front of Ray's naked body, pressed against his heat, Prudence fell asleep, exhausted and dreamless.

When Prudence asked about the car's funny smell, Rita plucked a candle of

Febreze from under her seat, waved it around. "Stuff's a miracle — I spray it on everything. Jasper hates my cigarette smoke, so before we go anywhere, I always shoot a bunch of this around, it totally covers the smell."

They were headed north, the last half of a seven-hour drive on a two-lane road in the middle of the Navajo reservation, plenty of time for Rita to educate Prudence about the Peabody Coal Mining Company dispute, the ruining of sacred land by strip-mining, the long-standing feud between the Hopis and the Navajos, the Hopis having sold water rights to Peabody, who had contaminated the water, using it as slurry for coal, the water table dropping lower each year, wells gone dry, livestock suffering, pastures parched, barren of animals, devoid of game. She talked about Peabody's harassment of Navajos on their own land, of elderly Navajo grandmothers being forced from their traditional hogans, their sheep poisoned by water turned toxic from uranium, all their firewood, sole source of heat, stolen. There was a near epidemic of cancer among Navajo teenagers because of uranium tailings left over from strip-mining. "The genocide hasn't stopped. It's just silent, hidden away in the courts of law and on the reservations." Rita's voice held a focused anger, a raw, impressive eloquence. Prudence turned to see if Ray was hearing any of this. He was in the backseat, stretched out, sound asleep.

"I didn't know this, Rita. I'm sure most people don't. Can't some of the younger Navajo and Hopi people become lawyers, fight this in court?"

"Let me tell you something. I did years of protest shit. I was at Alcatraz, I marched for Leonard Pelletier, I was at Wounded Knee, I've watched a lot of friends die. So has Jasper. There are lots of us old-politics warriors, and most of us are tired, real tired. Following the pipe, living the Sun Dance way, is best for me now. I do my battle on the spirit plane. I can't do the politics bullshit anymore. White government's too big, too powerful."

Looking out over vast miles of barren, parched reservation land, mesas and buttes rising in the distance, staring past the sere, cloudy plumes of dust rising around Rita's little car, Prudence thought of the centuries of genocide against indigenous tribes on both continents. She didn't know details, but she believed it had occurred, and up until now it had had nothing much to do with her. Now here she was, eroticizing the Indian man for white female consumption, adding to the romantic stereotype of the bronze-skinned, ebony-eyed, raven-haired "savage" of white women's fantasies. As the reluctant author of *Savage Heat*, wasn't she just one more insidious enemy, right up there with Peabody Coal?

Ray sat up in the backseat, yawning and rubbing his eyes as Rita pulled off the road and parked in the large, graveled lot outside the Hopi Cultural Center. "Best blue corn pancakes around, you two. Looks like the guys made it here before us." Rita pointed to the white van. "We're less than two hours from Pinon."

Inside the cultural center's restaurant, they sat at a large pine table with Jasper, Harold, Darren, Harrison, Lame Wing, and Marc and Heidi, a young white couple from Pennsylvania, schoolteachers at Grey Hills, along with a slender, nearsighted geographer from Kansas, passing through on his way to Seattle.

Over breakfast Prudence told Heidi, a grave-eyed young woman with long, straight chestnut hair, how she had driven up to Pinon for the first time a year and a half earlier, invited by one of her students to attend the Sun Dance. "I drove up alone, and my friend Ken Tsosie kept introducing me to all the people in his family, aunts, uncles, cousins, sisters, brothers, I lost track. I stayed at his parents' house, saw the last two days of the Sun Dance, and cried half the way home to Phoenix. I didn't want to go back. I thought I wanted to live on the reservation, how ridiculous was that? Still, if anyone had told me I'd be living with a Sun Dancer and coming up here to a pipe ceremony, I'd never have believed it."

After the final drive north on unmarked, rutted dirt roads, they arrived at the Sacred Mountain Sun Dance grounds. The winter skies were a dull pewter gray, and a hard, bitter wind whipped at them as they got out of their cars. The men's and women's sweat lodges were already under way, so they would have to ask permission to enter between rounds. Inside the car, Prudence and Rita struggled into long skirts and big T-shirts, took their towels, and waited with Heidi outside the women's *inipi*. When they finally crept in, on all fours, barefoot and single file, each saying *Mitakuye Oyasin,* we are all related, the sweat leader quietly greeted them. Prudence found space to sit beside an elderly

Navajo woman in a maroon velveteen skirt, her long silver hair bound in a neat bundle at the back of her head. She was praying aloud, a long, fervent stream of Navajo, while her two granddaughters, seated behind her, watched to make sure she was comfortable. The youngest granddaughter, twelve, would be this year's sacred pipe carrier, so special prayers were said for her well-being, her health and that of her family's. Prayers were spoken in Navajo and in English, traditional songs sung. At the end of the fourth round, when the flap was opened to let in cool air, Prudence saw, through the angled shaft of light piercing in, that she and Heidi were the only white women in the lodge. They crawled out with the others, stood up outside the *inipi*, and offered packages of tobacco as thanks to the lodge leader. Soaked and shivering, they hurried back to their cars to change into sweatshirts and jeans. Prudence had to pee, Heidi too, so they ventured down a small slope, finding a dense clump of cedar trees and took turns, squatting to pee, burying their bits of tissue in the silty, pale dirt, then hiking the short, sharp incline back to the car. Heidi's solemn absence of vanity in regard to her porcelain skin, limpid eyes and rich chestnut hair, her overall serenity, impressed Prudence.

"Will you and Marc be coming back in July for the Sun Dance?"

"We'll try to be here the whole four days. We've become pretty close to these people since we moved to Tuba City. That's how we met Rita and Jasper, through teaching at the school."

"What do you teach, Heidi?"

"Science and math. Marc teaches photography."

They wrapped fringed shawls around one another's waists, folding and pinning them to form narrow ankle-length skirts over their jeans. The cold, aggressive wind blew the shawls partially open as they walked to the bonfire to join the sixty or so Sun Dancers, relatives and supporters gathered in a circle. They stood on the women's side, near Rita, while Ray and Marc stood opposite, on the men's side. Prudence's shawl, a rich purple with silken yellow fringe, borrowed from Rita, slipped a little down her hips. She pulled it snug, rewrapping and pinning the fabric at her waist.

Prudence counted five white people besides herself, Heidi, Marc, the geographer from Kansas, Lame Wing and Harrison. The rest were native Sun Dancers and members of their families, supporters, all humbly dressed, the men in jeans, tennis shoes and nylon windbreakers, the women in sweatshirts or windbreakers, with long fringed shawls wrapped around their jeans or sweatpants. Waiting in a circle around the heat and sharp cedar scent of the fire, the people stood close, wind pressing against the women's backs, blowing hard into the faces of the men. Shivering, Prudence looked past the circle to the amber and violet-tinted mountains in the far distance, shrouded by a thin, shifting mist of gray. The wind threw sparks from the fire, and as she brushed a fat ember, still glowing, off the silky fringe of her shawl, the material loosened its hold around her waist again, one end trailing down, yellow fringe brushing the dirt, so that she had to hitch at it, retighten and repin the fabric. Respectfully, the circle of people listened as the Sun Dance leaders began to speak about spiritual preparation, the wind breaking apart their words, thinning them. The four leaders, including Jasper and Harold, stood near the row of sacred pipes, a white buffalo skull, its interior packed with sage, placed at one end. Several large tin cans with wire handles, filled with burning sage, sat on the ground, releasing bluish curls of pungent smoke into the air. When the male singers in the arena, seated around a great skin drum near the cotton-wood tree used in last year's ceremony, began their song, the people filed in, first the chiefs carrying the sacred pipes and buffalo skull, then the men, followed by the women, forming a circle around the sacred tree. A Navajo girl of seven, maybe eight years, lightly swung one of the cans of burning sage by its curved wire, stopping to let each person in the circle lean down, carry smoke to his or her heart. The leaders moved around the circle then, offering the sacred pipe to smoke, giving each person a sip of water from a hollowed-out gourd. *Wakan Tanka, Tunkashila, Onshimala . . . Grandfather Spirit, pity me, so that my people shall live.* When the prayers had ended, with the drums silent and the singing over, with the chill, insistent wind tossing hair and skirts and shawls, setting the grayish brittle leaves of the cottonwood chittering, everyone filed back to the bonfire to hear the chiefs talk about the responsibilities of the dancers and their supporters, the sacredness of this ancient Sioux rite, calling on each and every person to live in the strong, pure way of their ancestors, to honor past relations, those relatives who had danced, those generations of men and women who had suffered before them.

Squeezed between the young geographer from Kansas, whose name she couldn't recall, and the elderly Navajo woman she had sat beside in the sweat lodge, Prudence balanced a paper plate, buckled with carrot salad, fried chicken, mutton, fruit salad, fry bread and a handful of hard pastel candies, on her lap. She'd set a Styrofoam cup of orange soda on the clean-swept dirt floor by her feet. It was warm inside the hogan, crowded with sixty or more people, the air thick with the fragrance of burning sweet grass, desert sage and cedar. People sat on old mattresses laid end to end along the floor or, like Prudence, knelt or sat cross-legged on the bare dirt floor. The women who had cooked and prepared the food offered prayers before passing filled plates around, the very first servings going to the elderly men and women seated in chairs near the woodstove. By the hogan's open door, feral, bony-rumped dogs paced, sly, ravenous, and ready to fight for scraps of food. The smell of coffee, mutton and fry bread mixed with sage and sweet grass, with the dull, cold, gray of winter air, with the pinon and cedar firewood popping its hot blaze of sparks in the woodstove.

Since she knew the reservation's dirt roads and unmarked turnoffs best, Rita drove Ray and Prudence back to Jasper's that night, lurching over washboard hardpan and long miles of noisy, sliding gravel, before finally reaching paved roads slicing through flat black landscape. Eerie patches of low ground fog and sudden, rough swirls of dust tagged the headlights while around them pressed the deep un-mitigated darkness of a barren, drought-stricken land. Lit briefly by the car's swift-passing headlights, a herd of goats, startled to flash point stillness, a dead sheep, gut-bloated and stiff, then nothing, not even another car traveling in either direction. Rita stopped at the general store in Leupp, near the reservation's border, to get coffee and use the bathroom, the same place Prudence remembered stopping at on her first drive up to Pinon, the same place they had stopped at earlier that day. Leupp's was the only gas station and convenience store around for hundreds of miles. At the back of the store, the bathroom door didn't fully close, the light didn't work, the single toilet lacked a seat, and the plywood floor, soaked with black slime from an unrepaired leak, was littered with coarse florets of discarded toilet paper. People coming into Leupp's were mostly reservation Indians, Navajo or Hopi, trapped in a poverty so unrelenting it had a permanent odor, fouling and scabbing the air. Each time Prudence went into that little run-down store, a place stinking of urine and sour meat and sweet orange soda, she thought of articles she'd occasionally read, equating American Indian reservations with third-world countries, deep cuts of misery isolated outside the disposable culture of excess that was America. Each time, she felt ashamed to have ever considered, or even called herself, poor.

After Leupp, with Ray stretched out in the backseat, Rita told Prudence what she would need to have as Ray's Sun Dance companion . . . "plenty of sweet grass, loose tobacco, goldenseal powder to pack into his wounds, all your prayer ties. Are you remembering to give spirit offerings after you guys eat? You'll want to establish a really strong relationship with the spirits, so they'll be around to help you both, especially Ray, when he's out there suffering. You two should pray, smoke the pipe together as much as you can, it will bring you closer. There's work to do at Sun Dance, but a lot of time for prayer, too, you'll be sending your energy, supporting him with your prayers, sending your own spirit to give him strength. Amazing, when I think about it, how I happened to see Ray's artwork in this little gallery in Flag, and now I'm bringing him into the Sun Dance, and you've become like a sister, taking me into your home. Creator's ways are truly awesome."

They pulled up late in front of Jasper's house in Mountainaire. Lame Wing, Harrison, Harold and Darren were already back, planted along the dark, loamy row of couches watching *Full Metal Jacket*. Ray and Prudence had thought of sleeping over, going to a sweat lodge the next morning, then heading down to Phoenix. But as she was getting a drink of water from the kitchen faucet, Jasper came up to Prudence, his soft voice further muffled by sudden bursts of TV artillery, by the thunderous blaze of cinematic warfare coming from the living room. "Your daughter called. She wants you to call her right away. Something about a water leak in your house."

The phone barely rang. "Fiona?"

"Mommy, oh gosh . . . there's a flood in

the house, in the hallway. I'm throwing towels down everywhere, but I don't know what else to do. I think it's stopping, let me check. Yeah, OK, it's almost stopped."

"Where's it coming from?"

"The drain in the hall closet, where the hot water heater is? It started bubbling and flowing out of there, ugh, now water's coming up in your shower, my tub . . . my toilet just overflowed, it's completely gross."

Ray, who had been listening, calmly took the phone from Prudence, gave Fiona a few simple instructions, and told her they would be home in two hours, they were leaving right away.

Tempe, Arizona

The drive down the mountain seemed far, far longer and more tedious than the drive up. Around midnight, they pulled wearily into the driveway, and as Prudence stepped down from the van, Ray set one hand on her shoulder and pointed to the palm tree in the front yard.

"See that?"

"What?"

"An owl. It just flew out from that tree. There, it's on the roof now, near the garage."

A dark, indistinct shape lifted heavily off the roof, flapped slowly over the backyard, disappeared.

"I've never seen an owl here. Is that a good sign?"

"Not usually, no. But hey, let's go inside and help Fiona, see what the problem is."

"Why is it not a good sign?"

"Owls are usually considered messengers."

"Of?"

"Death."

"Oh great."

On his hands and knees, Ray ripped up carpeting, peeled up padding, and lugged the whole mess, soaked and dripping, outside, dumping it on the front lawn. He rolled back the hall carpeting that went into each of the three bedrooms as Prudence and Fiona sloshed through chilled black water, wringing out towels, rubbing mops across the brown concrete flooring, until finally, near dawn, with the windows flung wide throughout the house to let out the dank, reptilian stink, the three of them tried to get some sleep. Exhausted from the long drive and hard labor of pulling up the weight of soaked carpeting, Ray fell asleep in seconds, but Prudence, beneath the cumbersome weight of the buffalo robe, lay thinking of the owl, messenger of death, lighting on her roof. The flood felt sinister as well.

But the next morning, after calling her insurance agent to report the flood, and standing on the front lawn surveying the sodden heap of bath towels, the stained curls of carpeting, the ugly foam padding, all of it strewn like hurricane debris, it seemed to Prudence as if no unfixable disaster had befallen them, the flood was repairable, a minor nuisance. In the bright, optimistic light of morning, the grim portent of an owl perched on her roof seemed dismissible as well, an obsolete superstition to be put out of sight, out of mind.

Two days later, Prudence's momentarily stable finances were in ruins, and half of her house on the verge of full-scale restoration. Two damage inspectors, sent by Homeguard Insurance, short men in identical mole-colored suits, arrived Monday afternoon, tapping clipboards in dual rhythm, scribbling, clicking from room to room, tap dancers in identical hard-toed business shoes (gleaming red-brown cockroach shoes), fingering bits of carpet, running manicured hands down walls, exchanging cool, coded bits of information, *a Texas strain of mold, airborne allergens, fungus, water damage,* bearing thermometer-like devices aloft from room to room, measuring water seepage in her walls. By Tuesday morning, a man stood alert at her front door, persistently ringing the bell, gripping oversized books with giant black plastic handles in either hand. The pages of one book held dozens of carpet samples, stamp-sized rugs of varying density, plush, pile and hue, while the second, smaller book was dotted with hundreds of sample paint chips. With her hooded monk's bathrobe twisted around her and Ray's giant woolly socks on her perpetually icy feet, Prudence plunked, yawning and graceless, onto her white living room couch, and pointed blindly to one of the least offensive paint chips, Winter Barley, a color which, when later drying on her ceilings and walls, would show itself to be dove gray with a sick undertone of pistachio. She pointed next to a velvety little rug named Summer Oatmeal, milky beige with coarse flecks of brown and black, both her choices so blah (*barley and oatmeal, Mom, what were you thinking?*) they would prove a quiet, background irritant to everyone in the house.

On the heels of the paint and carpet sample man came yet another part of Homeguard's disaster relief team, this man having jicama pale hair, a sickly, drooped mustache and sad, elephantine eyes. He swung himself down from a high square van, *Helping Hands Restoration* marching in red letters along its white sides, and stood outside her door, thumbs hitched into saggy blue overalls. He was there, he said mournfully, to prevent mold, mildew and fungus. He was there to dry up her walls and floors, a thing which had to be done before the carpeting and painting of the bedrooms, hall, foyer and living room could even begin to take place. So Prudence let sad, doomy Oscar in. Racked by a wet, phlegmy cough (*Fighting mold and mildew*, he said, *makes me sick as a damn dog*), poor Oscar was feverish, sweating, unrecovered from the last case of pneumonia he'd picked up on the job. But he couldn't quit, he told Prudence, he needed the cash. Cranked up on antibiotics, Oscar worked obstinately, dying Oscar crept about Prudence's house on foam-encased knees, dismantling the lower half of her home, knocking off baseboards, drilling holes along the walls, plugging a spaghetti of lemon-colored tubing up and down the hallway, plastic tubing that snaked into bedrooms and bathrooms, tubing connected to five blowers, dehydrators the size of airplane engines, one in every room, one in the hall, another in her living room, engines that would soon be blowing, hallooing, trumpeting like the very windstorms of hell.

At the end of his difficult, feverish day, Oscar stood wilted in the foyer, the sun sinking prophetically, gloomily, behind him. "Warning, folks. When I turn all this on, it will be loud. Customers tell me the noise drives them absolutely nuts."

"How long do they stay on?" Ray asked, standing behind Prudence, sounding practical.

"Twenty-four hours a day, five-day minimum. I'll stop by every other day to check on your moisture level in the floors and the walls." As he talked, Oscar started plugging in each of the five blowers.

"Why are we doing this again?" Prudence yelled into his pale, drooping vegetable ear. He gestured for her to follow him outside into the front yard, where presumably she would be better able to hear his reply. Ray followed and began rolling up damp, spongy padding, stained hunks of carpet, stacking and carrying them out to the alley.

"Mold. There's a real bad strain of mold coming up from Texas. Mold and fungus? You get any of that going in your house from water damage, your whole family's liable to be sick. Hospital sick, mortuary sick. I've heard first-class horror stories." Coughing, hewing up phlegm, Oscar nodded at Ray, squatting down, furling up a warped, squishy length of hallway carpeting.

"He your husband?"

"Not exactly."

473

"Just wondering. You a schoolteacher? You remind me of a schoolteacher."

Prudence suddenly disliked Oscar, his noxious cough, his blowsome engines.

"I'm a romance writer. Ever heard of Danielle Steel? I'm just like her."

Oscar, seized by a paroxysm of coughing, with a little sideways wave, beat a panicky retreat to his truck, floored the engine and zoomed off. Hah. Scared off by one teensy word. *Romance.* She was sick of men forever asking if she was a schoolteacher, men telling her she had a schoolteacher's personality, a schoolteacher's smile. What was that supposed to mean?

Pausing outside her front door to admire her geraniums — red, circusy blooms monstrously healthy in their giant, unfired clay pots, Prudence snapped off a single dead, brittle bloom just as Rita's car purred up to the curb. Rita had missed it all — the flood, the carpet sample man, the tap-dancing insurance assessors, moribund Oscar with his fat tubing and jet engines. Rita hadn't seen the waterlogged half of the house, hooked up like an intensive care patient to a snaking mass of yellow tubing, hadn't seen the water gauges, mold-o-meters, dehydrators, or the dry half of the house, now a hodgepodge of furniture shoved into the center of rooms, chairs stacked all higgledy-piggledy on top of tables, carpeting rolled back, sofas shoved together in bulked, awkward congress. Lucky Rita had missed it all.

Above the din of the five dehydrating engines Prudence heard the phone, and stepped inside to answer it. Deleanor, wondering if Prudence had kept the Vietnamese ceramic garden seat from Saigon, she had just seen it listed in a Gump's catalogue for two hundred dollars more than Deleanor herself had paid for it back in 1976, and if Prudence didn't want it or wasn't taking proper care of it, Deleanor wanted it back. Prudence barked of course she still had it, though she had a dimly scotched memory of having sold it at one of several impromptu garage sales she'd held earlier in the summer, anxious to scour and rid her life of as many unnecessary, frivolous objects as possible, one of them being the Vietnamese garden seat from Saigon. Holding on to the phone, Prudence watched Rita walk into the house and sidestep a nest of tubing, holding two bags of groceries, a long baguette of French bread poking out of one sack, the blood-tinged corner of a pack of chicken wings out the other.

★ ★ ★

Wednesday, Prudence picked up the phone again, piecing out grim words through the windy nonstop onslaught of her five dehydrator engines . . . *Unfortunately, Ms. Parker, no coverage is provided in our contract for plumbing problems located more than ten feet beyond the foundation of the house* . . . Within an hour's time, as a direct result of sifting through the yellow pages under Plumbing Contractors, a motley parade of plumbers appeared, digging and delving in her backyard under the giant English walnut she'd always cherished (floating on her back in the pool, gazing up into its lofty Anglican branches), unaware of the treachery in its underground chthonic root system. In the end, the diagnoses of all six plumbers matched: *Your tree roots are clogging the orange pipe. You need to dig down, locate the exact spot, replace your disintegrating paper pipe with new pipe. Cost? Depends how far down, how long, how many yards of replacement pipe. Cheapest estimate? Couple thousand. Four to five more likely.* Prudence queried each drain man, hoping for a lone dissenting voice, but all six parroted one another, grim clones of doom. If it wasn't fixed, all six plumbers assured her, if the problem wasn't addressed, all that restoration going on inside the house would be for nothing. The flooding, the backup, the business of roots clogging the pipe would happen again. One year, one week, one hour, or with the next flush of the toilet, make no mistake, her house would flood all over again.

Prudence picked Plumber Five. He reminded her of the kindly father on *The Waltons*. He reminded her of her own father. Plus, he came with two polite sons in pressed white uniforms, pipe doctors, drain orderlies, one round and fat as an onion, the other skinny and gaunt as a discarded sucker stick. She liked how kind Plumber Five was when she wept a little over the news, handing her a square of paper toweling with pink teapots stamped on it. He and his boys, he assured her, would be back first thing in the morning to commence digging up her yard. They would locate and destroy the offending root, the evil root. As he comforted Prudence, his boys, Fat and Thin, began politely to shovel back the dirt they had just dug up with fossorial ease. Father Plumber supervised, giving Prudence a brief history of suburban orange pipe installation in the 1960s, pipe made of paper due to a shortage of lead due to the war in Vietnam due to the need for war supplies, orange pipe being a heavy grade of paper used mainly in suburban home construction. Thirty years later, everybody and their dog's paper pipe was falling apart, breaking apart, her own pipe specifically, sheared in half, in this case, by an English walnut root. Listening, Prudence scrawled her signature at the bottom of a plumber's release form, not bothering to read it. She gave it back to Father Plumber, busy blotting his brow with a neat square of pink-teapotted paper towel.

"Say, Mrs. Parker, you wouldn't by any chance be a schoolteacher? You strike me as a teacher. My wife Billie's a teacher. Special ed."

Since she liked him so much, Prudence came clean. "Yes, I am." Besides, it might reduce her bill, having something in common with his wife, Billie.

By noon the next day, the digging was finished, the culprit pipe located and replaced, the deep gouge in the grass filled in, leaving a nasty bald patch on the lawn beginning at the base of the culprit walnut, which at this point she couldn't help resenting for all the time and trouble it had cost her. Mr. Walton knocked on her back door, gouts of sewer mud on his work boots, a bill in his industrially gloved hand in the amount of $4,500. Prudence borrowed his pen with its chipped-off plumbing logo and signed a check in red ink, the exact color of blood, of hemorrhage. She was so collapsed by the bill's amount she forgot to offer Walton and his sons the iced Darjeeling she'd specially prepared earlier. Instead they had driven off, bandits in white, with all of the remaining money she'd earned from *Savage Heat*.

Half deaf from the roaring dehydrators (inspected earlier that morning by ever-dour Oscar, who prescribed another twenty-four hours), Prudence dashed about, ripping all five plugs from all five wall outlets. The house pulsed with a fearsome, library-cool silence, as Prudence hopscotched, picking her way through tangled yellow cord, finding her way to Fiona's bathroom, where she flushed the toilet three times to see if it really worked. She wept then, wailing for the last of her secret income, now swirling down the bowl into her newly installed piping before snaking out to the alley and who knew where beyond. The aftermath of Vietnam wartime shortages reaching her thirty years later, sabotaging her little moneyed step forward in the world.

An hour later, Ray came home and

found her at the dining room table, facedown on a page of scribbled calculations, dollar signs, pluses, minuses, financial calculations, certainly nothing he had any head for. On the other hand, he had just returned from modeling and had good news.

"Prunelet. Sugar. You asleep? What's wrong? Thinking too hard?"

Prudence raised a puffy, mascara-smudged face. There were marks on her left cheek from the buttons of her calculator.

"Wow, what happened?" He became aware of a distinct silence in the house, a beautiful, gorgeous nonsound. "What happened? The walls dry?" He pulled up a chair as Prudence sobbingly confessed (minus certain details) that she was, officially, devastated. Bankrupt. Financially ruined. She told him the cost of the plumbing. He whistled, patted her, made vague, sympathetic sounds. And yet — Prudence couldn't quite put her finger on how she knew this — Ray remained unruffled by her distress, safely outside her misfortune, his own wallet snug in his back pocket. Sympathetic, yes. Personally affected, no.

"I sold a painting, sweetie."

"You did?"

"Yup. One of the ladies in my modeling class went to the gallery, saw my work, really loved my one Hopi women piece. Sooo . . ." Ray produced a check from his T-shirt pocket, a lavender-tinted check with an imprint of flying saucers hovering over a midwestern barn.

"Wow. Five hundred dollars?"

"Yes ma'am, and she'll pay the second five hundred in June. So get dressed, wash your face, I'm taking my sugar britches to dinner!"

Prudence looked at her sheet of fiscal noodling — $4,500 plumbing plus $4,200 credit card debt left $300, most of which would go to replace the newly shot brakes on Fiona's car. That left $1,000, earmarked for Fiona's college tuition in the fall. Prudence took her tear-soaked legal pad, shoved it in her bill drawer, splashed water on her face, combed her hair, and went to Los Sombreros with Ray, who was so pleased to have finally sold one of his paintings, so pleased with his day, that she set aside her own troubles and listened to him outline plans for a series of desert plant and animal paintings — refusing to overshadow his artistic inspiration with her fiscal misery.

★ ★ ★

"Rats!"

"I thought Rita wasn't coming back until the weekend. With Jasper. To look for a house."

"That's what she said."

"Well, there goes our night." Ray reached over. "Button up your blouse, sweetie. Aw, don't cry. We'll just plug the damn blowers in when we go to bed, then you can make all the noise you want. I love it when you make noise, it turns me on. Sexy thing, you."

Coming in from the garage, Prudence, followed by Ray, nearly tripped over a large, empty animal cage in the workroom, its wire door gaping. The kitchen pocket door, usually open, had been slid shut.

Ray knocked. "Rita?"

"Hey guys . . . c'mon in. I just got home from the airport. Keep your voices low, poor baby's still freaked from her naughty, nasty plane ride."

Ray slid back the door. Peeking over his shoulder, Prudence saw a pearly pink scatter of raw chicken wings strewn across the tile floor.

"She just dragged one of the wings under the table, sooo cute, look, she's trying to bury it."

Ray knelt down, peering under Prudence's kitchen table. "Wow. How old?"

"Seven weeks. Isn't she absolutely gorgeous?"

Prudence sat on her tile floor staring at the creature under her table as it growled, slewed its eyes, and clutched a raw wing-stub under its paws. A flood, a broken pipe, financial ruin, now a baby wolf, not at the door, but in her kitchen, dragging morts of chicken around. What next?

"Her name, Nizhoni — that's Navajo for beauty. She's purebred, one hundred percent timberwolf, healthy as a horse, she traveled here just great, *didn't you, baby-kins, c'mere to Mommy, widdle waddle . . .* The wolf slunkered cautiously out, sniffed at Ray, ignored Prudence, snagged another chicken wing, then started frantically nipping and dragging all the wings into a nubbled little heap under the table before piddling on the floor. As Rita wiped up the spreading pool of strong-smelling urine with bunch after bunch of paper towels, Prudence suddenly recalled how she'd joined the Canadian and American Wolf Defenders League years ago, in her twenties, professing political allegiance to an animal she'd never even seen before. She was telling Rita this as Nizhoni slithered on her belly out from under the table, crept up, and nuzzled Prudence's face.

"Wow, that's cool." Rita cracked her neck, shook her hair, cracked her neck a second time. "First Rita Bragswolf, now a real timberwolf, tell you what, girl, you've got strong wolf medicine."

"Where's Boss?" Ray asked.

"Oh, they've met." Rita sounded annoyed. "He's acting like a big dumb mother hen. I went ahead and set up my fence panels on the patio, the ones I used to use for the horses. I don't want Nizhoni falling into the pool when I'm at work. Hope you guys don't mind."

Later that night, with all five dehydrators blasting, the wolf in Rita's bed and Ray asleep in hers, Prudence lay pressed under the buffalo robe, coming to an odious, unavoidable decision. To put herself above water, financially speaking, she would have to flesh out the second of Digby Deeds' chronologically ordered Savage Passion plots. She would be forced to write *Savage Arms*. Another ten thousand dollars and that was it, that was all, she vowed silently, poking Ray to stop him from grinding his teeth. No more P. T. Parker, author of Savage anything. Still, if she were honest, she had to admit she had almost begun to like the form, to find it, like any form, challenging. It was not as easy as one would think, as she had initially thought, to write a good romance. There was, if not an art, a definite skill in it. As Prudence lay beside Ray, imagining various opening lines for *Savage Arms*, she found herself strangely looking forward to writing her second (and last!) romance.

"You've got a what? A *wolf*? Isn't that illegal? Don't they eat children?"

"Fairy tale, Mom. Nizhoni's actually very shy."

"Shy my eye. What if you or Fiona goes outside to do your laundry one of these days, the thing hasn't been fed, it's asleep, dreaming of hunting, its instincts activated, you could both wind up wolf bait!"

To pacify her mother, Prudence drew on facts sketchily remembered from her days in the Wolf Defenders League, the timid nature of *Canis lupus*, how wolves were family creatures, mated for life, etc.

Her mother was unmollified. "What does it eat?"

"Chicken wings. Raw. And lots of them."

"Bones and all? Won't the bones puncture its stomach? With dogs . . ."

She pictured Nizhoni sprouting wings, two large flapping chicken wings, then abandoned her explanation of wolves' unique digestive tracts to answer the front door. Ah, Fiona! Her mother switched subjects.

"Did I tell you, Pruney? I fell down in the shoe store last week. Wearing one Ferragamo, I fell right across a glass table. The clerk, a terribly nice young man, called the doctor. Did you know they have doctors right there in the mall? The doctor made me sit down, brought damp paper towels for a small cut on my shin that bled like crazy, had me wait until I was sure I felt better. The salesgirl even brought me a cup of tea from their back room. Lipton, but still."

"How in the world did you fall across a glass table?" Prudence was alarmed by the frailty this suggested.

"Oh, I don't know, just got a little woozy I suppose . . . you know my cleaning lady's a Jehovah's Witness, and she keeps leaving these end-of-the-world tracts all over the place, she would have driven Walt up the wall, but she does a good job, especially on the toilets and the mini-blinds, poor woman's not the sharpest knife in the drawer, now where did I put that sauce container, where in hell's bells, Prudence, I can't find anything in this place anymore."

Moments after Deleanor's phone call had ended, Fiona told her mother an astonishing thing.

"She does, Mah. She honestly does. Grandma thinks you and Ray got married in a secret Indian ceremony. That time you two went up to the reservation? For the pipe ceremony? That's what she thinks. That you got married."

"For crying out loud!"

"You didn't, did you?"

"Fiona! We were at a ceremony! A religious ritual. It had nothing to do with me, or me and Ray. It was about the Sun Dance. I am not married to Ray, nor do I ever plan to be" (though like wishing for the idea of a dog, and not the real dog itself, Prudence did lately find herself wishfully considering the idea of marriage. It didn't help that she had spent so many sleepless nights conjuring up fictional romantic scenes and overheated descriptions calculated to lead with gravitational force and irresistible speed to the altar, symbolic or otherwise, of marriage, with its promise, its shill, of eternal bliss).

"OK, Grandma just got me worried. I told her I didn't think it was true, that as far as I knew, you guys weren't married.

Hey, I just stopped by to put a chocolate rabbit in the fridge. Kirby's refrigerator is the size of a toaster and it's crammed with potpies. That's all he ever eats, potpies."

"How awful. What do you ever eat, honey?"

"Salads. Or McDonald's hamburgers without the meat."

"Hamburgers without the meat?"

"Bread, lettuce, tomato, no cheese. I have them leave the meat off."

"And they charge the same price?"

"Yeah, I guess. I never thought about it."

Prudence sighed. Imagine being so unaware. *Non compos mentis,* her father would have called it. "Sure, hon. Put your rabbit in. There's plenty of room."

Holding her foil-wrapped chocolate rabbit, an Easter gift from Kirby, Fiona stood gawking in front of her mother's open refrigerator. One entire shelf was taken up with a plastic pillowcase of raw chicken wings resting in pinkish red brine. Watery chicken blood had formed a red, elongated pool on the shelf underneath. Beside the gallon of milk (cap missing) and a gigantic plastic tub of artificial crab salad hulked an open jar of fly ointment, the ointment itself a viscous, sallow jelly. Fiona cracked open the freezer door and looked cautiously inside. Three ovoid shapes, shrouded in black trash bags, bound with clothesline, lay in gothic formation.

"Mah? What . . . are those?"

"Hawks."

"Hawks?"

"Three frozen hawks. Ray's."

Fiona made an *eewh* of disgust.

Prudence dragged open the vegetable bin, removed three sprouting onions and one outlandish-looking Idaho potato. Taking the rabbit, she snugged it, firmly, diagonally, into the rectangular plastic cradle. "There. Safe and sound." (Where it would rest, a large, neglected candy, taking on the rank, smallish odor of onion, its existence nullified by larger, more troublesome events taking place in Prudence's house, beyond the hollow, dark world of the refrigerator, over the next three months.)

"Where is everybody?" asked Fiona. "It's too quiet." As if on theatrical cue, Boss missiled himself against the back door, his singular dull thud followed by Nizhoni's light, pleading scritchings against the dining room window glass. Meanwhile, Prudence was attempting to decipher Rita's extravagant scrawl across the back of a grocery bag propped near the phone, *Hey girlfriend, Ray, me and Jasper went to the Art Fair on Mill, Indigenous (Native band) playing, Love ya! P.S. If you have time, throw the kids some wings, six for Nizhoni, only four for Boss, he's getting fat, Thanx!*

The back door slammed. Fiona flew back into the kitchen with the velocity of a clown shot feet first from a cannon. "Have you *been* out there? Fat, buzzing flies, an ugly metal fence, your Italian flower pot smashed, that horrible wolf stink, and somehow Boss dragged out my paint palette and rolled around on it so now he's got these huge red and yellow splotches all over his fur . . . Mom, how can you stand this?"

"It's only for a little while, honey." Prudence sighed. "It really is temporary."

"You said that a month ago . . . That horrible woman's been here two months!"

"Well, she's having a hard time, she hasn't made enough money to move out yet. She's paying rent at least, so I figure the money helps with bills."

"Have you ever thought maybe *she* caused the plumbing bill — with all that *hair* of hers?" Fiona dragged something out of her back jeans pocket, handed it to her mother.

"Art Night at Metro. It's my performance piece. Can you come?"

"Fiona, sweetie. Listen. I know it's crazy here right now. Rita's basically a decent person, she's just having a really tough time. Much as I would like her gone, I can't toss her out in the street. I can't make her homeless. I cannot morally do that. We just have to wait till she has money to get her own place."

"Granted she's having a tough time, lots of people are, but what about you, Mom? The woman's overrun your house, not to mention Ray's stuff is all over the place." Fiona stuck her tongue out. "See? Bite marks. From holding my tongue."

"It will end, Fiona, I promise. And of course I'll be at your Art Night. I wouldn't miss it for the world."

"OK, well, I've gotta get to work. My new boss has been firing people right and left, so I can't be late."

Ray, Rita and Jasper rolled through the front door, each with a paper bag of groceries. "Hidey-ho, the gang's home! I'm going to get out my George Foreman Showtime and whip up a big ole country-style dinner. Chicken, mashed potatoes, gravy, apple pie, the works!"

"Chicken?" Prudence had a nauseous

mental rewind of all the raw bird wings, yellow, pimple-fleshed, clammy and flightless, holed up in her refrigerator.

Ray gave her a kiss plus a little scallop-pinch around the middle.

"Quit it. How was your day?"

"Boring. I missed you."

Jasper disappeared down the hall, leaving Rita to put away the groceries. He emerged, moments later, in black spandex swim trunks, his hair out of its braid, hanging in a V shape past his waist. A short, paunchy man with long, thinning, womanish hair, rat-a-tat-tatting on his chest, right between his fleshy breasts. "Anybody up for the Nestea plunge?"

"Not me, babe. I hate the water. I'll throw on my bikini, though, and hang out with you."

"Nephew?"

"Nah, I'm going to hit my easel. I've got an idea."

"Prudence?"

"OK, I'll sit outside a few minutes."

She sat in the beastly Arizona summer sun, watching Jasper dive off the diving board, listening to Rita yap on about her purebred Doberman back in L.A., how it had attacked and killed a neighbor's pet mule, how she'd driven the Doberman, its muzzle soaked in mule blood, to the veterinarian's to be put down, how the nurse kept exclaiming what a superb animal, didn't she want to reconsider? Rita's animal stories usually featured sudden attacks and peculiar mutilations. Now she was describing a story she'd seen on TV, a true story about five-foot-long parasitic worms in the Philippines, how people would try to rid themselves of the worms by standing around in bodies of deep water, ponds, so the worms could slither out of their itchy anuses and swim off.

The trouble was, Rita said, a lot of the worms slid half out, then climbed right back in again, kind of like sucking a strand of cooked spaghetti back into your mouth . . . Rita pooched her lips and made sucking noises as Jasper plopped in a chair between them, a white towel cast over his head like a nun's wimple.

"Whew. All that diving took me back to my old Mazola days."

"Mazola days?" Prudence asked.

Years ago, Jasper explained, he'd auditioned to be in a Mazola corn oil commercial — did she remember that old commercial with the young Indian guy diving off a high rock into a pool of water? Had she seen that one? That was him, in the commercial, doing the diving.

Prudence tried to remember a TV ad about corn oil. "Nope, can't remember."

"A lot of girls chased me after that. I was definitely a mini-celebrity."

"You still are, baby. You're still a gorgeous man."

How could Rita say that? Did she mean it? Ball-bellied, bandy-legged, his face brown and droopy, Jasper did not fall into Prudence's gorgeous category. Besides, wasn't he something far more important? He was Ray's spiritual mentor, a role model, someone to emulate and look up to, not the ex–Mazola man.

They wheeled with sedate, shiny grace, spun in calm, steady rotation inside George Foreman's famous roasting device. Prudence stared, mesmerized. "It's a Ferris wheel for dead chickens."

Rita laughed, spooning yellow globs of whipped butter into her mashed potatoes. She had changed out of her leopard-print bikini into a low-cut red tank top and tight capris in a red and white toile farm print (*Cheap Wal-Mart pants, sheez, goddamn barn's stretched right across my crotch!*).

Prudence stood near the sink, ripping up iceberg lettuce for salad, trying to answer

Rita's just asked question about the nature of her relationship with Ray. Prudence disliked relationship questions, but this time found herself confessing that Ray could be sweetly attentive one minute, cold the next, that the Sun Dance thing had helped a lot, but he could still be mean, how every time they disagreed over something, he'd say, *OK then, that's it, I'm leaving,* though of course he never did. Leave.

Rita stepped close, lowered her voice, her tone pleasant, though her message would not be.

"Listen, hon, I've known Ray for years. I love him and think of him as my little brother. But I have to tell you, woman to woman, what I see, just from living here with you guys. Ray cares, but he's not committed. This is definitely not a man who's committed. I mean today, while we were walking around the Art Fair, he kept pointing out all these different women, young women, *She's a hottie,* he'd say, *isn't she a hottie?* I didn't mention you, I just went along, teased, told him he didn't have a chance, just kind of joking around but maybe you need to ask what's he giving you versus what is he getting? I had a boyfriend like him once, Native guy, Buffalo Child, gorgeous, absolutely gorgeous man,

I supported his lazy ass for three years before I finally threw him out. One week later, he crawled back, asking me to marry him. I informed his sorry ass he had as much chance of marrying me as hell had of freezing over . . . I'm just saying, woman to woman, I think you need to be careful here. Take care of numero uno."

Prudence looked over at Ray, standing at his easel in the next room, his little bandanna slipping over his forehead. What *was* she doing? He lived in her house for free, came and went as he pleased, paid for nothing, was broke, he said, always broke. Meanwhile, he lived in a comfortable house (hers), ate decent food (hers), had sex with her (though not lately), and had the nerve to gawk at *hotties,* not to mention talk to the ones who called, the ones he met for coffee, movies, art advice.

"You OK?" Stirring a pot of gravy with one hand, Rita reached into the spice cupboard. "Garlic salt, this definitely needs garlic salt."

"I'm fine. Be back in a sec."

Prudence locked the door to her bathroom, turned both faucets on so no one could hear her crying. *Hotties, my flat ass.*

★ ★ ★

Plucking roasted legs and thighs off their Ferris-wheel hooks, Rita heaped up four plates with potatoes and gravy, salad, corn and chicken parts. They sat in the living room, plates on laps, Ray and Prudence on one couch, Rita and Jasper on the other. Ray held up his scoured dish, asking Prudence for seconds, patting her butt as she stopped to take his plate into the kitchen, *Thanks sweetie.* Prudence, on the other hand, wasn't hungry; she had left her greasy drumstick, glop of potato and pale scatter of salad untouched and began clearing dishes with quick, compressed fury. Jasper stood up, belching and shifting his jeans around, joking about his big stomach, then plopped back down to watch a Vietnam movie he had brought down from Flagstaff. Rita went outside to feed Boss and Nizhoni, hose off the patio and clean up the lawn, now her nightly chores. Irritated by the cinematic war sounds coming from her living room, Prudence was in the kitchen, scraping dishes, when Ray came up behind her, kissed her on the neck, lifted the dish from her hands. "Hey babe, I'll do these, you go relax."

Thrown off by the sweetness of *Hey babe,* Prudence paused at the sink, remembering *hotties,* what Rita had told her about *hotties.*

"Hey, I see you're starting to fill out those jeans a little, Prue. Getting a little jowly here, too." He patted her cheeks. "I'm not telling you what to do, but maybe you'd better lay off the sweets a little. I don't like my women starved, but I don't like a fat girl neither."

Ohmigod. That did it. Prudence disappeared into the bedroom, changed into her walking shoes, and sailed proudly forth, head high, straight toward the back door.

"Where you going, sweetie pies?"

"For a walk." Amazing. She sounded cheerful.

"It's dark. I don't like you walking after dark."

"Twenty minutes. I'll be safe, promise." She resisted slamming the door, merely pulling it closed before stalking out of the garage, turning blindly left, past the fire chief's house, the hydrologist's house, then reversing back, marching toward the Broadmor schoolyard at the end of the block, threading her way through a narrow pass in the chain-link fence. The schoolyard was a large, old-fashioned grassy field with a baseball diamond at the far west end, school buildings to the north, a row of tall, brooding Aleppo pines bordering the field on the south, and on the east, the side closest to Prudence's house, the side she had just entered, a playground with swings, straight and curly slides, cement crawl-tunnels, climbing bars like giant croquet wickets in graduated sizes, and at the center of all this playground equipment, presiding, giving welcome shade to children playing outside at lunchtime, stood one enormous, shaggy-armed Aleppo pine. Down its massive trunk Prudence slid, her back cradled against its comforting roughness. Running away from home. What home? She didn't have one. She had given it away. Lots of other people lived there now, with her permission. Within the tree's dark shelter, Prudence began to think. She could sit out all night, who would care? The last time she had run away from home, she had been ten years old and in love with her modest collection of Doris Day coloring books. One Saturday, barging into little Prudence's room, screaming *Pigsty!*, Deleanor had raised the sash on one of the prettily curtained windows, scooped up Prudence's prized coloring books, and pitched them like loose hay down the gray-shingled roof to the concrete driveway below. Traumatized, Prudence fled her room, bolted out of the house, vanished for an entire summer afternoon. The three times she saw her mother in the soft green Plymouth, searching for her, she scrunched behind a hedge, flattened herself against the side of a garage, scooted behind a tree, evading capture, until Eddie Archembeault, a scrawny, cross-eyed French kid, cycled up and told her she'd better get home, her mother was frantic, ready to call the police. Fifteen minutes later, at Deleanor's kitchen table, Prudence savored the sweetness of her mother's contrition in the form of two helpings of her favorite macaroni and cheese dinner followed by a sugared slice of homemade rhubarb pie with a double scoop of vanilla ice cream.

Now, however, Prudence was too furious, breathing too hard, swiping at her runny nose, to see much humor in having run away like a ten-year-old, punishing the mean grown-ups by disappearing. Hunched in the cool, needled dirt, stubborn and pouting, she saw Ray emerge from her house, stand in the driveway, look up and down the street. She glanced at her watch, its hands glowing faintly. Twenty-nine minutes.

She wasn't equipped for Grown-upness, hadn't been properly groomed. Fiona was intelligent, outspoken, independent, a solid young woman. Deleanor had succeeded as a blue-ribbon wife and green-ribbon mother. Sandwiched between them, Prudence felt defeated, compromised, dilute in character. She had been raised to repeat Deleanor's life, to be a housewife and mother with an average education, a career no larger than a hobby, certainly nothing to interfere with the real job at hand. But with college, the civil rights movement, the Vietnam War, the women's liberation movement, Prudence's consciousness had been raised straight through the roof, meaning she thought it unwise to repeat her mother's life. But how much headway could one woman make against biological imperatives, rooted archetypes, psychological imprints, cultural values, family rules? Nearly fifty, Prudence looked independent — a divorced single mother, college teacher, writer (one respectable literary book, one semi-lucrative romance). On the surface, she had attained modernity, maturity. Yet how many of her dreams, expectations and actions rose from childhood fairy tales, from Deleanor's domestic teachings and the constant signals of a patriarchal society? She only looked liberated. Didn't her current mess point to certain heart-shaped shadows, romance goblins, Martha drones and Hestian broom-sweepers, all taking up restless space inside her? Do you want Savage Passion? *Yes! No!* Do you want to be a wife? *Yes! No!* Do you want to be loved romantically, if not eternally? *Yes! No! Yes! No! Yes!* Betty Crocker inside, Gloria Steinem outside, biology itself indifferent, implacable, rolling up and over her, like a great noiseless steamroller. How could she throw Rita out, a woman with no money and no place to go? Should she boot Ray out, too, since he could be mean, was uncommitted and didn't contribute much beyond a dinner here, a movie there? Was the one good reason to keep him a moral one? She had given her word to support him in the Sun Dance. Could that be her decision? See him through Sun Dance, give Rita the same deadline, end of July, then out? She would claim her life back. Her spacious, silent life.

So many years lived on one street. La Diosa, the goddess. Fiona had gone to this very school, played on these swings and slides, sat under this very tree. Suddenly, Prudence saw Ray backing his van out of the garage, driving off slowly, in the wrong direction. She felt the weird, childish glee of invisibility. She could make this delicious feeling last, scotch around the opposite side of the Aleppo's broad trunk, camp there all night. Maybe then he'd realize what she meant to him. Or should she stand up, go back to the sidewalk, make it look as if she'd been out walking, forgetful of the hour, until, eventually, he found her?

She was walking east on Palmcroft when he pulled the van up, driver's-side window rolled down.

"Where were you? I was worried. Get in."

Having made up her mind to clear certain people out of her life in exactly three weeks, Prudence hopped in. Her decision had made her cheerful. "Lost track of time, I guess. It was nice out."

"Well, don't do that again. I don't want you out walking after dark ever again. Who's going to feed me?"

Feed you? Prudence thought scornfully. I have your eviction notice, buddy. Rita's, too. Getting down from the van in the garage, walking ahead of Ray, feeling independent, powerful, relieved, Prudence was surprised to feel Ray grab her arm, spin her around in the hot, dark garage.

"Prudence." His face was serious, his voice passionate. "I don't want anything to happen to you. I love you. I want to protect you, take care of you. You're my jewel."

She dived into his arms, her face pressed sideways against his chest. His jewel? A flood of feeling rushed up in her, but Prudence had learned caution. She kept silent.

He kissed the top of her head, several times, softly. "Let's go in. Watch TV with Jasper and Rita. He's driving back up north in a little while. C'mon, sweetie."

So Prudence found herself back in the darkened living room, Ray holding her tightly rescued on one couch, Rita and Jasper on the other, watching the conclusion of *Good Morning, Vietnam*.

Later that night, when Jasper and Ray were standing out by Jasper's truck talking, Rita sidled up to Prudence. "You should have seen him, girl. When you weren't back in exactly twenty minutes, little brother was pacing up and down until finally he just grabbed his keys, said he was going looking for you. The man's crazy about you. On the other hand, Jasper and I got in a fight, that's why he's leaving. We were sitting peacefully by the pool, I was looking at ads for places to rent, and all of a sudden the man got in a high holy snit because I wouldn't rub his feet. Can you imagine? Then he demanded I pluck out his mustache hairs with tweezers when he knows I have a phobia about facial hair!

After that he got huffy and said he was driving back to Flag. I just don't know what's gotten into him lately."

The yellow tubing and dehydrators were gone, her baseboards had been neatly replaced, a crew of painters and carpenters had descended for a week's steady hammering, stapling and paintbrushing. Her house had been put back together, new oatmeal carpet had been installed, fresh Winter Barley covered the walls. But this optimum movement and forward progress was spoiled by Rita's cutting across the front lawn one evening with a bag of groceries (raw fish for her, raw wings for the wolf) and a four-foot bouquet of purplish black flowers, hideous, spiked, warlike blooms.

"For you. Aren't they fabulous? Perfect for your dining room." So Prudence put them there, in her dining room, upright in a cylindrical glass vase, where they remained for over a month, too ugly to die, a blackening clump of amaranthine, nightmare blooms. She eventually bore them out to the alley one afternoon, dumping them, still alive, into the giant green trash can. Using the emptied vase as a short glass baton to shoo away flies, Prudence hoped to ride out the days of her bizarre life, days until Sun Dance was over and Ray and Rita could vamoose, scramola, be gone. Oblivious to her secret resolve, Ray kept busy painting, modeling, running with rocks, performing his rigorous daily series of two hundred sit-ups, push-ups, jumping jacks, and beading a large medallion to wear around his neck during Sun Dance. He went to a nearby tailor to have his ankle-length red cotton dance skirt sewn, made a pair of moccasins for himself with elk-hide soles and deerskin tops. He sunbathed nude every afternoon, face up, then down, on a towel beside the pool, slick with Banana Boat oil, earphones on. More often now, he sat completely naked on his towel, smoking his pipe and praying, while Boss, the ex-celebrity dog, lay stiff as a doorknob nearby.

On a Saturday in mid-June, Jasper Chee, Harold Martinez, Harold's wife Delphine, their oldest son Darren, four younger children, plus Lame Wing and Harrison, all stopped by Prudence's house, en masse, on their way home to Tucson from a ceremony meant to undo black magic that had been cast by certain enemies wanting to stop the Sun Dance. Navajo enemies.

Skinwalkers. In a peyote vision, the medicine man had seen objects buried in the dirt behind Harold Martinez's trailer, a human skull, pieces of Harold's clothing, strands of Delphine's hair. They must dig these up, the medicine man said, and burn them. The medicine man had pulled a snake bone out of Harold's right cheek, porcupine quills out of Jasper's neck, and a deer bone from Lame Wing's left shoulder.

Prudence served leftover chicken enchiladas, poured iced tea, reheated coffee as the men sat in her living room discussing evil spells, skinwalkers, black magic. When Fiona stopped by in the midst of this, Prudence put her to work carrying refilled glasses of iced tea and topped-off cups of coffee to the adults, soberly lined up along her two couches, in the living room. The four children perched at the dining room table, Delphine talking in a soft, worried voice as she and Prudence served them small portions of food and glasses of orange juice.

"It's been going on a long time. We've all been really sick, and Harold hasn't been able to work in three years. We have bad dreams all the time. I've washed the house down so many times, saged it, cleansed it, and now that medicine man's saying we need to dig up the curse he saw, burn the things he saw buried near our trailer."

"Do you know who's doing this?"

"We think it's this one Navajo man who's jealous of Harold, who wants his power, you know, as a Sun Dance leader." They returned to the living room, sat down with the men. Delphine spoke.

"Up there in Chinle, remember Harold, at the Sizzler, remember that time we saw him? That man? We were eating, and we saw him come in and stare real hard at us. That's the first time he shot us, Jasper too, with the quills and the snake bones."

Harold nodded, grunted slightly, held his plate out. Delphine got up to get him more food. Standing nearby, Fiona elbowed her mother and rolled her eyes.

As the children politely cleared their own dishes, Fiona invited them to sit on the floor around the TV and watch an old Marlo Thomas video, *Free to Be You and Me*, left over from Fiona's childhood. Bored by Marlo's bouffant hair and high-pitched chitchat, the littlest boy, Yellow Bull, went and stood in front of his father, who ignored him.

In the kitchen, the phone rang. Deleanor's voice on the voice message machine reminded Prudence that ninety percent of all sickness and disease begins in an unclean colon — she should consider a good colon-cleaning program. Prudence rushed into the kitchen to turn down the volume just as Fiona came in, wiping her hands on a dish towel. "I'm off, Mah, the kids are cute, but I can't handle seeing women waiting on men, it's too 1950s for me. And the way the men are all pissing on about black magic, bragging how many snake bones got pulled out of their necks, sorry . . ." She pecked her mother on the cheek. "I love you. I'll call later."

When Prudence came back to the living room, the men were standing up, stretching, clearly ready to leave. Delphine had started gathering up her children, while Marlo, in the background, chirped tirelessly, free to be herself twenty years ago.

From the front lawn, Rita, just home from running errands, cupped her hands, yelling to Prudence that she and Jasper would be back from Tucson later on, either that night or the next morning.

But Rita returned alone, and with grim news. One last ceremony was needed to destroy the powerful evil. Only one ancient medicine man, still living, knew how to break the spell of this particular black magic. The ceremony itself would cost seven hundred dollars. "Harold and those guys don't have two dimes to rub together. Shoot, if I had it, Prudence, I'd give them the seven hundred in a heartbeat, no questions asked. Harold told me he could pay me back when he gets his tribal check August 1. It would be a loan. I just don't have that kind of money."

Intrigued by the Hardy Boy drama of black magic, skinwalkers and spiritual warfare, Prudence clearly heard the word *loan*.

"I can do it, Rita, lend the money. It's all I've got, though, so I'll have to get it back by August 1."

"Prudence! My gosh, are you absolutely sure?"

Yes, she was sure. Rita called Jasper on her cell, telling him the good news, and Rita conveyed her fiancé's message. "Jasper says thanks and sends his blessings."

Electrified by her own magnanimity, Prudence scrawled out a check, ripped it from her checkbook, handed it to Rita. She avoided looking at her balance, which, minus seven hundred dollars, was barely enough to carry her until August 1, the date Harold promised he could pay Rita back with his tribal check. The loan amount had been siphoned from Fiona's college tuition money. But the need was urgent, the cause spiritual, and repayment certain.

Thrilled by her good deed, her sacrifice for the spiritual good of the Sun Dance, she woke Ray that night to tell him. He lay on his back, stared at the ceiling, then smacked his forehead with one hand, groaning. "I wish you'd waited to ask me, Prudence. I hate to tell you this, but you may never see that money again. Chances are good, in fact, you won't."

She explained about the loan, about Harold's tribal check in August.

"I'm sorry, hon, but I'll be amazed if you get ten dollars back. Your intention was good, but you don't know Indian people like I know Indian people. Don't forget, I'm one of them. What's called a loan, from a white person who looks wealthy by comparison, gets very easily converted into a gift. Calling it a loan saves face. I hope I'm wrong, sweetie, but I think you just gave away seven hundred dollars."

But these were Sun Dance chiefs, Prudence insisted, irritated by Ray's killjoy pessimism. Spiritual men. Men of honor. "Besides, their lives really might be in danger and they're so desperate. I wanted to help."

"I know you did, honey. I just wish you had asked me first."

His pose was unchanged, head resting on paws, ears pricked up, tongue ladled out one side, small eyes unblinking, staring straight ahead. That he wasn't exhaling with his usual melancholy, that he wasn't responding to Nizhoni's nudges and didn't raise his head when Rita shouted his name in increasingly worried tones, were hints he had expired, but the transit had been so subtle, so nearly imperceptible, that for hours no one realized Boss was truly dead.

"The flies were thicker, that was all," Rita sniffed that night, poking her artificial crab salad around, her eyes red and swollen. Boss was now in the trunk of Rita's car, wrapped in a flowered bedsheet, ready to be driven into the desert for a natural burial, which meant being picked apart by buzzards, coyotes, ants and the crematorial desert heat.

"She didn't care one fig about him, Ray. The minute Nizhoni got here, Boss was old hat."

Rita had sped off, Boss's corpse wedged sideways in the trunk, so Ray and Prudence felt free to mourn in their own way, criticizing Rita's neglect and pushing Nizhoni away whenever she sauntered up to them, nuzzling for affection. "Go away," said Ray. "You're spoiled rotten."

"At least he looked clean when he died."

"White as snow."

"We could have adopted him."

"Taken better care of him."

"Let him come in the house."

"Let him lie on our bed, sleep with us."

"No, Prudence. I draw the line at animals in the bed."

"With just Nizhoni, I guess that will make things easier."

"No. Boss was the easy one. He just lay there."

"Depressed."

"Depressed to death."

Sadly, they sat remembering poor Boss. Prudence, who thought of him as noble and granite-like, wept, imagining his regal, guiltless, huge frame dropped in the desert like a discarded Thanksgiving turkey carcass, picked over by vultures. Ray patted her on the back, lost in mournful musings of his own.

★ ★ ★

"Prune." Ray came into the bathroom, where she was flossing her teeth. "I have to drive down to Tucson and pick up Jasper, Harold, his whole family, drive them all up to the reservation. They've got a peyote ceremony to go to, plus that other ceremony, the one you footed the seven hundred dollars for? I'll be gone most of the weekend, so you and Rita will have to hold down the fort here."

"Rita's not going?"

"She can't. I guess no women are allowed."

"What about Delphine?"

He shrugged. "She's probably going along to cook, take care of the kids or something. I need to get my stuff and leave right away." He paused. "They want me in the peyote ceremony."

"Have you done that before? Peyote?"

"Nope. First time. Will you be OK here with Rita for a couple of days?"

"Sure, fine. I've got my end-of-semester dinner party tonight, over at one of my students' houses, then papers to grade. There's plenty to keep me busy."

"OK, good. I'm going to make sure they pitch in for gas on this trip. Hey, listen, if I get the chance, I'll talk to Delphine, emphasize the fact that you *loaned*, you did not *give* them, seven hundred dollars."

Leaning forward, her chin stubbed against the steering wheel, hands loose on the wheel at midnight-o-one and midnight-o-two, navigating cautiously, Prudence humped her little Rambler over the curb's soft rise, fumbled for the garage door opener, and as though she were watching a space launch at Cape Canaveral, watched the heavy door lift and tuck backward. Nosing the car in, she switched off the headlights, slid her keys out of the ignition, and sat numb, motionless and nearly sightless, like one of those human mock-ups for car crashes. She had drunk far too many Lost Virgins, Sheldon Pettipiece's homemade erotic cocktail, cassis with cherries. The interior of the car was spinning, and when she extricated herself from it, the garage was spinning, too, and when she used the wall for support, making her way into the workroom, the room where Ray painted and did all his bead- and leatherwork, even it was whirling. The floor looked very nice indeed, a place to rest against until the whirling lessened.

But the whirling didn't lessen, and Prudence got bored, lying on the carpet in the dark, her stomach belatedly objecting to the array of lascivious foods she had introduced into it, penis-shaped pasta with clam sauce, plump, juicy strawberries coated in chocolate, store-bought jelly roll cake, gooey caviar on champagne crackers, small white cakes molded like breasts with pink jujubes for nipples, and worst of all, something only Sheldon would declare erotic — corned beef — curling, grainy slabs of labia-colored pickled beef like so many nasty, wagging tongues. To top it all off, a sampling of exotic wines and champagnes, ending with a toast to Lost Virgins, everyone plucking cherries by their stems in slurpy, drunken tribute to their Questing for Eros class, a class that had hatched a late-blooming romance between Elaine Durrell and Sheldon, friendship between Jimmy Flores and Dwayne Bird, busy booking local performance space for their comedic piece, *The Penis Dialogues*, and from the look of Joe Harlinger and Tillie Tooter, nipping cherries off one another's stems, noses touching, a brand-new liaison, tumid with lust.

Prudence rose to her feet, wobbling, her head in one form of distress, her stomach in another. Since sleep was out of the question, Prudence deemed it interesting to check her e-mail. A spate of dry memos from the college, and a two-page chart from Deleanor linking birthdays with trees (*What Kind of Tree Are Yew?*), a predictor of destiny according to your birth date and the characteristics of your birth-tree. Having determined she was a fig, Fiona a pine and Ray an oak, Prudence was startled to see a white specter floating toward her from the unlit kitchen, sobbing piteously, choking on its words.

"That woman left three more messages! I've been checking his voice mail all night. She calls him Cubbie and herself Cubette, I can't believe it, those are Our Names! Not only that, a Vonda Lee called, complaining she hasn't seen Jasper in over two weeks, where was he, if he'd come over soon, she'd even pay him! Come outside with me. I need a cigarette. I'm just plain smoking myself to death."

Prudence sat outside with Rita, facing the pool and puffing inexpertly on the American Spirit cigarette Rita, with a shaky hand, had passed to her. Sensing her mistress's distress, Nizhoni burrowed her pointy, arrow-like snout in Rita's lap. Except for an XXXXLarge white T-shirt, yellow smiley face front and center, topped by an Indian war bonnet, *It's a Good Day to Die* printed underneath, Rita was apparently naked.

"How did your party go?"

"Oh, fun, I guess. I drank too much. Things are whirly. Kind of whoop-de-do."

"Man, if I wasn't a Sun Dancer, I'd get roaring drunk right this minute, that's what I used to do whenever a guy dumped me. This one time, I rode one of my horses all night in the dark, drunk as a skunk, it's a wonder I wasn't bucked off and killed." They smoked another cigarette each, Rita repeating she couldn't believe it, it couldn't be true, Jasper was her dream man, they were Sun Dancers, they led a morally upright life, he'd lied to her, who was this other woman? Prudence made sympathetic noises ending with a yawn and the suggestion they go inside, try to get some sleep. Nizhoni padded close beside, so Prudence suggested the wolf sleep with Rita in her bed, for comfort's sake. At her bedroom door, she watched the square gleam of Rita's white T-shirt, the dark, stealthy shape of a half-grown, leggy wolf float waftily together down the hall.

"Prudence, can you hear me? Good, because I'm out here behind the woodshed, I've only got a minute to talk. Listen. It's bad. It's really bad. There's a woman here with Jasper, apparently she drove in last night from Taos. I'm pretty sure they slept together in Jasper's room, they're both in there now with the door closed. Don't tell Rita that. She doesn't need to know."

"Is her name Autumn?" Quickly, Prudence told him about Rita's interceptions of Jasper's voice mail messages, three from Autumn, one from a woman named Vonda Lee.

"Yeah, I think that's her name. Spring, Summer, Autumn. Something like that. I confronted him last night, said I didn't think he was doing this thing right, that if he wanted to break up with Rita, didn't want to marry her, then he should be straight up honest and tell her. Be decent about it. Instead he's pulling bullshit, sneaking around, lying, hiding behind the supposed visions of a medicine man, saying he has to distance himself, that Rita's life will be in danger if he stays near her. That's plain bullshit, and I told him so."

"What do the others think? How are they acting?" (Fascinating, she thought. With all Ray's sneaking around, he condemns someone else's.)

"Nobody's saying much. I get the feeling they all knew about this chick."

A piece of pink notepaper rustled along

the kitchen counter, landed right under Prudence's nose. *What does she look like?* Rita looked imploringly at her.

"Ray, what does she look like?"

"Not to be mean, but try cow. She's huge. She has nice long brown hair, a pleasant face, but her butt, I am not exaggerating, is a barn with acreage. Her rear is the size of a Wal-Mart, I mean when she walks backward, she beeps. Complete opposite of Rita. This woman is big as an elephant and quiet as a mouse. Hardly makes a peep, traipses behind Jasper like she's his servant. And, get this, she has a brand-new Jeep Cherokee, a really sharp car she'll probably let Jasper drive up to the ceremonies. Hey, I gotta go, Prue, I don't want to get caught making this call. I'm in a pretty awkward position here. Everything OK down there?"

She shook her foot free of Nizhoni's slopping, slimy tongue. "Everything's fine, considering."

"I miss you."

"Miss you too."

"Looks like we're headed out, I see Harold hauling stuff out to my van. I'm not sure I trust either of these guys as far as I can wink. Hey. Tell Rita whatever you want, but not about them in the bedroom together. Prepare her, though. I'll be back at the house late tomorrow night."

"OK."

"Love you, sweetie. Bye." He hung up.

Prudence held the phone a moment. *Love you.* The words fell like drops of honey into her ears, making her insides light up like a pinball machine. Then she remembered Rita. Wrapping up her own happiness, tucking it away, Prudence went outside to find Rita slumped in her leopard-print bra and bikini underpants, cigarette in one hand, cell phone in the other.

At the news, Rita's howl, heard up and down both sides of La Diosa, signaled her admission into the street's informed sodality of widows, qualified not by death but by betrayal, not by the loss of a husband but by the loss of a fiancé and a life's dream. The fact that she was turning forty-eight in two weeks hardly helped (Prudence made a mental note to look up what kind of tree Rita was). "I'm old," she wailed. "He told me we were going to grow old together. I was looking forward to that, you don't know how much I was looking forward to growing old with Jasper . . . How could he have lied to me — the last

521

time I saw him, we made love — he told me he loved me — he had to distance himself, my life was in danger from black magic — he'd had a dream of me dead and buried — the medicine man ordered him to stay far away until the spell was broken. I can't believe this, he is the most beautiful man in the world, I gave up everything, I sold everything for him . . ."

Later, in a cold, sobering moment, Rita would calculate she had spent thirty-four thousand dollars on Jasper Chee — in three short years, she'd sold her house, three horses, a truck, scads of jewelry, all of it to pay his bills, his back taxes, and to buy birthday and Christmas presents for his four children, who lived across town with his ex . . .

Prudence repeated every detail she could remember from her conversation with Ray, leaving out Jasper and Autumn in the bedroom together with the door closed. After dissecting every particle of relayed information, Rita called Jasper's house in Mountainaire, but no one answered, so she left a string of messages beginning with a heartrending *Jasper, how could you do this to me? I trusted you, we were getting married, you told me you loved me, that when all this was over, we would get back together. Oh my god, I don't believe this. I don't believe you didn't even have the decency to tell me yourself, to let me find out in this horrible, horrible way* . . . The messages, initially pleading and bereft, turned angry, then bitter, vituperative and cost-conscious. She was beginning to realize the financial wasteland he had left her in. She began taking inventory of things he had that were really hers, camping equipment, camping chairs, a Coleman lantern, her foam bedroll. Prudence tried diverting Rita with tarot readings at the dining room table, but each spread of the cards gave off eerie, unfortunate forecasts of heartbreak, financial ruin, doom and betrayal. The facts hit harder, and Rita sank lower.

Handing over Kleenex after Kleenex, Prudence lost track of the hours. They sat on her shaded brick patio in their underwear, smoking. Nizhoni, appetite whetted by emotional crisis, slunk about the yard, catching and cruelly tormenting a series of pigeons. Seeing one fluttering, flapping about on the grass, near death, Rita rose, strode over to it, snapped its dark-ringed neck as though it were Jasper's, and flung the corpse, hard, over the fence. Still stuporous from her previous night's indulgence, Prudence sat passively, an Ear for the lengthy, checkered history of Rita's affairs with men, an extravagant, plentiful trail ending with Jasper, the one man she'd wanted to grow old with and be buried beside, a man who had just thrown her over for a fat, meek woman, a woman who owned a brand-new Jeep Cherokee.

"What did Ray say again? What did he say she looked like?"

Prudence skimmed past the long brown hair and pleasant face part, emphasizing the wide-as-a-barn image.

"I can't eat," Rita moaned with bitter self-pity. "I haven't eaten in two days. When I go into this state, I don't eat for days. I'll probably be a skeleton after this. I'll have to be hospitalized. I may die."

Prudence felt ravenous. She kept ducking into the house to cram a mixture of Frito-Lay's and M&M's into her mouth.

They sat on the same two plastic chairs in the shade of the patio, facing the blank turquoise pool, for hours and hours. Prudence felt sorry for Rita, plus she was genuinely shocked — she had thought of Jasper as Ray's spiritual teacher! What about that?

Toward nightfall, Rita ground out her cigarette, stood up, snapped the black elastic waistband on her leopard panties.

"Let's go to the mall. Wanna go to the mall? It's not that late. I need to get out. Will you go with me? I'm going stir-crazy here. You're a good friend, Prudence. I don't know how I can ever thank you. Too bad we're not lesbians, we'd make a good couple, hey? I'd have to be the man, of course. Nizhoni, haul your skinny butt over here. Drop that bird. Drop it! God, she's getting big, isn't she?"

Unfortunately, everything Rita saw in the mall reminded her of Jasper, of something they'd done together, something she'd bought to surprise him, somewhere they'd gone together. When a song came on over the sound system, Rita collapsed on a granite bench beside a planter of fake bromeliads and birds-of-paradise and wept openly . . . *Our song . . . we danced to that song, he called me his sunshine flower. Ooohhh . . .* shoppers gawked openly at the sight of a woman draped, shoulders heaving, over a planter in the brightly lit mall. They sat opposite a Karmelkorn shop, and Prudence was sorely tempted to buy herself a bag. As they passed a casket-length bright blue water massage tube, Prudence suggested Rita climb inside, ten minutes for ten dollars, it might help. Rita shook her head dolefully. "Besides," she began wailing all over again, "Jasper and I used to joke about buying one, having sex in one. We had the best sex in the world. He told me I was the sexiest woman he'd ever been with. He said I drove him crazy. I didn't tell you, but that day in the pool, when Jasper kept diving off the board, we had amazing sex, right there in the water."

"Where was I?"

"You and Ray went out for a walk or something. Remember when you opened the back door to say hi, and we were in the pool, under the diving board? Well, we were . . . going at it."

Passing a Cinnabon shop, Prudence inhaled greedily. Her face ached for pastry. She was feeling the first twinge of irritation since the Jasper crisis had broken over their heads in a huge, messy, drenching wave. She had been patient, listening to the same lament over and over. The self-absorption of the brokenhearted appeared equal to the self-absorption of the newly infatuated, proving there was an immense selfishness to romance all the way around.

Transfixed, Rita stopped before a shop window. Nearly tripping over her, Prudence followed Rita's fixed gaze. A leather horse, four feet tall, complete with miniature saddle, reins and a vicious look in its slightly crossed glass eyes.

"Oh god, it's calling to me." She turned on her heel, dived into the discount store. Sighing, Prudence followed.

Purposively striding through the jumbled, fluorescent-lit emporium of goods, Rita cornered a red-smocked clerk, a runty, fading fellow with one daring spike in his left ear. He trotted behind her to the display window, reached in, hoisted out the leather horse, and flipped it upside down so all four legs, rigidified, stuck up in the air. Locating a price tag on its groin, the clerk righted the horse in front of Rita, where it stood, rocking slightly. "Ninety-nine ninety-nine. The last one."

In the checkout line, Rita clutched the horse as if it were a life preserver. "Prudence, how much are those?" She pointed to a display of chili ristras, strands of red chilies three feet long, dangling by the cash register.

Prudence stepped out of line, came back. "Nineteen ninety-nine."

"Lift one for me? My arms are too full. No, not that one, two down. Right, that one. Perfect."

Using one of her dozens of charge cards, Rita purchased the leather horse and the ristra, signing the sales receipt with an illegible, swaggering scrawl. With Prudence lugging the leather horse, and Rita lightly swinging her ristra, they exited the mall, the horse's rump heavy as lead on Prudence's right arm, the smell of cheap, oiled cowhide in her nostrils. In the parking lot, Rita opened the trunk, turned, and hefted the horse from Prudence's aching arms, angling it so it poked in nicely, headfirst, before slamming the trunk shut. She turned to Prudence, tears practically boiling down both cheeks. "I sold off three of my horses to help that asshole. This symbolizes my new life."

"And this?" Prudence swung the ristra a little, its dry red skins rustling like cockroach wings.

"Oh that. I've just always wanted one. We can hang it in your kitchen until I get my own place. Wow. I guess I'll have to get my own place now, huh? Can't move in permanently with you guys, can I, ha ha?"

Sunday turned into a funeral with no corpse, no coffin and one principal mourner in a leopard-print bikini. Compulsively dialing and redialing Jasper's number, intercepting his messages — none from Autumn — aha! that meant she'd gone with Jasper to the ceremonies; all that bullshit about no women in the ceremony a big fat lie meant to throw her off! Rita talked on and on, hashing and rehashing, dialing and redialing while Prudence cooked. Cooking, during a crisis, she discovered, calmed her more than bingeing on candy. She made chili, cornbread, beans, tortillas, rice, since Ray said they would be back that night, and she presumed that meant the whole crowd, Harold Martinez, his wife Delphine and children, Lame Wing, Harrison, perhaps even Jasper (though surely not Autumn!), maybe even that crazy Zuni guy, Vince — who knew how many people would show up in her living room, expecting to be fed before the drive south to Tucson? The afternoon sputtered and jerked by, with Rita calling a girlfriend in California, Prudence alternating cooking with reading her students' essays, descriptions of oral, anal and basic sex, told from the viewpoints of various sexual organs . . . what had she been thinking, assigning such a thing? Where had her mind been? She marked an A on everyone's paper. How could you assign grades to a dyslexic vagina, a depressed breast, a singing testicle?

As the afternoon drained into sunset, Rita rehearsed and perfected her tragedienne's role: Loyal Woman Betrayed. She showered, washed her hair, changed clothes three times, appearing finally in Prudence's kitchen in a long black skirt, black shirt, black boots, black earrings, her signature red lipstick the sole horizontal exception to an otherwise funereal impression.

"You look good," Prudence said. Tragedy, she thought, was Rita's best cosmetic yet.

Rita smoothed down the front of her black skirt, tossed her hair, cracked her neck in two directions. "Should I wear my turquoise necklace? The one he gave me? A little guilt maneuver?"

"Not one thing more. You're perfect. Uh-oh."

"Ohmigod. What?" Rita peered out the kitchen window over Prudence's shoulder. Ray's van had just pulled up to the curb.

"They're here." Rita clutched at her throat. "I'm going to be sick."

"Be strong, Rita. Remember 'I Will Survive'? You have to feel just like that song. Remember? *Go on, go out the door . . .*" Smelling something burning, Prudence stopped singing, dashed to the oven, yanked out her cornbread muffins, their domed tops lightly scorched. Rita had edged back into the hall, concealing herself, an offstage position from which she hissed questions.

"Is he there? Do you see him? How does he look?"

Prudence watched the tired-looking parade straggle across her lawn. Even the children, looking glum, dragged their feet.

"He's not there, Rita."

"He's with her then. Ohmigod, he's with her. I'm going to die."

"No, you're not." Arranging her face into a pleasant blankness, Prudence opened the door.

The men lined themselves up along both white couches, sober as judges, while Delphine and the children settled on the floor beside Rita's outlandish leather horse, which cast a baleful, glass eye on the dour assemblage. Ray tugged Prudence down beside him on one end of a couch and squeezed her hand. Prudence was about to speak up, offer food, when Rita sailed with black magnificence around the foyer into the living room. Standing doomed and tragic in their midst, Rita waited one long dramatic beat before her voice — hoarse and ruined — broke the silence. "Where is he? Why isn't he here?"

Then she sank onto the couch, on Ray's opposite side. "Why?" Her composure suddenly dissolved, Rita began sobbing horribly, "Why has our brother done this terrible thing to me?"

Everyone looked uncomfortable, though no one, except Ray, looked sympathetic. If anything, Prudence observed incredulously, they looked annoyed. As if they wished they hadn't had to stop here, be put through this. And she'd spent her day cooking for these clowns!

"Excuse me, anyone like food?" Her voice, stern and clipped, startled everyone. Various relieved noddings, yes, yes, food would be nice.

So with Rita on the teary offensive, asking questions, determined to pry answers out of someone, Prudence brought forth bowls of chili, cups of coffee, singed corn muffins, flour tortillas. The men devoured everything, eating fast, grateful for the excuse to keep quiet. Even Delphine hovered over her children, making sure they ate.

It isn't our business, what our brother does in his private life. No, we didn't know he was seeing her. We knew nothing.

Lies, Prudence fumed. A solid wall of lies. They knew. Maybe not everything, but they knew. For the first time it occurred to her that Ray had been right. As Harold sidled in her front door, followed by Delphine, they had grasped both of Prudence's hands, calling her sister, thanking her profusely for helping them during such a difficult, dangerous time, thanking her exactly the way you would thank someone for a gift. Her loan to Harold Martinez, her seven hundred dollars, Fiona's college tuition, was gone.

Then Rita heard news from Lame Wing, information so outlandish she repeated it. "He wasn't there? Jasper didn't even show up for the ceremony, the whole reason he claimed he had to keep away from me? He wasn't even *there?*"

"We don't know why, but no, he never showed up." Delphine spoke evasively, her eyes lowered.

"Was he with that woman? Autumn? What kind of name is that anyway?"

Again, the wall of neutrality. *We don't know. What our brother does is his own business.*

Desperate for truth, she turned to Ray.

"He was with her, Rita, yes. They took off from the house in her car and didn't show up for either ceremony."

"Are you saying he's run off with her?

They've run off together?"

"I don't know, Rita. It looks that way."

She wailed anew, and this time everyone shifted miserably, while Delphine reprimanded one of her children for pulling on the stirrup of the leather horse, fetched another who'd scooted down off a chair, run into the dining room, and begun twisting doorknobs, trying, instinctively, to escape.

Prudence stood up and began snatching dirty dishes from people, piling them angrily in the sink. Cowards! No one but Ray telling the truth. So much for his "spiritual teacher." She wanted these people to leave, and wondered if Ray would still want to be part of the Sun Dance. As Prudence handed a fresh glass of orange juice to one of the little Martinez girls, who looked up and thanked her with sweet, unsullied innocence, she marveled at how it was children grew up to become such messy, selfish, confused adults. Including herself, she thought, chewing with peevish energy on a tortilla as Ray came up behind her, kissed her on the back of the neck, then went outside to stand around on the front lawn with the men while Delphine and the children waited in the van. Ray stepped back inside to let her know he had to drive everyone back to Tucson and wouldn't be home for another five or six hours.

Lurid details of Jasper's infidelity arrived daily via Rita's convoluted phone contacts. Not only had he been seeing *this Autumn chick,* as Rita referred to her (*barn,* Ray added), but he had slept with plenty of other women as well. With Rita in Phoenix, working hard, paying his bills, Jasper was up in Flagstaff sleeping around. With each fresh revelation, with each new woman's name, Rita lost more weight. She went to her job, couldn't work, came home early. She looked at the food Prudence set before her, but couldn't eat. She left bizarre messages for Jasper, who never answered. She went to a psychic who told her Jasper had multiple personalities and a major sex addiction. Things would get worse for this man, the psychic predicted. He would ruin himself.

Reluctant to call attention to something as banal as money, Prudence began to lie awake nights, fretting over how she would pay next month's mortgage and utilities, her six-hundred-dollar home warranty insurance, her overdue car registration and unpaid taxes — dry fiscal details compared to Rita's juicy, adrenaline-spiked drama. She tested her resolve to eject Rita and

Ray from her house after Sun Dance, found it wobbly, especially in regard to Ray, but still, somewhat anyway, standing.

Rita's destitute son, Colin, showed up at Prudence's house via the Greyhound bus station in downtown Tempe. He arrived from Oakland, California, fired, his left knee wrenched, all his meager severance pay spent on a one-way ticket. He arrived the same evening that Fiona, Kirby in tow, appeared on Prudence's doorstep because Kirby's apartment complex, The Jolly Roger, had had a bomb scare and was being methodically searched both by bomb-sniffing dogs and the FBI.

"Good thing I've got two couches," Prudence indicated a blanketed hump occupying the shorter of her two white sofas. "Fiona, you, of course, can sleep in your own room."

From the foyer, Fiona peered into the twilit living room. "Who is that?"

"Rita's son. He's on his way to a graffiti convention in Dublin."

"Dublin, Ireland?"

"His sister married an Irish wine importer and sent him a one-way ticket."

"Cool." Fiona sounded impressed. Looming behind her, Kirby shifted uncomfortably. Something, Prudence noticed, seemed to be glinting out of his lower lip.

"Kirby, have you got something on — or in — your lower lip?" she asked.

"Uh . . ."

"Kirby got his lip pierced two days ago and a thing . . . what is it called, Kirb?"

"Fourteen-gauge orbital."

"Yeah, he got a fourteen-gauge orbital in his lip and an eight-gauge vertical labret in his ear. I made him bring his sterilization stuff, he's supposed to clean the holes twice a day." Fiona returned her gaze to the dark comma motionless on the couch. "He looks awfully small. How old is he?"

"Your age maybe? I think Rita said he was twenty-one or -two. Between yours and Kirby's age. He *is* a bit short. Kirby, step into the kitchen so I can get a better look at you."

Kirby shuffled behind Prudence, then stood, as directed, beneath the overhead light. Aghast at the spike in his lower lip, Prudence was doubly dismayed by the black saucer in his lower left earlobe, the edges of which were swollen, pinkish red and angry-looking.

"Are those permanent? Do they ever come out?"

Kirby boasted that these were the first in a planned series of piercings, now that he was a CBMer.

"CBMer? I'm afraid you've lost me, Kirby."

Fiona, rooting through the refrigerator, her voice stifled and disdainful, explained. "Church of Body Modification. Make pain your friend. I personally think it's insane. Mah — there's nothing to eat!"

"Sure there is, honey. There must be."

Fiona pointed into the refrigerator. "Raw wings for the wolf? Sushi and yogurt for Rita? Fly ointment? A tofu brick, three cartons of soy milk and a sack of potatoes?"

"Colin's a vegan."

As if resuscitated by either his name or food status, Rita's son appeared in the doorway, rubbing his eyes and yawning loudly, a thing, Prudence noted, he had inherited from his mother, though in every other way he seemed nothing like her. Colin was short (less than five-five, Prudence estimated), and handsome in a D. H. Lawrence-ish way. Porcelain skin, straight dark hair, soft brown eyes, a sort of early twentieth-century bone structure. Nostalgically good-looking, handsome in a way that suggested to Prudence another era, a World War I British soldier, perhaps. He was also woefully skinny. More than anything, she would later speculate, it must have been his smile that so instantly enraptured Fiona. A lazy, sensual, beatific smile.

Dazzled, Fiona shook Colin's massively beringed hand while Kirby made subtle, repetitive adjustments to his mutilated ear.

"Anyone hungry? I can order pizzas." Prudence remembered Colin's vegan diet. "One with pepperoni, one without?"

Colin didn't eat pizza, thank you, but he wanted to thank Prudence for letting him stay in her home by cooking everyone dinner. "I love to cook." He smiled, devastatingly, directly, at Fiona. "I invent as I go. Spontaneous chefery. Give me a single solitary potato, I'll make a feast of it."

"The Jackson Pollock of food?" Fiona suggested.

"Right on, Fiona! Fiona is an Irish name, and it suits you perfectly. Listen, folks. Leave me on my own for one single hour." Raising up on bare pink toes, Colin began swinging open Prudence's cupboard doors, peering in. "I guarantee you will be amazed."

"Shall we go outside then, let Colin do his thing?" Prudence's tone was bright, indulgent, charmed.

Out in the yard, the three of them found Rita, hollow-eyed and chain-smoking, talking on her cell. Prudence pretended not to hear the hushed argument erupting between Fiona and Kirby over what time his ear and chin were to be cleaned. As she hung up, Rita waved her cigarette at Prudence.

"All arranged. Colin and I pick up a U-Haul tomorrow morning, head up to Jasper's place in Flag, clear out my stuff. Can you believe that asshole? He left a message on his voice mail that said if I didn't get all my shit out by this weekend, he would throw it out on the street. I've got the truck rented, the store space ready, all I need to do is drive up there. Thank god Colin's here. Creator's blessing. Hell, I'm looking for any ray of light I can find. Where is he? My son?"

"Cooking dinner for everyone," Prudence said.

"Oh god."

"Why do you say that? He claims he's a great cook. One potato, one ingredient, voilà."

"Yeah, well, be prepared. This is a vegan we're talking about. A boy who lives on soy sauce and last year's rutabagas. Even his shoes are made of reconstituted vegetable matter. In a famine, we could boil and eat his shoes."

"Maybe that's what he's in there cooking," Kirby har-harred. "His shoes."

Fiona leapt to Colin's defense. "I think it's admirable, being a vegan. You need to have incredible self-discipline, and it's about much more than food, it's this whole awesome philosophy of not harming the earth."

Rita blew a perfect smoke ring. "I'd frankly find it more admirable if Colin would stop getting himself in hot water all the time. He's been living in a walk-in closet in the worst part of Oakland, he's been shot at twice, his gay roommate-slash-landlord demanded sex from Colin when Colin couldn't come up with the rent — rent on a goddamn closet! That's why he left, apparently. And my god, have you looked at him? Pale as veal, skinny and weak, his knees all knobbed and swollen. Tell you what, I'm relieved he's going to Ireland. Let his sister worry about him for a while."

"Isn't he a graffiti artist?" Fiona asked.

"That's not art, that's defacing property." Rita sighed. "I blame myself. The divorce, then him living all those years with his father, a right-wing KKK Christian.

You know, when Colin was sixteen, his father enrolled him in Christian boot camp. Colin ran away and lived on the streets for three years before we found him."

The back door squeaked open. Colin, wearing Prudence's one apron, white eyelet with ruffled shoulder straps, stepped out, brandishing a rubber spatula. "Din-din, good people!"

All that could be heard was the clank and scrape of cutlery on Prudence's best china, an expensive botanical design left over from her marriage to Powell. Pink cabbage roses and butterflies. Her father had told her the Latin name of the roses, but Prudence couldn't remember it. *Gallica* something? At last, Rita spoke.

"Why is Ray missing this?"

"He's modeling. He'll be home around ten."

"Does he do nude modeling, Mom?"

"No, he's not comfortable with that. Though I understand models make more money if they peel."

The word *peel* sent Fiona into snorts of laughter. Kirby glowered and scraped, his face an inch from his rose-patterned plate. He had said nothing throughout dinner, and though silence was not unusual for

Kirby, still, Prudence realized there were variations, implications, *tones,* to his silence. His present tone was brooding, pouty. On Fiona's left, still in his ruffled apron, Colin ate cheerfully, quickly, checking everyone's plates, sending around bowls and platters of his spontaneous concoctions whenever it appeared someone's portion was diminishing.

"More sautéed tofu? Hummus, anyone? Shredded carrot salad?"

Prudence passed her plate. "A smidgen more shredded carrot, please."

"Certainly." But the pièce de résistance, the triumph, Colin announced, was dessert.

"Banana splits?" Kirby glanced up hopefully. "Sundaes?"

"No, my friend. Something far better. Stewed fruit. Compote, the gourmet term." Over a choiring groan of protest (even Fiona's), Colin addressed Kirby, his facial expression one of earnest pity for the unsaved, the environmentally impure.

"Kirby? May I ask you something? It puzzles me you would inflict such suffering on your body. Voluntarily disfigure yourself. I know it's a fad, there are scads of other kids like you, I call them human pincushions, but I've yet to understand the motive. Could you enlighten me as to the philosophy behind your self-injury?"

Fiona stood up and began carrying dishes into the kitchen, no doubt to avoid a potential shouting match. As it turned out, Kirby shouted while Colin employed a quaintly phrased, nonconfrontational defense strategy. Prudence and Rita sat listening.

"Let's begin with the Church of Body Modification. CBM. What religion is that exactly, what are your tenets of faith?"

"My wha?"

"Tenets — what is it they, or you, profess to believe?"

Kirby embarked upon a halfway eloquent discourse, eloquent because it was rote, thoughts and ideas he had adopted, borrowed, spouted. Eventually, however, he fell off-script and began to insult Colin.

"At least I'm not a bean-eating vegan. You guys are just flimsy excuses for men, you have soy milk for blood and soy beans for balls, sorry, dude, that's what I think. You guys are chowing your way to oblivion. Human beings are meat eaters. Go as far back as you want, to the dawn of time, all that shit, meat eaters bashed the brains of plant eaters every time. That won't change. Face it, dude. We're animals. Fucking animals."

"God, Kirby. Shut up." Fiona appeared in the doorway holding a cut-glass bowl of stewed fruit. "You make more sense when you keep quiet. And my mom doesn't permit swearing in the house."

Kirby ducked his head as if shamed, and for an instant, Prudence felt sorry for him.

"I apologize, Colin." Fiona set the bowl of compote down in front of him. "He shouldn't have insulted you like that."

"Oh, no apology needed. Kirby's simply expressing his opinion." Colin got up, went to the sideboard, brought back a glass ladle, dipping it into the cut-glass bowl, aswim with dark, felted blobs of cooked fruit. "Dessert, anyone?"

He looked so vulnerable, so dear in Prudence's apron, one ruffled strap sliding down one T-shirted shoulder, the cutwork hem brushing his hairy, short calves, that all three women pushed their bowls forward and spoke at once. "Fruit, please. Thank you."

Kirby's chin hung lower on his chest. "None for me." He wagged his head dejectedly.

Fiona glanced across the table. "Colin, will you be around tomorrow night? I have a show at my school. A performance piece. I'd love you to see it."

Rita picked a prune pit from her mouth, set it on the edge of her coffee saucer. "Colin, you're driving up to Jasper's with me early tomorrow. I'm getting all my stuff and bringing it back here. We'll have to pick up the U-Haul at six a.m., and it's paid for until noon the next day."

Fiona was lightly massaging Kirby's shoulders now, and because his eyes were blissfully shut, he missed the veiled look of disappointment exchanged between Fiona and Colin as they listened to Rita's plans.

A thought startled Prudence, sending her spoon, brimming with stewed prune, clanking into her dish — what if Fiona and Colin fell in love? What if they married? Conceived children? She and Rita would be linked eternally, as mothers-in-law.

"Mah? What? What's the matter?"

"The fruit. It's unexpectedly delicious."

Kirby rubbed open his eyes, releasing one long, pursy belch, then another. "Yeah, man, thanks. Even if I didn't dig it, it was awesome."

Colin's vegan feast had, it seemed, come to an end.

★ ★ ★

Prudence had gotten up to check both

the clock and the message machine. She checked on the two young men heaped on either couch, sleeping. Cavernous snorts followed by adenoidal snufflings rose not from Kirby, as she might have expected, but from the slight, vegetable-fibered Colin. Going into the kitchen for water and an aspirin, standing at the sink, she saw Ray's van approach, headlights guiltily dimmed. Three and a half hours late. Her latent paranoia, her jealous leap to the conclusion he'd been with another woman, was reinforced when she saw him come in from the garage, hair down, shirt open, his animal sheen of satisfaction quickly replaced by a vague, irritated reply to her question: "Open studio ran late tonight, a bunch of us sat around talking." Her suspicions deepened in response to his defensive tone. Defensive hostility, Prudence had read in a magazine article, was a sure sign of guilt.

"What now, Prudence. What's wrong now?"

"Nothing."

"Yeah right, you're suspecting me again."

Walking past him with her aspirin and water glass, she detected a faint, woodsy perfume. "You could have at least called,

Ray. I was worried."

"Look, if I need a mother, I'll drive back home to Texas. I told you I need my freedom, freedom to go where I want, when I want, to see who I want. I also told you I'd never do anything to hurt you."

"You also said you only tell me what you want me to hear, what you think I can handle."

Their old argument revived, word for ugly word, like a script they had both permanently memorized.

"Forget it, I'm not dealing with this. It's boring. Old and boring. I'm tired and want to go to bed." He stalked past her. She listened to the shower turn on. A shower at midnight? Washing off what, who? She took three sleeping pills on top of the aspirin, and since there was no other place to sleep, both couches taken, Fiona in her bed, Rita in hers, Prudence lay down, cautiously, in her own bed, curled on her side, feigning sleep. Ray got into bed naked, found her hand, and pressed it to his heart. Didn't a Sun Dancer have to be truthful, decent, a role model to others? She tried bolstering her trust with this line of argument, then thought of Jasper Chee, a full-blown Sun Dance chief, and all that he'd done to Rita.

Colin and Rita were up and gone by the time Prudence woke the next morning, groggy from the dreamless sleep of pills and from Ray, who had woken her in the night, bitten her shoulders, pulled her to him for quick sex, sign of innocence or guilt, who knew? Now, here he was, sprawled naked and gorgeous, asleep in her bed.

Fiona stood in the shallow end of the pool, wearing a vintage black and white polka-dot suit ruched at the waist. Kirby was tossing a stick to Nizhoni, who flipped it expertly with her nose, caught it in her teeth, and trotted back to him.

Prudence took her coffee and sat with her feet in the pool, near Fiona.

"Coming to my performance tonight, Mah?"

"I wouldn't miss it for anything, baby-cakes."

"Promise you won't act shocked even if you are?"

"I promise to be perfectly inscrutable. Poker-faced. Look at Kirby, will you? Rolling in the grass with the wolf. So cute."

Fiona dunked down to her neck and began threading her arms underwater like white, anemic strands of seaweed. "He's such a pimple, Mah," she whispered. "I don't even want him there tonight."

"So what kind of deal are we in for?" Ray peered furtively around as he trailed Prudence up a short flight of cement steps at the back of Fiona's school. He looked skittish, ready to bolt. Too many white folks. Hoping to ward off the inevitable speech, one she had heard so often she could hang it in a cartoon bubble over his head, Prudence answered.

"It's an art show for seniors. Fiona's class got permission from the school's director to set up their own show, advertise, promote, and run it like a real gallery. One of the local news stations is covering the event, they've already aired interviews with a couple of the kids on *Good Morning Arizona*. Tonight's show is just for parents, family, friends."

"Oh joy," Ray muttered, opening the school's back door and going in first. He wore his standard black T-shirt, blue jeans, black cowboy boots and black cowboy hat. The hallway leading into the school lobby was hung, on either side, with student artwork, labeled and modestly priced.

"I think Fiona's piece is downstairs in

the basement, Ray."

"Let's make it quick, then. Too many white folk."

Fiona's maze is made of burlap, a black honeycomb you wander without maps or guides, each "cell" a cloistral, dreamlike space. In the first, the floor is "paved" with sliced rounds of deli-meat, a soft tilework of headcheese, summer sausage and bologna, overlaid with a sheet of clear acrylic. In the second, on four walls of soft black burlap, hang cutout farm animals from children's books — pigs, cows, chickens, sheep — while a tape recorder plays a scratchy recording of "The Farmer in the Dell," mixed with the gruesome, piteous sounds of factory animals being slaughtered, *Heigho! the derry oh, the farmer in the dell,* whack. In the third cell, black and white scenes from *Big Band Dance Shorts* float against the black walls, young couples roller-skate in pairs, whirl in fancy circles and figure eights, hands clasped, the women's skirts fluttering, the men's hair pompadoured, unmoving, the eerie, monotonous gaiety of the long dead, the soft whirr-whirr of skates, thirties music, piano, trumpet, sax. On the floor, casually discarded, a woman's vintage evening gown, a beaded purse, a pair of old-fashioned roller skates, a black and white photograph of Gladys Plinth, Big Band dancer, aged ninety-seven. In the fourth cell, a buzzing chorale of identical black vibrators, their conductor a headless, nude mannequin with a green shock of carpet sample pubic hair. Covering the walls are still shots from a porno movie called *Rocco's Animal Training* — a plump blonde wearing a black face mask, a giant dildo strapped to her mouth, a dark-haired woman facing her, the dildo deep in her mouth, tears leaking out of the corners of her rolled-back eyes.

In the fifth cell, a jumbo, dinosaurian Easter egg, a "sugar egg" made of Styrofoam. It has an oval peephole; peering in, you see an Easter diorama of green coconut grass, jelly beans, yellow chicks, white bunnies, a chocolate crucifix with Christ in tiny Gap shorts. The voice of Martha Stewart, instructing devotees in the proper methods of dyeing Easter eggs, is underscored by the Mormon Tabernacle Choir's rendition of "Onward, Christian Soldiers."

The next cell comes with written instructions: sit on one of the two chairs provided and perform a Tibetan exercise called Floating the Tongue. Seated in one of two metal folding chairs, Prudence closes her eyes, focusing on her tongue, centering it, keeping it still in her mouth, concentrating the whole of existence in her tongue. Prudence and a second woman sit back to back, floating tongues.

Then four taxidermied squirrels, molting and scabrous, one in an aggressive vertical posture, the second posed as if running, right front paw raised, scampering past a 1950s living room constructed to rodent scale, a third perched on the edge of a red plaid couch watching TV, the fourth stretched full length on a floral sofa as if asleep, a tiny newspaper peaked over its face. Through a false window, a human eye stares in, startled, fearful.

The final cell in Fiona's maze contains a small, closed coffin on a simple trestle. A child's bier. You are instructed, in a recording, to place your ear anywhere on the plain pine box, imagine sounds of the coffin being made, its pine planks sawed, hammered, sanded, nailed. On all four cloth walls hang printed lists, the names, ages, and in some cases, blurry photos of Arizona children murdered by their parents or stepparents over the past three years. The names cover all four walls. In each of the photos, the children are smiling.

Exiting the labyrinth, Prudence saw other parents emerging, drained and shaken-looking. A line snaked down the hallway, kids waiting eagerly to go in, kids with blue hair, pink hair, multiple piercings, tattoos, combat boots . . . "my fifth time, it's so awesome," Prudence overheard one girl.

She found Ray waiting by an exit door. "I'll be right back, Ray. I need to use the bathroom . . ."

To her right, she heard familiar snuffling sounds, then a flush. Prudence came out of her stall to find Fiona blowing her nose by the sink, wearing a droopy, pink ballerina tutu, little green army soldiers glued all over it, and a tiara made of bottle caps and condom wrappers. She had on blue rubber clown feet.

"We broke up. He was here and he left."

"You mean . . ."

"We got in this huge fight and he left. I hate him."

"Why . . ."

"He knew this was my gig, and to start with, he showed up late, he wasn't even here when I needed him to help me set up. I had to get some other kids, last minute, to help. Then, when he did show up, he told me he couldn't stay, he had to go help his boss, that bod-mod idiot, with his so-called Evening of Perversion . . . God, Mom, you don't even want to know, it's so stupid. They do these multiple suspensions, six or seven kids at once, Kirby's getting so into it, now he's saying he's going to do that."

"Suspend? I know about that."

"You do? Isn't it completely ridiculous? They don't even know why they're doing it. So we got in this huge-ass, mother-ass fight because he insisted that suspension is *His* Art and that I should respect it, and that he's sick of everything always being about Me." She blew her nose. Prudence dug through her purse, tugged out a Handi Wipe from a soft blue packet. "Here, sweetie. Wash your face. Forget about Kirby. You're a big hit out there. Star of the show."

"Did you see it?"

"It's fantastic."

"You think? Mr. McGuff told me the modern art museum director wants to install it in her women's show next fall . . ."

"Wonderful! You see? Men are distractions."

"Let's not go that far. Is Colin here? Did you see Colin?"

"I think he's helping Rita get her stuff down from Flagstaff."

"I like him."

"I see that."

"He'd get exactly what my work is about."

"Maybe he can still make it — there's what, a couple of hours left?"

"Yeah, then the party at Heather's. I was supposed to go with Kirby. Oh — and get this — he wanted me to help out with the suspensions. I said I couldn't, this was *my* one big night. That's when he got ticked and left. He's completely changed since he got into this whole stupid body thing. He keeps saying he wants to shave his head, and I can definitely *not* handle that. I hate bald. Bald heads, hairy chests, yuck . . . do you know what time tomorrow Colin leaves for Dublin?"

"Noon, I think. You might want to get back out there, sweetie. Your fans await."

"Yeah, I guess. Is Ray here? Did he like it? Probably not. It doesn't have anything to do with Indians."

"He's here but I haven't had a chance to ask him yet what he thought. He gets claustrophobic, so we're just about to leave."

"That's fine. I'm glad you came by."

"Things will work out. With Kirby, I

mean. The main thing is you, Fiona. The men can just plain fall in line behind you. Plus Kirby's insecure. Think about it — you're going to college, he manages a pizza parlor. He's afraid to lose you."

"That makes sense." Fiona twirled. "Like my tutu?"

"Mmm. Especially all the little green army men. Makes me glad I forked out for those ballet lessons when you were six."

Ray located an alternate exit from the school building — a fire exit, so they climbed out to the parking lot without having to see or talk to anyone.

"What did you think of Fiona's art piece?"

Ray shrugged. "Pretty original. Not what I'd call art, though."

"Which part was your favorite?"

"The porno part. Did you know she knew about that stuff?"

"No, I was pretty shocked. That Rocco stuff is hard core."

"Hey baby, I've got some hard core for you when we get home." Ray nibbled lightly along Prudence's neck.

But when they got back to the house, Rita's U-Haul hogged the whole driveway, its back door rolled up, while Rita lay face-up on the lawn, arms akimbo, her back acting up, an old zoo injury. Colin struggled backward down the ramp, sweating and grappling with a massive, antlered elk head. Ray parked the van on the street and ran to help.

Scrambling to her feet, Rita popped her neck, then arched her back. "That's it, Prue. Bingo bango. Everything's cleared out of there."

"Did you see Jasper?"

"God, no. He made sure he was gone for the day, probably with that piñata-butt *chica*. I did leave one surprise for him to find."

"What's that?"

"All that ceramic dishware he supposedly made for our new house? I smashed it all over his kitchen floor. Bastard. Jackass." Rita broke into a loud, unattractive wail. "I loved those damned dishes!" Automatically, Prudence patted Rita's back and gave a small sympathetic coo. By the time Ray and Colin dragged down the U-Haul door and slid the bolt, Rita was sniffing, swiping her hand under her nose like a little kid.

"I'll throw everything in the rental space this weekend. For now, all my junk's gotta go either in the yard or in the house."

Colin stood before Rita, hand out, fingers waggling. "Keys, Mom."

"Oh right. I promised Col he could borrow the car to go to your daughter's art thing tonight. Be home early, son. You leave for Dublin tomorrow, and you still need to pack, get your stuff together."

"Done, Mom. I packed last night."

Ray drew directions for Colin, who revved up his mother's little car and zipped down La Diosa toward Phoenix. Prudence followed Rita, who wore a V-cut leopard-print tank top, black spandex shorts and zebra-striped rubber thongs, into the house.

Kirby had left three forlorn messages — he was sorry, he loved her, where was she? When the phone rang a fourth time, Prudence picked up.

"Kirby? She's not here. When she gets back, I'll have her call you." She hung up before he could somehow worm out of her the fact that her daughter had been out somewhere with Colin until 5 a.m.

"Look at all this *junk*," Prudence whispered to Ray, who was lounging in the living room watching a biography of Sonny and Cher. "How can one woman own so much junk?"

"She's rented a storage unit, re-member?"

"Well why didn't she just drive her stuff there, unload it there, not here, all over my house? This makes me crazy."

"I think she said the storage unit wouldn't be ready until the weekend. That's tomorrow. Just be patient a little bit longer, hon."

Ray clicked off the TV, went into the workroom, and began piling up gear for Sun Dance. Two tents, two sleeping bags, three coolers, food for Prudence, a lantern, two air mattresses. Prudence had to wade past Rita's junk, then Ray's, to get to the garage, get in her car, drive to school, lock herself in her office, eat a Mars bar, a Three Musketeers, an Abba-Zaba and a Nutrageous, one after another, as she churned out four more scenes for *Savage Arms*. According to Digby's plot formula, there were only thirty pages to go before ivory-skinned, flaxen-haired Tabitha could be swept up forever in the powerful, dusky arms of her Apache warrior, Lone Heart Hunter. Writing romance, Prudence was beginning to see its appeal. Look at the love lives around her, including her own. Who wouldn't want to escape such mess and disappear for two hundred or so pages

560

into an alternate world where passion, though wild, was destined to be tamed, where love, elusive and forbidden, eventually dozed by the hearth, a good dog, a loyal pet?

By the time Prudence came home from her secretive labor, it was dark out. She telephoned Fiona, who answered on the third ring, half asleep. "Hi, Mommy . . ."

"You're at Kirby's? I thought you two broke up."

"We're just friends now."

"Oh."

"Don't worry, Moolah, I'm fine. I got him to rethink shaving his head. I'll be home tomorrow morning . . . when does Ray leave for Sun Dance?"

"Early tomorrow morning."

"Just a sec . . . Kirby's in the bathroom yelling about his earring, it's stuck or something. It's the newest one," Fiona whispered. "It's infected."

She couldn't help it. Prudence was feeling left out, ethnically distanced and, as much as she hated to admit it, hopelessly white. Ray tried, kept pulling her back in, asking if she had enough sunscreen, plenty of long skirts and shawls, reminding her not to forget her moccasins, the ones he had made for her, drawing her a precise map with landmarks to watch for.

Late that night, after hugging Rita and wishing her a safe drive the next day, Prudence closed the bedroom door, got into bed beside Ray, who pulled her close.

"Where's Fiona, Prue? She OK? Didn't you say she'd broken up with her boyfriend?"

"She's fine. I talked with her earlier." If she had just kept quiet, they would have fallen asleep peacefully. But she added, "She's over at Kirby's. I guess she got back together with him."

"What an idiot."

"Who's an idiot?"

"Both of them. He's poor white trash and your daughter, I hate to tell you, is acting just like any other stupid woman."

Ray went on to criticize Fiona for having an idiot boyfriend who stuck holes in himself, to criticize Prudence for being permissive and weak, for having poor parental judgment and a weak character in general, until Prudence was racked by angry sobs, with Ray then accusing her of destroying his peace of mind on the one night he most needed his sleep, didn't she realize he had a long drive ahead of him followed by an ordeal she couldn't possibly begin to imagine, this was exactly why he never got involved with women, they screwed things up every time with their goddamned stupid emotions. Turning his back on her, he told her to quit feeling sorry for herself, quit whining and bitching, leave him alone so he could get some sleep, he had to be up and on the road in exactly five hours.

Prudence lay there, hating him. She especially loathed him for attacking Fiona. One innocent comment on her part, and all his old, mean self resurfaced, lashed out. She was stunned by his meanness, by his cool ability to simply turn his back on her and go to sleep. She worried about Fiona, about Deleanor, who had fallen again, this time on her patio, wrenching her shoulder. She worried about finishing *Savage Arms* on deadline, about money, about whether she should even drive up north now, if he still wanted her there, did she even want to be there, did she even belong, no, probably not.

When the alarm went off, it was still dark out. Ray moved swiftly, dressing and getting the last of his things together, while she lay quiet, still hurt, pretending to be asleep. She thought he had left for the Sun Dance without even saying good-bye, when he came in, closed the door, sat down, rested his hand lightly on her hip.

"Prudence. Prue? I was a complete ass last night, I'm sorry. I guess I'm pretty rattled by this, the Sun Dance, everything that's happened with Jasper and those guys, I don't even know what I'm doing anymore. If it weren't for Rita helping me out, I'd be completely lost. Look, sweetie. I brought my pipe. I'm really sorry I said all those things. Will you smoke the pipe with me, will you pray with me, before I go?"

They sat on the bed, passing the pipe, smoking, praying silently, a fragile thread of peace reconnecting them. Ray cleaned the pipe, slipped it back in the beaded deerskin bag, and stood looking down at her. Then he bent down, hugged her to his chest, hard, until she hurt.

"I love you, Ray."

"Why?"

She didn't answer. Loving him had never made sense, never been easy, never been a choice.

"Is Fiona taking care of the house while we're gone? Feeding Nizhoni?"

Prudence nodded.

"OK, I'll see you up there then. Drive carefully. Don't forget the map I drew for you."

Then he was gone. He and Rita were both gone, a foreshadowing of what it would be like after Sun Dance, after she'd asked them to leave, when they were both finally gone from her life. She got up and spent the rest of her solitary day pounding out the conclusion of *Savage Arms* (thanks to flaxen-haired Tabitha, Lone Heart Hunter's heart would be lone no more; Prudence took a strangely vengeful satisfaction, writing out a resoundingly happy conclusion, an ending that was ludicrous, fantastical and exactly right. For some reason she kept superimposing Sam Hill over Tabitha, and Holt over Lone Heart Hunter. What was that about, she wondered, and what could they be doing now, defrauding what government, inventing what cooked-up charity, and still smooching all over kingdom come?). Afterward, she celebrated by swimming naked in her pool, drinking a thimbleful of Pimm's, eating brownies and ice cream, and calling Trish to remind her about the Sun Dance.

"I'll be up there at Dine College, taking a course in Navajo translation, so I'll try my best to get over there, Prue. It's about an hour's drive from Tsaile to Pinon."

"I'd love to see you there, Trish."

"I'll try. I've never seen a Sun Dance,

though to be honest, I have mixed feelings about a Lakota ceremony held on Navajo land. There's this new pan-Indianism I'm not all that comfortable with. But that's me. I don't know if you've heard, but there's a bit of protest going on, up at the reservation."

"Over the Sun Dance?"

"Some of the more traditional Navajos, especially our elders, don't like it, don't like seeing all this Plains influence taking away from traditional Navajo teachings, the old stories that go with the land being lost, stories coming down from our ancestors. Don't get me wrong, Prudence. I'm curious about the Sun Dance, and for your sake, I'll try my best to get over there, at least for a few hours, and hang out with you."

Fiona and Prudence liked Mimi's Café, its French decor, Provençal prints, cottagey colors. But this evening the chain café was crowded, noisy and smelled of burnt onion soup. They sat on a small, bench outside, Prudence holding the little black box that was supposed to vibrate when their party was called.

The box vibrated.

Seated in a booth, they ordered and

waited for their sandwiches while Fiona regaled her mother with the many absurdities of her job in singles telemarketing. Rooting around in her Indonesian cloth purse, Fiona brought out her company's newest list of rules, uncrumpled it, and read aloud:

Top Ten Tips on How to Be a Big Dreams Telemarketer!

1. Be on time for Big Dreams!
2. Strive for improvement!
3. Take risks!
4. Search for new dreams!
5. Assume nothing!
6. Make customers warm up to you, not just our dreamy service!
7. Create challenge! Challenge creates opportunities for dreams to come true!
8. Never back off goals!
9. When it's time to go home, make one more Dream call!
10. Listen, listen, listen!

Prudence smiled, buttering her bread. "Do you think we could apply those rules to life in general?" She gazed gratefully at the waiter bringing her French dip sandwich. "God, I am so starved."

"It gets worse," said Fiona, "wait till you hear this week's script, what I'm expected to say to every customer who doesn't slam the phone down the second I start talking." Fiona began to read from a second sheet:

I know you have doubts, but if you'll give ten percent of your confidence, we'll cover the other ninety percent!

Singles are expected to take control of their professional lives, their education and their financial concerns. Why should one's love life be any different?

A one-hour consultation with Big Dreams could change your life forever, as it has for thousands of people!

Even busy people can make time for the RIGHT dream relationship!

"One hour can change your life forever? Pretty big claim."

Fiona's cell phone was playing "It's a Small World" in her purse. She dug it out and held it to her ear.

"No, I'm in Scottsdale. With my mom. I can't. I don't know. Only if my mom comes with me. Fifteen minutes, not all night. We will. You, too."

Fiona dropped her phone into her purse and sighed.

"Kirby?"

"He wants me to stop by this body modification place in Tempe. The owner's showing a new suspension video. I said I'd only go if you came with me."

"Me?"

"The place gives me the creeps . . . plus, who knows, you might find it interesting."

Prudence was looking at the young man seated one row up to her right. He had a shaved head, elaborate tattoos cloaking his bare arms, collaring his thick, pale neck, and a strange spike, like a fat silver toothpick, sticking through the flesh of one cheek. He wore a black T-shirt, *I Listen to Black Sabbath* printed in peeling cursive letters across the back. His demeanor was haughty, aloof, cool. Prudence leaned forward, tapped him on the shoulder.

"Excuse me."

The young man turned.

"Your tattoos. They're extraordinary."

"Thanks," he mumbled, turning back around.

Prudence addressed the back of his smooth, lustred, eggish head.

"Are you planning to suspend?"

He nodded curtly, without turning. She was embarrassing him.

"Well, I certainly think that is remarkable. You must have a great deal of courage combined with a very high pain threshold. Will it be your first time?"

Minutes later, Prudence held a scrap of paper with the young man's name, Josh, along with the date and time of his upcoming suspension. An invitation.

"Mom, how did you do that? That guy is the biggest asshole."

"I envisioned him as the innocent child he once was. I spoke directly to that aspect of him. Entirely telepathic, of course — it happens on an energy plane I can't quite describe."

Kirby stared at Fiona's mother, his mouth partly open, the stud in his lower lip glinting wetly.

"You're cool, Mrs. Parker. That was really cool. There's the owner, Gil Schwinn. He's doing a performance tomorrow night. He'll be mummified, suspended, then he'll get his eyelids sewn shut. He's famous for that."

Gil Schwinn, the man who would be having his eyelids sewn shut, was podgy, fiftyish and slab-cheeked, with home-sheared, thinning taupe hair, small brown eyes, tan pockmarked skin, dull brown shoes, duller brown pants, and a faded beige T-shirt with *Church of Body Modification* printed in glittery Gothic lettering across the front. As he introduced himself to his ten or so guests, his gaze kept darting, perplexed, to Prudence. He welcomed a late-arriving unisex couple, identically pierced and tattooed, with identically cropped, bristly black hair. Shoe brushes, Prudence thought, their heads look like two matching shoe brushes.

Gil Schwinn's ten-minute video began with a black screen and background heavy metal. Then Gil appeared, blinking into the camera, wearing his same brown outfit, looking like a food chain manager or an insurance claims adjuster, not one of the leaders of a movement advocating masochistic body rituals. Gil began by sharing a little of his own life story, how as a kid he'd stayed mostly in his room exploring new ways to pierce his flesh and tattoo his skin with tribalistic designs . . . how for a boy who'd grown up taunted, teased, beaten and persecuted, he's found himself, as an adult, at the center of a growing movement of young people finding spiritual strength and renewed joy through the ritualized modification of flesh. Prudence stared at the screen as Gil began to shove a variety of stainless steel hooks and skewers through a slender young man's bare shoulders and back. Ropes were attached, and at a solemn nod from Gil, four young men, assistants and fellow CBMers, raised the ropes in unison. Here Prudence hid her eyes, peeking just enough to see the young man swaying from hooks near a ceiling, his body undulating like a hammock, a beatific smile on his face. *Ritual modification allows me to gain a sense of peace I never knew existed. If it weren't for the Church of Body Modification, I might have always wandered the world wondering who I was and who I should be. Now I can honestly say I am finding myself more and more each day with CBM.*

"Kirby wants to do *that?*" Prudence whispered.

Fiona grimaced, nodded.

After a series of short testimonials by avid CBMers, the video ended. Gil snapped on the overhead lights, asking if anyone had questions about the video they had just seen or about active membership in the Church of Body Modification. Fiona stood up, gave Kirby a peck on the top of his head, and left the shop with her mother in tow.

"What did you think, Mah?"

"I don't get it, I mean I don't want to be judgmental, but I just don't see why you'd want to take a perfectly healthy young body and subject it to that kind of hideous torture."

"But how is that different from what Ray's doing? That whole Sun Dance thing sounds like self-torture. Fasting, piercing."

Prudence thought a moment. "But it's *for* something. The Sun Dancer spills his blood for the Creator, offers his flesh as sacrifice."

"Maybe that's what these guys are doing, they just don't have a tribal history behind them." Fiona sighed. "Personally, I find it disturbing, and I think if Kirby keeps going with this — well, I'm trying to get it, but it's dumb to me. Worse than dumb. Asinine."

"Have you talked with Colin?"

Fiona brightened. "He called last night — it was dawn in Dublin. He said the International Graffiti Convention is awesome, he's meeting artists from all over the world."

"He's short, Fiona."

"Oh, phooey. I love Grammy, but she's

off her bean there. I don't mind her *Parker women are three things: late bloomers, quick panickers,* and petite, *not short,* but her grudge or whatever against short men is a crock."

They went home, Fiona to grab clothes for Kirby's, Prudence to climb into a bed which seemed vast and chilly with only herself in it. It took a long while, but finally she fell into a hard, dreamless sleep.

"I'll be home in less than a week, Mom. I'm going up north to a Sun Dance."

"Sun Dance? That Robert Redford thing?"

"No, that's a film festival. This is a Lakota ceremony where the dancers, men and women, fast for four days and nights, dance, pierce themselves, pray. I'll be there as Ray's supporter."

Deleanor sniffed, a clear indication of her displeasure.

"It's an ancient, sacred ceremony."

"Well, I don't know why people in this day and age would do such things, it doesn't make sense to me. Sounds backward."

"I'm sure it does sound strange, but I'm still going. I'll pray for you while I'm up there, Mom, and I'll call as soon as I get back."

"Wild Feathers coming back with you?"

"As far as I know." Prudence tried to hide her irritation.

"Well, I'll be fine by myself. You go on to your pagan whatsit."

"I'll have Fiona call."

"Good, I love talking to Fiona, she's always so cheerful." Prudence felt a childish twinge of jealousy. Her mother preferred Fiona. Why couldn't Deleanor understand her, why did she always make Prudence feel guilty? Her father would have been tolerant, curious, even a little proud of his grown daughter's adventurousness. But Deleanor clearly felt disappointed by a daughter who could not stay married, had wandered off to keep poor company with an Indian and poorer track of her grandchild. No, her mother was plainly, vocally unhappy about her divorced, aging daughter's adventures.

Prudence woke groggy and stiff-limbed. She had difficulty packing — the task seemed drawn-out and tedious. She wasted long minutes standing in one spot, staring at clothing she'd tossed down on the bed. Six broom skirts, six T-shirts — long-sleeved, to protect her arms from the sun — one pair of leather sandals, lots of underwear, a separate skirt, T-shirt and towel for possible sweat lodges, a toothbrush, shampoo, toilet paper, prescription-strength sunscreen, extra protein bars, peanuts, jugs of water, vitamins. It was the general organization of these things that eluded her. It felt as if something was trying to block her from going, as if some etheric resistance dragged at her efforts to pack efficiently, lug things out to her car. She did manage to write a list for Fiona, what and when to feed Nizhoni, when to shut the pool pump off and turn it back on, collect the mail, take phone messages, inscribing her lifelong fear of fire in bold letters: NO CANDLES OR INCENSES*, TURN OFF ALL STOVE BURNERS AFTER USES*! She stopped mid-list. Did her resistance have something to do with Ray, with their weird, bitter fight the night before? Despite his apology, the memory of his words still cut to the quick. Was their fight connected to her sense of being in retrograde motion? Even putting two plastic jugs of water into her car felt arduous. It wasn't the heat. Prudence had lived through nearly a dozen Arizona summers, and even in July, the most hellish of months, she could function, perform simple tasks. She stood now before her small CD collection, incapable of deciding what music to take for the drive north. The air pressed against her skin like quicksand, quaggy and hot. She went over to Ray's collection, neatly housed in a structure of pale wood IKEA boxes, pick-ing out CDs of Bill Miller, 500 Nations, Robbie Rob-ertson, R. Carlos Nakai, music to reflect the scoured, isolate miles of reservation. Back in the bedroom, she pulled on, zipped up, then shucked off several sets of clothes before settling on a long floral skirt and blouse of pale green cotton lawn, deli-cately embroidered at the neckline and cuffs.

Finally, Prudence was dressed, the car packed, the house safely curtained and shut down, the list complete, and left for Fiona on the kitchen counter, when, unex-pectedly, the phone rang. It was Marc, the schoolteacher from Pennsylvania, calling from a pay phone outside Basha's grocery in Pinon with a message from Ray. Have Prudence bring the air mattress, his back was hurting a lot. The connection from the reservation was so poor she could barely hear Marc as she carried the phone into the garage, located the deflated air mat-tress, wedged it into the trunk just as the connection broke off and the line went dead. She walked the phone into the dining room, waiting to see if he would call back, and watching Nizhoni lope the length of the brick patio, back and forth, back and forth, a high-strung, skittish pacing. Beyond the patio, on the lawn, lay the morning's constellation of raw chicken wings. Nizhoni devoured two dozen wings a day now. In just weeks she had tripled in size, her shy, affectionate nature replaced by hypervigilant survival instincts, behavior useless in a suburban yard with a swimming pool, potted cactus and garden furniture. Sensing a human presence on the other side of the glass, the wolf reared up on long, spindly back legs, plunging her splayed front paws against the window, plumy tail walloping, whimpering and peering frantically inside — *Don't go, don't leave me alone.* Prudence turned guiltily away, went into the kitchen, put the phone back, fighting the negative lethargy inside the house, whatever it was that wanted to keep her from leaving. *OK, I'm hours late, it's past eleven, but I am leaving. Right now. I'm going. This instant. I am out of here.* She forced herself to get into her car, back out of the driveway, and head west, passing the empty schoolyard, making her way to the freeway, wondering if it could be true what Rita had said, that the spiritual power of the Sun Dance was so great, its influence so far-reaching, that those who were unprepared, not meant to go, or too weak, would be winnowed out, left behind. That might explain her bizarre fight with Ray the night before, the morning's strange torpor. It might even explain this, Prudence thought, later, trapped in a snarl of stalled cars outside Flagstaff. The Sun Dance, according to Rita, tested everyone.

Northern Arizona

Just inside the border of the reservation, Prudence stopped at the little general store in Leupp. Except for the cashier, a young Navajo woman in a faded red sweatshirt and blue jeans, the store was deserted. A radio, playing local community news, reported on upcoming weekend events in and around the Navajo Nation as Prudence made her way back to the dark, dank bathroom with the door that didn't lock, a saw-cut hole stuffed with toilet paper where the doorknob was supposed to go. She came out, paid for her gas, purchased crackers, candy and coffee, stepped back outside. The air was cooler than down in Phoenix, the sky an uncompromised July blue. A hot parching wind spiraled, picked up food wrappers and other bits of trash, danced them in lazy, fitful circles around the gravel lot. Prudence stood a moment, stretched, then got back in her car, driving her little Nash Rambler slowly through the tiny community of Leupp, passing the low-steepled Church of the Nazarene, a slump of chocolate brown HUD housing, a cluster of dingy white trailers, a short row of sloped heaps of chopped firewood, the Leupp elementary and middle schools, a water tower, and finally out on the two-lane road that would take her to the fading black and white sign pointing toward Kykotsmovi. There she would turn left, then right at the sign for Tuba City, passing through the Hopi reservation, First, Second and Third Mesas, the Hopi Cultural Center, crossing two cattle guards, then turning left at the inconspicuous, license-plate-sized sign for Pinon, a green, sun-bleached sign with a bullet hole shot through the letter *o*. Driving down a deep-gullied dirt road scarcely two lanes wide, Prudence was moving beyond the mind-set that built cities like Phoenix, traveling outside mainstream America, almost beyond linear time, and entering into ancient land, the scratched-out road devoid of traffic except for an occasional truck floating by, passing as if in a dream. The landscape was a wild, subtle mottling of reddish browns, golden ambers and small tufts of stubborn green growth, the iron-tinged green of cedar shrubs, the land itself peaking and falling, monotonous, a triumph of desolation, yet hinting of sacred stories, ancient histories and prehistories, overlaid with its most recent and terrible history of a people conquered, decimated, betrayed, returning first in individual strength, then in larger numbers, finally in whole populations. She passed stray huddles of sheep mixed with goats, herds of small, tough cattle, their bumped, flattened faces like the stony faces of pugilists, animals grazing along unfenced roadsides, moving with no haste or not moving at all but standing with the passive immovability of large blank rocks. Two dogs, one black, one tan, their snarled coats matted with burrs, stood ass-locked, unable to move and staring at Prudence as she drove past, their coupling evocative of a single forlorn beast, its two heads looking in opposite directions, a creature so resigned, absurd-looking and suggestive of the torment of desire that she laughed out loud. She passed horses with harsh, chalky coats and drought-staved ribs, passed broken-down trailers, hogans, and trucks haphazardly parked, as if they had dropped from the sky. And everywhere over the land floated an eternity of sky, pristine and lapidary blue. Compressed beneath such a heaven were ochre, umber and topaz shadings of earth, dusty grasses, the slow, gradual risings into square mesas or sharp buttes,

582

sandstone rock formations sculpted by centuries of wind, the untempered wind a constant lathe, turning mineral red, lustreless earth into bold, hypnotic formations. Rolling down the windows of her car, Prudence let hot, dry wind rush over her face and buffet her hair. The fenceless land unfurling beneath the sky's wide, elemental blue rendered her part of something other and vastly alive, some known exultation of rightful place, humble, solid, surviving. Prudence had felt this open up inside her the summer before, when she had driven these same roads, alone and for the first time. Going with Ray and Rita to the pipe ceremony in January, she had not experienced this, perhaps because of Rita's talking, perhaps because the windows had been shut against the cold. Then, she had looked only at the outsides of things, seen only raw gunmetal air, the brittle, skeletal ribs of grayed snow. But now, with the windows down, with hot desert air flooding over her like water, something primal, without language or desire or name, wakened in her, rushing out to meet the land, to join the sky. Occasional signs of modern life, dusty trucks parked outside cinder-block hogans, HUD housing clustered here and there, the uneven, jeweled flashes of tossed bottles, crushed beer and soda cans along the dirt roadside, seemed to be all that held her, kept her from vanishing, dissolving into the land altogether and ecstatically.

The final hour's drive crept along an even narrower, more deeply rutted road. Prudence had to roll up her windows to keep out clouds of reddish brown dust boiling up around her car. The road's earthen fractures, its hard-packed washboard clefts forced her to drive at a crawl, even steering at times through a stubborn, bedraggled drifting of sheep. Coming over a small, subtle rise in the land, she arrived, finally, in Pinon, its outskirts, driving past the newest sector of HUD housing, government homes cheaply built and jammed together, all painted a dull colonial blue. She passed the local school, Basha's grocery, an older subdivision of HUD housing, rows of governmental beige blight, its streets named A, B, C, D and E, its homes squat, dun-colored boxes linked by chain fences, bits of trash caught in the rough metal diamonds, feral dogs dream- ing in driveways or chasing cars, mangy, solitary, ravaged animals. The summer before, Prudence had stayed in a HUD house on G Street, with Ken Tsosie's family. Now she spotted the water tower to the west of town and decided to turn back to Basha's, her last chance to use an indoor bathroom (three toilets, all broken-down, swarming with flies), the people in the store, mostly Navajo families, staring at her with wariness (another white woman coming to do good that just as often ends up bad, another city woman free to leave whenever she tires of the Indian people's endless distrust of her). She couldn't help it, even though she smiled and was polite to everyone — she knew she was transient, treacherous scenery.

Back in her car, she turned off the main road, following hand-painted signs, thick red letters with arrows pointing the way to the Mountain Sun Dance. The road, almost a dirt path now, curved and rose through sallow, somber hills of pinon and cedar. There were no cars, no signs of life other than a solitary crow, brooding, perched like a black, tipping anvil, near the top of a cedar tree. Prudence was crossing into a world where she would mute herself, try to be helpful, humble, nondescript. She was painfully conscious of her hands on the steering wheel, their pinkness blotched with white — though Ray insisted he never noticed. Deleanor once suggested putting tan-in-a-can on the white parts, and Fiona sometimes teased her, calling her Pinto or Appaloosa. But here, on the reservation, Prudence felt almost freakish because of her vitiligo and the medicinal coatings of sunscreen she had to wear.

She slowed and stopped at the security point, a small wooden shed. As a group of young Native men, several on horseback, watched her car approach, one young rider jerked his horse around and abruptly galloped off. She rolled down her window, and told them she was with one of the dancers. They nodded as one of the young men, unsmiling, tied a strip of red cloth to her car's antenna, then waved her through. She recalled all Ray's jokes and judgments against white people, the sting of his prejudice, knowing he was not alone in his bias, and suddenly she thought of backing her car up, turning and driving straight back to the familiarity, the safety, of Phoenix. Yet her car kept inching down the dusty slope of road until the Sun Dance camp lay before her, and beyond, in the far distance, the majestic arm of violet-peaked mountains, sacred to the Navajo people. Within moments she spotted Ray's silver-blue van, and in a clearing protected by cedar trees, the small camp he had prepared, neatly situated on a sandy rise overlooking the Sun

Dance arena. Prudence parked her car and walked into the vacant camp. In the clearing was a small nylon tent, two collapsible camp chairs, a small fire pit, two giant coolers, and hanging from the rough, natural pegs of surrounding cedar trees, a trash bag, several towels and Ray's black bandanna. The mountain air had grown cool, the shadows of the fragrant cedars were lengthening, darkening. Tired from her drive, Prudence gazed down toward the arena and out over the imposing mountain range, purplish violet in the far distance. Last year's Sun Dance tree, with its faded hundreds of red, black, green, yellow and blue tobacco ties, had already been taken down, and everyone, it seemed, had gone deep into the mountains to find and cut this year's tree. Prudence sank down in one of the camp chairs, closed her eyes.

"Homegirl! Way to go!" Prudence struggled to wake up as Rita strode into camp. "Ray's on his way — he's been helping Victoria clean stuff out of her car."

"Victoria?"

"One of the Sun Dancers, an old friend of mine. We just got back from cutting the tree, it took all day. What a fiasco! Jasper and Harold were supposed to be in charge and so far they haven't even bothered to show up. Anyway, it's done."

Over Rita's shoulder, Prudence saw Ray, leaning against the side of a black sports coupe, talking and laughing with a young woman whose black hair fell in one blue-gleaming river past her waist. As if sensing her, Ray turned in Prudence's direction, then started walking up toward camp, Victoria close beside him, beautiful and light-stepped.

Upon actually seeing her, Ray's expression turned blank and cool. Behind him, Victoria, laughing, said she'd better get back to her family's camp. She waved and ran, lithe as a deer, down the slope. Prudence stood in the center of the small camp, feeling ludicrous and lumpish in her rayon flowered skirt, her damp, wrinkled green blouse, listening to Rita talk about Victoria, twenty-eight, a single mother on government aid with two children, one with spina bifida, and her father a veteran Sun Dancer highly respected in his community. Ray, who had given Prudence a perfunctory hug and dry, pinched kiss on the cheek, had walked over to his van. Taking a deep breath, she followed.

"Anything I can help with?"

"No, sweetie, I'm exhausted, though. I

have absolutely no idea what I'm doing. Jasper and Harold haven't even shown up, no one knows where they are, so the whole thing's been pretty disorganized. Victoria's been making sure I remember certain things. Actually, hon, could you fix me something to eat? Maybe some slices of meat over there in the cooler, a little cheese, no bread, or maybe just one slice? And can you wash my hair? I need it washed before I head down there."

So while Rita walked down to the camp kitchen to get a last plate of food before starting her fast, Prudence held Ray's flashlight, shining it into the van's shadowed interior so he could find last-minute things, shining it as he fastened a bundle of sage to the stem of his pipe with a slight strip of red cotton cloth. She fixed him a sandwich of cheese and lunch meat — he ate nervously, gulping, barely chewing. Afterward, he knelt on the ground and she poured water over his hair, rubbed in shampoo, then used a small plastic jug to pour streams of water through his long hair, rinsing it clean.

Ray dried his hair, then stood braiding it into a single gleaming rope. "See the truck coming in over by the east side? That's the tree, they're bringing the tree in." He put a long ribbon of tobacco ties, wrapped around and around a square of cardboard, into her hand. "Take these. I need you to tie these as near the top branches as you can. Tie them on really tight." Ray squeezed her hand hard, then left her to join the other men, fifty or so, lining both sides of the felled cottonwood's massive trunk, readying themselves to carry the two-hundred-foot tree lengthwise into the arena, raise it up, plant it securely in the spot prepared for it, the place where last year's tree had stood. This tree, like last year's, had come from Chinle, near Canyon de Chelly. There were not many of the old, sturdy cottonwoods left, Rita had told her. Each year it grew harder to find one healthy and strong enough to carry the people's prayers. Now, in the night's darkness, Prudence made out the shapes of men, women and even a few children gathering in the arena, a hundred or more. As the men carried the tree in and prepared to raise it up, Prudence ran to join the other women rushing forward to wrap the topmost branches with their long strings of prayer ties. She found a place as near the top as she could and, trembling a little, wrapped the hundreds of tobacco ties he had spent days preparing around the tree's heavily leafed topmost branches. When they had finished, she and the other women stood back as the men raised the tree, securing it so that it would stand strong, wrapped with prayers, new axis of the holy world for four days and four nights. Beneath a summer constellation of stars, the cottonwood's silver-pale leafed branches fluttered with red, blue, yellow, green and black tobacco ties, thousands of individual prayers, each made by a Sun Dancer, each offered to Creator. The people stood around the tree of life as prayers were said for the success of the Sun Dance, then a Lakota song of thanks was sung. Stanley Young Dog, the Mountain Sun Dance chief, urged the men and women dancers to get to their camps, get a good night's rest, there would be sweat lodges for them at four-thirty the next morning. Relatives and supporters were asked to pray for a good day tomorrow.

Crossing the sandy expanse and starting up the incline to camp, Prudence heard Ray call out. She waited until he caught up with her.

"Did you get the prayer ties on? Good, that's good. Rita's already left for the women dancers' camp."

He went to his van, got a few more

things, and then, as a seeming after-thought, came over, gave her a brief, emotionless hug before turning and walking off, vanishing down the hill into darkness.

Brooding and exhausted, Prudence dropped into one of the camp chairs. She was a burden, she shouldn't have come, these were his people, his culture, not hers. He should be with the beautiful young Navajo woman. Victoria. She should be his wife; they could be Sun Dancers together. Going to the van, Prudence slid open the side door and discovered the neat, comfortable bed Ray had made to surprise her. *He does love me. Why am I so quick to doubt that?* Changing into sweatpants, a thermal shirt, sweatshirt and heavy socks, Prudence crawled into the sleeping bag, haunted by the cool expression on Ray's face when he had first seen her, the perfunctory hug he had greeted her with, the abrupt, emotionless way he had taken leave of her just now. As she drifted into heavy sleep, images of slender, graceful Victoria mixed with images of herself, standing dutifully behind Ray, pouring water through his hair, in the pose of a servant, useful, dull, and loyal to a heartbreaking fault.

Hoka Hey! Hoka Hey! Sun Dancers! Wake

up! Hoka Hey! For the next four mornings, Prudence would be wakened in predawn darkness by this one strong reverberant cry — *Hoka Hey!* — followed by a single hollow thump from the giant hide drum in the arbor. Prudence's reaction the first morning was to draw the sleeping bag's nubbly felt lining close over her face. She felt cranky and mean-spirited. Her bones hurt despite the foam padding Ray had placed under her sleeping bag, and her feet felt icy. She desperately wanted to wash the film of dirt off her face and arms, but there was no water except what she could trickle out of a plastic jug. She needed to pee, but in order to do that, she would have to dress first inside the cramped van, hike uphill to the outhouse — it was too light out to use the bushes, and there were too many other families camped nearby, their tents half hidden among clumps of cedar. She could hear people beginning to wake, stir, unzip tents, and step outside. Prudence lay on her side, breathing warmth from the sleeping bag, feeling deeply miserable, unloved, wondering why she had come up here. She should have paid attention to that weird force, whatever it was, that had tried to keep her from leaving her house. She should have stayed home.

Pushing out of the sleeping bag, tugging off her socks and sweatpants, hunched on her knees inside the van, Prudence dragged on the same skirt she had worn yesterday, kept her sweatshirt and thermal shirt on, found her leather sandals, gritty with dirt, banged their soles together, and slipped them on. Brushing her hair and clipping it back, she slid open the van door and jumped down. Carrying a small roll of toilet paper, she trudged up to the outhouse, a three-sided box of pressed wood with a white bedsheet tacked across the opening. Stretching the sheet across the door with one hand, hiking up her skirt with the other, she peed, holding her breath against the stink and praying the sheet didn't fall down. Starting down the hill to the arena, Prudence remembered the shawl Rita had lent her and hurried back to camp to get it, folding and wrapping the dark green material tight around her hips, the band of silken yellow fringe hitting just above her ankles. Slightly hobbled by the tight wrap of the shawl around her hips, she started back downhill, seeing on her left, fenced off, the men's and women's camps, a scatter of tall canvas teepees and low-domed tents, the tarp-covered willow shapes of sweat lodges, the single bonfire which would be kept blazing throughout the four days and nights, keeping dozens of stones hot for the sweat lodges. She saw, as she walked, dancers starting to line up outside the northern side of the arbor, the men in narrow ankle-length red cotton skirts, the women in plain mid-calf cotton dresses. More than one hundred men and women stood, single file, in a long, motionless row, a black frieze of solemn forms burnished by the glowing light of dawn. With her sandaled feet sinking, slipping through the silken-grained dirt, Prudence arrived at the arbor's south side, and stepping out of her sandals, barefoot, entered the arbor's leafy shade.

Encircling the arena like the hub of a great wheel, fashioned of pine poles and a roof simply lathed and overlaid with leafy branches of cottonwood, the arbor, this first morning, held fewer than a dozen people waiting for the dancers to enter the arena, waiting for this first day of the ceremony to begin. To Prudence's left, six men, singers, sat evenly spaced around the massive hide drum, lightly holding their drumsticks, joking softly among themselves. The PA system came on with its crackling sound, someone tested the microphone system, and from a hundred yards or so away, Prudence could hear the generator's low hum kick on. In the arena, at its very center, the cottonwood tree rose two hundred feet, tobacco ties of red, blue, green and yellow fluttering from its silver-barked limbs, fifty or more piercing ropes neatly coiled and firmly knotted to the tree's thickest, strongest branches. High within its green, shimmering branches, a pole, laid horizontally, held the thunder-bird's nest, sacred doll and medicine bundle wrapped in buffalo hide. With sweet dawn air flowing over her skin, with her eyes closed, Prudence felt the vibration deep inside her as, at the signal of a single drumbeat, the six men began to sing, picking up strength and volume as they beat harder on the drum, their voices, still rough with sleep, given over to Lakota rhythms of the horse and the heartbeat, the ancient Lakota songs. As she and other supporters stood silent and watching, the procession of dancers advanced, moving slowly toward the eastern doorway, the rising sun behind them, the men entering first, single file, wearing red cloth skirts, sage bracelets encircling their ankles and wrists, their heads crowned with bands of sage wrapped with narrow strips of red cloth, each crown bearing two eagle spikes. Some of the men wore medicine bundles or beaded medallions; many held sage-wrapped pipes crooked in one arm. Coming through the eastern doorway, marked with its flag of yellow cloth, each man turned clockwise, lifting his arms to acknowledge the sun and piping on an eagle-bone whistle hanging from a leather cord around his neck. Some of the men were barefoot, some wore beaded or plain moccasins, all wore their long hair braided or loose down their backs as they moved in a solemn circle from east to south to west to north, pausing at each of the four doorways, the four directions. An altar lay to the west, a long berm of earth for the dancers to rest their pipes against, an eagle's-head staff planted to one side of the berm, a buffalo skull placed at either end. A third buffalo skull had been placed beneath the tree of life. The women dancers, holding sacred pipes, sage bands circling their wrists and ankles, sage crowns on their heads, filed in then, sixty or so, and were, like the men, of varying ages, from youths to silver-haired elders.

Searching, she finally saw Ray, pipe in his left arm, eagle fan in his right, wearing his blue-beaded waterbird medallion, his deerskin medicine bag swaying against his smooth, unmarked chest, gazing at the sun and shrilly piping — *heh heh heh* — on his eagle-bone whistle with its white eagle-down fluffs. She watched him lift both slender arms to greet the sun's imperceptibly measured ascent from the eastern horizon.

All hundred dancers, men and women, moved in a great, slow circle, lifting their feet in subtle rhythm, drawing energy from the earth, raising their arms, greeting the sun, honoring the tree of life, the tree's heart-shaped leaves green and slick with light, its still-supple branches flagged with prayers to *Wakan Tanka, Great Mystery, Great Spirit.* The second time Ray passed by her, he looked over, placed his eagle fan over his heart. *I love you.* She gave a slight nod back, wanting him to see how proud she felt, wanting him to know her jealousy, her misery, her selfishness, had fallen away. But he had already gone by, part of a continuously moving circle, pausing now at the south doorway with its flag of red cloth, raising his arms before moving toward the west doorway with its black cloth flag, the long earthen altar with its tobacco pipes, buffalo skulls and eagle staff, moving off toward the north, the east, the south, the west, circling, circling, one in a procession of dancers, part of an ancient, rhythmic lifting of feet and lifting of arms, a ceaseless singing and drumming, a realm, ever-moving, of song and dance and prayer.

By the end of four days, even by the end of the first, she would know each dancer, man or woman, by sight, by their plain and smaller differences, heavy, lean, old, young, prison tattoos, scars from old piercings, or like Ray, backs and chests smooth, unscarred. She would dance, feel the slight hip-sway, the wider sway of her shawl's yellow fringe, the air moving around her bare ankles, her bare feet against the earth, the drumming sonorous and powerful, its sounds as old as the distant mountains. At a signal from the chief of the Lakota nation, Edward Standing Elk, the singing stopped, the dancing stopped, and the dancers filed silently out the east doorway, following the outside curve of the arbor and going to rest in the lathe-roofed shelter prepared for them behind the altar, lying down to rest on shade-dappled blankets, the men on one side, the women on the other. This was a period of quiet, of rest, when supporters sat listening to those who stepped up to the microphone to speak in Navajo or English, sometimes Sioux, Spanish or another tribal language, to give messages, prayers, reminders of good conduct, no drawing, no photographing or videotaping, no jewelry, sunglasses or shoes, no food or drink out of respect for the fasting dancers. People came to the microphone with stories, teachings, songs of thanksgiving, testimonials of healing, confessions, apologies, portents, dreams. Sometimes no one spoke, and Prudence would hunker on the dry, cool earth, bare feet tucked under her skirt, unaware of any passage of time other than the bright, constant arc of the jeweled sun across the blue desert sky. At a signal from the drummers, the single, hard beat of a leather-head drumstick against the drum, the dancers would stand up from their blankets, ready themselves, and file back into the arena.

On his second round that first day, as Ray moved past her, he made a slight fanning motion with his eagle fan, followed by a glance up toward their camp — *The hawk fan I made for you, bring it with you, down here, to the arbor.* When the second round had finished, Prudence slipped her sandals on and, shielding her eyes from the sun's white glare, trudged up the hot, sandy rise to camp to get the hawk fan he had made for her. As she climbed, she looked toward her left and could see directly behind the wooden structure of the camp kitchen. Several men were tightly huddled around a young, ocre red calf. One man, a boy really, held the calf by a rope halter, attempting to tug the animal forward. The calf balked and bellowed fearfully as a second man, perhaps the boy's uncle or father, raised an ax high and swung it down on the animal's head. The calf collapsed, and the others fell in on it, knives flashing. Prudence was glad, as she changed course, heading over to the kitchen to say hello to her friend Ken Tsosie, that she could not see the calf being cut apart, swiftly pieced apart from itself and rendered into meat.

In the open-air kitchen, several of the women, most of them Ken's aunts, prepared blood pudding, wrapping the slaughtered calf's white, chenille-like stomach lining around its other parts, binding the whole together with string, sticking a nail into it, cooking the pudding until it was firm. The rest of the calf was boiling in huge enamelware kettles. On one table were stacks of hot fry bread, Styrofoam bowls for blue cornmeal pudding, cups for coffee, cans of orange soda. At the back side of the makeshift kitchen was a wooden shed for supplies, and in the dirt-floored kitchen, a large cookstove, a portable sink for washing dishes and five or six cafeteria-style tables with benches. A small campfire burned, and a dark blue enamelware coffeepot had been set on top of a cooking grate over the low, constant flames.

Ken sat on a tree-stump chair talking with two of his younger sisters as his aunts carried large kettles of brushed aluminum and speckled enamelware, brimming with calf stew, posole, blue corn pudding and pinto beans, off the stove and over to the serving tables. Children ran about playing or sitting quietly with their Navajo grandmothers, handsome women with strong-featured faces, pink or yellow floral- patterned handkerchiefs knotted beneath their chins, their long hair wound into coils of silver at the napes of their necks, their thin bare ankles sticking out beneath the hems of dark velveteen or calico-print broom skirts, bare feet in tennis shoes, wearing long-sleeved velveteen blouses in rich, dusky plum or maroon or dark emerald, and jewelry of traditional design — necklaces, earrings, bracelets and rings of pure silver, coral, turquoise and shell. The grandmothers, clan matriarchs, were always first to be seated, to be served food and drink, attended to by adult children and grandchildren. Grandmothers in their eighties and nineties, speaking little En-glish, who rarely, if ever, left the reservation, powerful women who owned the land their *churro* sheep, goats and horses grazed on, respected women who knew the land's ancient history, its old stories and songs, elder women, bowed from hard work and shrunken with age, who were deeply and constantly cherished. Prudence thought of her own mother, half-shunned, overlooked by a society privileging youth and youth's careless, unearned perfection, a culture frightened of age, hiding its old people in rest homes with optimistic, reassuring names, paying strangers a minimum wage to care for basic needs, but never for their stories or their spirits or their hearts.

Ken stood up when he saw her, welcoming Prudence with a great, warm hug. He was a tall, heavyset Navajo man with a thick, tapering braid that swung past his waist, a round face beginning to crease from so much smiling, a man blessed with a constant good nature. When she had visited him the first time, Prudence had seen how members of Ken's large, extended family loved and depended on him. He was the stable center of their world. His two younger sisters, Corinne and Jennifer, welcomed Prudence with hugs as well, and then Ken reintroduced her to his various aunts. *My professor back in Phoenix, you remember her from last time?* She was greeted kindly, offered blood pudding, blue corn masa, calf stew and fry bread. Prudence thanked each of the aunts, explaining she was not eating that day, a friend of hers was dancing, and in support of him, she was fasting. Ken teased, had she lost her appetite from the sight of the calf's head, skinned and sitting on a bench outside the supplies shed, attracting a black mess of flies? Prudence laughed, *maybe so,* then carried a Styrofoam cup of fresh, hot coffee to Ken's great-grandmother, Sarah, greeting her with the one word she knew in Navajo — *Yah-tah-hey* — Hello. Prudence felt a little silly, saying her one *Yah-tah-hey* word, but when Sarah, in her yellow kerchief dotted with pink roses, looked up, took the coffee, smiled, and returned her greeting, *Yah-tah-hey,* followed by a long, gentle-sounding stream of Navajo, she was glad. Ken and his sisters teased Prudence for a moment, until Corinne provided the relief of translation. "My grandma says she likes your skirt very much, she says it was good of you to bring her coffee. She says to thank you."

After a few minutes more of conversation, Prudence left the camp kitchen just as families began walking over from various campsites ready to eat the food the aunts had spent hours preparing. A slight wind kicked up, the skies turned a cottony gray, and for a few minutes the sun vanished behind a thick, dense wreathing of clouds. Then, several steps from her camp, dizziness overtook Prudence, a light-headedness so severe she stumbled. Maybe fasting wasn't such a good idea. She pulled a quart of cherry Gatorade out from one of the coolers, gulped down half, ate a handful of peanut butter crackers, then sat, leaning back, until her strength returned. She recognized Rita's voice before she opened her eyes and saw her. "Well, that's it. I'm out. The minute he strutted into the arena, the minute I looked at that bastard, I started my moon. Started bleeding, just like that, at the sight of that hypocrite." Rita's face, painted with the reddish clay called *chee*, sometimes used by the dancers as a natural sunscreen, was streaked with tears. She wore a shapeless blue calico dress, a maroon shawl wrapped around her waist, sage anklets and bracelets, a sage crown on her long, loose hair. Plopping heavily into a camp chair beside Prudence, she plucked off her sage crown and set it in her lap, her bare legs thrust straight out in front of her. "It's obvious Creator's protecting me, bringing on my moon early, just like that, getting me out of there. Having to be in the same space with him for four days probably would have killed me."

"Isn't there supposed to be a moon camp for women to go to?" Prudence asked, offering Rita the box of peanut butter crackers. Rita plunged her hand in, pulled up a fistful of crackers.

"Hell no, those bozos don't have their act together enough to have anything like that set up for the women. Sure, there's supposed to be one, there's always supposed to be a moon camp for the women. As subchiefs, they're in charge of making sure it's all set up. Traditionally, Plains women on their moon would separate themselves, camp out together, sing, sew, talk. It's meant to be a powerful, good time, not a punishment or a negative thing. Women on their moon are basically too powerful for men to be around. But these guys don't have it together enough to honor that. There's a sign saying *Moon Camp* back that way, but the arrow on the sign points straight into the sagebrush, there's nothing set up. No, I'll stay right here in our little camp, thank you very much. I can watch the Sun Dance from here. It'll be fine. I still can't believe it. I mean the very second, the exact instant Jasper walked by me, acting the Big Shot, not looking at me, acting as if I didn't exist, it started, my moon, is that uncanny or not? Not to mention his bitch ex-wife, Carmela, is head woman dancer this year, so it really would have killed me to have to stay in there with those two for four whole days."

Rita picked up her sage crown, pressed it to her nose to inhale the smell, shook her hair, and lightly cracked her neck. "This was to have been the last of my four-year Sun Dance commitment."

"I'm sorry, Rita. You want food?" Prudence asked. "Are you hungry?"

"Nah. I left my pipe down there, guess I can get it later. Ray looks great, he's really doing great. I'm proud of my little brother."

After listening to Rita go on about Jasper, his vanity, his arrogance, his nerve, then sighing, say she needed to crawl into her little tent and lie down awhile, Prudence said she was probably going back down to the arbor for the next round of dancing.

"Little brother's piercing, right?"

Prudence nodded. "Yeah. Three months ago, he dreamed he was dragging buffalo skulls, so he's going to ask Chief Standing Elk for permission to do that."

"Well, I hate to say it, but because of Jasper, Ray might not pierce at all. He's going to wait, he told me, see how things go."

"Is Sun Dance a four- or a five-year commitment, Rita?"

"Four. You have to do at least four years in a row. What do you think so far? Awesome, isn't it? Now if we just didn't have Jasper and Harold gumming up the works. He never paid you back for that peyote ceremony, did he? Cripes." Rita yawned, stretched. "I'm going to creep into my teepee. I'm getting bad cramps."

Prudence slipped off her sandals and sat beside Heidi on the Mexican blanket she had brought, a muddy lavender weaving with black and white stripes. The dancers were resting in the shelter, except for two men who had pierced during the time Prudence had been gone from the arbor. They lay on the ground near the sacred tree, chokecherry sticks piercing their chests, ropes knotted to the sticks reaching far up into the tree's branches. A third man, heavyset, walrus-faced, sat in another part of the arena, near the tree, sticks driven through the flesh of his back, his ropes attached to a massive buffalo skull. Prudence could see the man's back, heavily scarred from years of dragging skulls, and knew he would sit all four days under the hot sun, the weight of the skull pulling his flesh. Beginning with these piercings on the first day, the suffering would intensify and spread as the supporters watched, prayed, and sometimes wept, sending strength to the dancers spilling blood, offering themselves in sacrifice to their Creator. At a signal from Stanley Young Dog, the singers beat down on the massive drum, calling for a new round. Heidi and Prudence rose to their feet along with the other supporters, more people gathering now, as several Native boys and girls passed by, lightly swinging cans of burning sage, pausing here and there so the people could cleanse themselves with sacred smoke. Holding her hawk-feather fan with its leather-wrapped handle, Prudence leaned forward, using her fan to cup smoke toward her heart, holding the smoke against her heart, praying for Ray, for all the dancers filing in, still strong on that first day, their faces coated with *chee*. When he passed by her, his gaze had already gone inward. He had begun the journey Rita had said he would go on, learning to die, to leave human time and cross into a mysterious space of holiness and rebirth.

He had taught her a little about the sacred pipe, practiced smoking the pipe with her, explaining the stem was male, the bowl female, how the two fit together in perfect union. When you smoked the pipe, you passed it to the person on your left, stem in your left hand, bowl in your right, you could pray by blowing smoke in each of the four directions, cup smoke against your forehead, bless yourself, or hold the smoke against your heart. She and Heidi were invited that first day to sit in a circle with others and share one of the dancers' pipes. With the hawk fan resting across her lap, Prudence passed the pipe as Ray had taught her, always to her left, giving thanks and offering prayers for everyone in the circle.

At sunset, the dancers returned to their men's and women's camps. Nights in the camps were for sweat lodges, teachings, quiet visits, sleep. Back in her own camp, Prudence tried to eat a sandwich but suddenly exhausted from the day, closed herself into the van and fell asleep until the second day's predawn call — *Hoka Hey!* — when she would wash, prepare herself, wrap her shawl around her hips, take her fan, and walk by dawn's light down to the arbor. She knew where to look for Ray in the file of men, spotting his blue-beaded medallion and medicine bag, his slim body, thinner now, his *chee*-painted face, his sage crown casting a slight shade over his eyes, and in his mouth his bone whistle, shrilling, piping, calling on the spirit of the eagle, the eagle's courage. She could forgive Ray his anger, which was fear, forgive her jealousy, which was fear, too. Here, during four sacred days, her heart and his would empty, split open, begin to heal.

In his role as subchief, Harold Martinez walked straight up to Prudence and indicated she had been chosen to step over to the south doorway and accept one of the dancers' pipes. She carried the pipe back into the arbor, inviting those around her, including Heidi, to sit and smoke with her. A late afternoon wind made it difficult to light the pipe, so one of the women helped her shield the bowl, cupping her hands so the flame could kindle. The pipe circled among the small group until the tobacco was gone, then the people stood and shook hands. Prudence returned to the doorway and waited quietly with the others as seven dancers moved forward in unison, waves of spirit energy radiating from their bodies, to receive their pipes, carry them back to the altar, cant them humbly against the low berm of earth.

Prudence was putting on her sandals, thinking to go back to the kitchen and help Ken and his aunts prepare dinner, when she saw Jasper and Harold, with hard, stern expressions on their faces, walking toward her. Bluntly, Harold asked if Rita was staying in Prudence's camp.

"Yes," she answered truthfully.

Jasper spoke. "She's supposed to be in the moon camp. She knows that. Go back up there, tell her to leave your camp, get her things, go over to the moon camp. Tell her if she doesn't leave right now, we're sending our young men to force her." They turned their backs on Prudence and walked off.

She found Rita sitting and talking with several young Native women, all of them laughing and drinking sodas, until Prudence explained how Harold and Jasper had just accosted her, coldly threatening to have Rita removed if she didn't leave camp on her own. Like a newly deposed queen, Rita rose from her chair and stared balefully down toward the arbor. "They are trying to destroy me. They are doing everything possible to ruin and ostracize me. He would like to erase me, make me disappear. Well, I won't go away . . ." The young women looked bewildered, then sympathetic, as Rita spilled everything — how Jasper, her supposed fiancé, had used her, taken her money, lied, been unfaithful, slept around, and was now, this very minute, subjecting her to public humiliation. "Look" — she gestured with ironic grandeur toward a barren expanse of land — "their so-called moon camp! There's nothing there. No tent, no food, no water. Nothing. It's a disgrace. They want me to sleep on cold dirt and die of exposure. Nothing less will satisfy them." As she grew more vocal, more agitated, a group of security guards, none over eighteen, appeared.

Disdainfully, Rita stood on the ledge of

the camp, gazing down at the young guards standing a few steps below, shifting uncomfortably, looking up at Rita, then down at the ground. One of them, presumably their leader, finally spoke.

"We've been sent by Jasper Chee to ask you to leave this camp."

"Sending boys as his henchmen. His goons."

"You've been asked to leave," the leader repeated.

"Where is my tent then? If I'm to be cast out, where are my supplies, my provisions? There is no tent over in their lousy supposed camp, no food — only a sign pointing into nothingness. That shows how much Jasper thinks of women, what respect the man has. None. Tell him I will not move one inch until a decent tent, food and water are provided for me. Otherwise I stay here. By the way, there are other women on their moon, staying in their camps, with their families. He's said nothing to any of them. No, this is personal. He is determined to humiliate and ruin me in every possible way. One of the girls here visiting me is on her moon. Why is she allowed to stay while I am forced out? One rule should apply to all. No, he is a weak man, wielding his bit of power, trying to destroy me, to make me go away. Well, I won't. You go tell him that for me."

The young man who had ordered Rita to leave looked miserable. The others, breaking rank, began to back down the hill, turn away.

"Look, I'm just doing what I was sent to do, come over here and —"

"From now on, you should be more careful who you take orders from. It's not your fault, you're young. But you go back and tell that man I have gone to his nonexistent moon camp. You tell him that."

Shaken by the ugliness of what had just happened, Prudence drove Rita — now dissolved into loud, bitter weeping — down a weedy, bumpy path toward the supposed moon camp. Both women got out of the car and gazed with incredulity at the site where Rita had been ordered to camp. A blue tarp thrown over several plastic jugs of water. A squarish area partially cleared of brush. That was all.

Rita sank to the ground near the tarp, sobbing. "I can't believe this."

After calming her, Prudence drove back to camp, found Ken Tsosie, told him what had happened (*Hey, everybody up here knows about Jasper Chee, he's had so many different women, it's all about money for him, once he's used up one woman, he finds another one with money)*. Ken asked his sisters and some of their friends to go help Rita set up a clean tent, while Prudence took one of the camp chairs, a lantern, crackers, peanut butter, fruit. By nightfall Rita's little white tent glowed in the distance, and though isolated, she was at least fairly comfortable. Prudence went back down to the camp kitchen to get her some dinner, and with a flashlight in one hand and a Styrofoam plate filled with mutton, potatoes and fry bread in the other, she navigated the starry darkness, treading through densely scattered sagebrush and pinon scrub. She had forgotten to take her shawl off, so the hem's silky yellow fringe grew snarled and studded with burrs and twigs as she made her way toward the little tent, its beacon luminous, shimmering, as if floating in the oceanic blackness of night.

By the next day, word was out about Rita's banishment. Women walked out to visit her, bring food, talk about women's issues. The moon camp was renamed goddess camp. Even the Mountain Sun Dance chief's wife, Rachel Young Dog, walked unaccompanied to Rita's camp and spent several hours there, hearing firsthand about the sexual treachery of one of her husband's subchiefs.

Prudence knew too many disillusioning things now. Unable to sleep that night, she worried whether she could separate human failings from the spirit of the ceremony, or was it all destroyed for her? But the next morning, as the dancers returned to the arena, raising wasted arms and gaunt, drawn faces to the rising sun, weak from fasting, from dehydration, what mattered, she realized, was the humility, the sacrificial grace these men and women were taking on. As they filed past, she felt the air surge as if electrified, the spiritual energy of the dancers so strong, so palpable and powerful, that she began her own third day lifting her arms, swaying slightly, pressing the hawk's wing against her heart, bowing her head before this man she loved, her heart too full to look upon his altered, suffering face, falling so deeply into her own prayer, it did not surprise or startle her to hear a stranger's quiet voice in her ear. *He's piercing this afternoon, he sent me to tell you.* She nodded, gaze fixed on the tree, already sending her spirit, the moment she heard.

How many times had she crossed this expanse, hiked this sloping incline, the dirt of a texture and siltiness so like deep sand that children, not many yards from the circle marked out for the Sun Dancers, tumbled and played, sinking hands and arms, knees and elbows deep into its soft cinnamon, powdery grain? How many times had she climbed back up to camp, her feet dirty in their open sandals, long skirt brushing her bare legs, her head down, neck bent from the pull of the final, steep ascent? As the sun approached its zenith on that third day, she returned to camp to get the small leather bag Ray had made for her, a rectangular bag of soft deerskin, with red, blue, yellow and white geometric designs painted on one side. Everything she needed was in that bag, sewing needles, sterile razor blades, small squares of red trade cloth. She sat in the open van, resting a moment, eating a protein bar, drinking a little water, only enough to keep up her strength. Twisting the orange cap back onto the plastic water jug, she glanced over at the small, tough cedar trees, and suddenly seeing a hunched shape in the low branches of the nearest tree, walked close until she stood gazing up at a boy of six or seven, perched as if he had flown from somewhere far away.

"Hello. What's your name?"

"Leroy."

"Leroy. Nice to see you up there. Care for something to drink? Let's see, I have 7UP and Coke — which sounds good, Leroy?"

"Coke."

She went over to one of the coolers standing in the shade of the van, opened the lid, pulled out one of the Coke cans floating in water, water that two days before had been store-bought ice. The can still felt cold. As she turned to hand Leroy his Coke (where he sat, above her head, in one of the rough-skinned lower branches), she saw a heavyset older Indian man with black-framed glasses trudging up over the rise, followed by a young man of perhaps twenty, slender, lithe, his thick black hair falling past his shoulders and framing a face so startlingly beautiful, Prudence thought she probably appeared foolish, staring.

Leroy's father, Leland, introduced himself, accepting the can of 7UP Prudence handed him. He introduced the young man as Ambrose, and Prudence gave him a can of soda as well, inviting all of them to rest in her camp. With a tired sigh, Leland sank down into one of the camp chairs. From his perch, Leroy swung his bare legs, gulping soda, while the young man, Ambrose, walked down the hill and sat, his back against a low cedar, its trunk twisting nearly sideways out of the soft, rolling dirt. Prudence sat in the remaining camp chair, listening to a story she would share, days later, with Ray. Leland, it seemed, was a single father, a Sun Dancer from a camp somewhere up in northern California. Several months before, he had been driving with his son across the Navajo reservation, heading back to California after visiting relatives, when he happened to see a young man sitting cross-legged alongside a desolate stretch of road, head bowed, not even looking up as Leland passed by in his truck. As Leland glanced back in the mirror, something about the young man's utter dejection caused him to slow down, back up his truck, and ask if he wanted a ride. Ambrose, it turned out, was so drunk Leland had to help him stand. He put his arm around him, half lifting him into the truck's front seat. He was messed up, he managed to tell Leland, lost, no family, no home, he didn't know what to do with his life, didn't care anymore, wanted to die. Leland, who happened to be an addictions counselor, also happened to have an extra sleeping bag in his camper. So now, six months later, this exceptional-looking young man whom Leland had saved from drinking himself to death was traveling with Leland and Leroy, visiting all the different Sun Dance camps around the West.

"Does he want to be a Sun Dancer?" Prudence asked.

Leland tilted back the soda can, drained it, crumpled it with one hand. "Yes, he does. I'm teaching him. I like to think how I was driving along in the middle of nowhere with my boy here, saw this young man, a kid at the point of destroying himself, throwing his whole life away, when I stopped, picked him up — and who am I? Nobody really, a counselor, a Sun Dancer, somebody with an extra sleeping bag in the back of my truck. Ambrose has been traveling with me and Leroy, he's been part of our family, ever since."

Prudence invited Leland to help himself to whatever food was in the coolers, bread, peanut butter and jelly, slices of meat or cheese, whatever the three of them wanted, then took her deerskin bag and walked down to the north side of the Sun Dance arena.

Finding Marc and Heidi sitting together

under the arbor, Prudence gave them each a sewing needle, a razor, a few small squares of red cloth. A white woman, a dark blue batik sarong wrapped around her hips, stopped by, asking if anyone had an extra razor blade. Prudence gave her several, plus sewing needles and squares of cloth. Prudence waited in line behind Heidi and Marc as two Sun Dancers, men, stood side by side, one slicing a bit of flesh from each person's arm with a razor blade, the other swiftly enclosing it in a small prayer bundle of red cloth to be taken to the tree. Marc, long trickles of blood shining down each arm, stepped out of line so Prudence could step up next, the right sleeve of her shirt rolled high over her pale knob of shoulder. Accepting the sacred pipe, cradling it in her left arm, she closed her eyes as one man used her blade to cut flesh from her bared upper arm, the second man swiftly folding and tying it into the offered square of red cloth. Returning the pipe and thanking the two men, she stepped away, twin rivulets of blood snaking down her arm. Her prayer had been for Fiona, for her mother, for the soul of her father. Her flesh, in its square of red cloth, one prayer among the thousands of tobacco and flesh offerings, supplications, entreaties and dreams, tied to the tree of life.

★ ★ ★

The suffering he had prepared for, the suffering she dreaded, happened so swiftly, the piercing happened so quickly, in the midst of the dry, shimmering afternoon heat and the broad swirl of dancers, the singing of men, the hypnotic, monotonous pulse of drumming, that if Heidi hadn't taken Prudence by the arm, turned her toward the sacred tree, if she hadn't said *Look, they've taken Ray,* she might have missed him sinking to his knees, forehead pressed into its trunk, praying, as one of the Sun Dance chiefs — Jasper! — holding a scalpel, sliced just inside his right shoulder blade, pushing one of the chokecherry pegs he had made himself, polished, the width of a man's finger, into the cut, pushing through the gaping flesh and out the other side, cutting a second slit, pushing a second peg through the meat of his left shoulder. She might have missed the two men lifting him to his feet, leading him by the arms, half stumbling, half running, past the seven massive buffalo skulls, roped together, spaced several feet apart, a child of three or four years perched on top of each broad, bleached skull. She might not have seen how the Sun Dance chiefs knotted dragging ropes to the pegs piercing his shoulders, might have missed how, with the ropes fully tightened, the chiefs stood on either side of him, one fanning him with a great eagle-wing fan, both talking to him as he stood leaning forward slightly, beginning to test the weight of the skulls. Through the high white glare of sun and the drifting veils of dust raised by hundreds of bare and moccasined feet, dust released from the earth's brown skin, looking past the shadowed shapes of dancers, past other men now piercing, she saw as he accepted the eagle-head staff, used it for leverage, placing one foot ahead, using the staff to try to step forward, straining, pulling, re-straining, re-pulling, the weight of seven children hunching like solemn toads on each of the skull's broad bony seats. Individual muscles bowed out from his narrow calves as he bent deeper, pulled futilely, with all his strength, the skulls with their human burdens stubbornly rooted as trees, as small mountains, unmoving. Through the drumming and singing, she heard men who had already pierced shouting stern encouragement, one continuously fanning him with the eagle wing. She saw Victoria, in her plain brown dress, her face with its coating of *chee*, a wreath of red-wrapped sage on her head, her hair a black river down her back, saw her press a small bundle under his nose and hold it there, speaking to him, dancing beside him, encouraging him, and felt ashamed of her earlier suspicions, her jealousy. The men shouted, their voices harsh as he struggled, bent nearly to the ground, pulling, the weight behind him unmoving. She felt as if she would buckle, faint, lose consciousness. She felt helpless to stop what was happening to him. He had eaten and drunk nothing for three days and nights, he was reed thin, his ribs showed, he could not do this, no man could do this, should be made to do this. She despised these men torturing him, hated the humiliation of his failure — look — his legs, so thin, the calf muscles bulging, straining beneath the red cotton of his skirt, the skin of his shoulders tenting up high where the pegs ran through — she could not bear this, seeing this. Then, with his whole weight pitched forward, nearly to the ground, the skulls shifted, suggested motion or the thought of motion, and the line of skulls, roped together, started, scarcely, to move, to notch shallow troughs in the sandy dirt as the seven children ran back to families awaiting them in the arbor. He pulled then, dragging skulls. He began to walk forward. As he drew nearer, as he pulled she saw his face, its hideous rictus, lips drawn back in a grotesque agony, teeth square, shining, jutting from the gauntness of his face, one leg stopping, pausing to gather inhuman strength, something beyond the mere strength of flesh to drag the roped, heavy burden of bison skulls. When he was only a few feet from her, an unbreachable distance away, he lifted his head to gaze directly at her, raise his staff to her. She felt her chest split from sorrow, pride, terror, love. She delivered her whole spirit then, sent her whole spirit out to him, grateful for the beautiful young woman walking beside him, offering soft words of encouragement, grateful for the dancers fanning him, praying with him, thankful for the young boy, running behind, reaching down to turn the skulls, keeping them straight as they plowed the dirt, the tip of one horn catching, its weight flipping the skull upside down and the boy stooping down to right it — *Your body dies out there, dancing, you meet your spirit, become Spirit* — she remembered Rita's words. It happened in front of her then, the moment Spirit came into him, she saw the tremendous flash of Spirit in his eyes, giving him strength to pull seven massive skulls attached by ropes to two wooden pegs piercing his shoulders, dragging his burden four times around the arena, a thing incredible, beyond endurance. As he pulled his burden, made his agonized way around the circle four times, other Sun Dancers ran to the tree, knelt to pray, were pierced through the chest and helped to their feet, running backward then, stretching out the ends of their ropes, leaning back, arms flung wide, returning to the tree, kneeling, praying, helped to their feet, running backward, pulling hard on ropes fastened to their chests, their skin peaking, tenting, until the pegs broke from the skin, the ropes flew, and bright arcs of scarlet blood flashed against the sky, the drumming and men's singing going on, unceasing, the singing up of Lakota ancestors, of forgotten history, of time beyond telling, of time outside time.

He had stopped near the eastern doorway and begun hitching at his long red skirt, a stiff, compulsive, plucking motion he seemed unaware of, picking at the cloth with thin fingers as if to free his legs for pulling, though the skirt dropped again and again to his shins. When it seemed as if he could not move, all his strength spent, he did move. Again the skulls began to furrow the soft, pale dirt. Again he paused at each sacred doorway, raising the eagle staff, gazing up into the sun, his crown of sage slipping, a hot glaze of sweat over his face, returning west where his ordeal had begun. Having dragged his burden of seven bison skulls four times around the Sun Dance circle, he had still to break free, and in a final excruciating agony, with men dancing hard around him, raising their knees high, shouting words of courage, two suddenly seized him by the arms and pulled so hard his skin broke and the ropes snapped backward, the bloodied pegs flew backward, then fell into the dirt. Free, he ran three times around the circle, pausing to raise his staff to the north, to honor the north, then running straight toward her, his face transfigured by a supernatural fierceness, pointing the head of the eagle directly at her heart and giving one great guttural cry, piercing and final, his eyes shooting into hers with a light golden and silver at once, his eyes, really, those of a god's, and she heard God through his broken flesh, heard the sacrifice God asked of her, then God's messenger was gone, running, stumbling, blood flowing in streams down his back, the people in the arbor who had watched bowing their heads, hands over their hearts to honor this young man who had walked his own hard death, died for them, carried their prayers to Spirit, carried them all.

He was on the opposite side of the circle, she could no longer see him, when she felt a hand on her shoulder. Trish stood there, crying. "Did you see? When Ray was pierced, a redtail hawk circled the tree three times, then flew north."

Carrying a paper plate of mutton, fry bread, beans and two squares of thickly frosted chocolate cake over to the moon camp for Rita, they talked, Trish saying she had to drive back that night to Round Rock to attend a ceremony for her uncle, who was sick with cancer, but that she would try to make it back tomorrow, the fourth day.

Rita crawled out from her tent, stretching and yawning, thanking them for the plate of food. "God, I was starving. My moon's been over a day now, but hey, I'll wait one more day, just to be sure. Wouldn't want to get in any more trouble with the Two Big Cheeses, haha. Did Ray pierce?"

Prudence nodded.

"I knew it. I was lying down, listening to

the drums, kind of singing along, when all of a sudden I felt little brother piercing. How'd he do?"

"Amazing, but I don't think I can talk about it. I don't know if I can ever talk about it."

Rita laughed. "I don't think anything about the Sun Dance can really be described. Or should be. But I'm proud as hell of my little brother. Hey, this mutton's tasty, you guys want any? OK, all mine then."

Prudence and Trish stayed visiting awhile before heading back to camp.

"You OK, Trish?" Prudence thought her friend looked tired. Some sadness seemed to slow her walk.

"Not really. I'm having trouble with that guy, that good-looking Navajo security guard I told you about? Turns out Mr. Available's married with four children."

"No!"

"Yes. My friend Dorlinda told me he chased her around till she got wise, started checking around, asking questions. Seems he has a habit of picking up women who don't know much about him, has affairs with them, lets them pay for food, hotels, the gas in his truck, then one day he stops calling, stops showing up, melts back into the woodwork. He's run through a slew of women like that. Yours truly was his latest."

"That's terrible."

"Yeah, well, I did a lot of thinking on the drive over here from Tsaile. I'm tired of wearing my heart on my sleeve and getting hurt. I still want to find the right man, I'll never give that up, but I'm going back to my poetry, to my writing, putting my energy into that, not into love affairs that start out right and turn out wrong. I can't take the hurt anymore. I'm too old for it, and it's too humiliating. I'll be over in Tsaile the rest of the summer, teaching, so I've signed up for another photography class. I'm thinking of writing a book of poems about Canyon de Chelly, with photographs to go with it."

"Meaning you're going to take better care of yourself."

"Exactly. I'm really glad I got to see Ray, though. I can see why you love him so much."

"Even if he's difficult?"

"Yes, even if I'm not especially comfortable with a Lakota ceremony held on Navajo land, and even if I have been angry about the way he treats you. Watching him pull those skulls like that, what he did was just so incredible, so brave, it even gave me the strength I needed to break from one more dumb guy I thought walked on water." Trish gazed down toward the arena, empty now, the dancers resting inside their shelter. "You can feel the spiritual power down there, almost touch it, it's so strong. I'll try to make it back, I'll be at my uncle's tonight, so I'll try to stop back tomorrow before heading back to Tsaile."

Prudence sat at the base of a tough, craggy little cedar tree, looking out at distant mountains, thinking this was Trish's home — stories of Spider Woman, the Twins, these stories were hers, had come from the people who lived here. Trish had once shown Prudence her Navajo wedding dress, black wool with a traditional red border, woven by her mother and worn with a handmade silver concho belt and hand-stitched white deerskin moccasins. She had once invited Prudence to a Yeibeichei ceremony in Rough Rock, held on a freezing January night, in snow-flecked darkness, with only a small cedar fire to light the dancers. Prudence had read Trish's poetry about Indian boarding schools, about her life as an educated modern woman caught between the white and the Navajo cultures. All this was her people's land, weighted with stories and mysteries, an ancient, still-living land. What would it be like, to be given life by the land you stood on, the mountains rising in great protection around you, to walk the same earth your ancestors had walked, their stories still living in your blood? She tried to imagine and felt only the colorless but cherished thread of her own small history, running back to her parents, her grandparents, before vanishing altogether.

While Rita spent a last night in her moon/goddess camp, Prudence lay awake in the van, thinking of the bit of flesh, cut from her arm, wrapped in red cloth. That piece of her was out there now, separate and tied to the Sun Dance tree. Ray was somewhere out there, too, apart from her. Human flesh. Perhaps no one belonged to anyone, and everything was God's. Named by her parents, she owned nothing really, could claim nothing and no one. If she let Ray go, wouldn't she be loving him more than she had ever loved anyone? Wouldn't she be loving him purely, without desire, as God loved the world of his creation?

Hoka Hey! Prudence burrowed into the

warmth of her sleeping bag and fell straight back to sleep. When she finally sat up in the dim, stifling interior of the van, she saw by the sun's slant in the sky it was late, not yet noon, but late morning. She had missed the first rounds of dancing, had not been there, he would be wondering where she was. She dressed awkwardly, on her knees, pulling a long red cotton skirt up over her sweatpants, tugging the pants off, leg by leg, putting on her last pair of clean underwear, peeling off the same T-shirt she had slept in every night, one of Ray's. She put on last year's Sun Dance T-shirt, then her jean jacket, slid back the van's side door and sat yawning, groggy, breathing in air sharp with the scent of cedar. Inching on her sandals, she took up her roll of toilet paper and padded off to the outhouse, thinking of going down to the camp kitchen afterward to get some coffee to help her wake up — she had had no coffee for three days now. Stepping into the outhouse, she bundled up her skirt, bunching it in one hand to hover, butt just above the plywood lip of the toilet, holding her breath. She peed, wiped, and as carefully as she could, pushed aside the sheet, now limp and dirty, and stepped back down. Back in camp, she washed her hands, rubbing soap on them and rinsing with the little bit of water remaining in the plastic jug. She rinsed off her face, too, and smoothed on sunscreen, her movements lethargic, her body moving like cold syrup. The arena was quiet, the dancers resting, and she could hear a woman on the microphone praying in the slightly burred, soft, rolling cadence of Navajo. She trudged down the hill, the powdery dirt hot under her sandals, dirt slipping between her feet and the leather soles, the sun bearing down, already as scorching as it would be by noon. Tempted to chastise herself for missing half of the fourth day, she didn't. She had needed the rest.

The arbor was crowded — each day, more people arrived to support the dancers — she found a place to stand, wedged between two large Navajo families. Monotony mixed with a thick charge in the air, a sensation she could only compare to that fused, sparky feeling just before lightning struck. She was breathing holiness. For three days, energy had been drummed up from the earth and called down from the sky, faces turned sunward, bodies spilling blood, this energy had accumulated, and pulsed around her now as she stood under the shaded arbor watching a small boy straighten fallen prayer sticks, slender pine dowels tied at the top with narrow strips of red cloth, used to mark a boundary around the circle, the sacred hoop within which the dancers moved. The dancers lined up, filed solemnly in. Ray passed before her, skeletal, his red skirt riding the jutting bones of his hips, staring into the sun, bobbing his head, shrilling on the eagle-bone whistle. She saw, as he passed, the piercing wounds on each of his shoulders, packed now with goldenseal, wounds which would, over weeks and months, turn into shiny raised scars.

This round of dancing, the announcer spoke into the microphone, would honor all the grandmothers. A dozen or more Navajo grandmothers were escorted into the arena by members of their families, led to the tree of life where they stood, indomitable women, as weathered and tough as the roots of the cedar trees, in long broom skirts and long-sleeved shirts, shoulders like bent knuckles, floral kerchiefs over their heads, long hair pinned in flat coils against the napes of their necks. Stanley Young Dog, accompanied by his wife, Rachel, came to the microphone asking people to honor these grandmothers for their wisdom — *Without the old people and the children, it is said by our people, the circle is not whole* — prayers were said, followed by a song of honor, then the grandmothers were led back to the shaded arbor to sit on lawn chairs, surrounded by children, grandchildren and great-grandchildren, generations begun when their own young women's blood had spilled, so many years before.

A second round was called to honor war veterans. Soldiers from four wars — World War II, the Korean, Vietnam and Desert Storm wars — were asked to come forward, accept pipes to carry back and share with the people, then return, blessed by these warriors, to the Sun Dancers.

She expected him to be weakened from his ordeal. Instead Ray was dropping out of line, giving words of encouragement, fanning dancers with his eagle-feather fan, moving with brilliant energy. During the next round, a mourning round, when those who wished to pray for the dead in their families came into the arena, she saw him give his head a rough little shake, as if resisting, then let his head fall back, letting go, weeping openly, the old grief and guilt breaking open, spilling out. She knew the beaded medicine bag around his neck contained bits of Erroll's flesh, hair, blood. She knew he had carried him into the Sun Dance, had pierced for his brother, dragged skulls for him, seeking forgiveness. He wept for him now.

After the mourning came a healing round for those people who were ill or wanted healing for members of their family or for friends who were gravely or chronically ill. These people, moving into bright hot sun and standing behind prayer sticks bordering the dance arena, were given water to drink from a hollow gourd, the pipe to smoke, then a physical blessing from each of the hundred or more dancers filing past. Ray blessed each person, brushing their opened palms with his eagle feather, his face transformed, radiant with compassion.

After the rounds for the grandmothers and the warriors, the rounds for mourning and for healing, the dancers went into their shelter to rest. Prudence, her skirt folded around her, sat listening to the various people stepping up to the microphone, to the calls in Navajo or Lakota, and to their English translations, for generosity, courage, honesty, compassion. She heard warnings of hard times ahead, of old Lakota prophecies of difficult times to come, of Mother Earth cleansing herself. She listened to calls for the people to live in a sacred manner. She felt content, heavy-bodied, she could remain in this place of peace forever. Feeling a light touch on her back, she turned as Trish squeezed in, sat on her left side.

"Hey. Can you stay for the feast?"

"My mother's asked me to help her out at home, and I need to drive out there before dark, the road to her place is really hard to find at night. But I can stay a little while, until the end of the ceremony."

There were more rounds of dancing, a final frenzy of piercing, the dancers' suffering at its peak, four days in the hot sun, dancing, with no food or water. Some of the men and women became sick, bent double, dry-heaving, vomiting up nothing, kneeling by the tree or lying down, or fanning one another as they danced, one lifting up the other's long hair, fanning the bared neck, or if someone wavered, ready to faint, the one behind fanned that dancer. Suffering was shared.

Late in the day, as the dancers shuffled wearily past at the end of a round, a tall eagle spike worked loose from one of the men's sage crowns and, lifted by a breeze, blew straight down, landing between Prudence and the woman sitting on her right, a dark-haired woman with pale, translucent skin and dark glasses. The feather fell between them, slightly out of reach. An eagle feather falling to the ground was never good, Prudence knew that, but she didn't know what was supposed to be done about it. The woman on her right was staring at the feather, too. Prudence spoke first.

"Do you know what we're supposed to do?"

"I'm not sure, but . . ." The woman stretched out her hand, picked up the feather from the hot sand, and when one of the cedar boys came by with his bucket of burning cedar, she instructed him to go tell one of the leaders she had one of the dancers' eagle feathers. The boy ran off, and not long after, one of the chiefs came over and took the feather, thanking her, saying it would be blessed and returned to its owner. The woman, whose name was Diane, was from Pine Ridge in South Dakota. Her oldest son was dancing his final, fourth year. "And I couldn't help but notice" — Diane pulled up one sleeve of her blouse, uncovering a multitude of white splotches on her arms — "you have the same skin disease as me. Vitiligo," she said. "I've had it seven years now, and it's over most of my body. I'm sorry, but I guess I couldn't help seeing it on your hands."

With the quick, specific intimacy of people who discover a misfortune in common, they talked, comparing histories and symptoms. Then Diane mentioned her youngest son's suicide two years before, how the death of her nineteen-year-old son, Black Horse, accelerated the disease. "As if I was trying to erase myself, disappear completely. Black Horse was handsome, artistic, athletic, a perfect boy. Of my three sons, I loved him best." Since his suicide, she had sat in her house, not sleeping, not eating, the world lifeless, motionless. She had died too, and could not find her way back. "But I came here for Grey Lance. I promised him I would. My daughter is here too, she's on her moon, so she's in the car, she can't come down here. Grey Lance is dancing for his little brother, for his spirit, but it's hard, it's so hard for me to be here."

Strange, they agreed, after Prudence shared what she knew of Erroll's death and Ray's sense of guilt. A feather falling brought us together, our skin brought us closer, and now, the death of brothers. Quietly, they wondered over the gift of such swift, unexpected friendship.

Near sunset, people hurried down from the kitchen, emptied out of their camps. All of the men's and women's piercings had been completed, the ropes hung slack from the tree, men who had lain four days and nights on the earth, pierced, had been released. The drumming started a final time, the singing, the dancers coming in for the last time, arms raised, bone whistles shrilling, mimicking the eagle's cry, the drum pounding like the earth's own heart, like the sound of horses thundering across the Plains, the air immense with prayer, dense with holiness, brightly electric with joy. Standing between Trish and her new friend, Diane, Prudence surrendered to the wave upon wave of holiness flooding outward from the circle, from the dancers and the tree of life instructive above them all, its heart-shaped leaves paling, its still-bright prayer ties of yellow, red, blue, green, the sun lowering to earth, casting a rich gilt sheen of gold and reddish gold over everyone.

Swept up in the rhythms, the humble

gestures, feet lifting and falling, hips swaying, mouths praising, arms lifting, faces upturned as in a trance, forming one last great line of pageantry, surging forward, retreating back, surging forward, ebbing back, then, with restrained joy, the dancers, one hundred men and women, filed out the east door, emerging reborn from the same door of sunrise they had entered four days earlier. Led by Edward Standing Elk, then Stanley Young Dog, Harold Martinez and Jasper Chee, they moved outside the arbor's south side where hundreds of family members and friends formed two lines with an aisle between for the dancers to walk down, to touch the hand of each and every person, to give away a sage bracelet, a braided circle of sweet grass, to touch someone's forehead or heart with their pipe, give a blessing. One by one, the dancers were thanked for their sacrifice. People wept, *Thank you, thank you,* the dancers all radiance, still giving off some high, otherworldly heat, their eyes not yet returned from another realm, not earth's yet. Shaking each dancer's hand, too full of emotion to speak, she was seeing holiness everywhere, thanking these men and women who had emptied themselves to bring God down into a dark, pitiful world, bringing hope, giving strength. Diane, wearing her sunglasses and a large straw hat to protect her skin, broke down weeping as one of the dancers, an elderly man, his eyes closed, face luminous, stopped to place his eagle fan over her heart a long moment before going on. On Prudence's other side, Trish, with quiet dignity, extended her hand to each dancer passing by, thanking each one respectfully, solemnly.

"Prudence" — Trish turned to her — "do you see Ray? He's nearly here."

He had leaned out from the line, as if searching for her, then vanished behind ten or fifteen dancers still ahead of him. More dancers passed by, she saw him lean out again, spot her, then, in a sudden, swift burst, break from the line and run to her. Before she knew it, he was embracing her, hugging, thanking her, breaking down crying, and with a motion so swift, thrilling and pure — she understood she would recall its deep blessing forever — he raised the crown of sage from his long black hair and placed it in her hands, pressed into her hands the crown he had suffered beneath. Then he was gone, moving down the long line, shaking hands with dozens upon dozens of people, a line ending at two long tables where small paper cups of juice had been set out for the dancers, breaking their fast now, beginning to laugh, joke, trade stories, to reenter the familiar goodness of their earthly world.

Grateful for Trish's steadying hug, *My god, that man loves you*, holding Ray's crown, crying, she shook every hand, looked into each face, each shining, pristine soul, these men and women of all ages, each a story, a history, a personality shaped by blood and consequence, God shining in equal measure from each one's flesh, binding them in a holy manner that would fade, diminish, become memory and the shadow of memory, until next year's dance and the dance after that, the circle widening and gyring, widening and gyring, following the sun's direction and the Lakota legend of White Buffalo Calf Woman's coming into human flesh through the spilling of human blood, the emptied self a vessel of spirit for a brief time of miracle, miracle receding into memory, memory restored to miracle through ceremony. If any human word could be forged of breath and vibration to describe what had taken place here, that word, spoken in any language, formed on any tongue, would be love.

★ ★ ★

She introduced Ray to Diane before she left with her family for the long drive back to Pine Ridge. Trish congratulated Ray again and then left for her mother's home in Round Rock. Rita emerged from her exile, strong-spirited, and walked to another camp to visit friends while Prudence and Ray attended a feast prepared by the families of Sun Dancers who had just finished their fourth year of commitment. Watching Ray from the corner of her eye as they sat together on a plain wooden bench, watching him laugh, talk animatedly, devour three full plates of meat and potatoes which she gladly served him, feeling his sudden drop in energy, then feeling his hand wearily pat her thigh through her skirt, his voice in her ear, intimate, loving, he was tired, he wanted her to go back with him to their camp. They walked back, where the night continued with Ray talking to Rita, Marc and Heidi, describing his experience, answering their questions, how he'd felt being pierced, dragging skulls, how he felt now. Finally — and it seemed she had had to wait forever — she was alone with him, inside the van, pressing goldenseal powder, saffron-colored, acrid, light as dust, pressing powder with her fingers into the wounds on his shoulder blades, wounds so deep she could see layers of raw flesh shining beneath the darkly browned rind of his skin. Quelling her own faintness, she pressed in the goldenseal, taped a square of clean white gauze over each wound. They lay down finally, and held one another. Ray fell asleep in her arms almost at once, and she held him lightly, aware of the heat of his skin, of the bones beneath the skin, giving thanks for this beloved body, scarred, sacrificed, returned, giving thanks for the flame of his soul, still soaring.

The next day brought a gradual reimmersion into normal time, some pleasant visiting between camps, the taking down of camps, pulling down tents, packing up coolers, the loading of trucks and vans, final hugs, long good-byes, exchanges of addresses — Sun Dancers came from all over — Texas, California, Oklahoma, Utah, Montana, New Mexico, Colorado, South Dakota, Canada, Mexico, Central and South America — Native people, she had learned, did not live by the federal boundaries of states, or by the former lines of colonies now called nations, but by a flow of tribes and tribal events — an underground flow, a migratory movement invisible to anyone other than indigenous peoples. Five hundred nations, living tributaries flowing beneath the predominantly white skin of America, and even though Prudence was descended from those western Europeans who through force, treachery and disease had decimated the Indian populations of North America, though she could never fully understand what it was to be one of them, still, she was modern witness to these peoples' subterranean, ongoing life, witness to a Native people resurgent, enduring and proud.

Tempe, Arizona

With Rita behind the wheel of Prudence's little Nash Rambler, following the van, they left the Sun Dance grounds, bumping cautiously along dirt roads, traveling first through Pinon, the Navajo and Hopi reservations, stopping at the little store in Leupp, heading toward Flagstaff and down into Phoenix, the seven-hour drive one slow, spiraling fall out of one world back into another until they were turning down Prudence's street — La Diosa — and Ray, who had insisted on driving his van the whole distance, braked to a stop in the driveway, walked into her house, into her bedroom, lay down on her bed and collapsed. She would spend the next two weeks guiding him back, helping his body heal and gain strength, though it was hard not to grow light-headed at the sight of his wounds, cleaning and dressing them several times a day, the seepage of pus mixed with blood, bandaging, pressing goldenseal over and over into the red, weeping craters of flesh.

Caring for him, respectful of the strength of spirit in him, Prudence had forgotten sex until their second night home, when he woke her, biting gently along her shoulders, then pushing into her, talking to her, loving her, calling her by name, so different, so changed, his heart open, their bodies in a rush of energy, a merging so intense Prudence could only lie near him afterward, stunned, tears streaming . . . This man who had pulled seven bison skulls from two pegs in his back, his body bent to the ground, legs shaking, hitching at his red cloth skirt, teeth jutting out from his skull, pointing the eagle staff directly and with a fierce cry at her heart, demanding she become holy by becoming strong, own herself, love herself, this same man was in her bed now, his weight on her again, and for the first time since they had met and known one another, living nearly a year together, for the first time and with genuine passion, he called her name out loud.

From that moment on, their bed would be a place of coming together, a place of rest, of some argument and occasional illness, a place of passion and succor and abiding friendship; the crown of sage he had worn and given her as tribute, hung as

650

remembrance and tribute, above their bed, a place of learning to dream and to listen and, above all, to love.

"It doesn't sound right, Prune. From what you tell me, that Sun Dance thing you went to sounds barbaric. It sounds, forgive the pun, savage."

"I'm sorry, Mom. Maybe if you had been there, seen for yourself. It's so hard to describe. I could simplify it by saying I felt really close to God."

"I tell myself God hears our every thought, God knows everything. I talk to God half the time and to Walt the other. He must know how I miss your father, how some days I just want to give up . . ." She trailed off.

"Mom, there's another side. You're healthy, you're in amazing shape, and Dad left you well taken care of. Financially, I mean. He didn't want you to have to worry about anything, he told me that."

"I know, I know, I know. I walk around this place bumping into things, I'm busy counting my blessings so hard, the same ones over and over." There was a silence, her mother fighting tears back. "I just don't want to die here."

Where do you want to die? Was that the

whole issue for her mother? Death? Fear of death? The unknown? Well, who had a choice? Her father certainly hadn't. Hadn't chosen. Prudence had found proof, evidence in Walt's weekly TV guide, where he had circled the programs he'd intended to watch that afternoon. Falling dead among his roses, he'd missed a biography of Marilyn Monroe, he'd missed *Gardener's Hour* (a repeat on easy organic mulching methods), the Tiger Woods Open and *Wheel of Fortune*. Obviously, he had looked forward to sitting in his plaid armchair, watching his circled shows, not to dying while spraying soap solution on his most recent infestation of green aphids. She thought how far she was from the Sun Dance after only one day, how difficult it was to practice compassion, kindness, generosity, service. Far easier to contemplate the future attainment of goodness, to take pleasure in picturing one's future self, perfected and saintly — yet here she was, calling Deleanor to let her know she was safely home, then feeling impatient, angry, insulted, worried, a whole, messy brew of volatile emotions compared to the calm soul-strength she had felt in the arbor. The vision of herself — actions and words rising seamless and pure from an endless well of spiritual bliss — eroded and cracked. All she could do on the phone was conceal her irritation, mask her fear, skirt troubling issues as deftly as her mother did, repress her honesty the way Deleanor had taught her, by a lifetime of example, to do.

"You won't die there, Mom. You're going to live to be over a hundred, and you know it."

The first thing Prudence saw coming home from dropping Fiona off at the airport, turning down La Diosa Street and into her driveway, was all Rita's expensive camping equipment, looking as jumbled as if it had been hurled from the heavens, strewn along the east side of Prudence's house, a glittering feast, prize rummage for thieves. Rita had just found a small rental house in downtown Phoenix and was moving out, one carload at a time. She had also begun dating a Hopi kachina maker who did radio voice-overs for Indian casino commercials, and found a new "job," signing up for an advanced pyramid scheme to help market an internationally famous brand of vaginal sex cream. Earlier that morning, with her newly purchased King Tut CD sarcophagus lashed, face-up, to the roof of her Civic, its painted head facing forward, like the clumsy prow of a ship, Rita had stuffed other items, like the leather horse, the plastic kiddie pool and Nizhoni, into the interior of her car, and buzzed off to her new abode. With Rita migrating, busily moving her things to her new place, driving back and forth, Prudence's house was beginning to feel spacious and oddly quiet. She already missed her daughter. Aside from this morning, driving Fiona to the airport to visit Powell for two weeks, she had only seen her once since the Sun Dance, heard about her final breakup with Kirby, how he had met some girl named Trash Cookie at a suspension performance, a girl, Fiona snorted, with so much metal on her face she looked like an Ace Hardware close-out sale, how he'd dumped her for T.C., though Fiona kept insisting, on the way to the airport, she was happily rid of him. "He'd gotten gross, anyway. Kirby used to be so fun, we'd play games together, be silly. Now he's all into shaving his head, tending his stupid, self-inflicted wounds like a great big baby. Trash Cookie, Dirty Oreo, whatever her name is, Vanilla Waste, can have him."

"Are you looking forward to seeing your dad?"

"Yeah, actually. These new friends of his, musicians from L.A., are into electronic laptop music — they compose music from the sounds of laser eye surgery, liposuction, vomiting, pretty wild stuff. Anyway, they're hiring me, while I'm there, to help in their studio. Dad said they just got some kind of big grant to combine laptop music with performance art — so I can help out, earn money for a ticket to Ireland."

"To see Colin?"

Hopping out of the car at the curbside check-in, backpack over one shoulder, Fiona blushed as she leaned in to kiss her mother, and pushed back both short sleeves of her T-shirt to reveal small tattoos on each arm. "I got these while you were at Sun Dance. The red one, *Sannt*, means greed in Gaelic. The green one, *Truas*, means compassion. It's yin-yang without the gender shit. Colin has the exact same ones, so now we match. It's our life philosophy, what's evil, what's good."

Oh boy, thought Prudence. "That's nice," she said. "I love you, sweetie. Say hi to your father."

Fiona blew Prudence an airy kiss, "Love you, too," and was gone.

Waiting for traffic to clear, Prudence watched as her daughter adjusted her backpack, stepped confidently into line, and began chatting with a perfect stranger, Fiona nearly that now, a stranger, a confident, artistic young woman, ready to take on the world. Prudence felt an ache so sharp she actually gasped out loud, flashing back to four-year-old Fiona, gathering King Alfred daffodils into her small arms on an April afternoon, two-year-old Fiona sitting in the shower at Prudence's feet, puddling and plashing water with starfish baby hands, ten-year-old Fiona sitting on the couch with Prudence, reading books, toes touching, sharing cups of cocoa — memories flashing up with such sweet clarity Prudence missed the first clearing in the traffic lane, swiping tears from her face, trying to concentrate, blinking hard, steering out into traffic, merging, not daring to glance back, even once, at her grown-up daughter.

The house on La Diosa was empty of Rita, even her camping gear gone, carted away either by Rita, her new boyfriend or suburban thieves. Skittish, chicken-eating Nizhoni was gone, too, and Boss, poor thing, long gone, to vultures. Fiona going to her father, newly tattooed, then off to Dublin, then art school, college, who knew. The house held just Ray now, Ray and Prudence, with their newly peaceful, spiritually grounded life.

★ ★ ★

Coming in from the garage to the kitchen, Prudence automatically and out of habit, pressed the voice mail button. Message one: Deleanor, wondering if Prudence wanted a low-fat recipe for osso buco, and she wasn't sure she should have, but she'd accepted a golf and dinner date with her new neighbor, a retired acupuncturist from Seattle named Dr. Wu. Message two: Trish, wanting to get together for dinner and a movie, she had news, a younger man in her life, an Italian film student, Federico, making a documentary on Navajo life, with Trish as his main subject. Three: Fiona, from the airport — *If Kirby calls, whatever you do, don't answer. When I get back, let's have a day together. Love you, Moomers!* Four: Ingrid Blixen, executive editor of Zebra Romance, calling to confirm Prudence's flight time into Houston tomorrow, along with her reservation at the Ritz-Carlton, she could hardly wait to meet Digby's chosen successor to Mildred Crawley, the talented new author of *Savage Heat* and *Savage Arms*, the entire Zebra staff could hardly wait to hear Prudence's keynote speech at the Twentieth Annual Romance Writers Convention, this year's conference promising to have the largest turnout yet of published and aspiring romance writers from around the world . . . Prudence bumped the volume down, pressing one ear to the machine to hear the rest of Ingrid Blixen's message. Why had the woman called her at home when she had given *specific* instructions to Deedee Grind, Blixen's assistant, to *only* call her office at school! Having promised herself this was the last secret, the very last lie, Prudence had fibbed royally, telling Ray she had to go out of town for a college teachers' convention. After Zebra Romance had offered Prudence three thousand dollars for a twenty-minute keynote speech, how could she say no? She had found the black-and-white-striped letter among a stack of mail after they'd gotten home from Sun Dance. Ray knew nothing of *Savage Heat*, much less *Savage Arms*. Her life as a romance writer had gone undetected for nearly a year now, and Prudence had sworn that after this one conference in Houston, after this one high-dollar speech, she would quit the whole thing. She knew the gist of her speech — starting with her chance meeting with Mildred Crawley in the Tempe library lavatory, her visit to Casa Crawley, how she had become reluctant heir to the famous Savage Passion series. Ingrid Blixen wanted Prudence as this year's speaker for two reasons: one, brisk sales (*Savage Heat* was turning out to be Zebra's runaway summer title), and two, Prudence's personal story, a story, Ingrid felt, that would inspire conference attendees, most of whom nursed a dream of standing where Prudence now stood, at the pinnacle of Zebra's historical romance list. If a middle-aged, middle-class college instructor and single mother could reap success on her very first try, why couldn't they? Prudence had agreed to speak on one condition: that they *not* call her home number and that any subsequent correspondence was to be sent to her office at the college. She intended to confess eventually, spill the whole story to Ray after she quit, after her three-thousand-dollar speech in Houston. She even hoped he might find the idea of her writing a Native American romance funny, even complimentary, since the physical descriptions of Blazing Eagle were largely based on him. But all that was ruined — both Prudence's plans and her intentions behind those plans — because of Ingrid Blixen's damning voice mail message, a message Prudence could tell had been heard, already listened to.

★ ★ ★

His deathlike stillness, the rigidity of his posture, so reminiscent of Boss, worried her a little. A lot. She opened the back door, cleared her throat.

"Hi."

He did not turn around, merely raised one hand. In that hand, glinting wickedly in the sunlight, was the gold and fuchsia spine of the new paperback edition of *Savage Heat*. She hadn't even seen that version yet.

It had been four decades since Prudence had felt that *Uh oh, deep trouble* sensation in her groin, not since grade school, when she'd been packed off to the principal's office for stealing a coveted Chinatown pencil from Donna Kuby's locker. Years later, shame still enshrouded the memory of that stupid pencil, a bobble-headed china doll with a silken turquoise tassel, the shock of being caught stealing, the shame of doing something wrong, the humiliation of being sent to the principal's office, creating that low, awful thrumming in her groin, the exact same sensation she had now, looking across her yard, seeing Ray dangle *Savage Heat*, the glitzy new paperback edition, from his graceful, oval-nailed brown fingers.

Taking a deliberately deep breath, she walked over, sat before him, a remorseful, rueful penitent, eyes lowered, hands clasped in her lap. This was bad, she thought, but still salvageable.

He dangled the book, his fingers loath to touch it, holding it by one precarious corner as if it were contaminated, a source of communicable disease. He was wearing dark glasses, so she couldn't tell if he was looking at her or not. Leaning forward, he dropped the lurid paperback into her guilty, thrumming lap.

Overhead, Prudence heard the crazed chirping of peach-faced lovebirds who lived in the hydrologist's palm trees next door, small green birds with rosy chests who had escaped from a large cage somewhere and now lived extravagantly, noisily, in the palms next door.

"Care to explain?" His tone was opaque, unreadable.

The book lay on her lap like a rectangular, lightweight dead animal. She flipped it to conceal the cover's image, a brawny, breechclouted Indian embracing a flame-haired vixen, her Victorian schoolteacher's dress half off, bosom exposed, throat arched vulnerably back. But the opposite side was no better, the same tawdry image, underwritten with fat-fonted, hyperbolic praise for *Savage Heat*: . . . *bold, heart-stopping love, a rousing tale of sultry passion . . . a proud warrior finds love in a turn-of-the- century schoolroom . . .* Prudence repositioned her book, spine down, white pages up. Her pages. Her words. He sat still, ominously silent, his dark glasses reflecting the telephone pole in the alley behind her yard.

She spoke with soft, careful precision, confessing her deception (the exact story, though slanted for opposite effect, as her planned speech at tomorrow night's Romance Writers Convention). She began with running into Digby Deeds in the bathroom of the Tempe library, then accepting his invitation to tea at Casa Crawley, turning down his generous offer to inherit the lucrative Savage Passion series, but with collection agencies hounding her, in fear of losing her home, of having to declare bankruptcy, her desperate last-minute decision to begin secretly writing *Savage Heat*. And who could miss the amazing coincidence — having been offered this once-in-a-lifetime opportunity to make money by filling in the plot blanks of a romance with a Native American Indian as the designated love interest — the coincidence of Ray Chasing Hawk, Comanche Indian, arriving simultaneously, synchronistically, heroically, on her doorstep! His coming to visit her was surely a sign, a stroke of destined luck. She also thought it fairly harmless, one silly book. (*Then two.*)

"When did you find time to write? When did you write this crap? Where was I?"

"Asleep. I'd get up while you were sleeping, go into that middle bedroom. Though since Rita moved in, I've been writing in my office at school." Uh-oh. He didn't yet know about the second romance, *Savage Arms*. Or did he? She couldn't remember.

"All those so-called curriculum meetings?" He sounded sarcastic.

Prudence hung her head. "Yes, I was in my office, writing this stupid thing. I hated writing it, Ray. It's so stupid. I loathed every sentence."

"What about the other book? The lady on the phone referred to another book."

"*Savage Arms*? It's a sequel, coming out next month. But that's it, Ray, that's the last one, I swear. I never told you because I was too embarrassed, but it was the only way I could see to pay off my debts. I was planning to fly to Houston tomorrow, get paid three thousand dollars for a twenty-minute speech, then quit. I thought you didn't need to know." She hesitated. "I'm sorry."

He stretched out one hand, waggling his fingers, wanting the book back. She handed him *Savage Heat*, cover down. He flipped it over, studied the cover, opened the book to its last page, and with sarcastic, agonizing emphasis, read aloud:

"Let us be together, my beautiful captive, my small white woman. Let me show you just how much I love you. Let me show you now."

Rebeccah watched Blazing Eagle undress. First his sleek, muscular chest shone in the moonlight, then his warrior's thighs, between which stood his throbbing strength, a coppery velvet sheath, ready to pleasure her in every way. Blazing Eagle removed his moccasins last, dropping them to the floor beside the bed of rabbit fur upon which Rebeccah lay naked.

"Love me, my woman," he whispered as she clasped her snow white arms around his dark, strong neck. "Make the sun rise in my heart. Light the path of ecstasy inside me." His jet black eyes burned with fiery passion as he brushed her ruby, heart-shaped lips with his.

Then Rebeccah whispered words that would ring true for the rest of her existence as a Comanche captive turned wife. "Oh, Blazing Eagle! With you all time and reason are lost. There is only you, my love. Only you, I swear. Forever."

He tossed the romance back to Prudence, lightly, as though it were slippery, a thing made of slime.

If he loved her, Prudence reasoned, he would understand. He didn't have to like what she had done, but he could certainly understand. He might be angry she had kept a secret from him, but eventually he would calm down, understand her reasoning, poke fun at the ridiculous passage he had just, with tight, sarcastic fury, read aloud. When you think about it, she told herself, if you look at the situation in just the right light, it's hysterically funny.

"What can I say, Prudence. You have betrayed me. No, worse. You have betrayed us both. I believed in you. My mistake. I have never trusted white people in my life, but with you, I made one reluctant exception. You persuaded me to rethink my prejudice, my hatred of white people. I trusted you, and look what shit you made of that trust. You thought I would never find out, and no one would be the wiser. Hey, pay off your debts, maybe have a little money left over, make life easier. Maybe, like you said, you meant to tell me later on. Maybe you thought I would find the whole thing funny, some kind of crazy joke. Well, it is not a joke. This is white garbage, white woman's pornography. Trash, pure and simple. The worst part, the part that hurts, is how it perpetuates all the goddamn stereotypes of the Indian man — savage warrior, loinclothed creature of lust serving a white woman's pleasure. Yet another way to damage my people, to insult Indian men and denigrate their women. I take what you have done, what you have done behind my back and without my permission, very seriously. I take it as betrayal. Fly to your romance convention, Prudence Parker. Give your speech. Collect your money, your three thousand dollars. The damage is already done. I am no one's savage warrior, no one's tamed animal. No one owns me, least of all you. I hadn't told you this yet, but at the Sun Dance we were counseled to get rid of those things in our lives that no longer served us, to let go of people and things that stood in the way of our spiritual growth. I had been thinking a great deal about that, about what to give up, what to let go. I never thought it would be you, Prudence. So go right ahead, do what you need to do for you, and I will do what I have to do for me. When you get back from Houston, I will be gone, my things will not be here. I don't know where I'm going or where I will stay, but I can no longer stay here with you." He reached down, tugged a small package out of the hip pocket of his jeans, opened it. "Here. I made these earrings as a surprise, to thank you for all you have done for me since I met you, for supporting me at Sun Dance. They're made of abalone, leather, elk tooth. There's a pair of beaded moccasins, too, on your bed. I've never made a pair of moccasins for a woman before in my life. I know you think I've been sneaking around, cheating on you. There has been no Other Woman like you seem to think. The women I've been meeting are friends, that's it. I hid from your jealousy, your insecurity, your distrust of me, that's all I did. Keep these, Prudence, I made them for you, but I can't stay here anymore, I have to go."

She kept her head lowered, his words pelting like stones, stinging. At one point she thought to object, to say, Well you've sure used that stereotype to your advantage, what about all those women always calling you, always giving you their phone numbers, what about all those Indian costumes you dress up in . . . but she said nothing. Both of them had changed, grown, Ray most of all. She didn't raise her head until she heard him stand up, heard the back door open, then close, until she was sure he had gone into the house.

What had she done? Traded him for the

paperback in her hands, a romance novel she had intended never to show him? She thought of running after him, falling to her knees, begging his forgiveness, but she knew his disgust for theatrics, knew an emotional scene would only ignite rage in him, hysteria in her, create a worse catastrophe. She thought of going into the house and asking him to calmly hear her out. She would repeat her story, place greater emphasis on her financial plight, but he was impatient with repetition, especially when her idea of poverty, compared to the poverty he had grown up with, the poverty most Indian people suffered under, was fairly indulgent and relative to race. Her one hope lay in letting him go. If she left him alone, he might cool off, might reconsider, relent. Holding the earrings he had made for her, she sat listening to the raucous, promiscuous, ironic din of her neighbor's lovebirds, the soft cooing of the mourning pigeons on her roof. Finally she stood up, left the damning book on the patio table, and went inside, checking in the several places he could usually be found, on the couch, in bed, painting or beading in the workroom. But the house was yawningly empty, vacant of his presence, as if he had never lived there. She opened the door into the garage. His van was gone, the blank parking space accusatory. Prudence broke down sobbing. Her bills were paid, yes, debts cleared, yes, but the price was too high. She wailed, not caring who heard or how long or hard she cried.

Paced, waited, paced, waited. Glanced out the kitchen window. Packed, unpacked. Lay awake. Took a triple dose of herbal sleeping pills, dropping into a rocky, nightmarish sleep. When a dark green taxi pulled up late the next morning, Ray had still not come home. At the airport, she checked her luggage, sat waiting to board her plane. Some foolish hope kept her looking around, searching for his familiar figure. The man she loved now judged her as treacherous, a spiritual obstacle, a white person like all the rest, not to be trusted. Prudence had never felt so low or sad or ashamed of what she had done in her life.

Houston, Texas

He waited at the passenger gate wearing maroon livery with gold braided trim, holding a sign over his head, *P. T. Parker, Romance Writers Convention*. With tired and grateful relief, Prudence sank into the plush black leather upholstery of the waiting limousine. Her driver chatted all the way from the airport to the Ritz-Carlton — how much he loved his job, the celebrities he met (Rodney Dangerfield most recently, and before that, the Dalai Lama and Alan Greenspan's granddaughter), say, she must be somebody pretty special herself, judging by the size of the convention. Quite a few ladies, a whole *lot* of ladies, hundreds maybe, already there, all fans of romance novels. "My wife eats up those books, those romances," her chauffeur shrugged. "Me, personally, I like a spy story with a good-looking woman thrown in as bait, or a good war story, doesn't matter what war, but my wife, she goes for the type of book where the gal gets the guy in the end, he's usually some rugged outlaw he-man type, and she's the prim-on-the-outside/wild-on-the-inside schoolteacher . . . Harr," he laughed, showing little gray teeth. "I know better than to mess with my wife when she's reading one of those romance deals, you learn to stay out of her hair."

"Why do you think she reads them?" Prudence asked. "Does she say why?"

"No, she don't say why. An escapist thing is my guess. Life as women would like it to be."

"Hmm."

"You write those books? Romances?"

"I wrote one. No. Two."

"Well, I take my hat off to anybody who can just sit down and write a whole book, I don't care what kind. I'll have to tell my wife I met you. That your real name, P. T. Parker, or is that the name you write under? I'll tell her, and maybe she can go to the store and buy one of your books."

Yes, that was her real name. She asked for his wife's name and address, wrote it down on the back of her airplane ticket. "I'll send your wife my books so she doesn't have to go buy them."

"Oh my, she'll be tickled to death." He

squinted up at her in the rearview mirror. "I probably shouldn't even tell you this, but she's always wanted to be one of those writers herself. Says she's read so many hundreds, she could write one in her sleep. She even took a couple of writing courses at the community college, night courses, and last year got a poem in her high school alumni magazine. I guess that's really her secret dream, to write like you do, write one of those love stories."

"Well, tell your wife I'm sending her mine. And tell her I said to just sit down on the chair and write one — it's not that hard. If I could do it (*so easily slit my own throat, destroy my life*), anyone can."

"Say, I will, I'll tell her that. Here we are. What'd I tell you? A lot of ladies."

The black, mirror-polished limousine glided to a stop under the Ritz-Carlton's massive granite portico. From inside the limousine, Prudence, her forehead pressed against the tinted glass, watched droves of women, drab sparrows spruced up in bold pantsuits, flashy scarves, hair tinted a little brighter, trundling flowered suitcases, or splurging on hotel staff to do it for them. P. T. Parker readers. Parker fans. Good holy lord.

"You sure you're all right, Ms. Parker?"

He opened the door for her, one pudgy, liveried arm gallantly extended. "You look a little peaked."

"I'll live, thanks. I just didn't sleep well last night." Taking his arm, standing up from the limousine, Prudence pressed a twenty-dollar bill into his hand, what did money matter now, she'd seen enough of it, maybe he would treat his wife to dinner out. She looked into his honest, cheerful eyes. "Truth is, I'm having a little trouble in the romance department. Funny, huh?"

"Oh, now. A lady as attractive and successful as yourself, you must have guys falling at your feet."

"I frankly don't want anyone falling at my feet. If a man fell, I might feel obligated to pick him up. But thanks for the compliment, Mr. . . . . I'm sorry, your name?"

"Burkee. Don Burkee. Like turkey. My wife hates the name."

"What's her name again, I'm sorry?"

"Daisy, Daisy Hallowell Burkee. Sounds like a writer's name, I always say."

"Well, tell Daisy I'll send her copies of my books, autographed, I have your address here on my ticket. And, Mr. Burkee, thank you for everything. You've been a wonderful, kindhearted human being."

With that, Don Burkee got back into his

limousine and drove off, leaving Mildred Crawley's heir, P. T. Parker, to make her way into Houston's Twentieth Annual Romance Writers Convention. She was lavishly welcomed by members of the hotel staff, shown her suite with its excessive floral arrangements, a green cellophane tower of fresh fruits, and gold, pink- beribboned box of Godiva truffles, along with a handwritten note on zebra-striped notepaper welcoming Prudence to Hous- ton, inviting her to order anything she'd like from room service, her reception would begin as scheduled at five o'clock in Ballroom C, with her speech to follow at seven o'clock in Ballroom A.

Grabbing the box of chocolates and kicking off her shoes, Prudence dropped facedown on the king-size bed, the trapunto quilting of the white bedspread pressing against her cheek. Rolling over, she slid the dainty pink ribbon off the Godiva box, lifted the lid (which came off with a prim, reluctant sigh), stuffed a seashell truffle into her mouth, and began to cry. This was fame. She bit into a second truffle. A conch. This was what success and hundreds of women paying good money to listen to you — P. T. Parker, doyenne, literary mistress of the Savage Passion romance series — was like.

When the phone rang, shrilling and startling her awake, the room had grown dark. What if it was Ray, calling to say he wasn't angry anymore, calling to wish her luck. She located the phone by its angry winking, red-domed light, plucked up the receiver. *Ray,* she whispered. The voice of Ingrid Blixen boomed into Prudence's right ear. "We thought we'd better ring you up, honey — it's a quarter past five, your reception's in full swing, and there's a roomful of loyal readers down here, dying to meet you."

"On my way," Prudence said, plunging the phone down and standing, all in one frantic, uncoordinated twist of movement. Dashing into the huge marble bathroom, big enough for an extended family, she switched on the overhead chandelier light and peered into the mirror. God.

Approximately seven minutes later, dressed in a black velvet broom skirt, matching velvet blouse and wearing the shell earrings and beaded moccasins he had made for her, Prudence stepped out of her lavish suite, hurried down the plush carpeted hall to the elevator, and stood waiting beside a full-color blowup of

Savage Heat's cover. Three minutes later, she arrived in front of Ballroom A, where two more *Savage Heat* posters were displayed, her name flowing over the top of each one in huge, florid gold letters. She peeked into the vast room — dozens of white and gold, elaborately dressed circular tables, a gold-beribboned copy of *Savage Heat* at every place setting — she allowed herself a moment's pride, seeing her book everywhere, her name everywhere, before turning away and heading down the richly lit hall to Ballroom C, where still more blowups of her book's cover greeted her. Fashionably late, P. T. Parker walked into her reception and was engulfed by fans. As Ingrid Blixen, dressed in a silk zebra-striped pantsuit, skillfully extricated her from less important guests in order to meet journalists, reviewers and one movie agent, she whispered that P. T. Parker had taken the romance world, quite literally, by storm. "You have become the long-awaited voice for a whole new generation of romance readers, you are at the helm of the modern romance."

"You think?" Prudence was genuinely curious. In *Savage Heat,* and even more so in the soon-to-be-published *Savage Arms,* she had simply taken the skeletons of

Digby's plots, reset the bones and told the paradoxical truth, at least as she was experiencing it, about love.

Deedee Grind, speeding over with a glass of merlot for Prudence, chirruped, "Passion, more passion, we at Zebra Romance celebrate every woman's right to full, carnal, orgasmic passion."

"Fascinating," said the male movie agent, vaguely discomfited by Deedee's outburst, a minor gaffe Ingrid Blixen expertly covered by turning to the agent and divulging the adorable fact that P. T. stood for Prudence True. She then checked her jewel-studded watch and exclaimed it was time to proceed to the banquet in Ballroom A.

"You probably won't be able to eat a bite before your speech, but I wanted you right up here with us — feel free to order whatever you like later from room service. I'm simply thrilled you've agreed to be here," Ingrid said, rapidly escorting Prudence down the hotel's broad, red-carpeted hall to Ballroom A where she would be seated among the various executive editors and publishers of Zebra Romance. She sat at the table of honor, beneath a formal stage backed with heavy gold brocade curtains, where in less than an hour's time, she would step up to a podium and begin to speak. Prudence slid her overcooked asparagus spears around, dipped her fork in and out of her garlic mashed potatoes, poked at her dry filet mignon, drank down as many cups of coffee as their table's white-jacketed male waiter could manage to pour for her. Most of the time, Deedee Grind and Ingrid Blixen, sitting on either side of Prudence, dressed in matching zebra-striped silk pantsuits, forgot her presence entirely, busily discussing in-house troubles and triumphs, gossiping about who'd seen who fornicating in the stairwell over the weekend, whose marketing husband had run off with whose editorial assistant, then turning to Prudence with forced enthusiasm, acknowledging the rare animal in their midst, the main attraction, their bread and butter, the author du jour, who really (Prudence imagined them thinking) was rather dull in manner and quite peculiarly dressed. With twenty minutes remaining until her keynote, and feeling the diuretic effects of far too much coffee, Prudence excused herself to go to the ladies' room. She also wanted to be alone for a few minutes, to go over her three-page speech, neatly sheathed in a manila folder, inked over with corrections and amendments, messy in comparison to Zebra's conference programs, hundreds of shiny red trifolds with florid gold lettering and red silk tassels. Prudence simply wanted to find a bathroom stall, shut herself in a moment, and pray for the strength not to think about Ray, not to succumb or panic or hyperventilate or go unconscious onstage. After all, her readers had read *Savage Heat* and wanted more of her, not less. In less than fifteen minutes, hundreds of fans would be eating hazelnut torte and looking to her for advice, inspiration, entertainment. She was, for the moment, their queen.

Prudence bolted herself in the furthest stall, a marbled space the size of her bedroom at home. When she felt calmer, clearer, she emerged from the stall, washed her hands, glanced at her face, impossibly flushed and pale at once, and stepped out of the bathroom. Heading in the direction of Ballroom A, clutching her manila folder, Prudence glimpsed a figure in the distance, at the end of the hotel's hallway, a slender man in a black cowboy hat. Then he was gone. Couldn't be. Couldn't have been. It was just her frayed nerves and nervous heart, playing tricks.

"You write in your book by fire's light," *he said, looking from her to her thick-leaved journal. "Why is this, Rebeccah? Why do you leave Blazing Eagle's bed to spend time with this, this book? And why did I first find you in the forest, traveling alone? This is not common practice for white woman, is it?"*

"No, it is not a common thing for a white woman," she uttered softly. "It is not commonly recommended. But I am not like most white women. I am different. Like you, Blazing Eagle, no different from you, I like to . . . explore."

P. T. Parker
Savage Heat

Following Ingrid Blixen's extravagant, florid introduction, a portrait so over-wrought Prudence scarcely recognized her-self, she managed to mount the stairs without tripping and reach the podium with its small reading light, glass of water and bulb of microphone. She stood a mo-ment, looking out at the sea of faces (*Cliché, of course, sea of faces, but really it was like that, a sea, or raft of bubbles at the top of the sea, all those pale, eager faces bobbing on the froth, several hundred women, their wor-shipful applause dying down now, surflike, who on earth were they? Unavoidable, this cliché of the sea, try another: their faces beamed up like so many common buds, turning toward her, their newest sun, hundreds of late, hopeful, emergent blooms).* Prudence suddenly saw these women not as enemies or fools, not as the drab sparrows she had once so unkindly named them, but as an entire generation, her generation mainly, though overlapping into her mother's and Fiona's as well, of women striving to please, to do as they had been encouraged to do, marry, bear and raise children, take jobs outside the home, do everything in their lives conscientiously and well, now in this ornate room (Ballroom A!), searching for some misplaced part of themselves, selves as neatly tucked and folded away as fine linen, and too often mislabeled Him, mislabeled Romance, True Love, Happily Ever After. The silence was complete as she gazed out over her audience to the furthest end of the room, and saw him enter through a set of tall, gilt-trimmed double doors — the slender build, the long black hair, the pure, androgynous face, the black hat with its beaded band, the one he'd worn the night he'd arrived on La Diosa, her goddess street, just now removed and held respectfully in his hands. He bowed

681

slightly, acknowledged her standing before him on a stage brilliant with light.

Prudence smoothed the cover of her folder, opened it and scanned the opening lines of her speech, lines typed days before and now made important-looking by the brass podium light. She shut the folder, looked out at her audience, and with a dawning confidence in the truth of what she was about to say, began to speak, her voice gaining volume, filling the room. Her speech was short, and Prudence ended it by announcing she would not be writing any more romance novels, that *Savage Arms*, due to be published in the coming season, would be her last. Applause slowly emerged from shocked silence, then opened into questions, questions Prudence answered as honestly as she could. She urged the women in the room to discover their own lives, their own journeys, to not live vicariously through romantic dreams that only a few profited from. Standing before a roomful of women she did not know, she told them they were each their own truest and longest love story. At the head table, Zebra's staff sat stonily, revealed as exploitative manipulators of female loneliness, purveyors of stereotype, cashing in on the myth of the savage warrior, a lusty, untamed Indian man, wise in nature's ways.

★ ★ ★

Seated at the book-signing table set up for her, her right wrist cramped from inscribing more than one hundred copies of *Savage Heat,* Prudence turned as the line diminished and spoke to Ingrid Blixen, standing, glacial and fixed, to one side of Prudence's chair.

"I've decided not to accept payment for tonight's speech, and I won't be staying at the hotel this evening. My friend" — here, Ray, who had been leaning against the stage, straightened up, tipped his hat — "my friend will be taking me home tonight."

Ingrid Blixen spun on her heel, and in a blur of zebra stripes left the ballroom. Though it was past nine-thirty, with hotel staff taking down banquet tables and chairs, half a dozen women still waited for P. T. Parker's autograph, murmuring among themselves, comparing the book's cover to the Indian dressed in black and standing before them. Finally Prudence finished signing and the women left with their books, some glancing back a last time, wondering.

"Good speech," Ray teased her. "No notes."

"I wrote two speeches and didn't use either one."

"You spoke the best way. From your heart."

As Prudence stood, rubbing her sore wrist, Ray caught her in his arms, held tight. "I'm so sorry, baby. I've been doing a lot of thinking, and we'll talk more later. But I was wrong, really wrong, to be so harsh with you." He kissed her. "C'mon. Let's go home."

"Home?"

"The ranch. I flew in this afternoon. I've got Mom's truck here."

She picked up an unsigned copy of *Sav-age Heat*. "Last chance for an autograph."

"For my mom? I hate to say it, but she'll probably love it."

"Will she know you're the passionate Comanche hero?"

"Will she know you wrote it? Who was supposed to have written it in the first place?"

"Mildred Crawley, actually Digby Deeds."

"Right. Crawley/Deeds."

"One problem."

"What's that?"

"My name's all over the cover. See?"

"P. T. Barnum?"

"Parker, you goof. P. T. Parker."

"Hey."

"What?"

"Nice earrings. You looked pretty sexy up there."

"You're not half bad yourself, Blazing Eagle."

"Watch it, white woman."

"Comanche captive."

"You said it. Let's go, P.T. What's 'P.T.' for anyway, part-time?"

"Ray. I mean it. I'm not writing any more of these things."

"Write short stories, like you used to."

"How did you just do that? Read my mind?"

"My secret. Leave me one secret, sweet thing."

With the windows rolled all the way down, the truck's dark interior flooded with the dense, redolent fragrance of a Texas summer, the fine smell of horses mixed with sweet rainfall and thick summer grass, alfalfa, clover, oat grass. Empara's horses grazed, white manes and tails shimmering and starry in the black fields. Prudence could make out the dark square shapes of barns, the solidness of Joe and Empara's brick house, the yellow porch light left burning. She looked toward the fenced, tree-studded darkness, remembered the wooden swing she had sat on months earlier, pushing forward and back, confused and sad, a journey ago. No ideal religion, she thought, no perfect love. Only forgiveness, the bliss of now, the heart's remembrance.

"Paradise."

"Hmm, sugar britches?"

"Nothing."

Ray parked his mother's truck near the house. Three white mares, grazing nearby, raised curved, lily-cool necks, watching as a man and a woman got down from the truck, found one another and stood embracing a long, quiet moment, long enough for the mares to lose their mild curiosity and return to cropping the summer's fragrant, night-drenched grasses with broad, velvet-soft, hungry mouths.

ROMANCE⋆ READER⋆ SURVEY

After you have finished a romance which you liked, what do you most often do with it? (Remember, check only one.)

____ a. I put it on a bookshelf to keep although I sometimes lend my romances.

____ b. I throw it away.

_____ c. I give it to a friend or relative. (Do not check this one if you only lend your books.)

_____ d. I donate it to the library or to charity.

_____ e. other (please specify)

— Janice A. Radway,
Reading the Romance: Women, Patriarchy, and Popular Literature

About the Author

Melissa Pritchard is the author of three story collections, *Spirit Seizures*, *The Instinct for Bliss*, and *Disappearing Ingenue*, and two previous novels, *Selene of the Spirits* and *Phoenix*. Her numerous literary awards include the Flannery O'Connor Award, the Carl Sandburg Award, the Janet Heidinger Kafka Prize, as well as fellowships from the National Endowment for the Arts and the Howard Foundation at Brown University. Her stories have appeared and been cited in numerous anthologies, among them *Prize Stories: The O. Henry Awards*; *The Pushcart Prize*; *Best American Short Stories*; and the *Prentice Hall Anthology of Women's Literature*. She is director of the M.F.A. Creative Writing Program at Arizona State University and is on the faculty at Spalding University.